Remy thinks life after high school will be easier. He'll go to California Pacific for a year while he gets a handle on his HIV, then after Michael graduates from high school, they'll blast out of there for colleges—and life—on the East Coast. Then Remy visits Boston and everything changes. He realizes he likes CalPac. Turns out, Boston doesn't have anything for him beyond one of the biggest regattas in North America.

Life grows more complicated when he gets home. He can't find a way to tell Michael that he's just blown their plan for their lives out of the water. Then Remy's CalPac coaches drop a bomb on him. Those rowing officials who have been watching him? They are recruiters for the national team, and his coaches want him to try out. They'll even let Lodestone coach him. Now he has to choose, school or crew, CalPac or Michael, and he still hasn't told Michael he can't transfer. Is there even a place for Michael in his life? Somehow they have to withstand training at the highest levels and having different goals. Will love hold them together...or tear them apart?

ALL THAT IS SOLID MELTS INTO AIR

The Lives of Remy and
Michael, Book Two

C. Koehler

A NineStar Press Publication

www.ninestarpress.com

All that is Solid Melts into Air

Printed in the USA

ISBN: 978-1-64890-215-4

First Edition, February, 2021
Originally Published in January 2016

Also available in eBook, ISBN: 978-1-64890-214-7

WARNING:

This book contains sexually explicit content, which may only be suitable for mature readers, and homophobic slurs.

Dedicated to the memory of Steven Keith Marschke (May 23, 1963—April 8, 2015), who was in his way my own Peter Lodestone.

Chapter One

So far, I'd made it halfway through the first semester of my freshman year at California Pacific, and you know? I had to admit that it didn't suck. I know, I know, that was a bizarro thing to say about one's choice of school, but there's something you had to remember. CalPac was most assuredly not my choice of school. I made some very...I'll call them colorful...choices the summer before my senior year of high school, and the gods of indiscriminate love rewarded me with HIV. It almost killed me—mostly because I neither told anyone but my brother and my boyfriend, nor did I seek medical care—but my parents made a decision I resented at the time: rather than sending me across the country to Boston University, as I wanted, they spoke to the men's crew coach at CalPac. Between their persuasion and some fast talking from my high school coach, the ever-awesome Peter Lodestone, I wound up going to the local private university in the Sacramento area with a full-ride scholarship so long as I stayed brilliant in the boats. Mom and Dad's idea was that I spend my first year in college at CalPac as I learned to quote, unquote manage my condition, and at the end of that we'd discuss transferring.

I flipped out when they dropped this bomb on me, and I dropped an R-bomb on them in return. R-bombs. That's what Michael affectionately called my rages. They're like daisy cutter cluster bombs but involved words and caused a lot more damage. All my plans—all *our* plans, as Michael and I had our future worked out—gone, just like that. But my parents knew me well, surprisingly enough, or at least knew my temper, and to take the sting out of it, they made a contract with me: in return for my cooperation, they gave me a notarized promise that at the end of my freshman year I could transfer to the school of my choice. Or maybe the school of my choice that chose me back might be a better way to phrase it. At the time I felt so sure of my future. Row my seat, keep my grades up at CalPac while I applied to BU, and bide my time while Michael finished high school. As soon as he graduated, I'd transfer so fast people behind me would get pneumonia from the wind in my wake. Michael and I would stay on the same schedule on the East Coast. That was the Plan. I'd worry about NCAA eligibility later.

Oh, and then there was my father's edict that despite the fact they lived across the Yolo Causeway from CalPac, I would live in the dorms. That went over well.

"You've got to make the break, Remy," my dad had said.

As I recall, I made a face. "Dad, no. I'll be what, fifteen miles from home? How much of a break could I possibly make?"

"Trust me." Dad snorted. I remembered that clearly. "Once you're there you'll realize we might as well be on the moon. It'll seem like a world away, and one more thing—you can come home *maybe* once in a while, but under no circumstances will your mother and I allow you to come every weekend."

"What? Why not?" I think I whined.

Then Mom jumped in. "That seems a bit harsh, Steven."

"He'll never make the transition to any kind of independence if he does, Dina. He'll be more likely to drop out, and he's too good a student to allow that. I can show you the research if you want."

"There's research?" Mom had sounded surprised, and I didn't blame her. Dad could be autocratic sometimes.

I still saw Dad nodding. "You bet there is, hon. This isn't me being arbitrary, for once."

"Then I agree," Mom had pronounced before turning to me. "We want you to stay close to home to make sure you learn what you need to know about your HIV from Dr. Kravitz, not to create a state of permanent dependency."

So, there I was at CalPac and living in the dorms. There was one thing I was absolutely unprepared for when I agreed to all of this with my parents.

I loved CalPac.

No matter how much I held myself back, no matter how hard I tried to cultivate a "just passing through" attitude, no matter how hard I tried to remember that Michael and I dreamed of life together on the East Coast, I grew more and more attached to this small private school among the leafy greenness of Sacramento. That proved to be a major roadblock to my plans for escape, to the Plan. The campus was beautiful. Unlike some local schools I could name, the buildings at CalPac didn't look like poured-concrete monstrosities or cheap interpretations of New England campus Gothic. CalPac's campus was a place all its own, its architecture unique, suited to its environment, like the building committee actually listened to the school's Architecture and Design Department instead of whatever was trendy when new buildings were approved. The result was a campus at peace with its host city and the surrounding geography. Okay, some of it stuck out. The Art Department owed a little too much to Dalí and whatever came after postmodernism, and the History Department looked like a Renaissance palace in the Florentine style, only smaller. The scale was all wrong, and it made me giggle every time I walked by. But mostly everything worked.

I hit my second roadblock not long after I moved into the dorms, only I didn't know it. More of my obliviousness to everything that didn't involve rowing shells and oars, I guess. This was hardly a revelation. Michael and Goff both had teased me about that for years, telling me I needed a keeper. I'd been counting on Michael fulfilling that role. I knew I would always find my way to the boathouse—whatever boathouse I was currently rowing out of—but the rest? I needed firm guidance, and how lucky was I that Michael liked to provide firm guidance? My pants always got a little uncomfortable when I thought about Michael and his firm guidance too much.

Anyway, my plan to bail when Michael finished high school also meant I at first held myself aloof from collegiate life, so maybe that's why I missed all the signs that my roommate at the very least thought I was an asshole and more likely hated me. I promised myself I'd get my head out of the clouds one of these years. But the air was so much fresher up there...

I thought we had had a decent roommate-type relationship, although I had no real grounds for comparison other than what Goff, as I called my twin brother, Geoff, and his girlfriend, Laurel, told me. Okay, Laurel lucked out with her roommate. A month into the fall quarter at UC San Diego and, according to Laurel, she and Olive were as close as sisters. Goff and his roommate were taking longer to warm up, but that's because Goff was pretty sure Craig was gay but hadn't admitted it to himself, let alone to Goff. Goff knew that once Craig came out it would all be fine. I tried to caution Goff not to push the issue, but he brushed me off. After all, what did I know, I was only gay. I was sure Craig would be subject to all manner of "my brother and his boyfriend" stories in the coming months. The thought of meeting this guy made me cringe.

Anyway, Brady Watts and I might not have hit it off like Laurel and Olive, but we were at least cordial. Or so I thought until one afternoon. Brady and I waited outside a classroom in the Life Sciences building for our fresher seminar to start. CalPac trotted all freshpeople—yes, it's that liberal and averse to gendered language—through a series of half-semester seminars. They were part breadth requirement and part help choosing a major and included the social sciences (boooring), life sciences, physical sciences, and humanities. CalPac was a semester school, so we started our fall semester in early August and ran sixteen weeks until the middle of December. We had barely started our second eight-week seminar, life sciences, obvs. I already knew the life sciences were for me.

So anyway, a bunch of us were waiting for class to start, and I wasn't the only one with earbuds in, listening to my jam. I was, apparently, the only one not blasting said jams.

I heard someone say, "Stuck-up asshole."

That someone was Brady.

Ouch. I tried not to let it show. I clenched my jaw, instead.

Then I got angry.

It was not as if he and I never spoke. We both spent time in our room. He knew why I got up stupid early in the morning and why I went to the gym every afternoon. He knew where I was from, just as I knew he hailed from LA, hated Sacramento, and wasn't adapting well to college. He knew I had a twin brother whom I missed terribly, and I knew he had a little sister who had died young from an anaphylactic reaction to antibiotics. The only thing I hadn't told him was my serostatus. If I ever cut myself and bled everywhere, then I'd tell him that too. What more did he want from me?

I shoved all of this aside. I had a class. I'd deal with my roommate later. Thank God I was a master of compartmentalization.

Later that evening, after I'd returned from weightlifting and seeing Michael, I faced Brady. It's not like I had a choice. He glowered at me when I came back to our room.

Seriously, he looked up from his reading when I walked in. Then he went right back to his studying with the most dismissive glance ever. Not even Michael looked at me like that when we were on the outs before my senior year of high school. If looks could kill...

Of course, back then Michael had ignored me too studiously for it to count. Me, I'd shoved things into tidy little boxes in preparation for my first Youth Nationals.

I noted with a certain humor Brady was cramming for the next life sciences quiz. I barely cracked the book. I didn't have to. I was acing the class. Like I'd told Mom once, Davis High had prepared me well for college.

After dealing with a duffel bag full of smelly gym clothes, I checked the dry-erase board to make sure everything on it was out-of-date. For reasons of its own, the housing office thought each room needed such an accessory. Personally, I didn't care why our room had a dry-erase board. I merely welcomed a canvas on which to make my point. I pulled up a handy meme I'd saved on my phone to refer to and started drawing. After a few minutes, I felt Brady's eyes on me. Mission accomplished.

Then I kicked off my shoes and sat down on my bed.

"What's that?"

I smirked, looking up at the picture of a donkey stuck in a hole in the ground. "It's an asshole."

"A what?" Brady acted like he didn't know what I was talking about, but really? An ass in a hole? C'mon, buddy.

This wasn't my first time around the block. When I wanted to make a point, I made it stick. "I'm not an asshole...you asshole."

Brady flushed. "I don't know what you're talking about."

"Yes, you do. I heard you before fresher biology seminar today."

I met his eyes and then stared, unflinching, unblinking. I'd faced my own mortality. A snippy college freshman didn't compare.

Brady started shaking and breathing heavily, only glaring at me harder. "Do you have any idea how hard it is for me to live with you?"

"Uh...no?" I wasn't expecting that. I'd thought I was pretty easy to get along with. I kept my things on my side of the room. I was quiet and clean. What else could anyone ask for in a roommate?

"You never talk to me. Did you know that? We have no late-night dorm room bull sessions. We don't go out for beers, we don't get high together, you're an asshole," Brady continued.

I rolled my eyes. It's a bad habit of mine, one I've never succeeded in breaking. "You do know I'm here on an athletic scholarship, right? We're both underage, so don't even talk to me about alcohol, and smoking of any kind—really? World-class rowers have the highest VO_2 max of any athlete, and before you trip out at the thought of having to look something up and accidentally learn something, two things. One, putting it crudely, VO_2 max is the measure of how much oxygen an athlete can extract from a lungful of air, and two, I really do have a shot of being that good. So yes, I'm that much of a straight edge, and no, we're not going to bond doing any of that shit." There went that eye roll again. "As for late-night bull sessions, we'd actually have to be friends for that, and calling me an asshole in public isn't likely to bring that about in a hurry either."

"Can you even hear yourself?" Brady's voice rose. "You're so patronizing. It's...it's like you're not even human or something. You're this unstoppable machine who marches out and gets what he wants."

I sighed. "It's called having goals. You should try it."

"You are such a...such an asshole!"

This grew more tiresome by the minute, only now I was losing my temper. "You've said that already."

By this time, he'd jumped up from his desk to confront me. We both realized at the same time exactly how much shorter he was. If he decided to take a swing at me, it'd be the shortest confrontation in the history of everything. Seriously, I had seven inches on him.

He looked up at me, hopefully reconsidering his plans for the immediate future. "I'm failing our biology seminar, and...and you never talk to me, and you're gorgeous, and you don't even look at me, and you're probably some kind of fundamentalist creep who's about to pound me."

I stared at him. "I...what?"

Brady pointed at my neckband. It was a tight-fitting leather collar given to me by Michael, studded with metal. Hanging from it was a metal plus sign, plus for poz. A cross was the last thing it was, if only because I was pretty sure Mom's parents were born Jewish. Since she was never bat mitzvahed, we'd lapsed hard. "You're really, really wrong. My boyfriend lives in Davis. You've met him, so what the hell are you talking about?"

"That figures." Brady slammed his hand into the wall.

I laughed. I couldn't help it. "Dude...you don't know the half of me. If you did, you'd never say those things." Brady exploded again and moved to storm out of the room, but I was lightning fast. I grabbed his arm. "Don't go, not if you're serious about help or getting to know each other."

"And whose fault is not knowing each other? You bailed on those roommate mixers." Brady jerked his arm out of my hand, but at least he stopped reaching for the door.

I sighed. "Those things are terminally stupid, and you know it. You never would've learned the things you seem to want to know at those. I actually think you're a nice guy. Or did. So, you're failing biology seminar. Did it ever occur to you to ask for help? Because I'll be honest— I haven't heard a thing out of you."

He didn't say anything at first. Then, "No."

"Did you go to the tutoring center or talk to the prof?"

More silence.

"Riiight." I rolled my eyes again. "Let's look at your quizzes. I'll see if I can help, because there's another quiz coming up, you know."

So little Brady was gay. I hadn't noticed any signs, but then again, he wasn't made of carbon fiber and was therefore unrowable. I told him nothing else about my life, my condition, or anything else of substance, certainly nothing about Michael. After tonight he was on a need-to-know basis. Brady would have to earn his way in.

Chapter Two

One thing that took some getting used to about college was the schedule. Maybe I should say the schedules. It still felt weird being able to take off whenever I had the time. I arranged my schedule around my practices and around when Michael was in school and *his* practice schedule. Why not? Since I had that kind of flexibility, I'd be a fool not to take advantage of it. I could've even skipped class, but I didn't have the balls. If my classes bored me, I might be more inclined to experiment, but I loved school, and then there was that rowing scholarship. My coach kept an eye on my grades.

So, I was essentially done with my afternoon when I drove out to the Cap City boathouse, even though Michael wasn't done with practice. It felt like coming home to hang out there, like putting on an old pair of jeans or maybe a favorite hoodie. It fitted right. Cap City's boathouse was next to UC Davis's and CalPac's boathouses in West Sacramento at the Port of Sacramento, a body of water charitably called a lake, Lake Washington. The port appeared incapable of turning anything resembling a profit, and cargo ships were rarae aves, leaving the crews more or less unmolested. Surprisingly, the big ships and the shells got along fine. As the big ships passed, the water went up and then the water went down. Their propellers were so deep under water that the wakes were submerged far beneath the surface. No, it was the tugboats operators who refused to play nicely. The tugs kicked up three-foot wakes when they were allegedly idling, and despite state maritime law, they did nothing to mitigate those wakes when in the presence of unpowered watercraft like rowing shells. Jackasses.

But the tugs were nowhere in sight as I wandered down to the dock to watch the boats come in. The junior varsity boats appeared to be in front, and I'm sure Michael would have something to say about that. It was late September, and the Head of the Charles was in a month. CalPac's practices were intense. In fact, we had three more weeks of that ball-busting intensity before we started our own pre-Charles taper. While Cap City's junior crews wouldn't be heading east, there were other races, including Cap City's own Head of the Port next weekend. That the JV were in front doubtlessly meant they had won a scrimmage, and if there was one thing varsity hated, it was losing to junior varsity. I'd have to gauge Michael's mood before I said anything snarky.

In the meantime, Coach Lodestone drove his launch toward its berth at the dock. A huge grin split his face as he called out, "Remy!"

"Coach Lodestone!"

I waved as I loped over to his boat. This man had been responsible for some of the greatest triumphs of my young life, as well as helping me through some of my most challenging times. He was a mentor, a father figure, a friend. So, it wasn't like he was important to me or anything. I rowed varsity under him for three years—okay, maybe not under him in the way some of my more overheated fantasies might have had it—so in many ways he helped to shape the man I was becoming.

I helped pull Lodestone's launch the rest of the way in. Cap City forbade coaches driving their launches all the way into their berths. Apparently, the club's board frowned on ripping the bottom out of the boat by forcing it up onto the dock with the engines.

As important as Lodestone had been to me, and as much as I was doing a member of his gentlemen's crew—being done by?—I'd been somewhat shy about showing my face around here, at least since I stopped helping with the learn-to-row camps at the end of summer. I lived inside my head, but sometimes I didn't like to examine my motives too closely. I didn't want to think about making a break from the most important four years of my life to date. My father's a therapist. I learned a snootful growing up about the stages of childhood development, and when Goff and I were in high school, we couldn't turn around without hearing about how it was another step in the separation process. If therapists' kids were nuts, it's because their parents made them that way. I didn't want to think about separating from a place in which I had learned so many lessons about life. I didn't want to think about making a break from a place where I had grown up.

Then something else occurred to me. What if I had avoided the Cap City boathouse up until now because I was pulling away from Michael? It had occurred to me before, and I had discussed the matter with my own therapist, but I sure as hell wasn't going there right then.

I faked a smile as Lodestone jumped out of his launch. He grabbed my hand to pull me into a bear hug. Guess I wasn't the only one with familial feelings. "Remy, it's great to see you! Where've you been?"

"Oof. You might consider leaving a rib or two intact, Coach Lodestone." Seriously, dude, ease up.

Lodestone shook his head. "You could call me by my name. You know, since you don't row for me."

"I thought I did." I pretended to be puzzled. "Your name's Coach, right?"

I blinked at him in innocence, an innocence no one on that dock believed for a shred of a second.

Lodestone stared at me. "Angels and ministers of grace, was that a joke?"

"No." I held my face expressionless, even though it about killed me.

"How I've missed you." Lodestone laughed hard. "Do you know none of these boys have the stones to bust my chops?"

"Shocking. I see Michael's rowing varsity."

We both lost it at that point. Lodestone, seeing some potential in me, had encouraged me to ride along in his launch so he could show me rowing from another perspective. I learned an incredible amount from those ride alongs, including that a certain now-varsity rower wouldn't be stuck in JV for long. When I pointed this out to Lodestone at the San Diego Crew Classic one year, he grew rather testy. I stood my ground, and I think he respected that. It helped that I'd been right, because Michael now rowed at seven seat in the gentlemen's varsity A boat, a boat that was most definitely not going to be first back to the dock.

I could've watched Michael row all day, although he was obviously tired. Every so often I noticed a slight hitch in his stroke, nothing unusual at the end of a long practice...for a rower of lesser skill. I noticed Lodestone noticing it too. I thought about needling Lodestone, but I also thought better of it. That was none of my business. What was my business were those muscles glistening with sweat in the golden light of a September afternoon, those and the way his deep breaths highlighted the planes of his face. We might've met when we were both in high school, but we had both grown. My own maturation barely registered when I looked in the mirror. I mean, who observed himself on a daily basis, right? But Michael—Mikey—I paid attention to. Two years of puberty had been very good to him. He was now taller than I was and far heavier of build, and I fucking loved it. Let's be honest, I'm subby, and our physical differences worked very well together.

By the time Michael's boat landed, I stared openly. He looked up and smiled, so yeah, I'd been caught. Neither of us cared. I guess a few of the other guys noticed.

I had only graduated the year before, and some of them recognized me, acknowledging my existence with a nod or a wave, but they had other things to do, like carry the oars to the oar racks and otherwise prepare to get the boat back into the boathouse and wipe the water off it. I didn't recognize one or two faces. They ignored me, and I returned the favor.

"I said," Lodestone repeated, snapping his fingers in front of my eyes, "are you going to Boston?"

I blinked. "I'm sorry, I heard some annoying, buzzing sound. Did you ask a serious question?"

"And the ego has landed." Lodestone shook his head.

I blushed. "It's not ego if it's true." I looked at my former coach. "You didn't train me to row a novice boat. Junior varsity, freshman walk-on."

"Damn straight," Lodestone said.

"As it were."

Lodestone gave me a shove toward the boathouse. "Go help your boyfriend wipe his boat down, and you'll be out of here faster. And out of my hair sooner."

*

We headed back to the CalPac campus to clean up. The time of day was a busy one on campus, so we couldn't fool around in the showers, and I never could figure out Brady's afternoon schedule. Maybe he didn't have one. But that made it even hotter when we got back to my room after Michael's shower and he spun me around and pushed me up against the door.

"Grab the shelf," Michael growled in my ear as he dropped his duffel bag.

There was a shelf above the door, and—gaaah, he licked my ear as I reached up—I loved being tall. I strained to reach it, standing on my toes, leaving me under a bit of tension and vulnerable to whatever it pleased Michael to do to me.

"I love it when you're like this," Michael whispered, his lips pressed against one ear.

"And how is that?" I rasped.

He pinched my nipples. Hard. "Vulnerable."

Michael knew how to rob me of thought and in the shortest time possible. We didn't always have the leisure to take hours to explore our limits. Sometimes fast, hard, and hot was better, and this looked like one of those moments.

Michael's fingers danced over my chest and back, strumming me like a guitar, playing the songs we both craved, the brighter melodies of pleasure and the darker bass of pain. I never asked him where he stashed those toys or bought them in the first place. That was his secret, those clamps and the other things we lacked the time for right then.

He unbuckled my jeans, letting them fall to my knees. I canted my ass as he caressed it. We both needed this, I thought, as he smoothed my underwear down my backside. Then I gasped as he slapped it, first once side, then the other. Gasped and moaned as he set up a rhythm, nothing too punishing, but we also knew I'd feel this for a few hours. The barest thought made me shiver.

"Somebody likes this." I looked back over my shoulder to see Michael smirking at me.

My breath came in shallow gasps. "I don't think I'm the only one."

"Never said you were, and I'm about to like it a whole lot more."

Michael stopped and spread some soothing lotion over my pleasantly glowing ass. As he tore open a condom he swore under his breath. I didn't know where he stashed it, and I didn't care. He wasted no time in opening me up, and I cooperated fully. I shuddered when he made contact and almost let go once he was fully seated in me, his pelvis planted firmly against my well-spanked butt.

Michael grabbed my hair and yanked my head back. "I never said you could let go, did I?"

"N-no."

He growled, and it went right to the root of me. I almost came right then. "No, what?"

"No, sir."

Then Michael started moving, and all was for the best in this best of all possible worlds, at least for that moment.

Neither of us lasted long after that.

Michael moved quickly to clean me up afterward, wiping us both down with his damp towel.

I grunted with discomfort, even pain, as I massaged the ache from my arms.

Michael was on me in a short second. "Are you okay?"

"My arms are a little stiff." I wouldn't meet his eyes.

He pulled me to his chest. "That means you can barely move them. Rem, why didn't you say something?"

"Because we were both enjoying ourselves, and because I didn't realize how much they hurt until we stopped." I rested my head against him, listening to his heart.

"Oh, Rem, what am I going to do with you?" He kissed my forehead gently. He rubbed some more lotion into my backside before pulling my briefs up and then my jeans.

After we were both dressed again, we sat on my bed, and Michael rubbed my arms as I leaned back against him. I could never get enough physical contact from him. "So...something happened."

"Oh?" I was amazed at how much freight he loaded that one word with.

I tensed up, and I felt Michael respond in kind. "Um...it's about my roommate," I said, telling him about my recent exchange with Brady.

Michael listened in silence, slowly resuming his massage. "Did it never occur to you he was crushing on you? I've seen this for a while now."

I was thoroughly nonplussed. How did I not see these things?

Michael shook his head. "That's it, I'm coming over after practice tomorrow and studying with you. It looks like I have to make things clear to this Brady person."

When he did that, I felt stupid. It used to be cute, but it wasn't anymore. Now it only grated on my nerves. I was honestly not an idiot, and I had the test scores and grades to prove it.

"You might as well bring some stuff with you to keep in my dorm room. Maybe shower supplies and a change of clothing or two." I nodded at the duffel bag. "While I approve of the things you seem to have secreted away in its pockets, maybe we can keep some of them here too."

Michael sighed. "You know my parents won't let me stay over."

"Doesn't mean we can't push the edges of your curfew."

Michael made a face. "I hate that word. It makes me sound so..."

"Underage?"

"Thank you."

"It's the truth." I gave him a pointed look. "The last thing I want is your parents showing up and reminding me of that fact. Once was enough."

"Oh jeez, don't remind me." Michael shuddered. "That was only the worst day of my life."

The worst day of his life? I could have thought of much worse days that he'd been involved with—starting with confronting my parents about my serostatus when I was in the ICU—but being woken up by his parents in my dorm room when it had been clear that being woken up was not a euphemism? Not even in the top five.

But yes, one evening early in CalPac's semester before Davis High had started for the fall, Michael had tried to spend the night with me. That was it—spend the night. None of the little games Michael and I were so fond of, if only because we had never managed to find a safe place to play them. Without privacy it was surprisingly difficult to find a place for Michael to tie me up and dominate me, something that frustrated us both. So there we were, spooned up and dead to the world, when his parents managed to gain access to my dorm—it wasn't that difficult—and marched their way right up to my floor and room and pounded on the door until Michael and I woke up at the late hour of ten thirty on a Friday night. Fortunately, Brady was out at some party, so we were spared that bit of mortification.

Then Michael caught my arched eyebrow and blushed. "Oh. Yeah. I'm sorry, but you know what I mean, right?"

I nodded and hoped he'd grow out of this phase. Soon.

He sighed. "You know they're very supportive of our relationship, Rem—"

"As long as we don't actually have sex."

"As long as we don't have sex," he repeated softly. "I'm sorry. For some reason, the fact that you're in college is a barrier they can't get past. Never mind that at this time next year we'll be on the East Coast and doing whatever the hell we want."

"I spent the night in your room after the senior ball. We fucked like bunnies—"

Michael flinched. "Yeah, about that. They don't actually know that part."

"You have got to be kidding me. How could they not?" This was news to me. We hadn't been particularly quiet, although now that I thought about it, he did cover my mouth with his hand a lot. At the time I thought he was just dominating me. I narrowed my eyes, thinking. How many other dots had I not connected?

"The music, for one thing. They know I listen to it at night, so they're used to it. I also took care of the evidence and made sure they'd never find it."

I sighed. "So, we can study and hang out together but not really anything else?"

"There are times like tonight, and we make out whenever we can," Michael said. "Don't forget that."

"But not actually make love like adults who're in a long-term relationship?" I smiled to take the edge off my words.

"You could always ask Lodestone if you could chaperone my regattas," Michael said with a wicked grin.

I laughed. I had to. "I think he'd see through that."

"Yeah, but until he did, think of the fun we could have."

"I've never been a fan of quickies."

He looked crestfallen.

"I'm sorry. I didn't mean it like that. What we did was hot, don't ever think otherwise."

Michael held me for a while. Then something occurred to me. He'd sworn under his breath while opening the condom wrapper. I'd assumed it'd been part of our lovemaking, but I also knew he hated condoms...

"Michael...you're still taking the Truvada, aren't you?"

He sighed. "Yes, but... Why do we have to bother with both? I hate condoms. I've gotten through Truvada's side effects. It's not the most pleasant drug."

"Because I refuse to take any chance with your health." We'd been over this so many times. "My viral load is currently in the undetectable zone, and I do my best to make sure it stays there. I'm also tested regularly. You know all of this. But if something changes before the next test, I don't want to be caught—and you exposed—unawares."

"Yeah, but both..."

I sat up and faced him. "Truvada puts you into the high nineties in terms of protecting you, assuming you take it regularly, but condoms? They're only about seventy percent effective. You know that. Did you know they've never been approved by the FDA for butt sex?"

"I...no. I didn't." Michael looked surprised. "Somehow they don't mention that in our safer sex classes."

"No, they never do, but condoms do one thing Truvada and my meds don't do—they protect against other infections."

"But if you're not sleeping around and neither am I, then we're neither of us at risk for anything a condom would catch other than HIV, right?" Michael looked at me slyly.

I groaned and not in the good way. The cold hard reality was that so long as I took my meds as prescribed and my viral load was effectively zero, I was far safer a sex partner than a lot of people because I knew my serostatus. "I hate arguing with intelligent people. No, you're right on that score but, Michael? I'm terrified of anything happening to you, of me being responsible for anything hurting you."

"I get it, Rem, I really do." Michael caressed my face.

I leaned into his touch. "Why can't we—"

Then the lock clicked, and Brady walked in. He glared at us, and I felt Michael tense. I knew Michael disliked him. That might've been too soft a word. Loathed? I tried not to invest that much energy into someone I didn't care for.

So much for a round two. One of the things I liked about being young was the short refractory period, but not that night. "Shall we hit the dining room? That protein bar you ate in the car on the way back from the boathouse has to have worn off by now."

Unlike what I'd heard from my friends about a lot of college dining halls, the dining room attached to my dorm fed us well. While Goff told me he'd already lost five pounds due to a general refusal to put more of that slop in his mouth than he had to, I could tell that the so-called freshman fifteen was a thing at CalPac, and I'd have to watch my step, or I'd pack it on. So, Michael did not mind at all when I took him "out to dinner" at my dorm's cafeteria from time to time. It was faster and cheaper than many restaurants and better than fast food.

Still, I think we both wanted more for dessert but knew we weren't going to get it.

Chapter Three

I started therapy during my senior year of high school, not long after my parents found out about Josh Brennan. Much to their surprise, I asked for it.

"This is too much," I had said when my parents once again prepared to beard the dragon (that would be me) in his lair, in this case when they'd gotten wind of the latest wrinkle in my reign of error that summer. Detective Nakimoto had been true to her word and had never said a thing to Mom and Dad. The district attorney, however, had been another matter, and after a letter arrived in the mail, the shit—a whole manure pile—had hit the proverbial fan. "I need to talk about this—all of this—with someone who's paid not to get personally involved."

"You—" Dad had looked thoroughly confused, I remembered that clearly, like he had expected more resistance.

Mom had at first looked surprised, then amused. "He asked for a therapist, Steven."

"But—"

"Can you recommend one, or shall I help Remy to call our HMO tomorrow?" Mom had said.

Dad had eventually sputtered to a stop and then helped me find a therapist he thought would suit my needs and personality. I'd been seeing Alicia Lopez, LCSW, ever since.

"So, how's the trial going?" Alicia asked me during our next session, a handful of days after Michael and I had enjoyed ourselves in my dorm room.

She meant the trial of Josh Brennan, the one-time intern with the adaptive rowing program at Cap City, the one who'd hit on me one day while I was de-rigging a boat before a regatta, the one who I lost my V-card to, the one whose indiscretion alerted Coach Lodestone and eventually Coach Sundstrom that something was going on between the two of us.

The one who had broken my heart if I had to be brutally honest about it.

"I've only had to testify those few times, but I'm learning a lot of things I never needed to know," I said.

Josh was the one who, as it turned out, liked any number of boys younger than I was at the time of our relationship. That was why the DA had contacted me— and my parents.

I had not, in fact, been an isolated thing where Josh had been concerned, so while he might've been protected from legal jeopardy in our relationship by Romeo and Juliet laws, Detective Nakimoto and her team had uncovered a number of other relationships that failed the stink test. I was only unique because he had thought I was in college. I guess everyone liked variety once in a while.

Alicia steepled her fingers. "How are you doing on overcoming your guilt at not stopping Josh?"

I struggled with that, which was why she asked. Maybe if I'd figured out what was up, I might have stopped Josh and spared other, younger guys what I'd experienced. I'd been virtually an adult when he and I had gotten together, but those other guys? Not so much. That's what haunted me.

"It's been a slow process, and some days are better than others," I said.

"That's to be expected. What I meant is, how are you doing at remembering you were little more than a child yourself at the time?" She gave me a pointed look. Did therapists have any other kind of look?

That made me squirm. "I felt grown-up at the time."

"I know you did, Remy. We always feel grown-up at whatever age we're at."

"You *are* grown-up."

She laughed. "I'm glad you think so. I'll be sure to let you know what I want to be when I grow up when I've got that figured out."

"Does my dad know you feel that way?" I thought adults were supposed to have their acts together, or at least the ones I trusted to help me keep mine that way.

"What Steven and I discuss is our business, Remy. Suffice it to say we all wear many hats and play many roles. 'Therapist' is only one of mine, just as 'father' is only one of your dad's." Then Alicia grew serious. "The point, Remy, and one I hope you'll continue to think about, is that you were barely seventeen. You weren't an adult, although you felt grown-up. A generation or two back, you wouldn't have reached your legal majority until you turned twenty-one, and colleges stood *in loco parentis*. My point is—"

"In the Middle Ages, men reached their majority when they were fourteen," I said. I don't know why I brought that up. Maybe it was a dodge, an attempt to deflect the truth of her words. On one hand, I knew she was right. On the other, I'd been racked with guilt ever since I found out about Josh's other conquests and that I'd been the oldest. All those boys... If only I'd known, maybe I could've done something.

Alicia sighed. "And they were old men in their forties. My point, since it appears I need to spell it out, is that by our society's rules, you were a minor yourself. No one expects you to have done anything heroic, no one—"

"No one but me."

"No one but you." She didn't say anything for a long moment. "That's why we're here, so you can go a little easier on yourself."

She didn't get it. No one did. I clenched my hands into fists.

"Look, had Josh known I was in high school, his attentions wouldn't have wandered. How's that for a kick in the pants? If I'd been honest about my age, that creep's eye would never have strayed and neither would mine. Don't you get that?" I said loudly.

Alicia didn't say anything. What could she say?

"I've known this for a while." I wanted to scream. "While there was a definite squick factor, I can accept it. I didn't think I was being molested then, and I don't feel that way now. That's not why I'm in therapy."

"Then why are you here, Remy?" Alicia said softly.

I glared at her as my pulse raced. "For fuck's sake, I'm in therapy to deal with my rage over the fact that if Josh had known my real age, I probably wouldn't be poz!"

I wasn't angry with Josh. I was angry with myself.

I could have heard the proverbial pin drop, and its noise would not have been a tinkling chime but the door of a bank vault thundering closed.

"I did this to myself, and my meds remind me of that every goddamn day."

Alicia scrambled to keep up. I could see it in her face. "And why do you think that's the case?"

"Don't you get it?" My lips curled in contempt. "If I'd kept Josh's eye, if he hadn't embarrassed me, if my coach hadn't connected the dots, Josh wouldn't have gone looking for other playmates, and I wouldn't have run amok like a bug chaser on Grindr. You don't pick the bug up from a water fountain or a toilet seat, you know."

Given where I'd tricked, a public bathroom had probably been involved, but you can't pick up HIV that easily. Jeez. If I let myself go and really think about this, I'd consume myself with fury.

"All right," Alicia said. "I'll bite. How would your life be different if you'd stayed with Josh?"

A bark of cynical laughter escaped me. "I wouldn't have HIV."

"You can't know that."

"Oh, for fuck's sake… You can't say that."

"Neither can you."

She was good, I had to give her that.

"What? That doesn't even make sense."

"All you can say is that you wouldn't have picked up HIV from whatever trick you picked it up from. You don't know you wouldn't have caught it from someone else. You don't know that you wouldn't have contracted it from Josh. You don't know that he's not where you got it in the first place or that you didn't spend your post-Josh summer infecting your other partners," she said patiently.

I stared at her, mouth agape.

"You did know that he's HIV-positive, didn't you?"

I couldn't process what she said. I slowly shook my head.

Alicia flipped to a section of my very thick file. "I have a copy of the detective's report since you were a minor—by the skin of your teeth—when I started treating you and it was deemed important to your care. A précis of Mr. Brennan's record is right here, including his HIV status."

"What—" I cleared my throat. "—what does this mean?"

"It means that you can't be sure where you picked up the virus. Being angry at someone for giving it to you is a huge waste of emotional resources." Alicia leaned forward and looked me right in the eye. "You *are* HIV-positive. It means that being angry at yourself for being poz is the biggest waste of energy I can think of. You have it. Build a bridge and get over it. Tilting at this particular windmill will not help you maintain your health or help you to reach your life's goals."

Wow, mind blown. I sat back in my chair as Alicia watched me with hard blue eyes. "Aren't you supposed to be nice to patients?"

She laughed. "No, I'm supposed to help them. You've been flirting with self-pity for a while, now. I can't stand self-pity."

"So, what do I do?"

"I can't stand whiners either."

I rolled my eyes, waiting.

"Look, Remy, you're the only one who can help you. I can guide you to certain insights, but you still have to do the work of figuring out that rage is only hurting you. Brennan doesn't care, and neither does HIV. If Brennan cared, he'd have used condoms or have left you alone in the first place. People like him are narcissists, chasing their own pleasure, and let me tell you something. They will never find it, which is why they move from victim to victim. There's something else you need to realize too. The virus itself is barely alive. It's incapable of feeling anything, so it doesn't care either."

I found myself nodding. "I can accept that."

"Good," Alicia said, "because you don't have a choice. Your only choice is between acceptance and unhappiness. Let me tell you something else you don't have a choice about accepting. The past is over. You can't rewrite it, and so far, time travel is nothing but a figment of science fiction and theoretical physics. Neither will help you. For next time, I want you to work on letting go of it. Every time you find yourself dwelling on 'if only I hadn't done that,' I want you to be aware of it. Don't blame yourself for thinking that way, don't worry about the fact that you've done it, only be aware of it. We'll work on replacing it with other thoughts later. Do you think you can do that?"

I thought about it. Don't dwell in the past, because it's already over and done with and will only make me unhappy. I knew what she meant. I'd been obsessing over the events of last summer more and more, and other than spinning my wheels, I'd achieved nothing. Now that Alicia called my attention to it, I saw her point.

I nodded. "I think so."

Alicia pulled out her appointment book. "Now, can you make it next...?"

*

In early October Coach Ridgewood, the JV men's coach, called me into her office. I liked her. She wasn't as intimidating as Frank Pendergast, the men's varsity coach. He tried to be intimidating, I thought, whereas

Joanne Ridgewood was naturally approachable and more effective for it, at least in my opinion.

I knocked on her office door. "You wanted to see me, Coach?"

"Yes, come in, Jeremy." She typed a little more into her computer, presumably saving what she had been working on. "Have a seat."

She stared at me for a moment, not long enough to make me edgy or anything. "So. You and sculling."

"What about it?"

"I know you come out here and scull every afternoon."

She definitely had my attention. "Yes, ma'am. I hope that hasn't been a problem. It was dumb luck there were those Hudson singles and a crying shame they weren't being used more often."

Coach Ridgewood smiled. "Why would it be a problem, Jeremy? You're putting in extra time in a boat. Besides, I spoke to Peter Lodestone over the summer, so I knew what to expect." She sighed. "Competence in a single makes for better rowing in the sweeps boat. I think it's great that you're a skilled sculler, and that's why I was asked to speak to you. You've never been to the Head of the Charles before, right?"

"No, this is the first time. I rowed for Cap City in high school. While the masters sent boats, the juniors didn't. We put our travel money into the Crew Classic and the Youth Nationals." I still couldn't talk about the

Nationals without thinking about one of my teammates dying on the operating table as I won his race for him.

"I know about those races. I was there, watching," Coach Ridgewood said softly. She knew.

"The second year no one died." Thank God.

"Way to set that bar high, Jeremy," Ridgewood said. "How would you feel about entering a second race as part of a quad?"

Ignoring that, I stared, openmouthed. "The Charles. As a sculler. Won't...that is, aren't the races the same day?"

She shook her head. "Nope. I checked before I agreed to approach you."

"Wow. Um...sure. I'd love to." Sweep rowing in the big boats was all well and good, but sculling? I would always love it more.

"Great! Now for the fine print. There are no collegiate sculling events, and ordinarily you cannot row more than one event at the Charles. They're very strict about that—no one, not even cox'ns, can row more than one event. That said, the Directors' Challenge events are the exception to that, but these events go to fund the regatta's endowment, so oddly enough they make an exception."

I rolled my eyes. There it was again... "Self-interested much?"

"Tell me about it." Ridgewood smiled. "Lodestone asked me to approach you. He and three friends from Cap

City usually row a quad in the Directors' Cup Challenge, but someone dropped out at the last minute."

"And they want me to fill in? Why didn't Lodestone contact me himself? It's not like he doesn't know how to reach me." I sounded peevish to my own ears. I wondered what my coach thought.

Ridgewood nodded. "I know, but it's because I'm your coach now, and he didn't want to do anything that might affect your performance the next day in the main event. I can see how it'd look bizarre from where you're sitting, but between coaches this is considered good manners."

"Oh. Okay, then."

"So glad you approve," she said dryly. "It may also raise questions about your NCAA eligibility. I'm still looking into that, but I think we'll be in the clear. You'll blow their age handicap, but they knew that when they asked for you."

I slumped in the chair. "Wow. I'd never thought of that."

"And there's no reason why you should have to. That's why you have coaches. You're a freshman. You'll be entered as a member of Cap City, and you'll have to pay your share of the entry fees for the quad yourself."

"That seems reasonable." And it did. This would have nothing to do with CalPac. Why should the team pay?

"I knew you'd see it like that. That said, we'll transport everything on the school trailer, ours or UC

Davis's. It won't be a problem, so don't give it a second thought."

"Guess I'd better talk to Lodestone next time I'm at the Cap City boathouse." I gathered my things to leave, but Ridgewood stopped me.

"There's one more thing," she said.

"Oh?"

"There are points awarded for—" She paused, choosing her words with care. "—let's call it unusual or humorous rowing attire, so be prepared for Lodestone or his friends to suggest...well, anything."

I laughed. "I can't wait to see where this lands. Thanks for the heads-up. And for approving it in the first place."

Chapter Four

Life continued with the extra race and the extra practices on my mind, and a whole lot more besides. I couldn't say my situation with Brady improved noticeably. I made an effort to be a more aware roommate, but Brady apparently wrote me off after his blowup. I still tried to tutor him for our biology seminar, but it was like trying to teach a pig to sing. It wasted my time and annoyed the pig. If forced to guess, I would have said he had stopped trying. Oh, the muttering with his friends and their pointed looks continued, but any actual effort? That went down the dorm garbage chute along with pizza boxes and the bedroom trash.

Brady did, however, try to make it very awkward whenever Michael spent any time in our room. I couldn't imagine what he thought that would accomplish. Sure, he could bring his friends over while we tried to study together and generally be obnoxious, but he overlooked the fact that I had friends, too, and they came in multiples of eight; nine if you counted the cox'ns.

It came to a head one morning after practice. We were all hanging around the boathouse, at least those of us who didn't have to jet back to campus for classes or other reasons. I liked the CalPac boathouse. I hated to admit it, but it was much better than Cap City's cluster of three smaller boathouses that were always too small the moment renovations stopped. CalPac had only the one house, but it was huge, with enormous twin bays. CalPac had money, and it showed.

That morning I could not have cared less. I only wanted to stretch out after my row and maybe curl up under one of the boats and sleep for a hundred years or so. Concrete couldn't be that hard, could it?

"You okay, Jeremy?" Robbie, the junior varsity team captain, asked me.

I shrugged. "Yeah, why?"

"Because you look like shit. You need to get more sleep. We leave for Boston, like, the day after tomorrow. This is so not the time to be partying." Robbie was a tall guy, we all were, but while he was shorter than me, he was bulkier, and I tried to stay on his good side.

"I wish I were partying, because that would mean I was getting laid too." I shook my head. He was right. I was dead tired. "It's my roommate. He's decided I'm an asshole because I'm getting a better grade in biology seminar and maybe because I didn't notice he was lusting after me."

A couple of the guys in the boat snorted. They'd already learned that if I couldn't row it, it didn't matter. "Dude, seriously?"

I shrugged. "That's what he told me when he was yelling at me."

"Don't you have a boyfriend?" Robbie looked upset. He took relationships seriously.

"You've met him." I sat down on the ground and started stretching. If this was to be an inquest, I might as well put the time to good use.

Robbie looked at the other guys. "What d'you think, boys?"

At some unseen signal, a bunch of them nodded. Kev, the stroke in my JV boat, frowned. "I'll round 'em up. When were you thinking?"

"Tomorrow" was Robbie's curt reply. "There's no point in letting this get out of hand, and Jeremy needs his rest."

Kev—Kevin—looked down at me. "I'd say it's already out of hand. Next time something's wrong, Jeremy, speak up. We're a team, on and off the water."

"Do I want to know what's going on?" I looked up from a deep hamstring stretch.

Kev grinned. "You'll find out, but your reaction will be more genuine if we don't tell you."

Then suddenly Robbie loomed over me. "This roommate—what's his name?"

"Brady."

"So, this Brady or whatever it is, he knows you've got someone." Robbie looked like a thunderstorm. It was a statement, one last verification by the headsman before the axe fell.

I stood up. "He does. Michael's been to my room many times. In fact, that's part of my roomie's current MO. He and his friends try to make us as uncomfortable as possible. When we study, they make noise. When we're together—and no, not like you think—they do what they can to drive him out. Michael seems like a strong guy, but he's younger than I am, and while he doesn't let on, he's still a little intimidated."

"Didn't you say this guy was gay?" Kev looked perplexed, and I couldn't blame him. It didn't make much sense to me either.

"No, I said I failed to notice he wanted me, but I guess it was implied." I yawned. "I like to think I'm somewhat good-looking, but I'm not delusional. I won't be coaxing straight boys down out of the trees any time soon."

Kev snorted. "You're funny."

"Looks aren't everything. I don't think Brady's happy here, but at this point the number of fucks I give will fit on the head of a pin. If he tries to come between me and Michael, I will break out a level of crazy that will make his worst nightmares seem like his happy place."

My teammates on the JV squad stopped talking to stare at me.

"Dude," Kev said, "that was out loud."

I shrugged.

"Damn," the JV bow seat, Colton, whispered. "I want someone to feel that way about me."

"Try treating your girlfriend that way and see what happens," DeShawn, our two seat, said with a certain amount of disgust.

Robbie nodded, his mind made up. "Understood. I won't tell you when to expect us, but I'll need a copy of your room key."

Because nobody expects the oarsmen's inquisition? He was straight as an arrow, but the biggest drama queen I'd ever met. Apparently, we weren't just a team; we were a gang. I was cool with that.

Fortunately, my ride had waited for me. When the team captain lowered the boom, we lesser mortals waited. Or something. I was tired and hungry at that moment, and never mind the taper. At least we were done with twice-daily practices, so I might have a chance to catch up on some sleep before we left for Boston.

I'd rowed plenty of head races in my time with Capital City Rowing Club, but there were head races and then there was the Head of the Charles. Or so I'd been told. I'd never actually rowed it. Originally rowed on the headwaters of rivers, all "head race" meant was it was a longer race than a sprint, five kilometers instead of one or two, an endurance piece instead of an all-out race like the Crew Classic in San Diego. Head races were more forgiving, more psychological. In a sprint, if you missed a stroke, you might lose the race, but a head race? Not a problem. You had five thousand meters to make it up while you picked off the competition, one glorious stroke at a time. I loved head races.

I was one of the younger members of the JV squad. Walk-on JV rowers weren't unheard of at CalPac, but we weren't common either. I was nervous, but then, so were my boatmates. I had one advantage over them, however: my rowing headspace. It might take a fair amount of effort to get my attention for anything unrelated to rowing for a while, but they'd adapt. I wondered if Lodestone had warned my new coach. They'd find out in Boston.

The next morning my shock lasted only for seconds when the entire junior varsity squad let itself into my room and scared the crap out of Brady.

"What the fucking hell are you doing to Jeremy!" Robbie screamed through an old-school conical megaphone. That Robbie stood inches from Brady made it all the louder. "He's got the biggest race of the season in less than a week!"

"Gaaah!" shrieked the no-longer-sleeping Brady.

But Kev had somehow gotten his hands on a powered megaphone. And had it cranked all the way up. "The next time you try to intimidate Jeremy with your pathetic little friends, we'll bring in the novices. They're not housebroken, they don't smell very good, and their manners suck. I don't like novices. They make me angry. You make me angry when one of the rowers in the engine room of my boat is too tired to perform well because of your antics. You don't want to make me angry."

Robbie looked dyspeptic. "And knock off the bullshit where Jeremy's boyfriend's concerned. That makes me cranky. It makes me cranky when Kev has a problem because someone's upset one of his rowers. You've made me cranky twice. Do you want to find out what happens when you make me cranky for the third time?"

All Brady could do was stare in shock.

"Kev, he's not answering me." Robbie lowered his old-school megaphone for a moment.

"Maybe he can't hear you," Kev said through his purloined powered megaphone. If God spoke to mortals, he would sound like Kev and that powered megaphone. I would've enjoyed this if it weren't making me deaf.

"I—" Brady squeaked.

Robbie glared. "Speak up, asshole. What do you have to say for yourself?"

Brady's eyes were as wide as saucers. I had always thought that was just an expression.

"If you can't speak, then listen. I don't care if you're in a frat, I don't care if you play some other sport." Robbie leaned on Brady's bed so they were eye to eye. "Rowing is huge at CalPac, and there will always be more of us. Next time you have an issue with your roommate, try dealing with it like a grown-up. This isn't High School Part II: the Ashtray Years."

"And this is grown-up?" Brady said, finding his voice at last.

Kev laughed. "This is having a team at your back, and Jeremy knew nothing about this."

"But...Bratty?" Robbie said.

"It's Brady."

Robbie shrugged. "Whatever. Knock this shit off, especially intimidating his boyfriend. They're not doing anything gooey. Your hot roommate came preinstalled with the boyfriend functionality module. Deal with it."

*

Brady's domestication made life more bearable, but even though Michael felt less intimidated in my room, we didn't spend much more time together, Michael and I, those last few days before the Head of the Charles. The CalPac contingent left for Boston in two days, and I had already moved into my regatta headspace.

Michael kissed my forehead before he said goodbye to me. "I hope you have a safe trip, and you know I'll be glued to my computer watching the races in real time, but I've seen you in your headspace. There's not a lot of room for much else."

"I know." I sighed. "I'm sorry. Thanks for being so understanding."

Michael pulled me close. "It's who you are, Rem. It's part of what makes you so effective in a boat. Has the rest of your crew figured it out yet?"

"They're starting to. Lodestone knows what to expect, of course, and I think Coach Ridgewood has figured it out, but the guys? They're clueless."

"Wait until they see you walking the race-course." He laughed.

"Or see me going over the course map with the cox'n. Have you seen the course? It looks like a snake that's been through a laundry mangle." I shook my head. "This will be a tough one."

Michael kissed me again. "I have every confidence in you. Text me when you land, okay?"

"Absolutely."

What I hadn't told Michael, or anyone else, was that since I would be in Boston, I planned to arrive a day early and take a tour of Boston University and talk to the admissions office about transfer requirements. As I had more or less decided on biology as a major, it made sense to look at the offerings in the various biology programs. Lastly, and I shouldn't say most importantly but let's be honest, I wanted to talk to the men's crew coaches, even knowing how busy they would be right before the Head of the Charles.

Obviously, my parents knew about the trip. They agreed that it made good sense to check out the school as I would be in Boston. In fact, they applauded my thrift at combining the two trips and viewed my insistence on handling this myself as a sign of growing independence and maturity. A shrink for a parent—gotta love it.

Yet for some reason, they called me home for dinner the night before I left. The same people who had told me flat-out that I couldn't come home to do laundry, and that returning to the nest because I was homesick would not be allowed, now demanded my presence for dinner. Suspicious much, Remy?

"Since I'm coming back to Davis for dinner, is it all right if I invite Michael?" I asked when Mom called to set up the command performance.

"No, that wouldn't be a good idea at all," Mom said. "We'll keep it in the family."

I think in this culture we're educated to ignore our gut feelings, the little voices at the back of our minds that tell us to watch out, tell us not to go into that dark room after we hear a creak, calling, "Hello? Who's there?" The gut instinct that screams, "Don't go down into that basement, you fool!" Sure, if we listened to those, there'd be no teen horror movie genre, but the world could live without it. If I'd listened to mine, I'd have invented a midterm or something. Instead, I walked into a trap. Parents as ambush predators. Who knew?

Sure, it started out fine, food and banal conversation, the little catch-up things you endure when you haven't seen each other for a while. Most of it revolved around my brother. Of course, Goff and I spoke or e-mailed each other daily, frequently both and usually more than once, and that didn't include texting. If I couldn't reach him, I'd talk to Laurel. I knew more about their lives in San Diego than our parents did, that was for sure. I'd already flown down to visit him once.

Oh, and Goff's roommate? Gay as a daisy.

Then my dad glanced at my mom and sighed. "Look, Jeremy, we called you here tonight because we have something serious we need to talk to you about."

"We think you're too dependent on Michael and that maybe you should see less of him now that you're in college," Mom said.

That rocked me back in my chair. "Wow. What a great thing to lay on me right before a major regatta."

"It needed to be said." Dad sounded defiant.

"But right now? Thanks, Dad." I exhaled noisily. I hadn't realized I'd been holding my breath. "Why do you say I'm too dependent on Michael?"

Dad stared at me like I was crazy. "You spend an inappropriate amount of time together, for starters."

"Define inappropriate." They may have taken me by surprise, but I intended to rally and push this back. What a bunch of fuckery.

Dad didn't answer, but Mom said, "We've heard from the Castelreighs. They're worried you're exerting an undue influence on Michael."

"Okay, so if you won't define 'inappropriate,' maybe you can tell me how I'm exerting an 'undue influence' on Michael, who is—by the way—the aggressor in our relationship." I had to admit I thoroughly enjoyed Dad's flinch. If you can't stand the heat, don't give your gay son a chance to bring up his sex life, old man.

"He spends the night at your dorm," Dad said.

I sighed. "No, he most certainly does not. He fell asleep there once while I was studying. His parents came to get him at ten thirty, which, by the way, isn't late for a high school senior. As you should recall, Goff and I stayed up way later than that when we were studying."

"He's younger than you are, Jeremy," Mom said. "Nothing you say can change that."

I laughed. "When you're right, Mom, you're right. Yes, he's younger than I am. He was last year, too, and no one said anything then."

Dad looked exasperated, but what did he expect? For me to roll over and take it? They had crappy arguments. "We're worried about your dependence on him. We know he stood by you when you were so sick, but you don't owe him fealty."

"You make every important decision based on what he wants, dear," Mom said. I squinted at her. She never used endearments like, well, "dear."

"In fact, he makes those decisions for you." Then I saw Dad sneak a look at a file card he had hidden under his salad plate. Wow. If this got any more farcical, we'd be in an Oscar Wilde play. *The Importance of Having Your Act Together Before Attacking Your Son's Boyfriend*. I could already see the unfortunate Mr. Wilde crumpling this draft up and throwing it in the circular file.

"He does not! Seriously, can you even hear yourselves? I'm too dependent on Michael, yet I apparently exert undue influence while doing dastardly things to him after hours in the dorms. While being his serf. Can you at least get your story straight, as long as you're using a crib sheet, I mean." I snorted in derision. "I hate to break it to you, but when I said the aggressor, I really meant the debaucher. Yes, Mom and Dad, that's right, I'm a total bottom, and I get off on pain. So, if any debauching is being done, Michael's doing it, and you know what? Talking about it gets me hard enough to scratch granite."

Dad cringed. Okay, that wasn't suave, but I couldn't have cared less. "Jeremy, you chose your classes based on when he was available."

"And so do a lot of other people at CalPac! What's wrong with taking care of my responsibilities when Michael's in school? And have you asked for a side-by-side comparison of Geoff and Laurel's schedules? Because let me tell you, they did the same thing. So, I'm left asking myself, why am I being treated differently? I'd have thought you'd have ridden the poz pony to death, but maybe not. Am I still being treated like my judgment's no good because of the summer I turned seventeen? Or is it because I'm gay? I'll leave you to think about that, and in the meantime, this conversation is done."

I pushed back from the table. Someone was upgrading his service cabin on the way to Boston tomorrow, that's all I had to say about this meal. I recalled that when they forced me to go to CalPac rather than any of the schools I'd wanted to, I promised to make them pay. Looked like I'd be making good on that threat. I called the airline as I drove back to campus.

Chapter Five

I enjoyed the flight to Boston. It was a real novelty to have enough leg and shoulder room. I wore my wind shell, the waist-length, more or less waterproof anorak in team colors that would identify me faster than anything as someone in town for the Head of the Charles. Someone in the first-class cabin commented on it, as did one of the cabin attendants. But when I deplaned in Boston? Whoa. Adrift in a sea of rowers, or so it seemed. I read somewhere that the Boston area had the greatest concentration of colleges and universities of any place in the country, if not the world, and that Wednesday before the Head of the Charles, Boston looked as if every single one of those schools had fielded teams for the regatta. It was awesome.

But BU itself—I didn't know what to say. I'd fixated on it sight unseen—the school itself and the crew. The school looked amazing, and so did the biology programs. I knew my grades would pass muster. While there were some programs I would be ineligible for as a transfer student, BU still offered plenty of options. I sighed a little at that. Biology and medical education as a major sounded great, because somewhere along the line I'd gotten the notion of going to nursing school in my head and couldn't shake it loose. I could still go to nursing school, obviously, but a combined degree program like that sounded amazingly cool. I tried to put it in perspective. Yesterday I had known nothing about such a program, and I'd been perfectly happy to study biology or some permutation thereof, so I needed to chill because I suddenly found out about something I couldn't have. If I told my therapist that, maybe she'd pat me on the head.

As I wandered over to the race venue after the tour of the school, kicking at fallen leaves and trying to enjoy the brilliant show of color I'd never see in California, I tried to face the fact that something didn't *feel* right about...what? I couldn't quite put my finger on it yet. I hadn't seen much of the city, but there was a vibe to it, an energy, the likes of which Sacramento would never have. Said vibe could be good or bad. I'd have to learn to live with snow, and that prospect failed to thrill me. I had yet to speak to the rowing coaches, maybe that was it.

I walked along Massachusetts Avenue—or Mass Ave, as I'd already learned to call it—and tried to see myself here. I couldn't. I tried not to think about what that meant for the Plan Michael and I had hatched, him in Providence or New Haven, me here. *Good luck with that, Rem,* I thought. *This was only your future with your boyfriend far from disapproving parents.*

Despite the hurly-burly of race preparations, the BU coaches were actually quite willing to take a few minutes and talk to me, especially once I mentioned I was thinking about transferring. While Lodestone wasn't around at that moment, he had already arrived in Boston and stopped by, apparently. He had worked his now-usual magic and told them about my performances at the two Youth Nationals I'd raced in, as well as about my mojo as a walk-on junior varsity rower for CalPac. I wondered when I'd stop being grateful to Lodestone for all the things he did for me, and then I realized that maybe helping people out was something friends did for each other and one day maybe I'd be in a position to help a friend out. That's how you paid people back—you did good things for others in your turn. While the varsity coach was friendly, the JV coach gave me his card, and I promised him I'd keep him posted about my transfer plans. He promised to watch my races.

After meeting the BU coaches, I was too scattered to walk the course in my headspace. For once I was too unsettled for my prerace ritual. I had no idea what to do about that either. Eventually I found my way to where the CalPac trailer was parked. Maybe I could help re-rig boats. The mindlessness of re-rigging always settled my nerves.

And there was Coach Pendergast. Great. I was actually kind of afraid of him, but maybe—hopefully—that was only his reputation. What else was there to do?

Suck it up, dude. I stood nearby. "Excuse me, sir."

He looked up from where he was stretching. "Oh, hello. I literally just got here. You're on the JV, right? The sculler."

"Yes, sir." I laughed nervously.

"What can I help you with—?"

I held out my hand. "I'm Jeremy Babcock."

"Franklin Pendergast."

"I got here yesterday and finished what I needed to do today. I'm looking for something else to occupy me for a while," I said.

Coach Pendergast glanced significantly at the trailer next to them. "Well, the varsity rowers aren't supposed to meet here until tomorrow morning, but I think you and I can keep ourselves out of trouble for a while."

"Coach Ridgewood isn't having us meet until tomorrow at 1:00 p.m., and I'm too distracted right now for my usual prerace rituals." I started pulling out slings for the quad I'd be rowing.

"And what," Coach Pendergast said, "would these rituals be?"

Aw jeez, I'd set myself right up. "I usually walk the race-course at least once so I'm prepared for anything thrown at me. Based on the map, Anderson Bridge looks the worst."

"That is a wise thing to do, young Padawan, but let me show you something." Coach Pendergast made gimme motions, and I handed him my map. "Anderson looks bad, but there are worse perils along the banks of the Charles.

"There are two other bad bridges besides the Anderson, and all three bridges have their issues. First, after you launch, there's a dogleg, not unlike what we row on at home. Think of it that way, and you'll be all right." Pendergast pointed it out. "When you come out of it, look for the Riverside Boat Club on the Cambridge side of the river. You can essentially ignore the River Street and Western Avenue Bridges. I'm assuming you won't be rowing in the stern of the quad? If you are, Peter Lodestone's a bigger sadist than any of us realized."

I chuckled. "No, sir. I'm rowing at two. I shouldn't get into too much trouble."

"We can only hope. Next comes the Weeks Footbridge. It'll have people sitting off the edges, but they know better than to drop things on rowers."

"That's...different."

Pendergast chuckled. "That's not the half of it. The real problem with Weeks is that if your cox'n or bow seat isn't careful, you can easily add a good two hundred and fifty meters to your course. This is where experience comes in, and probably one of the reasons why you're not rowing bow in the quad."

"That and the fact that you don't want someone who's never rowed the course steering your boat."

Pendergast gave me a long, hard look. "You're an unusual person, Jeremy. You've achieved a lot at a young age, and yet you don't seem to have let it go to your head."

I thought about that for a few moments. "I'm not sure I'd say that, to be honest. It's more like we're not discussing that right now, and I'm very pragmatic. I know myself, and I know what I can do."

"I see." He appeared to think about that. "That's an interesting discussion, and one we'll have to come back to sometime, particularly when you make varsity. At any rate, after you clear all of those is when the course geography gets dicey. First you'll come to the Anderson Street Bridge." Pendergast looked up from the map. "It's right here. Can you see it?"

I squinted at the map. Could they not make the print bigger? "Yes, I think so."

"Anderson's tricky because it has a narrow opening, and to do it right, your cox'n—or your bow seat in the case of the quad—has to be on it, but that's not where collisions usually occur."

I gulped. "Collisions?"

"Yes." Pendergast grinned. "Collisions. I bet you've never been so glad not to row bow. Collisions usually occur at the Eliot Bridge."

I frowned. "Coach Ridgewood has had us practicing sharp turns for a month to be ready for it. It's that horrible?"

"It is indeed." He pointed to one of the bow-loading fours on the trailer. They looked strange without their rigging, the boats. "My cox'ns call those fours 'coffin ships' because if they hit anything, they're goners, and the Eliot Bridge? There's a very good chance of hitting the bridge or another crew if they're not careful. In a stern-steered boat, what will hit will usually be oars, or if the cox'n's terrible, the bow. In a bow-loader?"

I nodded. "Yes, I see. Coffin ship."

"Look at your map again. You've made it past Anderson, and there's a wicked dogleg. Your cox'n or your bow seat in the quad is going to be calling for one side to row harder than the other to keep the boat turning."

"That's basically a 180-degree turn." I frowned at the map.

"A *blind* 180-degree turn, and then you go through the Eliot Bridge."

Ugh. I was suddenly glad not to be a solo sculler and said as much.

"So, you walking the course prepares you by helping you to stay calm and being ready to drop power or crank it beyond everything you've got when it's needed." Pendergast smiled, as much as anyone can smile when someone's driven a boat trailer across the country. "So, tell me about you and sculling..."

When I finished, I realized it was a bit darker, and Coach Pendergast was smiling. "You're an interesting person, but as much as I enjoy talking to you, my own squad appears to be AWOL, and I need to find it. Or at least send out a text blast."

"I think I know enough to walk the course and have it make sense now. Thanks for your help." I could work with him.

As Coach Pendergast tried to find his rowers, I looked up...and met the friendly eyes of a rower from UC Davis. I wondered how much he had heard. Spilling your guts to your future coach is one thing, but to some stranger from another school? Suddenly I felt creeped-out and vulnerable.

I looked at the course map again, trying to find the nearest subway stop. They called it the T there. I'd come from BU, and that was a green-line T stop down near the starting line, but I'd been speaking to the BU crew coaches at the DeWolfe Boathouse on the Cambridge side of the river... Such a headache. New York City was laid out on a grid like they actually wanted you to find your way around, but Boston? Totally random because go fuck yourself, which, I was told, is a semiofficial greeting in these parts.

I felt my phone vibrate. I pulled it out of my pocket to find a text from Lodestone.

> LODESTONE: *Sorry I wasn't there to meet you. Marissa and I were getting settled. R U at the race-course?*
>
> ME: *I am.*
>
> LODESTONE: *Great! Meet you at the rowing expo in ten?*
>
> ME: *Perfect!*

That solved one problem. But as I walked away, I glanced over my shoulder, and that guy was still looking at me. I had a boyfriend. I shouldn't even be looking at other guys, should I?

*

Since I loved sculling, it only stood to reason that I'd love rowing in a double or quad, which was sculling with one or three other people, respectively. But ZOMG, rowing a quad during practice—even practicing sharp turns—couldn't hold a candle to rowing one during a race, particularly a race as tricky as the Charles. For one thing, the power. I'd never felt such power, not even in an eight. A men's eight at full steam was a dreadnought—big, heavy, and when it's up to speed, unstoppable. A sculler found that out the hard way at the Charles several years ago, when he was run over by a collegiate men's eight going all out. The sculler's innards became outtards, and if that accident had happened anywhere but there, the guy would've died. The Charles River isn't all that clean, and add to that the horrifying trauma of evisceration... But some of the best hospitals in the world are in Boston and Cambridge, and the sculler went from debris to the operating table in an amazingly brief amount of time. For all I know, he had a lifetime invite to row at the Head of the Charles. If not, he should.

But if a men's eight was a dreadnought, the coxless quad we rowed was a clipper ship—pared down to the bare essentials and built for speed, carrying nothing but the four people rowing her and moving with a velocity and grace the larger boats couldn't match. I fell in love with the quad almost immediately, which I supposed was only natural.

As it turned out, I knew the other three rowers, if only by sight. Lodestone obviously, and I had at least met

Brad Sundstrom. I'd never met Adam Lennox, but given how tall he was, he certainly stood out around the Cap City boathouse. When we met that Friday morning for a quick practice row—they knew I had other obligations—one of the hottest gingers I'd ever seen accosted me. He was older, with gray touching the hair at his temples. It didn't detract from his looks; far from it, it screamed "seasoned beef." He walked with a slight limp, which explained the cane.

He grabbed my hand, pumping my arm up and down like I was a well and he expected water to come out. "I cannot thank you enough for this. Would you believe these fools were giving serious thought to shoving me into the empty seat?"

The freakishly tall guy—Adam—sighed. "Tell the nice boy who you are, before he runs away and we have to go find him."

Ginger blushed. "Sorry, I get a little excited sometimes. I'm Owen Lennox. The giant over there is my husband, Adam."

"Hi, Owen, I'm Jeremy Babcock." I tried not to laugh. "I've met, or at least seen, your husband, but it's good to put a name to the face. But why are you thanking me?"

"Dude, are you blind? I limp and use a cane."

I felt my face heat right up. "I assumed you can row, or they wouldn't do it."

"I can row, but not on this level, and thanks to this bum leg, I'll never row at this level." Owen seemed pretty cheerful, but I happened to glance at Adam while Owen was speaking. Adam looked like he was in the mood for dismemberment. They had a story to tell, but it wasn't my place to ask. "So, you being here? Gives them a chance to win and spares me from humiliating myself. I owe you a beer. Are you old enough to drink?"

"No, but I won't tell anyone if you won't."

Adam frowned. "Pete, I thought you said he was varsity."

"I said he was varsity-*caliber*." Lodestone smirked at Adam. "Actually, I said he's better than that, but don't let him know."

"He's standing right here, Pete." Brad shook his head as he looked up from where he was adjusting the foot stretchers on the boat.

Lodestone looked right at me. "Oops."

"Can we launch?" This was getting tiresome and more than a little embarrassing. "And are there *any* heterosexuals at Cap City?"

"Sure," Owen said. "Just because I haven't seen them doesn't mean there aren't any."

"That's pretty shaky logic, you know," I said to Owen.

He shrugged. "What can you do?"

Brad elbowed Lodestone. "He'll do fine."

So, with that, we launched the clipper, a Cap City quad named *Wind Racer*. True to her name, she flew before the wind coming in off the harbor. With Adam and his long reach at stroke making us all stretch to match and Brad in the bow to keep us on course, we spent the first half-hour learning one another's rhythms. In actuality, that meant me learning to fit in with them, since they knew how to row together. It took me longer than I thought it would, but we eventually clicked together as a crew.

"So, wait," I said to Brad's husband, one Drew St. Charles, as we fetched the oars. "Those three came out here to row in the Directors' Challenge? And nothing else? That seems kind of extreme."

"With you in a collegiate race, they can't row anything else," Drew told me quietly. He'd been busy this morning, working on our "fun" race apparel.

"Damn, I'm sorry." I felt like crap. "I'm keeping them from really enjoying this weekend."

But Drew shook his head. "No, you're allowing them to be here. Don't get me wrong, I was the first to suggest finding someone who could commit to both races—nothing personal, it's only logical—but it turns out that most of the guys who're here in the masters or seniors sweeps events are lousy scullers, and all the women scullers are entering their own boats."

"Oh." I hadn't expected that.

"I actually looked all this up online. There are mixed boats allowed, but they have to be two men and two women, otherwise they're ineligible for medals, and that would never do. They're such competitive boys." He gave me the beady eye. "Something tells me you're one too."

What could I say? "Guilty as charged."

Drew laughed. "Good for you. You're honest. So many people try to deny that sort of thing. From what I saw of practice, you at least have something to back it up. In any event, they wanted to row a men's quad, and by asking you, they get to do that. I know you've got a busy day ahead of you but try to get some rest blah blah blah. Pete will no doubt get all coachy on you, but if you're as good as he says, you know this. After you're done with your CalPac practice—expect me to take a ton of pics to send to Nick, by the way—come find us. We'll have us a cackle or three and then you'll launch."

I found myself liking Drew. I could tell he'd be high maintenance, but then, I was too. We can smell our own. Maybe that was why he clapped his arm across my shoulders as we walked back to the other guys. We already felt like we were a team.

Wait, did he say Nick? As in Nick Bedford? Holy moly.

*

When the four of us pulled into the dock at the end of our race, I discovered we had far more than Drew, Owen, and Marissa Lodestone rooting for us. Word had spread, and all the CalPac and Cap City rowers had turned out to cheer for us, not only my JV teammates. It was pretty cool to realize that some of those people hanging off the Weeks Footbridge were cheering on my boatmates and me. Owen told me that by the time we neared the finish line, we had quite the following, and not just people from our various teams either.

"People like a good show," Owen said, "and with those getups Drew put together—"

"Everybody loves a gay unicorn. Don't deny it." Drew smirked. "They'd better get points for them too."

"Good job, guys!" Lodestone congratulated us once the boat was de-rigged.

I wasn't sure what to make of that. "We missed an automatic invitation to return next year by the skin of our teeth. We're thrown back into the lottery."

"Let me tell you something about that lottery," Brad said. "It's not nearly as random as they pretend it is. Where did we start? I mean, what was our bow number?"

I thought about it. "Thirtysomething?"

"Right," Adam said, apparently picking up the job of cheering me up. "Where did we finish, Remy?"

"I don't know, actually."

Adam thought for a moment and then laughed. "I don't either. Owen, where did we finish?"

Owen checked his phone. "Unofficially, I think you finished eleventh."

"So, what that means," Lodestone said, "is that we passed over twenty crews. That wasn't three men at or over thirty, Remy. That was you. You may have killed our age handicap, but you more than made up for it. I can almost guarantee this boat will be coming back. Now we have to find a way to tell Hal he's fired."

Drew leaned in close. "They've never advanced that far in the pack. Ever," he said in a stage whisper.

"Ouch!" Brad clasped his hands over his chest like he'd taken an arrow to his heart.

"Oh, cut it out, you big baby. You're the one who explained age handicaps to me." Drew sounded tough as nails, but I also saw him give Brad a tight hug and big kiss on his cheek moments later. All I could do was smile at that. I hoped Michael and I would be there someday.

Michael. Our plan. Talk about throwing water on the buzz. I'd avoided thinking too much about it, but BU wasn't going to work. As much as I lived for crew, I couldn't live on it, not really. Sure, there were professional rowing bums, and apparently a moving company in the area that hired rowers to facilitate the rowing bum lifestyle, but I needed more out of life. I needed not to think about that right now, not with another, arguably more important race tomorrow.

Then I looked up, and somehow there he was again, the UC Davis rower. I knew he wasn't stalking me. The Davis trailer happened to be next to CalPac's and Cap City's, but I saw him again, the same good-looking fella at the UCD trailer, who saw me right back. He smiled and I? For some reason, I smiled in return.

"Good job," he said. "That was fantastic to watch. But...are you a member of Cap City or do you row for CalPac?"

I laughed uneasily. "I rowed at Cap City for four years, but I go to CalPac now."

"That's cool."

Then the clock started ticking. Someone had to say something. Or maybe it was just me.

"I...um, have to make a phone call." I sounded lame to my own ears.

Did he look disappointed? "I'll see you later, I guess."

I started walking away, but I made sure my "Hey, babe" when Michael picked up could be heard.

"What was that about?" he said.

"Someone from UCD is getting a little too friendly, and while I'm perfectly willing to be neighborly, there are limits."

I buckled my collar back on as we talked.

Chapter Six

"You back with us, Mr. Babcock?" Coach Ridgewood said as my boatmates and I put our boat back in slings after our race. After two races, I understood what the big deal about the Head of the Charles was. The course was horrible—I'd rowed on far better courses on the West Coast. The weather could be garbage—people told me stories of snow during the regatta, and unlike the benign weather for my quads race yesterday afternoon, the weather today was the suck. A cold wind had come roaring off the Back Bay last night, making racing miserable, but not miserable enough to shorten the course. Yet in terms of competition, the West Coast had nothing to offer like this, and that—plus the rigors of the course—was why the Head of the Charles ranked. Now I understood.

I cocked my head to one side. "I didn't go anywhere."

Kev snickered. "Don't ever change, Jeremy."

"You've been a bit distracted." Coach Ridgewood smiled when she said it, but that didn't stop the other guys from laughing.

"Oh. That. That's not distraction, Coach. That's me in race mode."

"Your coach at Cap City mentioned something about that, but I have to admit I didn't believe him," Coach Ridgeway said. "Peter Lodestone sings your praises very loudly, you know."

I blushed. "He's always pushed me to be more than I am."

"I'm sorry. I didn't mean to put you on the spot. It's been a while since I've seen anyone that single-minded."

Ridgewood left to do something besides embarrass me, and I endured the good-natured teasing of my teammates. They didn't mean anything by it, and I knew it made me a better rower. I was sure they had their own prerace rituals. Simply because I hadn't seen them didn't mean such things didn't exist.

CalPac had a large presence at the Charles that year, JV A and B boats, as well as multiple varsity boats. I hadn't paid them much attention since I didn't row varsity. It sounded conceited, but every time I thought "I don't row varsity," I always appended a "yet." Maybe it was conceited, but I was also the only person on either CalPac squad invited to row for another club. That probably meant something, but I was still tripping on lactic acid and too drained to figure it out.

As we finished de-rigging our rides, we made sure the riggers themselves were secured together for transit but otherwise left the boat alone. There would be a mass loading of the shells later, but someone had the master trailer-loading plan, and it wasn't any of us. We had some free time, and everyone scattered, everyone but me. I loitered around the trailer, trying to figure out what to do. Call Michael? I'd missed him this weekend, and it would've been sweet if he'd been here, although I guess "watching your boyfriend race" wasn't much of a reason to miss school, although touring colleges was, and he certainly could've toured BU with me. Call Goff? I'd have called my parents, but I burned incandescent with fury whenever I thought about them, so calling them may not have been the best of ideas. If they wanted to know how the races had gone, they could look the results up online.

I felt the skin on the back of my neck prickle and looked around. Coach Ridgewood was speaking to Coach Pendergast and someone I had never seen before, someone in a USRowing wind shell. I didn't think too much of it. USRowing was a major sponsor—to say nothing of the insurer—of the regatta, and with the sharp turn in the weather, people had dashed for the merchandisers, of which USRowing was again one of the major ones. Half the people along the banks of the Charles that day had some kind of USRowing gear on to ward off the cold. I was tired—drained, more like it—and the fact that one or the other looked over at me meant nothing. People had been looking at me all weekend, and I'd been looking right back. Hot people positively infested this sport, and with all the eye-fucking going on, I was surprised we managed to put any boats in the water, let alone row them.

Speaking of eye-fucking, as I looked around, who did I happen to see? The rower from UC Davis, and naturally I was caught. I blushed, of course, and looked away, but he'd seen me, and we both knew it. I checked to make sure my collar was in place; it was, but with my wind shell zipped, it was out of sight.

I pretended to find my CalPac-branded gym bag all-consuming, but within about fifteen seconds, I felt him behind me. Taking a deep breath, I squared my shoulders and turned around. A bit taller than I was, he had dirty-blond hair and blue eyes and broad shoulders supporting a muscular torso. He was even hotter up close. I tried not to drool.

He coughed. Could he be as nervous as I was? Why did this matter? "Hi."

"Hello." Jeez, could I sound any dorkier? And how could I get out of this and save face for both of us?

"I...uh...saw you and thought I should introduce myself," he said. He was as red as I was. That made me feel better.

"Seeing as how we're practically neighbors and all." Yet somehow neither of us had gone looking for Cal State Sacramento. I held my hand out.

"Right." He shook my hand.

"Right."

So, we stood there for a moment shaking hands. No names were exchanged.

"Oh!" he said. "I'm Josef, but everyone calls me Randy." It sounded like Yosef.

"My name's Jeremy, and that makes perfect sense, Randy." I let go of his hand.

"I'm sorry, my middle name's Randolf." I tried not to notice how cute he was when he blushed. How the hell was I going to get out of this? I was done with worries about saving face and was seriously considering flight when my phone went off to Eve 6's "Inside Out." Because SoCal may be where his mind was, but it sure wasn't his state of mind. Goff! Thank goodness. Yeah, we had a hard time saying goodbye this summer.

"Girlfriend?" Randy said. Fish much?

I shook my head. "Boyfriend." I smiled. "It was great to meet you, but I gotta take this."

Saved by the bell. Or ring tone, as the case may be. I shouldered my bag and waved Randy a cheerful farewell as I headed for the nearest T station. Ugh, I get myself into the worst fixes.

"Goff. Thank God."

"Germy! Congratulations, baby brother! That was some amazeballs—"

"You have no idea how happy I am to hear your voice."

Goff paused. "Now what did you do?"

I explained my most recent awkward situation. Goff laughed.

"It's not funny!"

"No," Goff struggled to get out, "you're right. It's hysterically funny. I can't wait to tell Laurel."

I made the only sensible reply. I blew a giant raspberry into my phone. Then I wiped the spit off it.

"Seriously, Rem, I watched both of your races. You looked great, at least what I could see. You were fast."

Goff always knew what to say. "Thanks, brother mine. Both races felt good, even if they felt totally different."

"So, which one was your favorite?" I heard noises in the background, women's voices. He was probably over at Laurel's dorm. Big surprise there.

"If I had to choose?" I thought about that for a few moments. "Probably my race in the quad. You know how I feel about sculling, and something about that race felt pared down to basics. It was four scullers and a sleek, fast boat."

"Rem, you were dressed as gay unicorns."

"Only three of us were gay unicorns. Lodestone was a straight unicorn."

Goff snickered. "I can't actually believe we're having this conversation."

"Speaking of conversations..." It all came rushing back. "I needed you to have my back last week. Jeez, the parental units were after me about Michael."

Goff didn't say anything at first. Then he sighed. "Do I even want to know?"

"No, probably not, but if they'll get after me about Michael, they may get after you about Laurel. I can't think what set them off." Thinking about that dinner made me queasy, and that wasn't good. I had a bunch of calories I needed to replace, and right then I couldn't face the thought of food.

"Why don't you start by summarizing the convo?"

So, I did. "Basically, they think I plan my life around Michael."

"Dude, you do."

He did not go there. "I do not!"

"Rem, he makes every important decision for you," Goff said. "You're entirely too dependent on him."

I found myself about to scream in my brother's ear, so I took a few deep breaths. "Michael doesn't make every important decision for me, Geoff. He doesn't. What he does do is help me clarify my thinking, and I do the same for him. That's not dependency, that's being boyfriends."

"Okay, Rem, I've never wanted to get into this, but you know me and Laurel are close—"

"The word is whipped, Geoff." I couldn't figure out where he was going with this, and my suspicions were on high alert.

Goff sighed in my ear. "If you must call it that."

"It's true."

"Then you need to listen to this, because you're way beyond that, and Mom and Dad are right."

"The hell you say."

We always had each other's backs. Always. Growing up, Goff had an easier relationship with Dad than I did, especially after I overheard him saying some particularly uncomplimentary things about me to some of his friends on the phone. About the nicest was changeling, but even though Goff didn't understand why Dad and I butted heads and why I hid everything from our parents, he didn't question it. We were brothers, and that was that. So, this? This was the closest he'd come to betrayal in our eighteen years together.

"Rem, Michael's become a crutch for you. I remember perfectly well you sitting down with the CalPac fall course schedule this summer and matching your schedule against what you thought would be Michael's school and crew schedule, all so you'd be available when he whistled."

What the actual fuck? How could he say something like that? "Why does everyone keep harping on that?"

"Well, for starters, it's weird. Not even Laurel and I did that. I scheduled my classes when they worked for me, and she for her. We spend a lot of time together, sure, but we're here for an education."

"Bull. Shit. The only reason you two didn't plan your schedules together is because she told you what to take and when to take it, and don't deny it. I've been down there. I've seen your calendars." I thought for a moment. "As for me and Michael, that's not making him a crutch, that's me having a more flexible schedule and making sure we have some time together."

"Maybe people—me and Mom and Dad—would let it go if we knew for sure it wouldn't happen again, Rem. What happened? You used to be so...so fierce, and now it's like you're scared to do anything without Michael telling you it's okay."

Maybe I'd been so fierce last summer because I'd had to be, because I'd been semicloseted, and I hadn't thought I'd had anyone on my side. No one had stood at my back, and I couldn't even have counted on my twin brother. Looked like maybe I counted on him too soon.

Maybe I didn't trust my own judgment anymore because—hello—the last time I did, it resulted in me contracting HIV. But could I say these things aloud? No, I could not.

"Just because Michael's still in high school doesn't mean—"

"Doesn't mean you should set your life by him. It doesn't mean you should dump that kind of responsibility on him. Rem, he's not even eighteen yet! Give him a break."

"What's *that* supposed to mean?"

Goff sighed. "It means you're dragging him into college life before he's finished high school. It means you're still stuck in high school. It means," he plowed on relentlessly, "that you've stopped living for you and live only for Michael. I may be whipped, and yes, it's a foregone conclusion I'll propose to Laurel when she tells me to, but I'm still my own man. When did you stop being yours?"

Goff's words hit like body slams, each harder than the last, each coming so fast I barely had time to process it before the next one flew at me.

"He saved my life," I whispered.

"No, Rem, he didn't."

"But—"

"He didn't, Rem. He really didn't."

Okay, now Goff was full of crap. "When I was in the hospital—"

"If you hadn't gotten sick, you'd have told Mom and Dad sooner or later."

"But I did get sick."

"And I told them." Goff paused. "Rem, he kept you company, he gave you strength when you needed it, but he didn't save your life. You did that."

"But I love him," I said softly.

"That's great, Rem. He's a fantastic guy…but try not to lose yourself. I think that's all Mom and Dad are saying. It's what I'm saying. You used to be as tough as nails. You're not now. What happened? That's what Mom and Dad are reacting to."

There was so much I could not tell Goff, let alone my parents, so much I longed to articulate but didn't dare. My parents and brother were supposed to be the people closest to me in the world, right? Instead, they were the people I hid my cards from, the people I would never tip my hand to. Families were so messy. I knew on one level I was so lucky to have the family I did, regardless of how angry they made me, but on another level, recent events caused me to hold them at arm's length, there to stay for… I didn't know how long.

"I have to go. My coach is giving me evil looks." I disconnected the call without giving him a chance to say anything.

I called Michael immediately.

"Hi."

"What's wrong?"

"Everything. Nothing. I...I wish you were here."

Michael sighed. "We talked about this. There's no way I could be there."

"I know, but maybe all this shit wouldn't seem so vivid."

"Uh-oh. What's going on?"

"My parents are on the warpath because they think I'm too dependent on you, and apparently my treacherous brother thinks they're right."

Michael didn't say anything for a while, long enough that I'd have thought he had hung up if it weren't for his breathing. "I have to admit I think they may kind of have a point."

"They have a point. Well, fuck me with a chainsaw, why didn't you say so?" So that's what it felt like when the bottom dropped out of your stomach.

"Calm down, big guy. It's not a major deal. You seem to be naturally subservient, and I'm naturally dominant. You depend on me, and I take charge and take care of you. It's the natural order of things, and it seems to work pretty well." I wanted to take comfort in his words, I truly did, but something held me back. "Now I want you to do something for me. It'll probably be easier if you're somewhere without a lot of witnesses."

I looked around. Not too many people, for all that I wasn't too far from the race venue. "Yeah, it looks clear."

"Good, then I want you to put your arms around you like you're hugging yourself."

"That's absurd."

"See, the thing is, princess, I'm not there to do it myself, and you sound like you really need a hug right now. You sound like you need more than that, to be honest, but this proxy bit only goes so far," Michael said. "So, be a sport and play along?"

I had to smile. "Okay, arms around me."

"Now close your eyes and pretend I'm right there with you, putting my arms around you, and loving on you," Michael whispered in my ear. "You looked amazing out there. We watched some of the races at the boathouse, you know."

"Really?" That made me feel better.

Michael laughed softly. "A Cap City Juniors alum and our coach racing at the Head of the Charles? Are you kidding? We had a huge monitor and live video streaming. We made a party of it. But oh my God, those costumes? Who was responsible for those outrages?"

"Coach Sundstrom's husband."

"I've heard people call him Twinkerdrew." Michael giggled. "Isn't that horrible?"

"Yes, especially since he was such a sweetheart to me before the race when I was feeling like I was a lousy substitute they scraped up at the last minute."

"Good, I'm glad he set you...um, straight on that score because, Rem? I got chills watching you. You've always been good, but I've got to tell you. You're heading for great, and I'm not saying that because I'm your boyfriend."

"Thanks," I said, sniffling. Damn cold Boston air. "I miss you."

"Me, too. You'll be home soon, and I'll be waiting at the airport for you."

I smiled, my earlier bad mood slipping away. "I'm glad someone will. With my flights not coinciding with the rest of the team, I figured I'd take a shuttle back to school."

"I don't think you'll have to worry about that," he drawled.

"Oh?"

Michael chuckled. "It's not like I'm going to say anything."

"Tease." I had to admit, however, that I was feeling much better for speaking to him.

"You know it." Michael must have sensed my improved outlook too. "Are you doing better? You sound better."

I smiled. "I'm better, thanks to you."

"I think you'd have cheered yourself up eventually," Michael said.

"Maybe. Or maybe I like hearing your voice."

"Text me when your flight's on the ground?"

"Will do."

We made our goodbyes, and I disconnected the call. I had to wonder, I thought as I went to meet my teammates, if this was what Geoff had been talking about. Then I tried to put it out of my mind.

*

I spent the flight home Monday brooding. I'd had a great weekend filled with amazing rowing and good times. I wished I could've spent more time with the Lodestones and the rest of the people from Cap City, rather than my teammates from CalPac, but as head-in-the-clouds as I was, even I knew how impolitic that would've been. You have to dance with the one who brung you and all that. I could always visit the Cap City contingent back in Sacramento, after all, maybe even jump in on some practices. All I had to do was ask.

That said, I couldn't have been great company. I pled fatigue, and since I was the only one who had rowed in two events, no one could gainsay me. In reality, I was sulking, and it was a relief to be dropped off at the airport by Lodestone. I could quit pretending to put on a happy face after what was a great debut at the Head of the Charles, because my plans with Michael had gone up in smoke before the regatta started. My pie-in-the-sky school, the school my parents promised I could transfer to, the school for which they have given me a notarized note containing said promise, was clearly not for me. BU offered a lot, but not to me, and that's where my troubles started. If I were only looking to transfer, it would be no great loss, but Michael and I had hung a great deal on the two of us attending school together in New England.

I had a lot to talk to Alicia about at my next appointment.

Chapter Seven

I hit the tarmac running when I returned from Boston. Sure, Coach Ridgewood had given me and the rest of the crew notes to show our professors so they didn't think we had cut their classes, but that note didn't make the homework vanish or prevent the semester from marching along in its stately progression toward midterms and, eventually, finals. In other words, I had a great time rowing on the East Coast over a long weekend, and the payback sucked.

I still had therapy, and that was a good thing. I wonder if Martha Stewart tried to copyright that phrase. Not that I'd pay her royalties or anything. I also had all the problems I had when I'd left for Boston, too, plus some new ones.

"So, tell me about Boston," Alicia said.

We stood side by side in her office, looking out of the window at the city below. Her office sported a great view. I had no idea how she accomplished anything.

I sighed. "How about I start with my parents' ambush before I left?"

"Yes, I think that would be a good idea." Alicia gestured for me to take a seat in the big, sinfully comfortable armchair she provided for her patients. It beat the trite stereotype of a couch, I supposed.

"I thought it was a bit off to be summoned to dinner..." I started.

Alicia nodded. "Is that how it felt?"

"Yes, definitely. Before school started, my parents went through a whole song and dance about not coming home very often, how I'd never make the break if I came home every weekend blah blah blah, and then to be told to come home for dinner? I felt like I was being called on the carpet for something, and subsequent events bore that out."

I continued to tell Alicia about that evening, almost reliving the events, it was that real in my memory.

"So, how'd that make you feel?"

I frowned. "Well...ambushed, like I said. Even though I knew something was off-key about the whole thing, I had no idea they were going to go after Michael."

"Did they go after Michael, or your relationship with Michael?"

Sometimes I hated her coolly unflappable demeanor, that and her insight.

"Our relationship, I guess." I thought about it. "Their arguments were internally contradictory. As angry as I was—as I am—I realized that at the time. They told me I'm too dependent on him, and that he and I spend an 'inappropriate' amount of time together."

"'Inappropriate'? What does that mean?" Alicia frowned.

I shrugged. "Wish I could tell you. Dad never defined his terms."

"I can see why you're frustrated, Jeremy. I'm surprised you didn't get up and leave," Alicia said.

"This all happened so fast that there wasn't time. Anyway, then my mom started in. She claimed that Michael's parents had told them they thought I exerted an undue influence on him."

Alicia flipped back through her notes. "Wait, I thought he was an undue influence on you?"

"That's my parents. They think he influences me too much." I was starting to enjoy this.

"Now I know why you roll your eyes so often. Please continue."

"Then my parents and probably the Castelreighs accused me—us?—of spending nights in my dorm, which has never happened, by the way. The one time Michael fell asleep while I was studying, his parents came to get him at 10:30 p.m. I had to remind Mom and Dad that this is not particularly late for a high-school senior to stay up. Geoff and I stayed up much later than that when we had exams."

"So did I." Alicia laughed. "Pretty much anyone on the college-admissions track does. Do go on."

"Right. Then they objected to the fact that I'm older. I was also older when we started dating, but no one had any problems with the age differential then." I thought for a moment. "Then they argued that Michael makes my decisions for me, based on what, I'm not sure, to be honest. Neither they nor Geoff liked the fact that I chose classes this fall based on when Michael was busy at school and in practice, leaving my afternoons free when he's free. Is that some kind of felony I don't know about?"

"You'd have to check with Detective Nakimoto about that, but I don't think so." Alicia thought for a while. "You've mentioned your brother. Why don't you tell me where he fits in where all of this is concerned?"

I made a face. "Ugh, he's on our parents' side, and the biggest hypocrite on earth. He admitted he'd propose to his girlfriend when she told him to, and their schedules match despite his avowal otherwise. Yet when he called me to congratulate me on the races, he spent the time lecturing me about Michael."

"Can you sketch that conversation for me?"

"Jeez, do I have to? He's on my shit list right now."

Alicia shrugged. "He's a very important person in your life, more so than your parents. Given that you said he agrees with them, I think it might be valuable to hear his reasons. Just the highlights. I don't want to put you through all of that again."

"Yeah, yeah, I got it. Let's see... I summarized the fight with our parents, ending with their accusation I plan my life around Michael. Then he agreed. He doubled down by saying I was way too dependent on my boyfriend."

Things like that made me the moody, broody asshole everyone knew and loved. When I got out of there, I intended to plug in and listen to nothing but Joy Division for a week. Anyone who wanted to talk to me could take a number and wait until I surfaced.

"So, tell me what you think Michael does for you." Typical shrink babble.

"I think Michael helps me clarify my thinking, but apparently I'm the only one." Then I thought some more. "Geoff tried to use his relationship with his girlfriend as an example of balance and health, but I had none of that. Given that he's all but grafted to his girlfriend, the irony was suffocating."

I didn't say anything for a few minutes as I tried to put my thoughts and feelings into words fit for polite company. Sure, I knew I could've sworn and ranted in therapy, but why be that person?

"Geoff plowed onward, claiming Michael's my crutch and that it wasn't normal for me to make sure my schedule allowed me to be free when Michael was. Then he said I used to be so fierce and asked what happened. He doesn't get that I used to be tough as nails because I had to be." My voice dropped and thickened as I tried not to cry. "When you're in the closet, you've got no one. You're it. I couldn't even count on him because he didn't know." I didn't say anything for a moment or two. I choked tears back, my throat tight. "I still can't count on him."

Alicia said nothing but handed me tissues and let me cry.

"They don't get it. I mean, when I got back from Boston, I thought I'd get my luggage and take a shuttle back to campus. No greeting, no fanfare, but when I cleared security, there was Michael and what looked like half the CalPac novices and the guys from the Cap City gentlemen's crew who had rowed with me last year." I sniffled. "They had a banner and everything."

"That's wonderful, Jeremy."

After I'd had a chance to regain my equilibrium, Alicia said, "Now I'd like you to try to put yourself in Geoff's place. Why do you think he might be so concerned?"

This was the part of therapy I hated—when she made me work for it. I thought for a while. I hated living inside my head so much because I knew what she was looking for. "It's like what we were talking about before, when I blamed myself for having HIV. I made a mistake and won't trust myself again. But those events were a year and a half ago, and I need not to let them determine the course of my life. Just because I'm a sub doesn't mean the guy in charge in the bedroom gets to make my decisions outside of it. I don't think I've turned control of my life over to Michael, I really don't."

"But Geoff does. Your parents do."

I curled my lip. "My parents are once again on a need-to-know basis where my life is concerned. They've gone too far, and the olive branch is theirs to wave, not mine."

"Understood. They were over-the-top, and from what you've told me, that was far from the first time. But please consider your brother."

I didn't want to think about my brother. I wasn't ready to forgive him. I wasn't sure I could, or even should. I knew he expected total acceptance of his relationship with Laurel. Propose to her when she told him it was time? Excuse me? He needed to hear that one out loud. Repeatedly. Sac up, Geoff. What about when it worked for you? What about cutting me some of that same slack? My relationship was worth every bit as much.

All I said was, "I'll think about it."

"So, you and Michael. One thing that cannot be argued with is that he's still in high school and you're only a freshman in college. You're both young, and while you're older than he is, do you really feel any wiser?"

I laughed. "Would I be here if I did?"

"Touché. In a way, since you like classical and literary references, you're like Romeo and Juliet, only it's to be hoped without the poison. You've already got the disapproving families."

Romeo and Juliet. That tripped a wire. Romeo and Juliet. Romeo and Juliet laws.

Josh Brennan.

Oh, sweet suffering—

I barely made it to the bathroom in time.

*

"Jeremy, are you in there?" Alicia sounded scared.

I looked at myself in the mirror. I'd been fairly well put together when I'd left my room that morning, but wow, not anymore. Pale, shaking, haggard. I should hurry back to my room. I'd break Brady of his stupid infatuation right quick.

I washed my face one last time and then took another swig of water to rinse my mouth out. Thank the fickle goddess of the ergs for sugarless gum. At least that would disguise my breath.

"Yeah, I'll be right out." I sounded like I was a thousand years old. I looked it too.

"Are you all right? What happened?" Alicia looked appalled when I emerged from the bathroom, like maybe she'd never sent anyone screaming to the bathroom to vomit before. I guess she didn't treat eating disorders or something.

"Not here," I said. "In your office."

I leaned back in the chair, trying to order my scattered thoughts, trying to make sense of what sent me racing to the bathroom to heave my guts out. "I'm Josh Brennan."

I heard Alicia squelch a gasp. You knew it was bad when you frightened your shrink.

"Can you explain what that means?"

I looked at Alicia like she was simple. She had Brennan's file; she told me that herself. "Star-crossed lovers, disapproving families. I'm older. Do the math."

Jeez, thinking about it made me want to hurl again, but there wasn't anything left in my stomach to come up.

"You're going to need to flesh this out for me, Jeremy, because it's not at all obvious," Alicia said.

How could it not be? I mean, it was a big ol' radioactive elephant in the corner.

Wasn't it?

I sighed. "It just is."

She nodded. "You obviously feel very strongly about this, and I'd like to come back to it."

"Yeah, I think that'd be a good idea." I rubbed my face. "I'll give it more thought, see if I can't come up with something more articulate, but damn, it's such an overpowering feeling. I wish I could put it into words for you."

"You're not putting it into words for me. You're putting it into words for you."

I tried not to grit my teeth. I knew she was right, but sometimes I really hated psychobabble. I wondered if learning to say things like that was an elective or a required course at headshrinker's school.

"We've got a bit of time left. What else happened on your trip to Boston?"

Alicia's office had clocks scattered on most horizontal surfaces. She and her patients could tell when time was running out.

"How do you know anything else happened in Boston?" Seriously, how did she do that? It was spooky.

Alicia sighed. "Because you're not paying me to be stupid, and because you're one of the most layered people I've ever met. If you'd rather save it for next time, I completely understand. This session has been fairly intense."

"No, you're right." I searched for the right words. "Have I told you about what I call 'the Plan,' for lack of a better term?"

"No, I don't think so." Alicia started making notes.

"Basically, Michael and I intended to go to the same school on the East Coast, or at least schools close to each other, for four years of rowing, studying, and...probably falling in love." I paused. "We haven't told our parents that's why we're looking at East Coast schools, but that's pretty much it."

"And the problem?"

"I looked at Boston University while I was there for the regatta." The thought of it made me tense.

She nodded. "That's the sort of eminently sensible thing I'd expect of you. So, what went wrong?"

"I realized it won't work. I don't want to leave CalPac and the West Coast. I'd planned to go to BU, while Michael is looking at Yale and Brown. Boston's a great city, BU's a brilliant school...but not for me..."

Alicia put her pen down. "And you don't know how to tell Michael?"

"I don't even know how to begin." I sighed. I'd only thought life was complicated last year.

"It all seems to come back to Michael, doesn't it?"

A horrendous thought struck me. "Does this mean my parents are right?"

"No, or at least not for any of the reasons you've brought up today. Michael's obviously very important to you, but that doesn't mean you're too dependent on him, or being influenced by him, or are influencing him to an unwholesome degree, or whatever else they've said. Nor—" Alicia paused to look over her glasses. "—does it follow that you're an abusive user."

I slid down in my chair a little more. "Okaaay."

"What it means, Jeremy, is that he's an important part of your life right now. It also means that besides the fact you've already moved into a different phase of your life, you're moving further into it, and maybe that the pace of change in your life is accelerating relative to Michael's, at least for now."

I found myself nodding. "That makes sense."

"It also means you have some tough conversations ahead of you, particularly if Michael's making decisions about his life based on this plan. You owe it him to come clean about your recent realizations, and you owe it to yourself to go through life with a clear conscience. You have enough on your plate without weighing yourself down any more than necessary."

I thought about that. I knew I needed to do it, and soon. But to me it sounded like the death knell for our relationship. I said as much.

"It might be." Alicia nodded. "For both of your sakes, I hope it's not, but you're also old enough to realize that nothing in life is static. How much change have you seen in the last year?"

"An awful lot." I admitted it grudgingly, but at least I admitted it. "I've seen it in myself. Hell, I've seen a lot in the last week, starting with the realization that my life isn't meant to be in Boston. I intend to visit it yearly for the Charles, but live there? I don't think it's the city of my life."

"I think you've made a lot of progress today, Jeremy. What I'd like you to keep working on is your conviction that you've become the Josh Brennan in your relationship with Michael," Alicia said. "Is there any reason our usual day and time won't work next week?"

I took the appointment card she handed me and shook my head. "No, it'll be fine."

And the last thing I wanted to think about was Josh Brennan, but I also knew it would be all I'd think about.

Chapter Eight

One great thing in my post-Boston world was a nice, warm Michael under my arm as often as we could arrange it. Given our heights, it could go either way, and truth be told, I liked being under his arm at least as much. Any time I heard Geoff's voice telling me that was being dependent on Michael, I used some of the techniques Alicia had taught me to switch mental gears. Yep, therapy was already paying off.

Fall in the Sacramento Valley had always been gorgeous and temperate, at least since the rains abandoned us more or less permanently, so we took to studying outside after practices, Michael and I. The golden tone of the light was incredible, and when it got dark, we either took it inside to the coffee house on the CalPac campus or to one of the readily available coffee shops scattered around Sacramento or Davis.

Michael looked up. "I either need to break out a flashlight or we're going to have to go inside."

"I'm starting to get cold," I admitted.

Michael was lying on his belly on the soft grass of the quad, and I was using his butt as a pillow. That was the problem with fall. The temperatures dropped as the sun went down.

I nodded toward the coffee house. "That all right? I'm getting hungry again."

"Sure, but I have to leave by nine. The olds are getting on my case again. I cannot wait to graduate and get out of here." Michael threw one arm over my shoulder as we headed toward the coffee house. "You, me, and schools far away from here."

There it was again. I needed to grow a pair and tell him already. Somehow it wasn't that easy. Maybe because it felt like breaking up? "Bring it on."

"I know it's not even Halloween yet, but do you feel like talking about the Junior Prom?"

I smiled thinking about last year. "Sure, what's up?"

"I feel a smirk. What're you laughing about?" Michael nudged my shoulder.

"My mother's antics at last year's prom." I laughed. How could I not? I held the door open for him.

Apparently, Michael thought so, too. "Awww jeez. I wouldn't have thought I could've forgotten that, but I did. That was classic. Can I presume we won't have to go through that this time?"

I snorted as we sat down at a table. "Yes, if only because I'm not speaking to them at the moment, and that doesn't look to be changing any time soon."

"You're not? What's going on, Rem?" He stopped laughing. He didn't even pull out his books.

"Do we have to go into this?" Dragging it back out into the light held almost as much interest for me as oral surgery without the benefits of modern anesthetics.

Michael looked concerned. He placed his hand on mine. "I think we do, Rem."

"Okay, so right before I left for Boston, my parents summoned me home."

"That sounds ominous." He made a face, but then, he knew my parents and knew what they were capable of when they got their backs up, especially my dad.

"I know, right?" Was I really doing this?

So, I bit the proverbial projectile and told him, a thumbnail sketch, at least. He didn't need to know the whole argument. I watched him, however, and I noticed something. Sure, he made all the right noises. He was a stand-up guy and the best boyfriend I could imagine, but his eyes. They didn't react. I'd like to think that telling him the crap my parents crapped out would elicit some reaction.

"You knew about this." It wasn't even an accusation. It was a simple statement of fact. "How?"

Michael looked guilty. "Geoff e-mailed me. He's worried about you."

"That's because I'm not speaking to him either."

That caught his attention. "What's going on, Rem?"

"He agrees with them, Michael," I said flatly.

"The hell? Your whole family hates me?" His mouth hung open.

I leaned over and kissed him. "Not my whole family."

"So, what is this about? I'm thinking your brother left out a certain amount of detail." Michael looked miserable. Sometimes I forgot he was only seventeen.

"A little, yeah." I moved my chair so I sat next to him. I put my arm around him and pulled him down. My man needed to be held, even if he didn't know it. "I don't know what's ultimately driving it, but the proximate cause is that everyone seems to think I'm too dependent on you because I made sure my classes are done by the time you get off the water."

Michael raised his head. "That's it? That's not what Geoff said."

"Of course, it wasn't. Did he say they thought you exert too much influence on me?" I paused. "Or I on you. It went both ways."

"Are you kidding me? That's the stupidest thing I've ever heard. It doesn't even make sense." Michael glared at me.

I shrugged, which was hard while I held him. "Don't shoot the messenger."

The part about not trusting myself to make real decisions in the wake of my colossal blunder the summer before my senior year? I left it out. There was some truth to that, and I didn't want to go into it then, and in any event, he didn't need to hear it. Besides, I already had one therapist and I didn't need Michael trying to step into that role.

"I know." Michael wilted. "I... How can I win against that?"

"Michael...it's not a contest." I stroked his hair. "You already won. You're my guy. They're my past. You're my future."

Could I still make that come true?

"What about Geoff?" Michael said, his voice muffled by my chest.

"Okay, that one's tougher, but he'll come around once he sees he's wrong."

Michael sat up and looked at me. "Will he? Come around, I mean?"

I kissed him softly. "I hope so. I think he's parroting what my parents have said. It's not like he's seen me much since school started this summer. And you've seen him with Laurel. Who influences who in that relationship?"

"Good point." Michael laughed, but it sounded weak, even tenuous. "Rem... I'm sorry. If it becomes a choice between me and your family—"

"No."

He started. I guess I sounded sharper than I realized.

"No," I said, softer this time. "Michael, this isn't a contest or some kind of gay *Sophie's Choice*. I shouldn't have to choose between you, if only because they're wrong and because you're not the one putting me in this position.

For allegedly supportive parents, mine are suddenly being the exact opposite of that. It's not my job to figure out why, and it's not your job to accommodate them."

I didn't say anything about his less than supportive parents, no matter how much I wanted to. My usually strong boyfriend was doubting and uncertain, and when it came down to it, scoring cheap rhetorical points was a shitty and unloving thing to do.

"So, tell me about your plans for prom." I made no attempt to be subtle. If this had been a teen comedy, the sound of a needle dragging across a record would be heard here. And who listened to records on turntables, anymore? Hipsters? Screw them. They don't watch teen comedies. Everything I listened to is digital and fits on my iPhone.

"Thanks, Rem." Michael kissed me on the cheek. He took a few moments to gather his thoughts. "Okay, so here's what I've thought of. Thanks to us, there are several more out couples at Davis High this year."

That warmed me to hear. As ambivalent as I felt about my high school experience, even at über-liberal Davis High, the fact that Michael and I had blazed a trail— no matter how narrow—for others helped put a shine on it.

"I've told you about Casey and James, right?"

I nodded. "I think so, yes."

"So them, plus two girl couples, and then a straight couple for the sake of diversity."

"Have I met any of the rest of them?" I knew some of them, at least, had to be juniors because it was the Junior Prom. Or maybe they were all giving money to Michael...who couldn't buy the tickets. I was pretty sure at least half of each couple had to be a junior. Huh. I wondered how we were going to swing this one.

"Tiffany and Stella were novices at Cap City last year, so was Matrixa, and Darren was JV, so yes, you either knew part of each couple or at least saw them around the boathouse," Michael said.

"There's that much to quell my social anxiety issues, at least. Next question—how are *we* going to get in?"

Michael smiled, the sparkle back in his eyes. "I knew you'd ask that. Matrixa is on the organizing committee. She's going to get us in."

"Even though I'm not even a student at Davis High anymore?" How could this not blow up in our faces?

"She promised." Michael sounded so confident.

I couldn't say much to that, but it didn't mean I wouldn't have alternate plans, just in case. There would be faculty advisors present, after all. I assumed sneaking upperclassmen and their college boyfriends in would be only a little easier than putting white rum or vodka in the punch.

So as Michael spoke and then as the books came out, I turned inward, thinking. Michael and I would be the oldest students present, obviously. No, *I* would be the oldest. I already felt like a babysitter around Michael's younger friends. What on earth would I have to talk to these children about? Rowing, I guess, but only the most vague and superficial aspects of the sport. The Head of Charles? They'd never rowed it.

Safer sex, at least to the boys? That ought to cover an awkward five minutes. Don't do what I did, kids! HIV is a gift that keeps on giving, and frankly the meds are a drag. Truvada? Ask Michael about the names he's already been called for taking it because I'm poz. What did safer sex look like for women? Dental dams? I knew no lesbians who actually deployed those. But wait, there's more! The other STIs are equal opportunity infectors, and the biggest one of all is the easiest to prevent. Yes, that's right, babies! Wrap that rascal, boys, unless you're ready to be called "Daddy."

I shuddered. I tried to shunt my thoughts onto something—anything—else. But some things were too deeply rooted to get rid of that easily. I couldn't brush this one aside with a few parlor tricks. It didn't matter to me what Alicia said, or what Michael might say if I ever told him about this, I truly felt like Josh Brennan these days, preying upon a younger man. It didn't help that both sets of parents seemed to think my relationship with my boyfriend was unhealthy or that I exerted an unhealthy influence on him. I wondered how much of it was AIDS-phobia? They had no idea how afraid I was of infecting Michael or how careful I was with his health. They didn't know that I beat myself up on a daily basis because I'd done this to myself. If I'd only been honest about my age, Josh wouldn't have wandered.

I sighed. Or he might have, after all. Rationally I knew that Alicia was right. Josh might've been the source of my infection. Or it could've been Todd, the guy I'd met online and hooked up with at that first Youth Nationals. Like I said, rationally I could never know, but on this subject I reacted emotionally, and emotionally I was terrified of doing anything to hurt Michael.

I obviously had more work to do, either in a journal or with Alicia or both. What burned me up about my conviction that in some manner I was no different from Josh was that this whole line of thinking was nothing new. I'd been making myself miserable with this for most of the fall semester. Obviously, I was still troubled by my disquieting realization about Josh Brennan, and it wasn't going to go away any time soon. Could I manage to come to terms with it, kind of like learning to live with the monster under the bed? It might still scare the crap out of me, but I'd get used to the chill in my guts?

I guess I'd have to.

*

Before I could worry about the Baby Shark prom and what sounded like some immature hijinks at the hands of my boyfriend's friends, I first needed to endure Thanksgiving. Seeing as how my parents had yet to so much as send up a smoke signal in the month since the Head of the Charles Massacre, I had to scramble for Turkey Day. What was slaughtered at the massacre? I'd say my youthful illusions, but I'd killed those off myself a long time ago. Maybe it was the fiction of family unity or the idea that my parents supported my relationship with Michael, or even that my relationships counted as much as Geoff's.

Anyway, CalPac closed the dorms. Those who weren't leaving campus or couldn't go home were herded into the one dorm that remained open, perforce to sleep in strangers' bedrooms. The thought creeped me out. So not suave.

Thus I was relieved one afternoon to find an e-mail from Heath Nichols waiting for me. Heath had been the nurse practitioner who'd treated me when I first started getting sick before I was diagnosed with HIV. I had e-mailed him when I'd been released from the hospital after I'd been so sick. I figured the man who had pushed for me to get tested deserved to know how far awry things had gone before I'd seen the light. I'd underestimated both Heath and his husband, Jerry Fortier. Both had flown right into "Mah poor *bay*-bee" mode and immediately adopted me as some sort of honorary nephew. By the time Geoff and I graduated high school, he had taken to grumbling about not having his own fairy godfathers.

All I had to say was "Be glad you don't need fairy HIV-fathers of your very own."

So, when Heath e-mailed to check up on me, as per his custom, I knew I could be completely honest.

My parents aren't speaking to me, and I'm not sure what I'm doing for Thanksgiving.

Within ten minutes Jerry called me. "What do you mean your parents aren't speaking to you?"

"Do you want the long version or the short version?"

"That bad?" I could practically see him making a face.

I sighed. "That typical."

"Save it for dinner next Thursday. You'll arrive after your last class on whatever day it is they spring you children from that asylum." Jerry made his typical busy noises in the kitchen in the background. Everyone knew who did the cooking in that family.

"I have classes Wednesday morning and then practice Wednesday afternoon." I loved these men so much, but I still wouldn't skip sculling for them. "Are you sure? You don't mind me crashing your holiday?"

Whatever he was doing, it hit the counter with a clatter. "I said it, didn't I? Get your lily-white ass over here after practice. After you shower, if you please."

"Thanks, Jerry." I had to smile. That was his therapeutic technique. All smiles and warmth until you crossed him. Then the orders started.

"I swear, you rowers will be the death of me. Did I ever tell you how that child Nick Bedford snatched from the cradle took ten years off my life?"

"No." Actually he had, but I loved this story. Nick Bedford was the legend who put CalPac's rowing program on the map, but among the gays? He was a god who walked the earth. No one talked about it, but the rumor was his husband was once one of his rowers, and that he had quit coaching for true love. Or twu wuv, if you were a fan of *The Princess Bride*. Which I was.

"Liar." Jerry laughed. "We'll see you next Wednesday. Wear something tight-fitting."

"Jerry!" I heard Heath in the background.

I grinned. I loved them so much. "They're all tight, Jerry. It drives my boyfriend insane."

"Where were you when I was younger?"

"Kindergarten."

Jerry sighed. "You're a cruel, cruel child, Remy Babcock."

"I know." I cackled with glee. I hadn't been this delighted in some time. It was funny how a single phone call lightened a sour mood months in the making.

I heard a scuffle, and then Heath was on the line. "Don't listen to him. Come over when you can on Wednesday. We expect you to stay through Sunday or whenever you can return to your dorm."

I thought of Brady. No real hurry there.

"Ask the boy if he can make anything," Jerry called.

"Tell him I make an orange-glazed cranberry relish because I refuse to eat anything that came from a can that jiggles like that." Seriously, yuck. "But one of you will need to furnish alcohol to a minor because the orange comes from Cointreau."

Heath snorted. "Of course, you will, honey. I wouldn't expect anything less from you. Kiss, kiss."

"Precious, precious." I disconnected the call. That locked Thanksgiving down but only put off the larger questions of holidays and family, since my fight with my family no longer looked like it would resolve itself quickly.

*

When I'd told Heath and Jerry that I'd be over after practice, what I'd meant was after I finished sculling. I had to relax somehow, after all. But thirty minutes into what I'd intended to be a ninety-minute row, I realized my mind was on everything but the boat. I knew I should've cut myself some slack, but the only thing I could think of as I turned the single around was "herding squirrels," only the squirrels were all my scattered thoughts.

Oh well, whatcha gonna do?

Michael's school took the entire week off, so after I cleaned up, he and I hung out at the CalPac boathouse for a while, at least until his continued absence would be difficult to explain to his parents. I schooled my expression into as bland a mask as possible, so score one for me. The last thing either of us needed was me picking a fight with the Castelreighs, but seriously, I failed to understand their animosity, although they'd certainly piqued mine. But Michael seemed like he was in a vulnerable place these days, and I didn't feel like I could ask him what their issues with me were. He might not know the reasons himself.

At least by the time the Dead Bird Derby itself rolled around, Michael's Thanksgiving holiday would almost be finished, and if he snuck out for the pretense of Black Friday shopping, we could spend more time together. I could meet him at the maul—I hated shopping, and the day after Thanksgiving? Shoot me—so he had some packages to show for his efforts, and then we could hit the water. Yes, that's all I thought about, but he knew that.

But first, the Dead Bird Derby. I had ingredients to buy.

I hit the grocery store on the way to Heath and Jerry's because nothing screams cray-cray like Trader Joe's the afternoon before Turkey Day. I thought this was a good idea? Seriously, never mind my relationship with Michael, this was why my parents should've questioned my maturity. Bedlam hardly covered it. It started with me parking on the street in a residential neighborhood six blocks away. Not a problem. With my canvas bags tucked under one arm, I'd make walking sexy again, and in any event, the Fab Forties was a brilliant neighborhood to be seen in. What passed for fall foliage was on vivid display, and so was I. Another thing I loved about the Fab Forties was its location cheek by jowl with the gayborhood, Lavender Heights. A funny name, really. The hills in Sacramento started much farther to the east.

I elbowed my way into the store and dove into the fray. Being tall but slender had its advantages, and I worked all of them. Reaching through the throng for bags of cranberries? Check. Snaking two organic oranges while others argued over them? Check. Holding my basket over my head when people figured out what I'd done? Deploying my thousand-yard death glare? Check and double-check.

"Don't even fucking think about it." Mom always told me a smile was the quickest way to make friends. Good thing I wasn't at TJ's to make friends, wasn't it? "Next time, keep your eye on the ball."

Oh, Trader Joe's, don't ever change.

I went in search of the sugar. I suppose I could've used something artificial, but it was one day a year, and I knew I'd work the calories off. What other people did was no concern of mine.

Then, because I needed to eat, I grabbed a tray of California rolls and some lime-flavored fizzy water.

"Dude, why're you carrying your basket up there?"

I looked around and found a TJ's employee looking at me, trying not to laugh.

"It keeps people from stealing things out of it."

He looked surprised.

I grinned. "Not expecting that?"

"No, and I don't say that very often."

I snorted. "I'm almost positive that didn't come out how you intended it."

The clerk thought about it and then slowly looked me up and down. "Don't be so sure."

Somehow being openly admired made me feel like my skin didn't fit or something, or that I was a boy thrust into a man's game. That made no sense, given my activities that one crazy summer, but there I was. I never claimed I made sense. "Uh...yeah, I'll be sure to let my boyfriend know you appreciate my hard work."

He winked at me.

I looked around for the checkout stands. They had to be here somewhere. Oh yes, where the lines were. Without taking my leave of Cruisy the Clerk, I made my hasty way to the checkout queue. I put the basket on one shoulder and then read on my iPhone until it was my turn.

I put my embarrassment behind me as I drove to Heath and Jerry's house, what they'd told me was a Queen Anne-style Victorian, one of the painted ladies in Land Park. If McKinley Park was the jewel of east Sacramento, Land Park made south Sacramento sparkle. I should qualify that—Land Park was south of Broadway, the area immediately south of downtown, not the area more properly called South Sacramento farther south. The latter was nothing more than suburban gangland. Land Park started as and remained a respectable residential neighborhood. In addition to the acres and acres of the park itself, Land Park featured the zoo as well as a number of famous residents who had moved in and out of the area over the years. Sacramento was a company town, and that company was the state government, but in addition to political figures of interest only to students of California's government, Land Park was or had been home to the author Joan Didion, as well as to members of the Deftones and US Supreme Court Justice Anthony Kennedy. I loved the selection of American culture that had called Land Park home. Secrets like that kept Sacramento from being irretrievably hopeless.

Over the years, Heath and Jerry had put in the work to turn the tatty, somewhat rundown Victorian they'd bought into a beautifully restored turn of the century Queen Anne. While not so grand as San Francisco's painted ladies, Sacramento's version still projected a certain charm from the city's earlier days. When I'd asked Jerry why the entrance was on the second floor, he had laughed. "Hon, there weren't always the levies. This city used to flood every single winter."

I always forgot about that. If you looked closely at the walls of the state capitol building, you could see the high-water marks.

When they'd acquired the house, they'd had to rip out so much ham-handed "restoration" that it no longer qualified for any kind of historical status or registration, so their hands hadn't been tied. Air conditioning, so important in Sacramento Valley summers, was no problem, and neither was adding an extra guest suite at the back. They'd made sure not to spoil the lines, so the city approved the plans. The planning agency recognized a rehab job when it saw one. I merely saw a beautiful house that had always felt like a safe port in a storm.

I pulled up in front of the house and then checked the street signs. Was it the right day to park on this side of the street, and when would I need to move my car? Ah, urban living.

As I grabbed my groceries and bag for the weekend, I heard the door open. "Why're you parking in the street, lily-white boy?"

"As opposed to parking...where?"

Jerry shook his head. "The driveway?"

"It seemed rude to presume." I always trod carefully around Jerry. I never knew when the switch would flip and he'd out-queen the ladies at Aspects, or Ass-Pecs as it was known. Also, it drove him crazy, and there wasn't much he could do about it because I was being nice and all.

He rolled his eyes. "Move your car, child. The city doesn't need your money that badly."

I smiled. He stood at the top of the stairs, arms crossed and toes a-tapping, watching me. I'd won this round, but there was a long weekend stretching out ahead of me.

After I put my things in one of the guest rooms, the three of us—Heath, Jerry, and myself—spent a quiet evening *en famille*, eating dinner and playing board games. I supposed we could've gone out, even to the aforementioned Ass-Pecs, but when it came down to it, games were more fun, and we could make hogs of ourselves with the Chex mix without anyone judging.

The next day I slept in. Such a luxury. I couldn't remember the last time I'd missed sunrise at the port. That didn't mean I wasn't sitting at the kitchen table with a mug of coffee in my hand when Heath stumbled in at what he obviously considered an obscene hour.

"What're you doing up so early? Isn't this supposed to be a holiday?" Heath mumbled, his brain still mired in sleep. "And shouldn't you be sleeping in?"

"I already slept in. Now I'm enjoying coffee and the paper." And trying not to laugh at my host. I kept that to myself.

Heath squinted at me. "If I'd have known you could both sleep in and be up so stinking early, I'd have let you deal with the turkey."

"That'd work out fine—if I had some clue what to do with it. Other than eat it, I mean." I turned my attention back to the comics. Yeah, I'm that lowbrow. That Satchel, poor earnest dog that he was, always on the wrong end of that horrible cat's stupidity.

Heath bumbled his way deeper into the kitchen, presumably looking at the recipe or incantation or whatever it was Jerry had set out for the turkey. He was sure swearing a lot.

"Problem?"

He sighed. "Only that I don't need to do anything with this damn bird until two hours before we intend to eat it."

I glanced at the clock. "So, you're up this early for no good reason?"

"None whatsoever. Well, I can take my meds, but other than that and the dubious pleasure of your company, no."

I buried my smile in my coffee cup as Heath grumbled his way back upstairs. Me, I planned to contact Michael and see if maybe he might be interested in meeting at the Cap City boathouse, him or maybe Lodestone, if Marissa wanted him out from underfoot. Unless Lodestone planned to cook or unless they were traveling. I knew Peter's family lived up in Washington, but I thought Marissa's people lived locally. I tried not to be as self-absorbed as people accused me of being.

I glanced at the clock on the microwave. I knew my fairy HIV-fathers had planned dinner for much later in the day, so I could scull as well as lounge about for a while, which is exactly what I did.

Chapter Nine

When I'd left for the boathouse, no one else had stirred, and no one had arrived. When I returned there was a strange car in front of the house, and I suddenly wished I'd had a chance to clean up. Alas, the Cap City boathouse wasn't nearly as nice as CalPac's, but CalPac's was closed for the holiday. But I had to scull. I needed to, if only to get the stench from yesterday's attempt off me.

"Is that you, Remy?" Jerry called from the kitchen.

"Not if I'm meeting anyone!" Seriously, what could he be thinking? He was gay, I was gay. He knew the score.

"Jerry!" Heath hissed.

I heard unfamiliar voices laughing. Someone said, "We row, we get it. Let the man shower, Jerry."

Rowers. "We." That ruled out Brad and Drew, although they were supposed to be here for dinner. Drew didn't row, and they didn't sound like Adam and Owen. As nervous as I could get around strangers, I was afire with curiosity too.

I showered and dressed in reasonable haste. I debated shaving, but decided I had the right amount of scruff going on. At least Michael had thought so when he was nibbling on it after our row. Dressed in a comfortable pair of jeans and a Michael-approved polo shirt—he liked 'em tight—I went downstairs. Strangers to encounter and cranberry relish to make.

When I entered the kitchen, conversation stopped, and four heads swiveled in my direction. Whoa. Stranger danger.

Jerry grinned. "Thanks for joining us, lily-white boy. I was just singing your praises to Nick and Morgan here."

Rowers. Nick. Not *that* Nick, surely...

A handsome blond about my height extended his hand. "Since Jerry's apparently having more fun flummoxing you than being a good host, I'm Nick Bedford."

"Remy Babcock." I was shaking hands with a legend right there in Heath and Jerry's kitchen. I was surprised my mouth worked.

A taller man with darker hair and fairer coloring snickered. "I'm his better half, Morgan Estrada."

That clinched it. "He's that Nick Bedford, the one who made CalPac what it is, right?"

Morgan grinned. "Kind of a letdown, isn't it?"

"What? No." Jeez, could I sound any stupider?

"You've stunned another one of those poor children, Nick." Jerry laughed again. "You're going to have to move or change your name or something, if the mere mention of your name makes them plotz."

As long as it didn't involve my parents or Michael, I could recover quickly. "Only the gay ones."

"You're forgetting one thing. I quit so Morgan and I could be together without that hanging over the program you seem to think I magicked into being all on my own." Nick smiled when he said it. I could already tell he was someone I'd like.

"Isn't that sooo dreamy? Giving up your job for the man you love?" Morgan said.

I looked at Morgan closely. He made the lovestruck expression with the voice to match, but the eyes. They gave it away. "You're a bad man."

"I always knew you had a good head on your shoulders, Remy." Jerry was quiet for a moment and then he gestured with his half-full martini glass. "Hahahahaha! Somebody fix me a cocktail."

"I think someone's already had enough, don't you?" Morgan said in a stage whisper.

I shook my head. "You don't really expect me to get involved in this, do you? He knows where I sleep, at least for the next three nights."

Heath made me a sandwich since by that time my guts had a death grip on my spine, and then left me to visit with Nick and Morgan while he and Jerry continued to work on Thanksgiving in the kitchen. Jerry seemed to be in a queeny mood, and cranberry relish went together easily, so I made myself scarce. He could sharpen his fangs on someone else.

And so, the morning passed, at least until the rest of the guests arrived. I looked up from where I sat with Nick and Morgan when the doorbell chimed. More strangers...

"These are Brad and Drew St. Charles and their nephew, Freddie Cochrane," Heath said by way of introductions.

Or maybe not so strange. I knew Brad and Drew. I'd never forget how kind they'd been back in Boston.

"It's Fred," the sullen preteen with hair the color of fire groused. "Not even Philip calls me Freddie anymore."

I more or less ignored Fred, which was what I always did with ornery children, in favor of Brad and Drew.

"Remy! This is a surprise." Drew enfolded me in a hug. Then he held me at arm's length. "Have you gotten taller?"

"In the last month? Unlikely."

Brad smirked, which seemed to be his natural state. "C'mere, kid."

"So, it's safe to assume you know these reprobates, Remy?" Nick said as the rather large Brad had his arms around me. Seriously, Brad looked more like Peter Lodestone, who was built like a rugby player. Neither resembled the classic oarsman's build.

"You think?" Brad said.

"Stop bogarting the Brad." Morgan pulled me away. "I've known him longer."

"That may be true, but we rowed together in Boston. That's a bond you'll never understand." Brad stuck his tongue out at Morgan.

"We're best enemies," Morgan said by way of explanation.

Drew sighed. "Are they still beating that dead horse?"

"So it would appear." Nick shook his head. "I keep hoping they'll grow out of it, but it's been what? Eight years for you and Brad? It's not looking good."

"And nine for you and Morgan," Drew said.

Nick smiled. "About that, yes."

"Has Mrs. Estrada given up pushing for a wedding, yet?"

"You're kidding, right?" Morgan said from where he and Brad were bickering about some minor topic I hadn't been able to follow. Fred or Freddie seemed to have the right idea. He had dropped onto one of the sofas with an electronic device and was ignoring everyone.

Four old friends quickly shifted to conversational topics I knew nothing about, so I took the opportunity to slip into the kitchen and get to work.

"So, what do you need, Remy?" Heath said.

"For now? A citrus zester or Microplane and a plate to catch the zest." Not that I had a chance to cook often or was necessarily any good at it, but something about the ritual of preparing food soothed me.

After I had zested both oranges and moved on to the next step, Brad came in to work on his family's contribution. We chatted about nothing of any real consequence, the way people on the way to being fast friends do, when something occurred to me.

"Wait... Heath introduced you as Brad St. Charles, but that summer I got into trouble before the Youth Nationals, or even in Boston, you were Coach Sundstrom."

"I was Coach St. Charles then, too, because... reasons, but I've never been able to shake my old name around the boathouse." Brad looked miserable, absolutely wretched.

I had no idea what I'd said or done, but clearly, I'd fucked up in a grand way. "Brad...I'm sorry."

"Don't worry about it." But Brad vanished into the living room.

"That was so not suave. I screwed the pooch, and I'm not even sure how."

"Would it help if I said it's not you, it's him?" Drew said from the kitchen doorway.

I looked past him but couldn't see anything. "But—"

"Okay, yes, you kind of screwed up, but there's no way you could possibly have known. Brad and his brother Philip—"

"That'd be Fred's father—" I said.

Drew nodded. "Guardian, but yes. Brad and Philip's father was horrible. Like, trying to get one of his lackeys to bash me to get Brad to stop working for me and come back to the family company and resume dying by inches horrible."

I didn't say anything. What was there to say? But I was aware of my jaw hanging open.

Guess my father wasn't that bad, after all.

"Exactly. Brad still hates him with a passion that burns hotter than a million suns. So, when we married, Brad took my last name."

"Hence Coach St. Charles." Then something occurred to me. "Then why does everyone still call him Coach Sundstrom?"

Drew sighed. "Because getting everyone to take the name change seriously, even at gay-friendly Cap City, hasn't been easy."

"I'm sorry. I didn't mean to open old wounds. Or create new ones." I could never say that enough times, but I had to start.

"I know you are." Drew snagged a handful of olives off a tray.

"I'll apologize after I'm done with the cranberries and maybe he's had a chance to not be so angry at me."

"That sounds wise. I'll go calm him down before you do," Drew said, "but to be fair to you both, he's not so much angry as hurting. Some wounds never really heal."

When I'd finished, I went back to the living room. Morgan was saying, "My parents decided they were old enough not to fuss with Thanksgiving anymore. So, they handed the torch off to my oldest brother, but he's in SoCal. I have the whole week off, but Nick doesn't."

"It's my holiday to work," Nick said. "We'll see them for Christmas and hopefully expiate the Catholic guilt they're sure to heap at my feet."

I made my best effort to apologize, but Brad appeared deaf to my words.

"So much for recreating our Charles quad," I said quietly.

"Are you telling me my company's not good enough for you, child?" Jerry glared at me.

"Did those words pass my lips? No, they did not. But I don't see you sculling."

I told Brad again how sorry I was, but he only looked annoyed.

"Whatever, little oarsman," Brad said.

Enough was more than enough. I'd accidentally waded into a swamp I hadn't known existed. I'd made my apologies, only to have them cast back in my face. Poke me with a fork and all that. I frowned. "Little? I'm not that much shorter than you are."

"Short enough."

I gritted my teeth. "Maybe, but it was my underage ass that dragged yours down the Charles River, and don't you forget it, old man."

I left the room at that point. Who knows, maybe I'd leave the house too. I was almost positive I'd left something at the boathouse, right? What I failed to understand was why it was "pick on the kid day."

Jerry laughed. "Don't worry about her. It's that time of the month."

But I swore I heard Brad say, "I like him."

"That's because he won't put up with your crap." Morgan, I thought.

I heard Drew say, "You should probably pull the stick out of your ass. I'm getting tired of this. He apologized, which is more than he needed to do because—hello?—no one ever told him about the name change, given that he was basically larval when it happened."

Heath sighed. "Jerry, I'm going to sew your mouth shut. If you can't be civil, you'll be sleeping on the porch."

"If you guys like him, you should probably go find him, because I'm pretty sure he said something about getting out of here."

Smart kid, that Fred.

*

"Jeez, you're hard to find."

I glanced over my shoulder and—holy shit. They'd sent Nick Bedford after me. Naturally, I missed the next stroke and almost took a bath.

Okay, that pissed me off. I was a better sculler than that—duh—so I returned my focus back where it belonged. The mighty Nick Bedford could match my speed if he wanted to talk.

"It's not like I'm hiding."

"Oh, yes you are." I was amused to note that Bedford seemed winded. "What do you think we're doing out here on the river on Thanksgiving?"

"I'm getting the stink of yesterday's row off of me." I could row and speak—shout, really—all afternoon, but him? It wasn't looking good for him.

"I'd say you've accomplished that." Bedford called to me over the water, but I gave him only part of my attention. Loaned, really. Mostly I paid attention to the water, giving it my anger and embarrassment and humiliation. If it was so important to Brad to use Drew's last name, maybe he could've and should've made that clearer years ago, instead of biting my head off in the kitchen. "Can you at least stop rowing so I'm not yelling?"

I gunwaled my oars and let the boat run beneath me, and Bedford did the same.

"So, why're you out here?" Amazing how quickly I got over my awe of this guy.

He laughed, a bit mordantly I thought, as he maneuvered his boat closer to mine. "I'm the only one who can scull well enough to catch you."

"That's actually kind of funny." Then something occurred to me. "Wait, Brad was in the Boston quad with me."

Nick smiled. "Yeah, a quad. It's a bigger boat, and a more stable one. That doesn't mean he's any good in a single."

I don't know if that was supposed to make me feel better, but it certainly amused me.

"Why're they such assholes?" I knew I sounded whiny but screw it.

Nick shrugged, a neat trick when he held oars to keep his single steady. "Can't answer for all of them, but Brad's relationship with his dad was toxic. I mean *really* toxic."

"Drew mentioned something about that. He had Drew assaulted or something? That's pretty messed up."

Nick snorted. "That's not the half of it. Philip, his older brother, took care of the senior Sundstrom, however."

"Oh?"

"Booted their dad out of the company he founded and then made sure his own henchman turned state's evidence." Nick made adjustments to his boat to keep it close to mine. "Oh, and then married the best cox'n I ever had the pleasure of working with. Now Philip, Stuart, and Fred are a happy little family and living the good life with money Philip swindled their father out of while Stuart finishes medical residency."

I laughed. What else could I do? I'd never heard of revenge so total, at least not in real life. "That's brilliant."

"It was." Nick nodded. "It changed the course of my life, you know."

Not what I expected to hear, and I was curious despite myself. "How?"

"I'd planned to coach for the rest of my career—"

"But what about the fact that you and Morgan—" I clapped one hand over my mouth, glad I had my oars held steady by my knees.

Fortunately, Nick only laughed. "I'd be lying if I said that wasn't at the back of my mind when I shifted gears." Then he sobered. "Seeing Drew in a pool of his own blood outside of Aspects, and then watching the slow months of his rehab, convinced me that physical therapy was where I needed to be, not coaching. I was very lucky that many of my grad school units transferred and that Morgan was patient."

I nodded and made appropriate noises, but all Nick's story really did was remind me I had no idea what I wanted to do with my biology major other than a vague idea of nursing.

And that as mad as my parents made me, they'd never tried to have Michael whacked. That was... something else, whole orders of magnitude worse. I mean, how messed up did you have to be to do something like that? Talk about narcissism.

Then I realized Nick was speaking to me. "I'm sorry, what?"

"I said, are we about done out here?"

I shrugged. "You tell me. I'm out here because I'm tired of being picked on. Are they tired of tormenting the young guy?"

Nick looked up at the sky. "They're sorry they did it and that it went too far. Does that count?"

"Honestly, I don't know. I've more than enough crap in my life right now without putting up with any more. I came to Heath and Jerry's to get away from it for a few days, not to be the entertainment." I thought about it. "I'd rather check into a hotel and eat room service than put up with any more."

That give Nick something to think about, I could tell. "You know Drew likes you. Brad feels horrible and is ready to make a pet of you to make amends. Morgan, who's always been too outspoken for his own good, was ripping everyone to shreds when I left, at least when Heath stopped to inhale, but be prepared, he also thinks stomping off is a bid for attention and may call you on it."

"Then you'd better sit on him because I'm done with that. I'm about to start telling people exactly what I think. Are *you* ready for that? Glass houses and all that." I didn't know how much clearer I could make it.

"There's something else I want you to understand." Nick looked me dead in the eye. "Everyone there who rows? On some level, they're jealous, even if they don't know it, but I can tell. You were better in high school than they ever were, and you're not done, not according to Lodestone. Not even close."

I set my oars back in the water. It was time to go. "That's not my problem, it's theirs."

"Oh, I get that. I'm not sure they do, but I understand perfectly. Human traits assort along bell curves, and that includes skill in rowing. You're so far to the right on that curve they can't even recognize it. Even the nonrowers there understand that in your field, you beat them in theirs. Think you can cut them some slack?"

"Why should I?"

"It'd be the gracious thing to do."

Fuck that noise. "You mean like picking on the young guy?"

"You can go through life angry, or you can learn that everyone makes mistakes and we all need a little slack sometimes, Remy. Even you." Nick shook his head. "What's it going to be?"

I didn't ask for this. I didn't ask to be a prodigy. I didn't ask for a bunch of older guys to be jealous of me or hung up about my so-called skill in a boat. All I wanted was to row my single and be with my guy, but everyone kept getting in the way of that. "I just want a place to belong. Why is that too much to ask?"

Suddenly Nick looked far older than his years. "That's what we all want, Remy. I can't tell you how many times I think I've found it, only to have it jerked out from under me. Give these guys a chance, not only to be sorry but to be that place for you. I can't say they won't let you down again. They're human...like you, but they've been there. Hell, they're still searching and hoping...like you. Let them give you shelter. They've got experience. Let them share it with you. They might save you from repeating their mistakes."

I snorted. "I'll make plenty of my own. Jeez, I already have."

A wave of hunger racked me. Not physical, although I was that, too, but emotional, I guess I could say. Shelter, Nick had called it. I wanted that more than anything. Geoff had once been that, to the extent that he could, to the extent that he'd understood his changeling brother. That ended a month ago in Boston. I'd felt rootless ever since. Michael tried, but he still sought shelter and identity of his own, so how could he help me?

"Yes, you have. So have they, but that's the thing. That's part of being alive. No man's an island and all that. Maybe you've been trying to be. Maybe that's why you take off and scull when things get too bad. Beats me, but maybe it's time you let people help you."

I wiped my eye under my sunglasses. "I've made a real hash of things, haven't I?"

"Nothing that can't be fixed." Nick smiled. "Are you ready to turn around?"

"Race you back to the dock?"

"Sure, why not? We might as well pregame all those calories we're about to eat. I get a twenty second head start."

I laughed as we turned our boats, careful not to get in each other's way. "Age before beauty."

He glared at me, but I noticed it didn't stop him from taking off.

Chapter Ten

I hadn't had the time to get too far down the river, but I'd been angry enough to row hard and fast, so racing Nick required strategy and none of this fly-and-die nonsense. At least I'd stopped taking off at the speed of light and then crashing and burning halfway through a piece, hoping to fake my way through the second half the way I had in high school. At long last it had been coached out of me. So, while Nick and I faced more than a head race in distance, neither of us felt the need to row at that intensity on the way back.

Not at first.

I mean, I had to catch up to him, didn't I? No sense in rowing to lose.

After that I simply kept rowing, not quite at race pace but certainly more than what I'd use for a casual holiday row. I felt Nick look over at me. I looked back. He narrowed his eyes and picked up his own pace.

Then it was on.

Okay, yes, I could be super competitive, and I knew from reading his bio that Nick rowed at UC San Diego as an undergrad before going into coaching. That sort of thing doesn't happen unless you've a competitive streak of your own. So, I spent the next thousand meters trying to figure out how this race could go. On the one hand, USRowing handicapped races by age for a reason, and not only that, college rowers never raced masters. On the other, I rowed yesterday, and I'd already pushed myself today.

Then I noticed that Nick had pulled ahead.

Idiot.

I'd been here before.

I took a deep breath and dropped my stroke rating, the number of strokes I took per minute. Then I stood on my foot stretchers and made each stroke as powerful as I could, using the slower stroke rating to catch my breath in between. We called it the recovery for a reason.

I grinned as I regained lost distance, stroke by stroke. I had to keep my head in the boat as I clawed my way past Nick. He might've been older, and he might not coach much anymore, but he clearly stayed in condition. Physical therapists, who knew. I needed to work for this.

And so, work I did.

By the time we saw the Cap City dock, Nick and I raced flat out. I heard noise in the background but ignored it. Fisherman along the shore, perhaps. Who else would be crazy enough to be out there on Thanksgiving?

But as I neared the dock—ahead, thank you very much—I heard someone, maybe Morgan, bellow, "Check it down! You're coming in too hot!"

I glanced over my shoulder and sure enough, I was far too close to the dock. I jabbed the oar blades into the water. Not far behind me, Nick did the same. I released one blade, the one closest to Morgan, turning my boat parallel to the dock. "Pull me in?"

Morgan grabbed the blade. Ordinarily I planned better and landed far more gracefully. "Thanks."

Nick had more warning and actually looked almost competent sliding into the dock. But I won.

I climbed out of my boat and rested on the dock. I hadn't inked racing into my day planner that afternoon, and I was content to lie there in the sun and catch my breath.

Then a shadow fell over me, and I opened my eyes. "Hello, Morgan. Thanks for the assist."

"You looked good out there." It looked like Morgan was trying not to laugh.

I smiled. "I love sculling."

"It shows. I hope you didn't make Nick work too hard."

"He found me without too much trouble." I deliberately ignored what he really meant.

Morgan rolled his eyes. "Good, good. Need a hand putting your equipment away?"

"Traitor!" Nick called from farther down the dock.

I laughed. "I think my answer had better be no."

"Nick's a big boy," Morgan said.

"I seriously don't want to know." I stood up and got to work removing the oars from their oarlocks.

Morgan shook his head. "Pervert."

"Hey," I said, picking my boat up from the water and lifting it overhead, "I'm not the one who brought it up. Heads up."

Once I made sure I wouldn't brain Morgan, whose presence, after all, remained a mystery, I walked up the ramp to the singles house. Somehow the Cap City boathouses always felt like home. No matter where else I rowed, I knew I'd always come back here. Maybe that was why the presence of Fred Cochrane didn't jump out at me immediately.

"Can you hurry up?" he said. "I'm hungry."

"Oh yeah, sure. I'm sorry."

It was only as I racked the boat that I stopped to think about it. Wait. Morgan *and* Fred? What the hell was going on?

I wiped my boat down in a hurry and turned to jam out of the boathouse, only to run up against Morgan carrying two sets of oars and Nick with his boat. Boats have the right of way, so I stepped aside.

"What's going on, guys?"

"We're putting equipment away." Morgan sounded like he was explaining things to a rather stupid child.

And people wondered why I was the way I was. "Morgan…"

"Remy…"

I heard Nick snicker behind us. Morgan and I both turned to face him.

"I'd love to watch the two of you face off sometime. It'd be the irresistible force and the immovable object, I'm sure." Nick smiled, shaking his head. "But right now I've got a head race to wash off—don't think I didn't notice what you did out there, Remy—and I'd really like to eat something at some point in time today."

I sighed. I hadn't actually escaped anything, unless I was willing to depart the boathouse directly for a hotel. It looked like I'd still be returning to the scene of the crime, after all. At least I was calmer for hiding at the boathouse for a little while. Sure, the same assholes who'd gotten their jollies by bothering me before would do it again, but I would wrap my row about me like a shield, and in any event, asses would bray whether I wanted them to or not.

I grabbed the gym bag containing my rowing kit and then flinched. I needed to do laundry in the worst way. It was more than a little whiffy. At this point I wasn't sure I'd make it through the weekend with clean workout clothes. Given that I'd adopted sculling as my primary coping mechanism, this presented a problem, at least if the holiday continued as it started. Oh well, take each day as it came, right? Alicia would be so proud of me. If I managed to pull it off.

"Remy, over here," Nick called.

I looked up, and Nick was heading to the CalPac boathouse. Huh. I walked across the parking lot that separated the two boathouses. Three, if you counted UC Davis's. "You have a key. Interesting."

"I like that. No silly questions about whether or not I have a key, just the assumption that I do." Nick hoisted his own gym bag as he unlocked the door and then dealt with the alarm system.

I shrugged. I couldn't say much to that, but Nick Bedford coached for Cap City...just like Peter Lodestone, who had a key to CalPac's boathouse. As far as deductions went, it hardly predicted a career in forensics.

"There's a reason for me to shower here rather than back at Heath and Jerry's?" I headed directly for the locker room. Unlike the Cap City coaches, I actually had a locker with toiletries in it, toiletries like fresh contact lenses.

"Okay, play along, will you?" Nick said, following me into the locker rooms.

At least that confirmed my suspicions. "So, you admit something's up?"

"I admit nothing. Nothing, I say!"

I peered into the mirror to pick my contacts out, deciding to skip more contact lenses, at least for the time being. "Scared of Morgan, are you?"

"Take your shower," Nick called out before he turned on the water.

I texted Michael, instead.

ME: *Happy Turkey Day. I hope your day's going well.*

MICHAEL: *It's OK. Grandparents and assorted other rels. Miss U. Howz yours?*

ME: *Miss U 2. Mine's... interesting.*

MICHAEL: *???*

ME: *Let's just say I beat Nick Bedford sculling and leave it there 4 now.*

MICHAEL: *Need 2 know deets. Call U later. xoxo*

ME: *xoxo*

"Remy! Shower!" Nick called as the water cut off. He wrapped a towel around his waist as he walked out of the shower. "Don't tell me you're shy."

"No, texting my boyfriend about today." I put my phone in my locker and grabbed my towel and shower caddy.

Nick groaned. "Please be merciful. We're not all assholes."

"All I said is that I beat you sculling," I called over my shoulder as I walked into the showers.

"Punk!"

I laughed as I washed away the sweat. Unfortunately, the cares remained, but then, that might've been asking a bit much of body wash and hot water. "Punk was over *years* before I was born."

"Stop that." Nick shook his head as I exited the shower. "I swear, you're one of the most difficult people I've ever dealt with. You remind me of *him*."

"Him? Him who?"

"Who do you think? Morgan. Try to keep up." Then Nick appeared to think about it. "Although now that you mention it, it could apply to Stuart or to Drew too."

"Okay, then." Lofty company, I supposed.

"Okay."

I wasn't entirely sure what Nick wanted but standing around naked—or naked under a towel—made me feel vulnerable in a way that wasn't cool. "Do you mind if I get dressed now?"

"I'm not stopping you." Nick stood in front of my locker.

"You kind of are." I pointed out that fact to him.

He blushed. "Oh. Why don't I go wait outside?"

"You do that. I'll hurry."

Nick baffled me, he and Morgan both. In one sense, they were legends, especially to any gay CalPac rowers. I wasn't the only one, only the noisiest. But meeting legends sure took the shine off them, and both had been acting squirrely since I reached the dock. As much as I'd enjoyed racing Nick, I needed to bring this holiday back under my control. Right then I didn't even control my own schedule.

Maybe I'd built the weekend's escape up to more than any four days could reasonably be expected to support, maybe not. Whether or not that was the case, I didn't think asking for basic respect made me a diva. I'd run it all by Michael for an outside perspective when we next spoke. I frowned. How spooked did I have to be that I no longer trusted my own perspective?

"Some time before Betty White dies, Remy? She's not getting any younger, you know!" Morgan called from the human-scaled side door of the boathouse.

"He's a real piece of work, isn't he?" I said to Nick as I exited the boathouse.

Morgan smirked at me. "Maybe, but you're finally out here, aren't you?"

With Morgan all but pushing me and Nick walking alongside like this happened every day, I was herded back to the Cap City boathouse, where I found a complete picnic waiting for me, and there I froze. Not even Morgan could budge me.

Brad turned around and greeted me with sad, knowing eyes. He held his arms open, and I broke. I fled into the sanctuary of his arms, my eyes filling with tears.

It was like...somehow Brad understood something I couldn't name myself. He got being the cat who walked alone, if I wanted to get all Kipling about it. Or maybe Brad knew what it was like not to be understood.

"That was me all through college," he whispered. "I didn't even understand myself."

"It's not that—"

"But it's close, isn't it?"

I paused and then nodded. "Close enough."

I felt surrounded by the safety he offered, he and Drew. Then Nick and Morgan joined, followed by Heath and Jerry. I looked up, and Fred rolled his eyes. I laughed. I had to.

That seemed to smooth things over, and we got on with the holiday. Back when it rained in the Sacramento Valley, Thanksgiving could be foggy and wet or cold and crisp, but the rest of that day shone sunny and bright, without even a hint of breeze to spoil things. I could tell who the rowers were. We were the ones looking out at the glassy water and sighing. Even though I had more than satisfied the rowing gods lately, a part of me twitched at the thought of not being out there to show my gratitude, but enough was enough. I needed to rest sometime.

Didn't I?

For the rest of the weekend, however, Heath and Jerry hovered over me like I was made of porcelain. What they didn't realize was that porcelain was surprisingly strong, whether it was a translucently thin plate or something like a toilet. Ever break a toilet? I didn't think so.

Such a flattering comparison.

But Heath and Jerry were both nurturers and my fairy HIV-fathers. Something called them into nursing, after all. Heath and Jerry, two of the best people I knew, Jerry's occasional prickliness aside. They were nurses, and I a biology major with an interest in health sciences.

Nursing. Suddenly I couldn't pry it out of my mind with books, video games, or Michael. It was something to think about. I already knew I didn't want to go into medicine, or rather, I knew I didn't want to be a doctor. I already knew nurses worked hard—damn hard—but it seemed to me that doctors worked far longer and took their work home with them, and I wanted a life.

But nursing.

I was intrigued enough to talk to Heath and Jerry about it when things died down.

*

Fortunately for me, Thanksgiving, regardless of how fraught it was, helped to diffuse some of my tension. I still worried that on some level, my critics were right and that maybe I was a bad influence on my boyfriend. I couldn't say anything about it to Michael, if only because we'd never have a rational discussion on the subject. No, he'd go from zero to furious in seconds flat, angry at me for thinking such things and angry at our parents for daring to suggest anything of the sort. Neither option fostered productive discussion, but not telling him weighed heavily on me. We're only as sick as our secrets, right?

Speaking selfishly, when it came to my performance on exams and labs and the rest of the head races left in the season, I was glad I compartmentalized like there was a prize for it. I shoved all the nonsense aside and focused on what was most important to me. Sure, Coach Ridgewood called me out for hunching my shoulders more than she used to, and food never really did sit right, at least not until the end of the semester, but I did well in school and rowed my seat in the boats. That was all I had, that and Michael. Anything else I wouldn't let distract me. Anything else that bothered me, I set aside and got on with life.

And to think, people gave me crap for being oblivious to anything that wasn't made of carbon fiber and manufactured by Vespoli Racing Shells or Hudson Boat Works. It was not that I was oblivious so much as I immersed in something to the point at which it became totalizing, so all-consuming that I had little time for anything else, and anyone who shared my life would also need to share that all-consuming passion. It struck me that evening, as I readied myself for the Junior Prom at Davis High, that anyone I shared my life with would also have to share that all-consuming passion or be willing to share me with it. No wonder rowers tended to pair up. I would need to find a man dedicated in his own way to something equally consuming. It wouldn't even have to be another athlete, only someone with a major obsession of his own. Otherwise, I realized, I would face a relationship full of strife and jealousy without actually cheating or dicking around. It would take a special man to fit that bill.

Because gay men without damage were thick on the ground? I'd already figured out those were rare. The gay student union taught me that much. There were more men like Brady than like Michael. I glanced over my shoulder while I fussed with the beautiful onyx and mother-of-pearl stud set my parents gave me for one reason or another.

I had put on the Judybats's *Pain Makes You Beautiful* CD while I got dressed. Me and '80s music. That would never change. Quietly, of course, because otherwise I could expect a barrage of insults from my charming roommate. Yeah, great party music. But it did. Make you beautiful. Pain, I meant.

I was so not looking forward to tonight.

"Aren't you getting awfully dressed up for what's basically a casual event?"

I looked at him, unsure what he meant.

Brady smirked. "Robbing the cradle. I didn't know that required formalwear."

I turned and squinted at him with the quizzical look that I'd learned made people squirm. It was part "Wow, you're that stupid" and part "I'll carve your tripes out as soon as I figure out the best way to accomplish that."

"Don't you have somewhere pathetic to be? Or a test to flunk?"

Brady's face darkened in anger, but what was he going to do? Kick my foot? I was seven inches taller and a lot more muscular.

"When I join a frat next semester, you won't be able to push me around."

Whaaat? I couldn't even get the word out without snickering. "I'm pretty sure I will."

"You heard me," Brady said. He looked like he planned to explode in the very near future. "I need reinforcement after those assholes roughed me up. So, I'm joining a frat. Probably the football frat."

"Roughed you up? This isn't the Sharks and the Jets." I rolled my eyes again. I really needed to stop that, if only because I was close to a headache as it was. "First of all, what my *teammates* did was as much of a surprise to me as it was to you. Second, and in case you forgot, it was in response to your harassment. Third, if you'd get over your stupid problems, peace and love and fairy dust would reign supreme in this, our dorm room."

He pulled out a pretend knife and pretended to cut his guts out. "Yeah, right."

If only. I smiled like the OxyContin had just kicked in. "You're probably right, but at least I made an effort after you pierced my veil of obliviousness. Didn't work, did it? Have you asked yourself why? Have you considered that the common factor in all your failed relationships is you? No? Then it's time you start."

Someone knocked on the door, and please let it be Michael. All this clever banter was killing me. I opened the door a crack. You'd think the doors in a new dorm like this one would have peepholes, but no.

I found Michael peering right back at me through the crack and laughed. We certainly thought alike sometimes. It made being with him so comfortable and so easy, like coming home and putting on my favorite pair of jeans, the worn ones that were soft in all the right places. I smiled.

"Hey, you." I opened the door all the way and pulled him in for a kiss.

Michael looked stunning. While he had looked amazing the last time we had gone to a formal event—my senior ball—he had clearly put on width in the shoulders, height, and muscle in the interim, nearly attaining a man's frame. We both had. It made finally buying our own formalwear practical. "'Hey, you'? What kind of greeting is that? I get all dolled up for you and all I get is a 'hey, you'?"

"How about, you look delicious enough to eat, assuming I can hold off long enough to get you into the men's bathroom?"

"Not bad." Michael swallowed audibly, the fire in my eyes scorching him where he stood.

I stepped toward him. "Or, before this night is over, I'll bend you over a table and teach you what it means to be a man? Twice."

"I'm going to hold you to that." I noticed that Michael's voice wasn't nearly as steady as it had been.

I didn't top much, but when I did...

"Jeez, you two. Enough already." Brady paused with a can of soda halfway to his mouth. "Does anyone care I'm about to vomit over here?"

"Don't pretend you're not going to start masturbating furiously at the thought the minute we're out of the room. Please stay off my bed this time." I wrinkled my nose at the thought. "You don't clean it up nearly as well as you think you do."

Brady's jaw fell open. "You are so disgusting."

"And you are so busted." It was true too. I owned a small black light. The evidence showed up quite clearly.

Michael looked back and forth between us. "You'll have to tell me about this later, Rem. Like the next time I need to make weight."

He handed me a small plastic box containing a flower wrapped in a purple ribbon. "If you'll hold this, I'll pin it to your lapel."

"Gardenia." I smiled at him as the heavenly scent reached me. "You remembered."

After Michael pinned the boutonniere to my lapel, I fetched a similar plastic box from the dorm fridge I kept on my side of the room. Normally roommates shared such amenities, but "normal" no longer applied to me and Brady. The next step would be putting a lock on it, I supposed. Actually, the next step would be speaking to the housing office.

"A purple rose? Where on earth did you find such a thing?" Michael said.

I shrugged. "It's a new cultivar, but it looks good with our ties and cummerbunds, does it not?"

"It looks fantastic, and so do you." Michael leaned over and kissed me on the cheek.

I made a show of examining myself in the mirror. Not bad, not bad at all. Despite the occasional issue with my meds and the fact that the second half of the semester had contained enough stress to kill my appetite, I still cut a dashing figure in my tux.

Actually, we both cut dashing figures. I pulled Michael over to stand next to me, linking our arms as I rested my head on his shoulder. "We look good," he said.

He checked his watch. "We should go if we're going to meet the others on time."

"You can take comfort from this, Brady. You will never—ever—look this good in a dinner jacket if you don't start taking care of yourself."

Brady paused with a doughnut halfway to his mouth. "Fuck you."

"I don't think you have to worry about that." I was so glad I'd never disclosed my serostatus to him.

Michael grinned at me as he helped me into my topcoat. "You're Cinderfella this time."

"You do drive a better pumpkin." It was true. The Castelreighs might be less than supportive parents these days, but when Michael qualified for an unrestricted driver's license, they had bought him a late model import with more power than was perhaps wise for a teenage male, no matter how responsible. When Geoff and I had left for college, I got our white Civic from high school and a new computer. He got a new-to-him used car and his old computer. Twins were hell on our family's budget. Michael was clearly an only child.

"Is this some kind of weird mating ritual? Because if it is, leave me the hell out of it."

Michael glared at Brady. "You should live so long."

"Let's go, before Bratsy here throws a doughnut at us." I half steered, half pushed Michael toward the door.

"It's so much different from the last time. No parents taking pictures, no limo..."

I didn't reply for a moment, choosing my words carefully. "No, you're right about that. I'm hoping to make it through the evening without statutory rape charges being filed against me."

He sighed. "I'm sorry, Rem. I don't know why they're being this way. It's one more reason for us to get the hell out of here next summer."

"I guess so." Liar liar pants on fire. I knew I hadn't said anything because I was afraid and because I couldn't stand to think about me and Michael not being...well, me and Michael, but at what point did fear turn into chickenshit?

Michael put his arm around me as we walked out of my dorm and down to his pumpkin, in this case an Audi A6. "Your chariot awaits."

Chapter Eleven

Dinner could have been worse. At least, as Michael had promised, I recognized some of the people who still rowed for Cap City's junior crew. Not that we were necessarily good friends, but I nonetheless knew the faces, and we had rowing in common. It beat making pained conversation with their dates. Casey and James turned out to be my saviors at dinner. Casey had a wicked sense of humor, and James told a droll story, and the two of them together smoothed over the rough parts. They were the only entirely nonrowing couple, yet I found them the most interesting of anyone there. None of this changed the fact that I felt ill at ease in unfamiliar circumstances, or in any way altered the stark reality that I was two years older than some of these people. It showed, and I felt it.

Michael leaned over to me. "Maybe you should take a picture of them, so you can prove you can talk about something besides rowing."

"Pest," I hissed.

He kissed my cheek. "You love it."

I blushed, but I also had to admit I did, and quite possibly him. The thought scared me. I mean, how would I know? I couldn't stand the thought of being with anyone else, or worse, him with anyone else. Michael had owned my heart since...well, since the summer before my senior year, and that was a fact. But telling him? The thought scared the crap out of me.

We made it through the rest of dinner without me stammering too much or burping into my soup or some other gaucherie. The other couples were their own problems, and I knew Michael was suave where that was concerned. No, Michael and I only had to worry about me and my innate gracelessness. Hell, there was a reason I rowed and didn't play basketball. It's not like I wasn't tall enough. It was because I could trip over my own feet on flat ground, and that's when I wasn't shoving them in my mouth. Oh well, whatever. Love didn't require a dexterity test, and Michael seemed besotted with me as I was, the poor fool.

We made it to the prom in due time, and I sweated the entrance like a whore in church. But Michael's friend Matrixa—seriously, what kind of nickname was that? At least, I hoped it was a nickname—came through, and we sailed right by Cerberus, i.e., the parent chaperone guarding the door. Since we arrived fashionably late, the dancing was already underway, and we melded into the crowd. What I loved was that while you obviously had to dance with your date, sometimes you could dance with pretty much anyone without pissing your date off, which was how I ended up dancing with Casey and James and how Michael ended up across the gym dancing with some other friends of his. I could see him, he could see me, it was all good.

For a short time, anyway.

I didn't notice anything different about Casey and James, but suddenly they were on me, and I mean *on* me. They started climbing me like spider monkeys—which was a neat trick, since James was almost as tall as I was—and trying to graft themselves into me.

Odd, but okay. I caught Michael's eye across the gym and then tilted my head to one side, widening my eyes slightly, a sort of "now what do I do?" gesture.

Michael shrugged and laughed, as if to say, "Go with it, I guess."

So I did, or tried, at least. I talked a good line, but really, I was kind of a prude. Maybe that wasn't the term. I'd learned my lesson after that disastrous summer when I'd caught HIV and tried to be chaste in acting on my desires. You know, don't drool openly, don't touch what doesn't belong to you, that kind of thing. Secondary chastity? Was that a thing? Michael was my guy, and I was his, and that was that. So, this freaking—for that was what it had become—with two other men or boys or whatever? That was—good God! They were hard as rocks, and one of them, Casey, pressed his cock into my ass.

Oh no no, that was it. I shot Michael a panicked look, but he shook his head and rolled his eyes. Why the hell was he not over here pulling these punks off me? Never mind that, it looked like I would be rescuing myself.

"Sorry, guys," I all but yelled to be heard over the music, "this isn't my thing."

Then James locked his hands around my neck and held on to me like I was an under seat floatation device and our plane was heading for a water landing. "Awww, we're having fun, and we want you to be fun too."

"Yeah, about that... I have a boyfriend. So do you."

James grinned. Then he ground into me. "We want to play."

"I don't." Seriously, where the hell was Michael?

I reached up to pry James's hands off when I caught Michael's gaze. He stared at me intently from where he and his friends danced. Oh, he was paying attention, all right. He saw every single detail. And liked it.

Then they went to town. Jeez, I was trapped in my own personal girly show, only they were boys. That was it, however. They were still boys, both juniors in high school, while I'd cleared my first semester of college, more or less. As hot as this could've been with older guys, it needed to stop.

Awww jeez. They were young and they were hot, and they were hot because they were young, and how could Michael stand me? Was he looking at me because this turned him on or because I filled him with loathing? How could it not when even I made me sick?

And then the ghost of Josh Brennan reared his head. No Ouija board needed, just my overheated imagination and maybe some kind of martyr complex. I felt like a pervert for even being there. Maybe the

Castelreighs were right. Maybe I had no business whatsoever dating their son. Could four months of college really make that much difference?

I looked up and met Michael's eyes. He still danced with his friends, but I held all his attention. His eyes burned into mine, and I realized I'd catch hell later. Somehow, he knew exactly what had been going on. But if that had been the case, why had he not intervened?

Then his upper lip curled up, not quite a sneer, not quite a smile, but showing a lot of teeth. Oh, this was primal. Someone—two someones—had intruded on his territory, and he would have to reclaim it. Suddenly I found it hard to breathe. I ignored the children. The only person who mattered to me right then was Michael, and I watched him stalk me. I stopped dancing, letting Casey and James do whatever they were going to do in their addled state. It and they weren't my problems.

As soon as I felt their pressure lessen on my front and back, I pushed them away. I saw only one person who mattered in that moment. Everyone else faded from view, objects to be negotiated in my attempts to reach him.

I took my first steps away from Casey and James, when one of the chaperones caught us all. "Jeremy Babcock? What on earth are you doing here?"

Of course, it had to be Gutslinger, the vice principal for discipline.

I scratched the back of my head. "I'm here with my boyfriend, who's still a Davis High student."

I had to project to make myself heard over the music, some thudding techno beat that suddenly didn't sound fun anymore.

"And who would that be?"

I looked at the vice principal like she was stupid. No one was that naïve, not and be in charge of discipline at a suburban high school spanning the socioeconomic spectrum.

"Are you serious?"

"You can't blame me for trying. Regardless, the school takes a dim view on alumni crashing—"

I held up my hands. "I didn't crash. My boyfriend and I paid for tickets fair and square, same as everyone else."

"But...aha! You were dating Michael Castelreigh last year, and I see him plowing through the crowd toward us, so there's a good chance you still are. Neither of you are juniors and you can't protest that," Gutslinger said.

One of the other chaperones had collared Casey and James, but they seemed to be having a fine time, nonetheless. I shook my head. When would I ever learn?

Gutslinger followed my gaze and apparently my train of thought. "I'm going to have to ask you both to come with me while we get all this straightened out."

I nodded. "I suppose we'd better. The party's over, regardless."

"So, how's your brother?" she said as we all walked to her office. Well, Michael and I walked, the other chaperone herded Casey and James.

"I don't know, I haven't spoken to him since the middle of October, when he took our parents' side in an argument. Before you ask, I haven't spoken to them either."

Gutslinger looked up at me. "You're an unforgiving sort."

"You're one to talk." My sense of humor, at least on that subject, had long ago run out.

"I never hold grudges, Remy, I only do my job. Every day is a new day, and every student under my care starts it with a clean slate. That doesn't mean I don't know which students will dirty their slates sooner than others, but I never hold grudges, and it's never personal."

"This is." I didn't elaborate, but I couldn't help looking over at Michael.

Naturally, she caught it. "Interesting."

Gutslinger sat Michael and me down in front of her desk, and then left us alone while she conferred with the chaperone holding James and Casey. "You two, sit."

I had to admit, her tone of voice was far harsher than anything I'd ever heard her use on me, either when I was a student at Davis High or that evening.

Then she came to us and pulled a chair around to our side of her desk. "Some days—or nights—I wonder if I'm too old for this crap. All right, let's get down to business. Are you the one who supplied them with whatever they're on? I'm assuming it's molly."

I shook my head. "Are you kidding? I didn't have anything to do with it in high school, which you know perfectly well, and I still don't. You can call my coach if you want. I've passed all my random drug tests."

I didn't think she expected that. "Hmmm. No, you were straightlaced in high school, that was for sure."

"As it were." My voice grated in my own ears. The reality of the situation was, she had no authority to detain me. Michael, on the other hand? She could make his life hell.

Gutslinger folded her arms across her chest and turned to Michael. I knew it for what it was—cheap theatrics designed to intimidate high schoolers. "I'm rather surprised to see you involved in this, Mr. Castelreigh."

My tough boyfriend no longer looked so tough. He looked like what he was—a scared high school senior called on the carpet for the actions of others. "I didn't know anything about what they were going to do. I only wanted to have a nice night with my boyfriend."

Damn, but Gutslinger looked mean, and he looked terrified. "And it didn't occur to you that breaking the rules to get him into the prom wasn't the best idea?"

"The rule about one of us having to be a junior didn't seem like a big deal," he said softly, "not when someone on the organizing committee said sh—he'd get us in. We didn't plan to cause trouble; we were just going to dance. It's not like there's anywhere else we can do that."

Gutslinger smiled faintly, apparently catching Michael's slip of the tongue. "You're right about one thing. There aren't many opportunities for people under twenty-one to dance in Davis, and I'm not personally thrilled about my students driving to Sacramento for under twenty-one nights." Then the smile fell away, and she was all disciplinarian again. "It was entirely possible that if you'd come to me, Michael, we might have worked something out." She held up a hand. "Possible, I say, not probable, and now much less probable for the senior ball this spring. That depends on how my investigation about tonight turns out, including those two. I don't tolerate drugs in my high school. At all. And, Remy, I'll need your coach's phone number. If you have indeed passed your drug screens, I'll consider the matter between you and me settled, because I have no legal recourse to go fishing for anything else."

You're damn right you don't. I didn't say that out loud.

She looked at me long and hard. "But Remy? Given the fact that there's an active lawsuit between your family and the school district, your presence here is at the very least in extremely bad taste."

Oh, that was it. "That lawsuit is entirely the fault of your coaching staff, and you know it. They were aware of the Americans with Disabilities Act and their responsibilities under it, but they chose to ignore them in favor of AIDS-phobia or whatever you choose to call it." The whole thing infuriated me. "Furthermore, that all came out in court and under oath. This school and this district have only themselves to blame. Right now, the lawyers are haggling over dollar figures, and yet I have in no way been ordered to stay away from my boyfriend's school, which you also know."

Gutslinger sighed. "I know it's their fault, which makes me furious. I was only ever on your side if you'll remember."

I stared into her eyes, wishing my glare were a drill. "So, don't start in on me like I'm the enemy. I didn't bring drugs into this school, and I don't know where those two got them. They seemed fine through dinner, but all of a sudden, they were on me like white on rice. Furthermore, I haven't led Michael astray, and I never thought doing an end run around the entrance requirements for the prom was a good idea." I glanced at Michael. "I am not, however, always listened to, but I do have a perfectly legal backup plan on deck, so the evening's not a total bust."

"I see you continue to be mature beyond your years." Gutslinger turned to Michael. "You're not off the hook yet, but I'm not going to call your parents either. I'd like to talk to you more on Monday to see what you know and to see why you thought it was a good idea to take your friend up on *her* offer to circumvent the requirements about at least one of the couple having to be a junior. Depending on your answers, you'll either be let off the hook with a warning, detention, or we'll end up having that talk with your parents, after all."

Michael groaned, but not in the good way. "Anything but that."

"Oh?" she said.

"They think I'm a horrible influence on their precious little boy," I said, none too kindly.

The vice principal made a face. "Because you're over eighteen? They loved the both of you before you graduated, Remy."

I nodded but didn't trust myself to speak.

Michael, however, said, "You got it in one."

"Now that," Gutslinger said, "is one of the stupider things I've heard for a while, and believe me, gentlemen, that's saying something. Michael is capable of finding his own trouble, and you, Remy, were only ever a good student and a restraining influence on those around you."

"Except the hardcore jocks," I muttered.

"Except for them." She squared her shoulders. "All right, you two run along. I obviously have bigger fish to fry tonight."

As we left her office, I heard her say, "Well now, boys, what exactly did you think you were doing besides dry humping Mr. Castelreigh's date on the dance floor?"

Chapter Twelve

We couldn't get out of there fast enough. "So much for showing you a good time." Michael sounded dejected.

I bumped his shoulder. "Hey, you showed me an interesting time. That's almost as good."

"An interesting time? As in, 'may you live in interesting times'?" He smiled—or tried. That told me I needn't worry too much.

I stopped and pulled Michael against me. "Are you okay? Really?"

"I will be." Michael sighed into the hug, allowing me to support his weight. "It's not how I thought the evening would turn out, you know? I had it all planned out. Dinner, dancing, then..." He coughed. I had an idea what came after that. "Oddly enough, being hauled into Gutslinger's office never factored into any of it, to say nothing of threats to call my parents. She knows we didn't do anything, so what's with this sword of Damocles crap?"

Classical references from a high school student. God bless Davis.

"I don't know, babe. Maybe it's because she can or because when it comes down to it, she doesn't know how to deal with our kind in any other way."

Michael lifted his head. "Our kind?"

"You know, well-behaved people. She spends her days with miscreants, so she assumes we all are."

"Miscreants? I like the sound of that."

I snorted. "I'm not sure either of us could be miscreants or malefactors if we tried. You never did say how you wanted the evening to go. How did you want it to go?"

Suddenly shy, he buried his head in my shoulder again. "How I want all our nights to go."

"And how would that be?" I thought I knew what he wanted, but clarity mattered.

Michael kissed my neck softly even as he ran his hands inside my dinner jacket and over my chest. "It'll sound silly."

"No, it won't." I kissed the side of his head. I meant it. I knew he felt embarrassed right then, although neither of us had done anything to be embarrassed about. Casey and James were another matter. I could only imagine how all those conversations would go on Monday.

"I want you in me tonight," he whispered, right before licking my ear.

Oh, my gawd—I had to lock my knees. Michael certainly had my number. We didn't switch very often, but if my guy asked, I had to give it to him. I turned and shoved him up against the bank of lockers we were near, and he groaned. I kissed him hard, teeth clashing as I showed who was in control, at least for that night. He fought me, as if he weren't quite sure how it worked. I grabbed his hands in mine and pulled his arms over his head, holding them there where it worked for both of us.

"Rem..." he whined.

"Yeah, babe?"

"I can't reach anything interesting."

I smirked. "We'll take care of that in a minute."

Then I kissed him again, more gently, as I ground our cocks together. We both groaned. We both knew where this was headed.

Then a door opened and closed. I dropped our hands in a panic. We looked at each other, our eyes wide, our trousers very obviously tented.

"Oh shit," I whispered. "Could we have picked a worse place?"

"Remy? I am not fucking in my car."

I snickered at the thought. "You've got a great car, and I realize that car sex is supposed to be some sort of staple of college life, but we're both way too tall. Come on, I've got an idea."

I grabbed his hand and, giggling, we took off before anyone could catch us.

"Where are we going?" Michael said. "We're not supposed to be anywhere else at school."

"I know, that's why we're heading for a particular place I know." I grinned. "Trust me. This place starred in some fevered fantasies."

I led Michael to a sheltered corner that everyone saw daily, but no one ever paid any attention to. It had caught my eye one day when I was a sophomore. The corner was an architectural oddity, a place where the very oldest part of Davis High abutted more recent additions, just not very well. Virtually everywhere else the newer buildings met the older ones they blended reasonably well, but not here. This little space appeared to be the one place where the new architects simply hadn't been able to make the new design match up to the old build. I didn't intend to argue. It was sheltered from the wind that had come up and totally dark. Anyone patrolling the grounds wouldn't see us, even if he walked right by.

"I had no idea this was here," Michael said.

"You could've plowed me here every day at lunch and no one would've been any the wiser."

Michael looked around. "So why didn't I?"

"Because I didn't have the guts." I pressed him back into the dark recesses.

"Speaking of guts, I really want this," he said, groping me, "to rearrange mine."

"Some catchers are so pushy." I started kissing him again, running my hands over his chest. Even through his shirt and undershirt, I felt how hard his chest was. Then I pulled his shirt out of his pants for better access. Some men shaved their chests, but not my Michael. I liked the feel—the sight too—of his chest hair. I loved to rest my head against it after he had taken care of me, but not tonight. My guy had requested something different, and different he would get.

Tonight, I was in the driver's seat, and he had handed himself to me. There was a trust there, an absolute trust, one I would die before abusing. It all reminded me of a Depeche Mode song, and since Michael had figuratively handed himself over on a plate, I went with it.

I turned him around and held him from behind for a moment. I rested my head against his back, enjoying the promise of strength, the potential for mastery and dominance. But sometimes even the strongest of men needed to be held, to be taken care of, to surrender control to one every bit as strong, one equally able to dominate. I knew that as well as anyone. Tonight was my night to drive, and I knew exactly what to do. I knew where I wanted to take Michael to make the drive a pleasurable one for him.

I lifted his arms up and placed them up against the wall, like I was about to frisk him. "Don't move them," I said, covering his body with my own, front to back, everything lining up.

Michael shuddered beneath me as I bit his neck. I planned to mark him, but that didn't mean everyone had to see it. Just me. Well, me and whoever rowed behind him at practice on Monday.

I scraped my teeth down the sensitive skin where his hair was cut short, tearing a quivering groan out of him. I allowed my hands to roam. It might've been dark, but they knew the major landmarks.

Michael huffed out a breath and rutted back against me. "Yeah."

I reached one hand down and dealt with his belt and pants, the better to drive around down there. Michael wanted it, and I did too.

I knew I needed to reach my destination before the radiator blew, so I eased his pants and boxer briefs down over his amazing ass. As much as I wanted to stare at it in wonder, it was December, and I didn't want any of his moving parts to freeze up—nor any of my own.

I pulled supplies out of my dinner jacket's pocket and made short work of suiting up. No discussion of our debate about his Truvada, my undetectable viral loads, or riding dirty. We spent too much time on that as it was. I was in charge, and that meant condoms. Wrap it before you tap it and all that.

Even with Michael's pants below the swell of his glorious backside, I moved quickly. I couldn't bear to leave him shivering, not from cold, at any rate.

"Rem..."

"I've got you." I plunged slicked fingers into him, loosening him for the ride ahead. Michael sighed in contentment, but I knew it was only temporary. I added more lube, gently working it in.

"You ready?" I positioned myself at his entrance.

He shoved himself back on me, and my head swam. "That answer your question?"

Michael was tight and couldn't handle the hard-shove-and-in method, no matter how horned up he thought he was. I took my time and made him beg. It sounded so pretty.

"Are you okay? I didn't hurt you?"

"Move, damn you!"

So, I did. Even though I was in him, Michael still topped me. While he might've been hesitant about asking for what he wanted and needed earlier, he appeared to have gotten over it.

"Right...there! Yes! Keep doing that."

Neither of us would last long, and maybe we didn't need to. We were sneaking around at a high school formal neither of us had any business attending and doing the deed in an obscure corner of the school. It was so hot.

So, I pistoned in and out of Michael like we both wanted and needed. There was no art, just taking my boyfriend where he needed to go that night, where he had asked me to take him, where I wanted us to go.

"Almost there, Rem."

"Right behind you."

He cried out, and then I did. I wrapped my arms around him, holding him as we came down.

"Right behind me? Really, Rem?" Michael said as I slipped out of him.

I tied the condom off and pocketed it until I could find a trash can. "I said that?"

"You did." Michael kissed my nose as he tucked his shirt in.

"That was horrible."

Once we were again dressed and presentable to the world—Michael had to retie my bowtie for me—I checked to make sure we would be unobserved. Sure that no one would scope us out, we slipped out of our love nest. Just two guys taking a stroll, right?

"Feel better?" I asked Michael.

He kissed my cheek. "Much. You said something about a backup plan?"

"You'll think it's stupid." Honestly, I couldn't think where I dug up my ideas sometimes. The bottom of the river?

"Not if you don't tell me what it is."

He had a point.

That was how we ended up in a sketchy theater in Sacramento dancing the Time Warp with a fine selection of our fellow misfit toys. Because *The Rocky Horror Picture Show* in formalwear? It was an immoral imperative.

*

We were in the middle of finals, Michael and I, and our "dates" consisted of studying together. Parallel play for the win!

True to her word, after a conversation that Monday morning with him, Gutslinger let Michael off the hook with a withering lecture about the foolishness of sneaking into the junior class's prom. We were both banned from the senior class's formal dance in the spring. Tiresome as that might be, neither of us felt the need to bother the Castelreighs with that. After all, we'd already been to mine and could always claim to be danced out. I already had plans to take him to an eighteen-and-over club in San Francisco the minute he turned legal.

The only blowback I experienced from crashing the prom was a summons from Coach Ridgewood. She called me into her office one afternoon toward the end of the semester. I found Coach Pendergast waiting for me. That couldn't possibly be good.

"I had the weirdest phone call from a vice principal at Davis High a few weeks ago. What on earth was that about?" she asked.

All I could do was sigh as I stood there in front of my coaches. "Long or short answer?"

"Short."

"My boyfriend thought it'd fun to crash a formal dance. Hilarity ensued. She thought I was responsible for bringing drugs, but I told her the kids could and did do it all by themselves. So long as my random pee tests were clean, she said she'd let it go. I went to Davis High myself, so she knows my word's good."

Pendergast shifted in his seat, looking distinctly uncomfortable. "You're dating someone in high school?"

"I was in high school when we started going out." I shrugged. "I didn't see any point to breaking up simply because I graduated." I couldn't tell if that mollified my coaches or not. "Am I in trouble?"

"No, not at all. I just thought it was a strange call to receive." Ridgewood moved a few stacks of paper around on her desk, although why I noticed that I didn't know.

"It was a strange conversation to sit through. Come to think of it, the whole evening was a little off-key, but I'm willing to bet that's not why you called me in." I shifted uncomfortably. Could they maybe move this along?

"No, it wasn't. Have a seat, Remy." Pendergast nudged a seat in my direction with his foot. He stared at me for a few moments. It was an appraising look. I'd received a few of those in my life, and they never made me comfortable. "It's not a secret, I don't think, that we've all had our eyes on you."

I blinked. "Actually, no. I didn't notice. As my brother or boyfriend or even my parents will tell you, if it's not made of carbon fiber, it's probably not on my radar. So okay, yes, I saw you both huddled with someone in Boston, and yes, Peter Lodestone talked to people about me both at the Crew Classic in San Diego and at the Youth Nationals, but nothing ever seemed to come of it, and I couldn't row it, so I ignored it, you know?"

Ridgewood and Pendergast looked at each and nodded. "That explains a lot," she said.

"You'd be surprised how wrong you are about that, Remy. Lodestone spoke to both Joanne and myself in San Diego and at the Nationals in Lake Natoma, and both she and I paid a great deal of attention to your performance at the Nationals back east."

Ridgewood settled back in her chair. "That's what we want to talk to you about—those people observing you. You started as a JV walk-on. It happens, but not often. The thing is, you're outgrowing JV too."

"Oh." I hardly knew what to say to that. "Um... thanks?"

Pendergast laughed. "He's totally unaware of exactly how good he is."

"That's the only thing that makes it tolerable, Frank." Ridgewood turned her attention back to me. "What we propose is this, Remy: you'll continue to scull in the afternoons with me, but in the mornings, you row with Coach Pendergast in the big boats."

"This is something of an experiment," Pendergast said. "We've never had a rower straddle two squads like this, but we've never had a rower with a chance at the Under 23 National Team, either."

I stared at him and then jerked my head around to look at Ridgewood. "I... Wait, what? I couldn't have heard you right."

"To which?" Ridgewood laughed. "I threw a lot at you."

"All of it?" Seriously, my mind defaulted to the test pattern. But they were wrong about one thing. I knew I could row, but hearing others say it freaked me out.

Pendergast leaned forward. "Some of those people watching you, not only in Boston but at both Youth

Nationals, were from USRowing. They like what they've seen, Remy, and they like the progress you've made. Right now, you're not there yet. But we think you could be by June. That's when the next selection camp will be held."

I sat back in my chair, stunned. The U23 team. My gears spun.

"Now here's the deal," Ridgewood said. "Here's the Real Talk. We're not being entirely altruistic, although we're obviously invested in your potential. CalPac's a new program as far as these things go. We've got money, and we're making a name for ourselves based on what Nick Bedford started, but you're the first rower with this kind of potential we've had. You're the chance we've been waiting for to establish CalPac in the first rank of rowing programs like Cal or the University of Washington or the Ivies. Helping you go the distance means we go the distance with you."

I nodded slowly. "That seems fair."

"It is, basically," Pendergast said. "The NCAA has a bad rep where student athletes are concerned—"

"Entirely deserved, in my opinion," Ridgewood said.

"Unfortunately, yes." Pendergast sighed. "We'd be walking a fine line with you in twice-a-day training even when the rest of the team isn't. We plan to work with the human performance lab on campus to keep a close eye on your lactate levels, among other things, to keep you from being overtrained. This wouldn't be easy, but I think this could be rewarding for all of us."

"If you do this, we'd like to contact your academic advisor to bring her into the loop. Can we do that?" Ridgewood said.

"I think we'd have to." That sounded safe to say, but then again, my mouth was back to the test pattern since my brain had cha-cha'd off to parts unknown. "So, what else do I need to know?"

Pendergast handed me a packet. "This is USRowing's information about U23 selection. Read it. Become one with it."

"In there you'll find information about the declaration of intent to compete, plus some other things you'll need to look over, including a stringent code of conduct. You seem like a straight arrow, so it shouldn't be a problem, odd calls from your old high school aside." Ridgewood handed me another, smaller packet. "You'll note here that the selection camp is in late June, and the Worlds are in late July. You have a little time to think, but don't wait too long. You're good, but you'll need to be great."

I nodded slowly. Why was it I could never stay still? There was always something to yank the rug out from under me, right? For once I wanted to lead a more sedate life. Living out the Plan with Michael, where we rowed our seats without worrying about setting the world ablaze, where we finished college without complications like brooding roommates or colleges that weren't what we'd hoped, where psychological damage never showed its ugly face, disapproving parents didn't poo-poo our relationship, that was what I wanted.

But what fun would that be?

If I accepted their challenge. For once, I needed to think about something related to crew. "When do you need an answer?"

"When you come back from winter break," Pendergast said.

Ridgewood nodded her approval. "I'm glad you didn't jump at this. While it's a tremendous opportunity, it's also a serious commitment."

"Something else to consider is the cost." Pendergast made a face. "I hate talking about money. Yes, the school has money, and yes, the rowing program has it, too, but this will cost a fair amount out of pocket. You'll need a coach lined up, and you'll need to pay him or her. Start thinking about who you want. Don't rule out Lodestone just because he was your high school coach."

That surprised me. "You'd let Lodestone have a hand in this?"

"He took you to the Youth Nationals," Ridgewood said. "Twice. You obviously respond well to him. We're in uncharted waters here. Neither Frank nor I are going to let ego get in the way, and at the end of it all, when your name's listed in the program, it's going to say California Pacific after it."

"What if I don't make it?" I chewed on a fingernail, because despite their opinions, this sounded like a long shot to me.

Pendergast grinned. "That's the beauty of it—you're eighteen. Even if you don't make it, you'll still be on

USRowing's radar. Seriously, Remy, you already have their attention, but this will make sure they'll watch you very, very closely for the foreseeable future. And you can keep trying for five more years."

"Since you'll have to submit qualifying scores for 2k and 6k erg tests, this will include a strict regimen of strength training and aerobic conditioning," Ridgewood continued. "I think we'd want to monitor you quite closely, including things like diet and sleep. To an extent, we'll all be making this up as we go along. Sure, Frank and I will consult the more experienced coaches on the national team, but this will be a lot of firsts for all of us."

I'd have to disclose my serostatus, I realized, because this would push anyone to the edge, let alone someone with my condition. I wondered if that would make a difference. Should I tell them now or later? Maybe I should talk to my own doctors before I made up my mind...

Then I realized they were talking again.

"...Selection takes place over five days in late June, so it shouldn't even interfere with your summer plans."

"Oh oh oh," Ridgewood said, "something else to keep in mind... If you make it, USRowing will pick up the costs for the world championships with the exception of airfare and hotel."

I sighed. "That means more private funding, right?"

"Yes." Pendergast grimaced again, apparently at the thought of money. "But if you make the world championships, I can almost guarantee you that I'll be able to shake scholarship money out of the alumni oversight committee."

"You'd be the first from CalPac to make it that far, Remy," Ridgewood said. "In a few short years, CalPac will have gone from fielding a single eight at the Pac Ten to sending a rower to the U23 world championships. They'll cough up, trust me. Frank may not like to talk about money, but if it comes to it, I'll have no problem juicing those people like ripe oranges."

Pendergast looked at the time. "Listen, we've sprung a lot on you that you need to think about, and I have to be somewhere in thirty minutes. Think about this, talk to your family, talk to your boyfriend, and anyone else who can help you put it in perspective, like Peter Lodestone. Then give us your answer when you come back from the holidays."

"For that matter, if you come to a definite decision—a definite *considered* decision—over the break, let us know, but the one thing we insist on is that you think about this long and hard." Ridgewood stood up, extending her hand. "I know how you work. Go sculling. You do your best thinking out there."

I laughed as I shook my coach's hand, and then Pendergast's. I guess he was my coach now too. "Guilty as charged."

I walked slowly toward the locker room, quiet now during the off-season. So much to think about. I pulled out my phone to text Michael. Even if he were in class, he'd find the text waiting.

ME: *I need 2 talk.*

Then I walked into the locker room, feeling like I'd stepped into someone else's life.

Chapter Thirteen

Michael knew me so well. When he found my text and couldn't raise me, he drove out to CalPac's boathouse and made himself comfortable.

"Thanks for waiting," I said as I walked out of the locker room.

He gave me a long hug. "I'm surprised you went out."

"It wasn't this foggy when I launched, and I had a lot to think about." I sighed.

"That's what I suspected, given your text and subsequent vanishing act. I texted Coach Lodestone to see if *he* knew what was up, but his sphinxlike response only told me that he did and that I should come find you." Michael shook his head. "One of these days he'll come right out and answer a question, and then I swear all of his teeth will fall out from the shock or something."

We wandered out to the CalPac dock to stare at the now-glassy water, once again undisturbed since I'd brought my equipment back to the boathouse. We sat down on a bench, and I filled him in on my coaches' perhaps Faustian proposal.

His eyes round with surprise, he could only say, "Wow."

"That's one word, yes." I stared out at the water, my mind starting to churn again.

"Um...that's fantastic?"

I tried not to think about the implications. "I guess."

Michael gently turned my chin so I faced him. "Don't shut me out, Rem. Tell me what you're thinking."

"I'm not shutting you out, Michael." I smiled, or at least tried. "I'm...yeah. Overwhelmed. This is huge. I don't know what to think, or even where to start thinking about it."

"First of all, I know you, maybe better than you know yourself. Right now, this very moment, stop thinking that you don't deserve this. Because you do. No one works harder at this sport than you. I know that, your teammates know that, and so do your coaches. Lodestone's always known it."

"How do you always know what to say?" I whispered.

He kissed me softly. "I *know* you. So what you're going to do now is accept the fact that this is something you're capable of doing—or will be with the kind of training I know your coaches will dish out—and think about whether or not this is something you want to do."

"It's going to cost a fortune."

"Define fortune."

"I don't have exact numbers, although they're surely in one of the two packets Ridgewood and Pendergast gave me, but above and beyond some of my expenses, I'm responsible for my coach's expenses too," I said. "While the school will cover some of it, CalPac probably won't pony up if I tap Lodestone."

Michael looked surprised. "They'd let you?"

"So they said. As they pointed out, he took me to two Nationals." If I'd had to choose now, I'd choose Lodestone. Not that I'd asked him. Or told him. But I'd known him for five years, whereas I'd known Ridgewood and Pendergast for a handful of months.

"A fair point." He put his arm around me.

I rested my head on Michael's shoulder, taking solace in his presence. I hoped he found something in mine, otherwise my parents would be right. How could I give this up?

"So, it'll be expensive, time consuming, and exhausting," Michael said. "Sounds right up your alley."

"That about sums it up, yes." I smiled. "So yes, I'll be rather busy over break. Speaking of break, what're you doing for yours?"

Michael looked down at me. He looked decidedly displeased. "Other than a visit with my grandparents in SoCal, not too much. Hoping you'll deal with your family."

I lifted my head up. "What? What's going on?"

"Besides nothing on your end? Geoff keeps e-mailing me." Michael pulled his shoulder out from under me. "It was one thing when I was on the sidelines supporting you through one of your apparently endless wars with your family, but now your brother's dragging me into it, or trying."

"Trying?" Suffering Christ, couldn't these people try contacting me directly? Sure, I'd shred the meat off their bones, but maybe they'd earned it. Cowards.

"I keep deleting the e-mails."

"An eminently sensible response, in my opinion. I'm sorry my brother's trying to put you in the middle." But something wasn't right here. "Yet somehow you're angry at me..."

Michael looked at me like I was insane, and who knows, by this time I probably was. "Because you started this!"

I cocked my head, because it was react with sarcasm or scream at the absurdity of his statement and bolt. "So, I should've rolled over when my parents said what they said? And when Geoff agreed?"

"I don't have an answer, but I know I shouldn't be in the middle." Michael looked miserable.

"I agree with you there, and I'm really sorry about that, but I didn't start this." Seriously, you'd think a guy on the honors track could've kept the details straight. It made me wonder what was really going on. "Add his address to your spam filters."

Michael shook his head. "That's not really going to solve anything."

"No, not really, but it'll give you some peace while I figure out what to do about my family." And crew, and my roommate, and my life in general. And there was the whole issue of what to do about the holiday break itself...

As if he'd read my mind, Michael said, "What're you doing for the break?"

I shrugged. "No idea."

"Wait...you don't know where you're going?"

'Bout time that sank in. Michael's lack of response had me worried for a moment.

"As you pointed out, the Head of the Charles Massacre has yet to be cleaned up."

"Has it occurred to you that your parents are waiting for you to call them?"

I gave him a flat look. "They're the ones who think you have too much control over me. Or that I'm a bad influence on you. I still don't have it entirely straight. Either way, they started this when they picked a fight right before the Head of the Charles. It's up to them to fix this."

"Maybe they're afraid to." Michael looked out at the water, no doubt thinking the same thing I did: what a waste. Flat water and too foggy to row.

"What do you mean?" I admit it. I was suspicious.

Michael slung one arm over my shoulder. "Rem, we both know you don't just hold a grudge. You find stray grudges in the mud beside the road, take them home, give them warm baths, and then nurse them back to health. Then, when you've raised them up nice and strong, you turn them loose on an unsuspecting populace. Your parents—to say nothing of Geoff—may not have called because by this time they know full well you've come to a righteous boil over this, and that the first one to wave the stick with a shirt on it in our direction will be met with a barrage of artillery fire."

"I don't hold grudges, Michael."

He looked at me over the top of his sunglasses.

"I only remember the facts. I'm right."

"I know you are, Rem, but that doesn't mean your family is eager to march before your one-man firing squad, and they've let this go so long that it's what it's become." I could tell Michael parsed his next comment carefully. "And right's not going to keep you warm over a cold winter break either."

With the fog sucking the warmth out of us even through our winter coats, I felt his point. That did not mean, however, I had any intention of conceding it, let alone contacting my parents. They started this, and they had to blink first.

"I suppose I could e-mail Laurel..."

Michael nodded. "You should. She could tell you how Geoff's doing, assuming he's confided in her—"

I looked at him. I didn't even have to say anything.

"Okay, you're right. Scratch that. He's told her everything. None of this should've happened in the first place."

"You've got that right. I didn't start this fight, but I'm going to make damn sure they finish it." I glared out at the water, as if I could somehow will the outcome I wanted.

Michael nodded. "I hear you. I'm also telling you there may be a whole lot of daylight between right and home for the holidays. I'd invite you home, but we know how well that would go over. What about grandparents? Aunts or uncles?" He gave me a funny look. "You know, I've never heard you talk about aunts or uncles."

"That's because Mom's an only child, and Dad's either alienated or irritated his brothers and sisters." Then the light bulb flashed on. Of course! Mom's parents, Grandma and Grandpa Fischer! Then it winked out again. I hadn't seen them in years.

"What? You looked elated and then not. What's going on in there, Rem?"

"For a moment there I thought I might be able to go see Mom's parents, but I haven't seen them in probably five years. Dad's always saying how expensive it is to travel to see them." Damn, so close.

"Where do they live?"

"Chicago."

"Didn't you four go to Europe right after you graduated from high school?"

I nodded. "Yep."

"You could spend two weeks in Europe but can't fly to Chicago? There are a bunch of direct flights from Sacramento to O'Hare every day." Michael frowned. "That's the dumbest thing I've ever heard."

I gave him my best "oh really?" look. "You've met my father."

"I don't know, Rem. They might be your best bet. I think you should call them anyway. What's the worst that could happen?"

"They could say no." That'd be the last thing I'd need, more rejection. But the more I thought about it, the more I saw his point. I had very little choice. I couldn't—wouldn't—impose on Heath and Jerry anymore. "I hate to spend the holidays so far away from you, but you're right. They're my best bet."

Michael pulled me into a hug. "I'll manage. It's you I'm worried about. You're not nearly as tough as you want the world to think."

"But only you know the truth." I rested my head on his shoulder again. It was one of my favorite places these days.

"And that makes me the luckiest fella on earth."

After that, we found ways to warm each other up despite the fog.

*

When I got back to my room, I chewed my guts out for a little while, and then looked up the phone number for Grandma and Grandpa Fischer. I had it in my phone's address book, but I wanted to be sure it hadn't changed, but no, there they were, Howard and Evelyn Fischer.

Geoff and I barely knew them, or so it seemed, but when I thought about it, I found I knew a fair amount *about* them. Mom's family was Jewish, but so lapsed she'd never been bat mitzvahed. While Grandma and Grandpa weren't Holocaust survivors, *their* parents had been or had escaped Germany before things turned grim, and when my great-grandparents had landed on these barbarian shores, they'd decided they'd had enough with religion, *all* religions. While Grandma and Grandpa had eased up on their parents' militant atheism, they never, so far as I knew, recaptured the faith of their forefathers. Foremothers? I was pretty sure Judaism passed through the female line. Anyway, the Fischers apparently never objected to Mom marrying Dad, an equally lapsed Christian of some variety or other. Sure, we made out like bandits in December, with presents for both Hanukkah and Christmas... Christmukkuh? The fact that we usually ended up having brisket around Passoverish was probably a coincidence, but the high holy days never happened at our house.

But a sketchy biography didn't equal knowing my grandparents. I frowned as I stared at their number. This promised to be nerve-racking. I sucked it up and dialed the number.

"Hello?" a man said, a cultured voice, but older. My grandfather, obviously.

"Grandpa? It's Jeremy."

Silence greeted me. I gulped air, scared. This had been a mistake, he didn't remem—

"Pick up the extension, Evelyn, it's your grandson."

I heard my grandmother in the background say, "Which one?"

"The fegelah."

My jaw dropped. "You did not call me that."

"Yes, he did. Howard, you did not call your grandson a fegelah."

"What does he want, Evelyn?"

"You can ask him yourself, Howard. What can we do for you, dear?"

This wasn't going well, not at all. I started shaking. Nerves, I guessed. "I don't want anything, really, except maybe a place to spend the holidays."

Dead air. Oh crap. "Never mind, it was a stupid—"

"Why aren't you spending it with your family, dear?"

How much to tell them? Might as well go big. "Because my parents are full of crap and I haven't spoken to them since the middle of October. Also, my brother's being a jerk."

"Your father's always been a bit of a hothead. You'll have to fill us in on the details when you get here," Grandma said.

"And?" Grandpa said.

I sniffled. I refused to cry, dammit. "The holidays get lonely without anyone."

"We'll send you a ticket," Grandpa said. "How soon can you get here?"

Wait...what? That tide had turned quickly.

"I don't even need a ticket. I've got my parents' credit card, and it's my determination to make them pay and pay good. I only wanted to be sure I'd be welcome. I'll figure out my itinerary and call you back."

Grandma snorted. "E-mail it, dear. It'll be quicker, and we can get to spoiling you that much sooner."

"But...we haven't seen each other in what? Five years?" I was more confused than ever.

Grandpa made an extremely rude noise, but Grandma only said, "That's not your fault, dear."

"Do you have a pencil and paper for the e-mail address?" Grandpa said.

I took down his e-mail and promised to get right back to them. In return they sent me a list of clothes to pack. What made me the most nervous was that Grandma requested a picture of my dinner suit. What was I in for?

But that was how I ended up spending my winter holidays in a penthouse apartment on Chicago's Gold Coast.

Chapter Fourteen

I left for Chicago after my last final, taking a red-eye from Sacramento to O'Hare. Michael took me to the airport.

"I'll miss you." He wrapped his arms around me. It was his turn to rest his head on my shoulder.

We stood downstairs in front of the check-in kiosks and desks where I'd already turned over my suitcase, since he couldn't accompany me beyond the security checkpoint. "I'll miss you too. It feels funny not to be with you at the holidays."

"Any idea when you'll be back?" Michael sounded so vulnerable, and I felt very tender toward him in that moment.

I shook my head and then realized that with his head on my shoulder, he couldn't see it. Then I felt stupid. "No, I've left the ticket open-ended. If things are dicey with my grandparents, maybe before New Year's Eve. If not, sometime the week after, I guess."

As it was a week before Christmas, we were looking at a potentially long separation. If things fell apart in

Chicago, I could always stay in a hotel until I could get back into my dorm room, or even call my parents and make their lives hell by going home.

Michael lifted his head and kissed my cheek. "If I don't let you go, I'll embarrass us both by making a scene here in the airport."

I pulled his face toward mine. Then I kissed him full on the lips. I wasn't shy, and I didn't hurry. He was my guy, and I was coming to certain conclusions about my feelings for him, feelings I wasn't ready to share yet, but feelings I wanted to show him. When I broke the kiss, I said, "Make a scene."

I left Michael standing at the bottom of the escalators that led up to security and then to the gates. Just before he passed from view, I waved, a small, diffident wave. He meant so much to me.

With Michael on my mind, I slept the night away on the trip to Chicago.

*

The flight, technically speaking, took only four hours, but with the time change, I landed at a reasonable time of the morning. Reasonable, that is, if you kept rowers' hours. Grandpa didn't seem to think there was anything odd about picking me up at 7:00 a.m., however.

We hugged awkwardly outside of baggage claim, and then headed toward his car. "Your grandmother's at home. She never has liked early hours. She'll have breakfast for us and knowing her there'll be enough to feed a regiment."

Then Grandpa looked at me, and I mean he took a good, hard look at me, like maybe he hadn't noticed me. "Damn, Jeremy, you've gotten so tall."

"An epidemic of it swept my high school a few years back. Everyone I know came down with it." It wasn't as if Grandpa were short by any stretch of the imagination, but I guess it really had been a long time.

Grandpa stared at me for a moment, and then chuckled. "Oh, I'm going to like you. You were a very serious little boy, you know."

"I haven't had a lot to laugh about the last few years, I suppose. Dad and I spent my teen years butting heads, and he wasn't all that discreet with his words when I was younger."

Grandpa muttered something under his breath that might've been "asshole," but I pretended not to hear. I didn't want to think about the situation with the 'rents. Maybe Grandpa cottoned on to that because he changed the subject.

"So...uh, I thought college students were supposed to sleep until noon."

I chuckled. "I get up early to row. The time zone thing's thrown me, and I'm sure tomorrow morning will be ugly, but for now? It's not so bad, but I hope that breakfast includes coffee."

"I drink it by the gallon, so you've nothing to worry about." Grandpa clapped me on the shoulders as we approached his car. The hallways leading from the airport to the parking decks were heated, but as we walked out of the double doors, the cold hit me like a brick wall, and I swore like a well-educated sailor.

Grandpa looked at my jacket. "Did you bring any cold-weather clothing?"

"This is my cold-weather clothing."

"Then, my boy, you had better brace yourself and hope that coffee's strong enough to last until lunch, because your grandmother will take one look at that flimsy thing you're wearing and drag you to the stores as soon as they're open." Grandpa shook his head as I put my suitcase in the trunk of his Mercedes, shivering as I did so. "It's always the Californians."

I dove into the sedan as soon as Grandpa unlocked the doors and found much to my relief that it had some kind of fancy remote starter and was already warm. Miracle of miracle, the seat contained heaters. "Ahhhh."

I stared unabashedly as we drove along the 190 to the 90 from the airport to the neighborhood Grandpa told me was called the Gold Coast, what was once one of the most affluent neighborhoods in America. When we exited onto Lake Shore Drive, it appeared to me it hadn't lost any of that wealth. I craned my head up. "That's the skyline."

Grandpa laughed. "It is."

"And you live here?"

"In one of the high-rises, yes."

I nodded but kept my thoughts to myself. Living in Davis wasn't cheap, and most of my peers knew what our parents' houses would sell for, but I shuddered to contemplate what my grandparents' condo must cost. Somehow, I doubted they owed the bank for it either.

Then I looked around at ground level. It wasn't just snow. Oh no, ice was everywhere. Ice coated trees, stoplights, even some cars. Jeez. That was gross. Fine, play it that way, Chicago. I would never leave the condo.

"You're looking at the snow, aren't you?" Grandpa said, a smile on his face.

"The ice. Is it always like this?"

He laughed. "Sometimes it's worse. There's always," he said ominously, "thunder snow."

"I don't want to know." Sure, snow up at Lake Tahoe was fine. It slowed the drive down, and yes, deploying chains brought nothing but cold, wet irritation unless one had money to pay the chain monkeys, but even so, it could be a whole lot worse, like...thunder snow. What the devil? "Okay, I'll bite. What is it?"

"It's a thunderstorm with freezing temperatures, so the rain falls as snow. It can be pretty spectacular."

I slouched in my seat. "I pray I'll only ever be able to take your word for it. I hate weather."

"What is it with Californians and weather?" Grandpa said.

"Oh, that's an easy one. We never have any, so the slightest hint of it sends us all into a blind panic." I glared at the ice and snow.

"So, you never ski or snowboard?"

I shook my head. "Not very often. My coaches promised me that if I broke any limbs, they'd take care of the rest."

"Are you serious?" Grandpa shot me a look as we pulled into the underground parking garage beneath his building.

"I'm not, but I'm pretty sure they were." I thought about it for a moment. "When it comes down to it, I've already got one expensive, apparatus-intensive hobby. I don't particularly need another."

"Your grandmother and I can't wait for an update on your rowing," Grandpa said, parking the car. The trunk rose at a stately pace behind us. The car did everything at a stately pace, I'd noticed.

I grabbed my suitcase before Grandpa had a chance to. I'm sure he was strong and all, but I was decades younger, and my mama raised me better than that. Mom. These were her parents. I sighed. I was going to have to deal with Mom and Dad sooner or later. But not right now. I wanted, maybe even needed, a quiet holiday far away from everyone who wanted something from me.

True to Grandpa's word, Grandma indeed had a huge breakfast ready for us, and yes, that included industrial-grade coffee. Actually, she served espresso she made herself. She was a dab hand at it. If I stayed here too long, I knew I'd never be able to choke down another cup of Starbucks again.

I visited with my grandparents, nothing bigger than catching up on chitchat, like we hadn't seen each other since summer vacation instead of since I was thirteen or fourteen. Then Grandma pulled the trigger.

"So, why're you here, dear?"

I blinked, unsure what she meant. "Uh...to spend the holidays?"

"No, dear. Why are you really here and not at home? What's going on?"

Oh, that. I groaned. "It started in the middle of October," I said, explaining the Head of the Charles Massacre.

"Stop," Grandpa said, holding up a hand. "That doesn't make any sense."

Grandma frowned. "Your grandfather's right, dear. It's not even internally consistent."

"Don't blame me. I didn't make it up. The thing is, I think there's more going on, but I can't figure out what. Michael's pretty sure something's up with his parents, but they're even more opaque than mine." I sighed. I hated thinking about this, but I guess I had to.

"I hardly see how that's possible, but I've never met your young man or his people." Grandma took a sip of her espresso and frowned. She grated some chocolate over it and tried again.

"Your father's an asshole. He always has been. I can't think why our daughter's a party to this idiocy." Grandpa shook his head.

"Howard, you didn't call the boy's father an asshole."

He shrugged. "Why not? It's the truth. I can't figure out what's gotten into your brother, however, Jeremy. He's always been easily led, but this is extreme, even for him."

"Well, Jeremy always was the smart one. More espresso?" She might as well have asked Grandpa if he wanted more rocket fuel, because that's what this was. One more serving and I'd be able to see numbers and hear colors.

I didn't know how I felt about this. Sure, Dad was an asshole, dyed in the wool, and we were probably more alike than I cared to admit. But Geoff? I might not actually be speaking to him right now, but he'd been there since before we were born, you know? He needed to realize that what he had said was not only wrong but staggeringly hypocritical, but it took a lot to sever the kind of bond we had.

I looked up to find my grandparents watching me like the proverbial hawk.

And then it hit me, and I grinned. "I know what you're doing."

"And what would that be?" Grandpa asked, his eyes alight.

"You're pushing me back to my brother by making me defend him."

Grandma smiled into her tiny cup of sticky caffeine. "What makes you say that, dear?"

"And now I know where I get it from." I laughed. Seriously, all my life I'd never known exactly where I fitted into the family schema, but now I knew. My last name might've been Babcock, but I was a Fischer. Stirring the pot for the pleasure of watching it boil? Calling it like I saw it? Both sounded all too familiar. These qualities made me wonder about Mom, but I'd sink my teeth into that later.

"Get what from?" Grandpa looked at me suspiciously.

I smiled at them both. "Everything. Dad's called me a changeling on more than one occasion, but I'm not. I'm you two."

I was pretty sure I heard Grandpa mutter "jackass," but I let it slide. It wasn't like I hadn't said it myself.

Even Grandma frowned at that. "He's called you changeling, dear?"

"Oh yes, many times, that and similar terms. Admittedly not where he thought I could hear it." I shrugged. "I suppose it's a way of coming to terms with how different he and I are. It took Geoff a while to believe me, but he was there when I confronted Dad about it."

Grandpa shook his head. "Why didn't your mother put a stop to it?"

"I think she did once it was out in the open. She's always known Geoff and I had different relationships with our father. I mean, we're different people, right? But when I finally confronted Dad and he couldn't weasel out of it, she looked like she was going to bite his head off."

"Let's not worry about it now, dear. Finish your breakfast and get settled. By the looks of things, I'll need to take you shopping if you're going to survive for more than a minute outside." Grandma flicked her glance to the coatrack by the door where Grandpa had hung my apparently too-thin parka.

"You don't need to do that. I'll stay here the whole break. I need to recover, anyway." Seriously, it's not like I wore rags, but I certainly didn't live in this kind of climate.

Grandma's laughter sounded like silver bells. "And miss what Chicago has to offer? The Art Institute? The Field Museum?"

"Her chamber quartet?" Grandpa said. "Face it, she's going to take you shopping. It's easier to give in now. I speak with experience. What kind of suit did you bring?"

"Uh...none? Grandma didn't care for the one I sent her a picture of."

Then my grandmother squealed with glee. A dowager squealing. I hoped never to hear—or see—such a thing again. "I guess I'd better get ready."

*

Shopping proved to be every bit as ghastly as I thought it would be. After Grandma ransacked my suitcase to see what I brought with me—seriously, she took inventory—we set off to something called the Magnificent Mile, and zowie, they weren't kidding. The Mag Mile had everything, starting with the four malls that I counted and who knew how many freestanding stores. We started with a place to buy a warm parka along with a few sweaters thicker than the ones I used for layering. The whole thing made me dizzy. My grandparents were richer than God and moved in circles far more affluent than I ever would, because I'd never heard of some of these stores. These stores had clearly heard of my grandmother, however, because the salespeople greeted her by name.

"This is your grandson, Mrs. Fischer?" one of them, an admittedly hot guy, said as he latched on to my arm.

"That's right, he's visiting from California for the winter holidays," Grandma replied. She looked a bit put out by his sudden overfamiliarity with my person. Join the club, lady.

"So, tell me—?"

You want my name, do you? "Jeremy."

"How'd you get so big and strong, Jeremy?"

"Crew."

"Your girlfriend must love it."

"My *boyfriend* seems to appreciate it, that and the tight T-shirts." I met my grandmother's eyes and then rolled mine. She snickered. "But then, he rows too."

That sent the salesman into paroxysms of... something, which I used to extract my arm from his grip. "Charmed, I'm sure, but we'll be going." I extended my arm to my grandmother. "Shall we, Grandma?"

She took my arm, and we glided away. "You were very smooth, dear."

"I've had a certain amount of practice extracting myself from situations I didn't want to be in, but jeez, they're going to have to call for a cleanup after the way he was drooling." I made a face.

"You're a very handsome man, dear. People are going to react a certain way." She patted my arm comfortingly.

I glowered back over my shoulder. "Subtlety is everything, Grandma."

"Of course, it is, dear." She pulled out her phone and placed a call. "Hi, Sylvia. It's Evelyn Fischer... I'm fine, thanks for asking. Listen, are you busy? I'm downstairs with my grandson, and we've just had a run-in with one of your colleagues. We could use some help that doesn't involve salivating over him... Wonderful! We'll meet you by the fountain."

Grandma beamed at me. "Problem solved and without the digestive fluids!"

"Excellent!" I had to laugh. Dowager she might be, but there was nothing old about my grandmother.

In fairly short order, Grandma placed me into the capable hands of her personal shopper, an attractive woman I'd place in early middle age. Sylvia was born to wear knit dresses, and hers clung to every curve like sin.

Sylvia placed her hands on my shoulders, turning me this way and that. "Mm-hmm, yes, you'll be easy to dress. Take off your coat, hon."

I complied, and my grandmother took it from me.

"Okay, so I see strong legs despite those baggy jeans. Those have to go, by the way. They're a crime with a body like yours. Strong upper body too."

"He's gay, Sylvia." Grandma shook her head.

Sylvia gave my grandmother a withering look. "I have eyes, Mrs. Fischer, and I'm not stupid, but I can still admire the view. Now, what were you looking for today?" she asked me.

I looked at Grandma. "What're we looking for?"

Then Grandma told Sylvia what she wanted, and my eyes grew round. "Did I bring *anything* that passes muster?"

"Your underwear's fine, dear. Those Andrew Christian and aussieBum briefs don't leave much to the imagination, do they? But what, pray tell, is Nasty Pig? Do I even want to know?"

Could I possibly turn any redder? No, no I could not. Sylvia had the decency to turn away, but I could tell she was doing a herculean job of holding in an epic bout of laughter. "No, Grandma, you don't, but the rest? Michael likes them, and that's all anyone needs to know." Then I gave her a gimlet wink. "But my favorite? PUMP!, and you really don't want to know what that means."

Finally, it was my turn to make someone blush. "That's quite all right, dear. I think we can forego further discussion of things that won't see the light of day. But you should know I wasn't born old, and your generation didn't invent sex."

"Thank you." All the discussion of my undergarments almost—almost—distracted me from the subject at hand. "Do we really need all of that, Grandma?"

"Oh, this? It's not much, just a few things to keep you warm, plus a tuxedo for the parties we'll attend. Oh, and my concerts." She winked. "You'll be fine, dear."

And off she sailed, leaving Sylvia and me in her wake. "Just a few things," I whispered to Sylvia.

"Welcome to Chicago, hon," Sylvia whispered back.

Chapter Fifteen

After what felt like a marathon, we stopped for lunch. At least we weren't schlepping packages.

"They'll deliver everything to the house, dear." Grandma looked at her watch. "Probably before we return, except for your dinner suit. You looked very dashing in the claw-hammer coat, but it's completely over-the-top, and in any event, no one wears white tie anymore."

I was mortified my grandparents were hosing this much money around. It's not like I dressed in potato sacks or anything. Did potatoes still come in sacks? Try to stay on the rails here, Rem. Sure, I needed a warmer coat. I understood that. But the rest? I was so glad I'd fitted in some holiday shopping before I left town. "I feel bad that you're spending so much money on me."

"Don't give it a second thought, dear. This is how my friends and I compete, did you know that? For years they've been flaunting their grandchildren in front of me." She looked at me coyly over the rim of her coffee cup. "Can you imagine their dismay when Howard and I walk in with you in tow, and in that daringly cut dinner suit? My triumph will be long in coming, but all the sweeter for it."

Yeah, okay that was weird. "And my tux at home was...?"

"Boring. No offense, dear. I appreciate you sending me a picture and all, but it simply wouldn't do. Besides, think of how much fun you'll have with it later." Grandma thought for a moment. "Your stud set will work, of course, and your black wingtips will pair nicely with the sportier cut of what we bought today. Admit it, what we picked out for you today is so much nicer."

Grandma had a point. What I wore to that ill-starred prom was the basic model: black and white. Grandma bought me a much more modern suit in a midnight blue that almost had a bit of sheen to it. Think about the metallic blue in a magpie's feathers and then darken it to midnight. Give it an athletic cut—wide through the shoulders and tapered down to a narrow waist in the jacket; narrow waist in the pants, room in the thighs but otherwise hugging my legs—and that was what Grandma intended to package me in when she showed me off to her friends. I could wear it with the standard bow tie and tab collar, or with a regular shirt and tie, and knock 'em dead. Either way, I shivered anticipating Michael's reaction.

"So, when will you debut me?"

Grandma chuckled. "Tonight, dear. It's a small party, no more than a hundred people or so, a thank-you for a charity your grandfather serves on the board for. I think you'll be fine in a suit and tie."

"Oh, it's not a competition party?" You mean one of the ties I'm afraid to breathe on, let alone eat in the vicinity of? Those ties? I was quickly coming to realize my grandmother—and probably my grandfather—was a force of nature when armed with a credit card that probably lacked any kind of limit.

Grandma clapped her hands and laughed with delight. "See? You're getting it already!"

"I'm gay, Grandma," I said dryly. "This kind of thing's practically second nature, along with dressing to depress, the well-timed remark, and communicating with an arched brow. When the time comes, all you'll need to do is point out who you need impressed or cut down to size, and I'll take it from there."

"Well, then." Grandma looked like a cat who'd gotten into the cream. "We're going to have some fun before you have to go back to school. But the first competition party will be tomorrow night, and you'll be put through your paces, I assure you. We all will."

I smiled at her enthusiasm. Looked like I'd be resting up this afternoon and as much of tomorrow as I could, at least after I sneaked a workout in, plus whatever my grandparents had planned.

Grandma stood up. "Ready for round two? You're getting a precision haircut!"

I fired off a quick text to Michael.

ME: *My grandmother is crazy, fun but crazy xoxo*

*

The last twenty-four hours had been madcap, but suave in their way. I didn't know how else to define them. Grandma had been right. The previous night's party—reception?—hadn't been worth the effort of getting dressed up. We put in an appearance so people could fawn over Grandpa and put on the hard sell for more of his money. He'd deflect by introducing me, and then the three of us would move on, only to repeat the process again and again. I saw other people my age, sometimes with parents, sometimes with grandparents. We'd catch each other's eyes, smile ironically, and then be whisked out of range by our elders. What could we do? We were there for purposes of distraction, and we knew it. That's not to say someone else's son and I weren't playing at eye contact, however. We both knew nothing would come of it. Besides, I was spoken for and happily so.

After we'd been there an hour and half, Grandpa looked at his watch. "I'm so sorry we can't stay longer, but Jeremy only arrived this morning, and as you can see, he's all but asleep on his feet."

"I'm sorry, please excuse me—" I yawned for all I was worth. Some of it was even faked.

Grandma tut-tutted. "Oh, Jeremy, why didn't you say anything?"

I looked sheepish. "I didn't want to impose."

"I'm sure you understand," Grandpa said to whomever he was speaking with. I didn't care if Grandpa offended anyone, but I was well past the point of boredom.

That other guy shot me daggers as I caught his eye on the way out. I smirked and blew him a kiss. Suffer, buddy, suffer hard.

I waited until we were in the elevator before I said anything. "How was that?"

"Perfect, dear. Absolutely perfect."

But tonight's entertainment? It more than made up for last night's tedium. It started midafternoon when Grandpa brought us home from the Field Museum before 4:00 p.m.

"Your grandmother needs time to apply the war paint, Jeremy," he told me. Was it wrong to think it was one more reason I was glad to be male and gay?

"Howard, you did not say that." If looks could kill...

"I think he did, Grandma." I was starting to get the hang of life in these parts.

She rewarded me with a stern glare. "I see. Your time will come, young man. Time is a cruel master."

"Grandpa seems to be doing all right."

She threw up her hands. Good thing Grandpa was driving.

After we returned to the condo, I fitted in a workout in the health club located elsewhere in the building. Grandpa called down to make sure a pass waited for me at the desk. Despite the ergs in the cardio room, I chose to run on a treadmill. I erged enough, and it looked like I'd be doing a whole lot more of it in the next six months. Yeah, I hemmed and hawed, but I knew what my choice would be. Like there could be any other decision? Sure, I'd have to run it by my physicians, and that niggling question of money hadn't gone away, but in for a penny, in for a pound.

Cardio and weights. Might as well get used to them.

The gym's membership wasn't restricted to the residents of the condos on the floors above, and accordingly it drew its clientele from the surrounding upscale urban neighborhoods and offices. I ignored the people around me for a while, at least until I felt one too many pairs of eyes on me. At first, I chalked it up to being the new guy in the room. People have their routines, after all, and get used to seeing the same people at the same time. Made perfect sense.

Didn't it?

So why did people keep looking at me? It creeped me out.

I wished Michael were here. He'd know whether there was more to it or not, because as he and a number of other people never ceased to remind me, I never noticed things that I couldn't row. Seriously, I went to the gym to make boats move faster. That it made changes to my body was nothing more than a side effect that Michael appreciated and that made my T-shirts tighter. He liked my T-shirts tight.

It came to a head while I used the bench press. Okay, the bench press can be tricksy. You're lying on a bench with a bar perpendicular to your sternum, and your chest isn't flat. It actually curves down toward your throat.

If you drop that bar, it will roll down onto your throat and crush it. I mean, the bar alone weighed forty-five pounds, and if you're a power lifter you'd better have a spotter, someone to catch that bar before your arms gave out. The thing is, I wasn't a power lifter. Rowing requires lean muscle mass and endurance, not brute strength. Sure, at the level I hoped to achieve, some guys were big, but that was a fringe benefit. First and foremost, they possessed endurance. We all did.

I once saw something on one of those online sports forums, asking about what sport required the most cardiovascular fitness. It's not marathons, it's not long-distance cycling or swimming, it's crew. Don't get me wrong. All those athletes require exceedingly high levels of aerobic conditioning. But not only do world-class rowers possess the highest VO2 max of any athlete—the fact that I stood a decent chance of joining this elite in the next few years frankly scared the tar out of me—the sport was almost entirely mental. Yep, never mind the fact that Olympic-caliber rowers could extract the most oxygen per tortured gasp, they needed the titanic discipline not to psych themselves out.

Every race started with a sprint, which meant we started in an anaerobic hole—we started each race in the intense pain of a lactic acid burn. The precious mitochondria in every muscle cell—the energy plants that depended on oxygen—couldn't produce the fuel our cells needed, so they switched to plan B, feeding on glycogen and other compounds stored in muscle cells. The problem was, glycogen was a poor substitute for adenosine triphosphate—the usual source of energy for the body—and produced lactic acid, and that shit burned. Muscles that weren't working as hard—like our guts—shut down, while our legs and lats kept working beyond their capacities, and still the lactate levels climbed. As all that lactate-bearing blood flooded the only muscles working, as the other muscles shut down, blood shunted away from our brains, so thought became confused and our worlds tunneled. We didn't need to think. We endured, focusing on our cox'n's voice, and we pulled as we'd been trained to do.

Rowers had the highest levels of lactic acid tolerance of any high-performance athlete, and how did we push past that? Endurance training. Every practice, every erg piece, every session in the weight room built that endurance further. When people argued with me about whether crew was an endurance sport or not, my first impulse was violence.

Marathoners talked about hitting a wall toward the end of a race. Motherfuckers, we started there, thanks to those sprints at the beginning. Only it wasn't a wall, it was a deep well of agony, and we pulled ourselves through with mental toughness and the terrible fear of being the only one in the boat not pulling hard enough.

In the weight room that afternoon, I lifted a relatively light weight that I knew I could lift over and over again. That's how I built endurance, or one of the ways. So, when someone stood over me, his basket so close I could smell his sweat and musk?

So not suave.

"You shouldn't lift without a spotter." He looked down into my eyes.

I exhaled as I pushed the weight up and into his belly and then pulled one earbud out. "I'll be fine."

He grunted. "No, seriously…"

"No, seriously," I said right back, "it's a light weight, and you're in my way."

"C'mon, let me help you."

Then the pieces clicked into place. I knew he wasn't there to keep me from crushing my trachea. I sighed and racked the weight. He moved out of the way so I could sit up.

"I told you, I don't need any help. As you can no doubt see, it's a fairly light weight."

Overly Helpful quirked a smile. "Can I sit down?"

"No, it's a weight bench, not a park bench."

"Whoa, someone's cranky." Oddly enough, that seemed to spark something in his eyes.

"Someone's workout's been interrupted. Was there something you wanted?" I made to replace the earbud.

Overly Helpful smiled. He looked attractive in a mussed, sweaty, in-the-middle-of-a-workout way. "Yeah, I wanted to talk to you. I've been watching you since you walked in. You're a good-looking guy, and I've never seen you here before."

"Thanks." Okay, I didn't *always* need to be a dick about things like this. It always turned out that way, however, so I smiled. "I'm only here on winter break visiting my grandparents. I'm also taken. Thanks for the compliment though."

"That's the story of my life." He didn't look too crushed. "I was serious about the spotter, however. You really do need to be careful."

I shook my head at his persistence, but only in a good-natured manner. "You don't give up, do you?"

"Nope." He grinned. "My name's Rick."

"Remy. Fine, I'll finish my workout with you. I'll even meet you for workouts the rest of my time in Chicago if you want, but if you get handsy, be warned—I *will* drop the bar on you."

Rick gulped. "Yes, sir."

"No, Sir would be my boyfriend." I smirked at him.

Rick's eyes grew round. "Are you sure I can't tempt you?"

"I'm feeling kind of clumsy today, Rick."

He sighed. "I wish I could find someone like you."

"I'm high-maintenance and so focused on rowing I'm blind to anything that doesn't float. So long as I have access to a boat and water, I'm reasonably easy to get along with...until you piss me off. Then I stay angry, and my temper burns incandescent." I shrugged. "Honestly? You can do a lot better."

Rick sighed again, only it sounded kind of bitter this time. "You're not helping. How old are you, anyway?"

"Too young for you." Seriously, did he find these lines on bathroom walls in bars?

"You'd grow out of it," he said hopefully.

I shook my head, because really, enough was enough. "Weights?"

"So where do you row?" Rick asked as we got to work. I pointed to my shirt. "Do you like it there?"

I nodded as I finished my set. "Surprisingly. I'd only intended to be there for my freshman year before transferring, but it's working out really well."

"That's great." Rick switched places with me. "Wait...you're a freshman?"

I nodded. "I am."

"I can't believe I hit on a college freshman." Rick shook his head. "I need a shower with a loofah."

"I'll need industrial-strength soap."

He grinned. "Want someone to wash your back?"

"Get to work. I have someplace to be this evening." I started adding weight plates on the end of the bar in the hope that he'd get the hint.

Rick added plates to bring the weight up to his level. "You're relentless, aren't you?"

"Is there some other way to go through life?"

We made it through the workout, but at a considerable test to my patience, and I resolved to be at the gym when it opened from then on. Back up at the condo, I rinsed off and took a nap. After my nap I took a real shower, one that involved shaving so I'd look my best for my grandparents.

"Tonight's party won't include a formal dinner, Jeremy," Grandpa explained over dinner. "It'll be the typical buffet and booze rodeo affair, but nothing you'd call nourishing. We don't mind if you have a glass of champagne, but in general we expect you not to drink, as you're underage."

"Of course, I understand." I laughed. "Geoff and I have had fake IDs for years, and we haven't used them for alcohol yet, so you've nothing to worry about."

Grandpa looked nonplussed, but I hid my smile. "Some things never change," he said at last.

"Technology's made it a lot easier, however." They both looked at me. "What? It has."

"I'm sure, dear. I'm sure. We know you'll be on your best behavior."

"I haven't let you down yet." They didn't point out I'd only been here a few days. I appreciated that. In return I didn't roll my eyes at them. "Don't worry, alcohol isn't on my training plan."

They glanced at each other, but it was Grandpa who spoke. "We still hope you'll tell us all about that."

"And I want to. There's a great deal to tell." I smiled.

Suddenly Grandma looked like a predator. "Oh? Anything we can use for bragging rights, dear?"

"Actually, yes. I went to the Youth Nationals twice in high school."

She looked a bit let down. "Yes, dear. Your mother told us that. We're going to need more than that."

I stared at them levelly. Suddenly this social competition with me as a proxy struck me as bizarre on some level. Sure, I could play the game, but now I didn't want to. "I'm at CalPac on a full-ride crew scholarship, and I started school as a freshman walk-on to the JV crew, which is almost unheard of, then—"

"Yes!" Grandpa said. "That'll shut up that tiresome Henry Siciliano and his grandnephew who's on the football development team at Penn."

What, no fist pump? "I'm not done. I was bumped up to varsity in the middle of finals."

Grandpa's grin became beatific. "Excellent."

He sounded like Mr. Burns from *The Simpsons*. Creepy.

"I haven't officially decided if I'm going to do this, but I've been scouted by USRowing, and my coaches want me to train and compete for a spot on the Under 23 team, with the goal of rowing at the World Championships next summer. I have to give my coaches an answer right after break."

I watched my grandparents' eyes grow wide as I spoke.

"Oh, and I have a four-pointer. Can you work with any of that?"

This unseemly gloating? It couldn't be healthy.

I excused myself to put on my tuxedo. No way was I risking it by eating in it. Was this all I represented to my grandparents? A means of jockeying for position? They'd seemed so warm and welcoming. I'd come up with something positive to say about Geoff on the ride to the party, even if I had to lie, because I had no clue what his grades were or what else he'd been up to at UC San Diego. But they should be proud of both of their grandsons, not only the rowing impresario. I'd come looking for love and welcome, but I'd found money. Being an adult, I was coming to learn, was a very complicated thing.

Pictures were taken. I texted one to Michael, along with a brief commentary on the evening thus far. No reply. That worried me. He never failed to reply, and it made me wonder if I'd offended him in some way. So, I was walking into a society party—basically a shark tank—offended and worried. What could possibly go wrong?

Chapter Sixteen

On the ride over, my grandparents provided me a rundown of who we'd meet that night. They'd hired a car service to take us, partly for purposes of display and partly so they could freely imbibe. It sounded like one of those "events of the season" parties. All I knew was that we were all swathed to our chins in topcoats or wraps we planned to wear only for the length of the drives to and from. I shrugged inside the armor of wool. Rich people. What could I do?

At least we wouldn't be announced. I hoped.

"Mr. and Mrs. Snobby Asshole, and their pawn, Hapless Dupe." Yeah, I could see it now. Not suave at all.

We drove for a while, making only chitchat that meant nothing. Good practice for the evening to come, I supposed. Never had I wished more that my HIV meds contained a sedative.

The car had long since left the Gold Coast when it pulled off the highway, and before long we drove through a neighborhood—if that term applied to a place where mansions sat in splendid isolation, separated from their putative neighbors by acres and ivy-covered walls—where people's cooks drove ten minutes to get to next door to borrow the proverbial cup of sugar. At least the light displays looked tastefully understated. I made a mental note to compliment our hosts' gardeners when we arrived.

My grandparents' hired car waited in the queue to drop us off, but not for long. Apparently this class of people—or their drivers and valets—knew how to make short work of a traffic jam. I wondered what drivers did while they waited. Oh well, soon someone opened our car door, and we made our entrance. Once inside a butler quickly divested us of our outerwear, and that was that. I felt like I was about to be thrown to the wolves.

And the first wolf spotted us in record time.

"Evelyn! Howard!" squealed a woman in an unspeakable fuchsia dress. It left me speechless. Thank whatever dark power was responsible for its creation that she knew my grandparents, because I had no idea what to say. "I'm so glad you made it!"

"Pandora!" My grandmother opened her arms to greet her. "We wouldn't have missed it for the world."

The two women stopped short of touching and kissed the air roughly an inch above each other's cheeks. Maybe their makeup would've triggered a cross-reaction?

After Grandpa had greeted Pandora, he turned to me. "This is our grandson, Jeremy Babcock. He's visiting from California during his winter break from college."

Pandora shook my hand. "How do you do, Jeremy? You must be Dina's son!"

"One of them, yes, but please, call me Remy. My brother Geoffrey sends his regrets. He was detained at school over the break, a project he didn't quite finish in time." Okay, maybe not the best line to come up with off the top of my head, but I was determined my brother wouldn't be totally erased. I might've been mad—furious, even—at him, but we were still brothers.

Pandora tittered. "You never told me that Dina's boys had grown up into such handsome young men," she said to my grandmother.

"We hardly knew ourselves." That would've been my grandfather.

Pandora waved it away. "Come in, all of you." Still attached to my arm, she leaned in and said, "There are any number of people your age here, but I dare say you're one of the comeliest."

I looked good, and I knew it, maybe better than I'd ever looked before, but what was the point? Michael couldn't share it with me, and Geoff wasn't here to grumble with. I groaned inside. I so needed to resolve that issue. But I was the total package from my shoes to my glasses and hair. I didn't say that often. Actually, I'm not sure I'd ever said that. So why couldn't I sit back and rock it? Because I'm me, that's why. Instead, my grandparents' weird interest in anything and everything they could and would use to advance their social position ate at me, along with Michael's radio silence.

For some reason all I could think of were the lyrics to ABC's "Vanity Kills." That song told the story of a beautiful person entranced by her own reflection, a modern Narcissus, but Codeine Velvet Club's song of the same name? That one was a cautionary tale. Screw it. I was hot.

I tagged along with my grandparents for an unpleasant hour or so before they released me into the wild, which in a way was worse. As the three of us had circulated about the rooms of the enormous house, I'd felt the eyes of my peers on me and caught the calculating gazes out of the corner of my eyes.

I hated being alone at parties. What had Geoff called me once? The Ice Princess? That's what happened when I was alone in unfamiliar situations. I turned aloof and isolated myself. Oh hey, icy hauteur for the win! I was already halfway there, feeling like I was nothing but a game piece for my grandparents' social advancement.

So, I pulled out my phone and texted Michael.

ME: *I'm alone @ a party full of strangers. U know how I get. Save me from myself.*

As I had come to expect, he didn't reply. I sighed. Since I lacked the balls to read on my phone in a room full of people, I put it away. I knew no one, and while my grandparents' social climbing on the back of my rowing achievements weirded me out, I nonetheless was reluctant to embarrass them. They'd been so kind to me, after all...

Then I looked up. Someone met my eyes from across the room. My playmate from the other night. Had it really only been last night? Was this the rich peoples' party circuit or something?

So yeah, he was there, along with a cadre of the young and beautiful from what I presumed was Chicago society, or at least gathered from around the country by Chicago high society. I couldn't figure out my problem. It wasn't as if I'd see these people again once I flew home. Actually, that wasn't entirely true. I knew exactly what my issue was—incurable introversion. That, and the fact that I'd grown accustomed to hiding behind Michael.

But these guys? What were they going to do? Run to their parents and grandparents and whine, "Some guy in a dinner jacket snubbed me?"

No wonder I was in therapy. I still wasn't housebroken if I couldn't be taken to a party and behave for several hours.

Then I looked up from where I was trying to hide behind a light-festooned ficus tree. My playmate from last night approached. Not only that, he looked determined. So much for hiding deeper into the potted ficus.

"Hi," he said.

"Hello."

"So, who are you, mysterious cover boy?"

"What?" I laughed. I couldn't help it. It was such an absurd conceit.

"I am quite sure that I've seen you on the cover of *Paris Vogue* or maybe even *DNA*."

I gave him an *are you fucking kidding me?* look over my glasses. "As far as pickup lines go, that has to be one of the cheesiest I've ever heard. You write it yourself?"

"I was going to say *Architectural Digest*, because you're that well built, but I didn't think you'd fall for it." He grinned. "Are any of them working?"

That forced a laugh out of me. "Oh my God... You did not say that."

"I'm Lance. I saw you last night."

"I saw you seeing me last night. I'm Remy."

"As in Martin?"

"As in Jeremy."

"So, who do you keep texting?"

I froze as I reached for my phone. "I've only texted someone once since I've been here."

"I'm including last night."

"My boyfriend."

"That figures." His words sounded grumbly, but he really didn't look that put out. Alas, my reply only seemed to pique his interest further. "So where is he tonight?"

"Home, unfortunately." I didn't feel like talking about this, and Lance's Torquemada act only made me want to brick his mouth up with my fist.

Lance looked up at me. "You're a talkative one."

"For fuck's sake, what do you want from me? I've been dragged to a party full of people I don't know by my social-climbing grandparents who've packaged me for display and whose sole interest in me appears to be in using me for advancement. This whole thing is so far from suave that the light from suave will never reach it.

Meanwhile, my boyfriend won't reply to my texts or phone calls."

Lance only smiled more broadly as I lashed out.

"And you just sit there and grin like an idiot. What is your problem?"

"Because this is the most emotion you've shown since I first set eyes on you. I was beginning to think you were carved from marble. But, dude, what do you think I'm doing here? What do you think all of us are doing here?" He indicated a knot of other people our age. "My parents trot me out like a well-trained dog any chance they get. It's the same for all of us, which is why I came over here to get you. That's why I try to hide at school as much as I can."

"At least now I know the score."

Lance laughed. "You just figured it out?"

"Makes me sound kind of thick, doesn't it?" I grinned sheepishly.

"Kind of, yes. At least you look good in your tux."

I scratched behind my neck, a new nervous gesture. "It's hard not to look good in a monkey suit."

"Sure, sweetheart. Easy for you to say."

Lance turned out to be a funny, even sidesplitting, guide to the evening. A steady stream of trenchant commentary issued from his mouth as he cut this segment of society down to size. He left no one unskewered, not even my grandparents.

"That's kind of what I thought. They pumped me for information on the way over here, you know. If it had gone on any longer, I fully expected to start spitting out water."

Lance snorted. "That's hilarious."

"And yet kind of sad," I said.

"Now come meet the others. They'll wonder why I haven't brought you back." Lance pulled on my arm until I stopped digging in my heels.

He introduced me to...well, if they weren't his friends, at least they were people with whom he was acquainted from parties such as this one. I recognized some faces, but not too terribly many.

"Everyone, this is Remy. Remy, this is...everyone." Lance gestured expansively. A few people waved, more nodded, hardly the most rousing of welcomes, but then, we all knew the score. We were temporary ports in the social storm. Lance seemed genuine enough, but none of us would see one another after the holidays, and we all knew it.

Small talk ensued, and I actually had that glass of champagne my grandparents allowed. Much of the talk turned on comparing abbreviated biographies and humorous stories from school. Brady proved to be a rich source, and I showed no hesitation in mocking him. Well, him and that absurd prom.

"So, wait," someone said, "your boyfriend stood there and watched them?"

I nodded. "It annoyed me at the time, but now it's kind of funny."

"Sounds hot to me," Lance added.

"That was Michael's response. Later." I smiled a Mona Lisa smile.

"Yeah? So'd you get lucky?" Lance said.

I looked at him over the top of my glasses. "A gentleman doesn't tell tales out of school."

That certainly got a rise out of people. A few people looked bothered by the fact that I was gay, but I could not possibly have cared less. But... Michael. I sighed, and the conversation swirled elsewhere. I checked my phone without bothering to be subtle.

Lance looked over my shoulder. "No reply?"

"No, not that I expected any." I sighed.

"Trouble in paradise?" He looked genuinely concerned and not like a circling vulture.

I shrugged. "Our parents seem to be having issues, but we're fine. I'm not sure what's up with not returning texts. For all I know, he dropped his phone."

"Okay, I'm going to ask the obvious question, but why not call his landline? You'd have the answer to the dropped phone hypothesis and get over all this tiresome mooning around," Lance said. "For a guy who seems pretty sharp, I'm surprised you haven't thought of this."

"Because his parents don't like me?" I hated saying that out loud.

"So, is that a question or a statement?" someone else said. "Because if you're suddenly on the market, I'm in line."

Lance feigned outrage. "Dibs! I found him first."

"Yeah, hi. Right here. I can hear you talking."

"Good. It means we won't have to track you down. I'm Caden, by the way." Mr. In Line extended his hand.

I shook it. "Remy."

"I was kidding, you know. But...are you?" Caden grinned.

"No," I said, my voice as final as the guillotine's blade. Seriously, what was with these people? I'd been in bars less cruisy. "Do you people not get sex at school?"

The thundering chorus of "No!" almost deafened me.

"Then you're doing something wrong." I shook my head.

"Fuck you," Caden said cheerfully. "My girlfriend won't give it up like she should."

I stared at him.

"What? Don't be biphobic. I'm an equal-opportunity slut."

Caden was so honest about it I could only laugh. I felt bad for his girlfriend though.

"You're a bad man, Caden" was all Lance said.

"Yeah, but you love me anyway." Caden batted his eyelashes.

Lance grimaced. "Love is a strong word."

I gratefully let the conversation fall away from me, content to retreat into my own thoughts. I'd finally realized the source of the melancholy I'd felt all night. I'd only been separated from Michael for a couple of days, but I hadn't heard from him, and that was unusual. No returned texts, no calls, not even an e-mail or chat, and I missed him terribly. And *poof!* What remained of the magic disappeared from the evening. The sparkle turned back into tinsel, which was frankly on the tacky side if you looked at it too long, and the fairy lights were nothing but Christmas lights available three packs for ten dollars at any garden center. I was done with the evening. I had only to fake it until my grandparents were ready to be poured into the hired car.

As it turned out, Lance and Caden soon noticed my mental departure.

"I've got...uh, a little something to make the night pass better." Caden opened his coat to show a couple of joints in a sandwich baggie.

"That's not really part of my training plan."

Caden looked me up and down. "Triathlons?"

"Crew." I blushed hard. Really, any other tell, please.

Lance snorted. "Dude, at my school half the rowing team blazes up any chance they get. The other half drinks like fish."

"They don't row on my level." I refused to get into this.

"Whoa oh oh! Listen to you," Caden said.

I shrugged. "They don't. It's a statement of fact. I made varsity as a freshman. I have to decide when I get back to school whether or not to train for a spot on the Under 23 National Team in order to compete at the Worlds next summer. So...not a part of my training plan." I smiled to take a bit of the sting out of it. "There's not a whole lot that is."

"I can see that." Then Lance thought for a moment. "What's your boyfriend get out of this?"

I smirked. If they were going to rag me for not using, I might as well rub in the fact they weren't getting anywhere near me undressed. "My body."

"Yeah," Caden said, "but aren't you too tired to do anything with it?"

"That'd be for us to know and you not to find out, right?" I winked.

His smile fell. "I don't even get to watch, do I?"

I cocked one eyebrow at him as I revealed my collar. "Sir doesn't share."

Both Caden's and Lance's jaws dropped. I already loved doing that to people.

"You mean you—"

"A gentleman doesn't tell tales out of school, remember?" That Mona Lisa smile again.

"That is so unfair," Lance said.

I winced. "The pouting. It's not attractive."

"He's right about that," Caden said. "It'll give you wrinkles."

Lance pulled out his phone. "You two. Such bitches. Give me your digits. I want to keep in touch."

I laughed and complied. So did Caden.

"Since this is as close to a three-way we'll ever get with the Boy Scout here," Caden said.

Thanks to those guys, I ended up having a good time, or at least a better time than I thought I would after my grandparents demanded information about me. But I still missed Michael, and not hearing anything from him still bothered me. I made sure I didn't pine visibly after that.

Chapter Seventeen

The next day started the next afternoon. Mine started late morning with a workout in the building's gym, blessedly free of the Spotter. I might possibly have teased Caden and Lance with a workout selfie. All in all, I found the day quiet and peaceful. My grandparents didn't surface until close to dinner, which I took charge of. The only texts to violate my phone, however, were the outraged ones I received from Caden and Lance after dinner. Those consisted of one word each: "bastard" and "asshole."

I hated to think I'd grown accustomed to Michael's silence, so I distracted myself by writing a postcard. I didn't entrust too much to what was basically a public advertisement that I possessed the leisure and money to travel. I put a bit more thought into it than "The weather's frigid, wish you were here" but not much more.

Lance, Caden, and I traded party schedules after dinner and usually managed to find each other at subsequent affairs. They helped to pass the time until Christmas. We even met for lunch and shopping a couple of times. It gave me a chance to find presents for my grandparents.

"No word yet?" Caden said over lunch.

I shook my head. "I keep texting and e-mailing like normal, but it's scaring me."

"Dude." Lance sighed. "You've got to grow a pair and call him on a landline. So what if it's old school or you end up talking to his big bad parents?"

"Lance is right. If he's the stand-up guy you say he is, something's wrong. There's no way he'd dump you with a fade-out. That's what I'd do, and I'm a douche," Caden said. "Your Sir wouldn't do that. Damn. Do you really call him that?"

My eyes twinkled. "I don't know. Do I?"

They both looked hungry for a moment before they covered it up. Were we *all* subby bottoms who wanted it to hurt? I laughed. "No, but think how much fun you've had with that."

Lance threw his crumpled-up napkin at me. "Rude."

But Caden stared at me. "There's something he's not telling us, Lance."

"Maybe." I smiled demurely.

"Don't make me tickle you," Caden said.

I rolled my eyes. "I can outrun you both."

"You can't outrun your feelings, and right now you're feeling pretty low where your guy's concerned." Lance's arrow hit me right where it hurt too.

"I'll call, I promise. Now can we please get this conversation off of my failings and onto some of yours?" I glared at Caden. "So. You're a two-timing douche, you say?"

Lance laughed. "Yeah, tell us about that. Why do I get the sense you're in a frat too?"

"They kicked me out after I boned the president's girlfriend." Caden paused to make sure he had our attention. "And his little brother."

"I suddenly have the idea you don't mean in the frat buddy-system sense either." Lance met my eyes and shook his head. I couldn't tell if he found it hilarious or if it made him jealous. Interesting.

*

Christmas Day passed quietly. I'd assumed all that shopping would be my gift, but I had assumed wrong.

What had Grandma done, nipped off to the Apple Store while Sylvia had me trapped with the tailor altering my tux? "Here's my credit card. I'll take one of everything for my grandson." Because that's what it looked like. New laptops (regular and Air), new iPhone, a couple of new iPads? Check.

I'd already learned the futility of arguing with my grandparents, so there was no point in that, but there was no way I could accept all of this. Maybe Michael or Geoff needed something? I was worried about Michael and pissed at my brother, but I knew neither state would last forever.

Fortunately, I'd managed to slip a few things for my grandparents into my suitcase before I'd left Sacramento, and again after various shopping expeditions in Chicago. At least when I wasn't limited by my own lack of money, I liked to buy art or small antiques for gifts. They were difficult to return. Thanks, Mom and Dad! You're the ones who taught me that trick. I'm not speaking to you, but Grandma and Grandpa loved that Hiroshige print I found on the Miracle Mile and that lithograph I brought with me from Sacramento. The best part was, no one in their circle had anything like it, and I think that's what mattered at that point in their lives. They could buy anything they wanted, but one-upping their friends? That was the key.

Likewise, that small mirror from the antique store? Couldn't forget that. It didn't cost a whole lot, relatively speaking, but it predated the transcontinental railroad, according to the antiques dealer I bought it off before I left school. That meant it reached California the hard way, by sailing around the horn to get to San Francisco. There was even faint writing in different hands stating the names of different owners and dates, so I believed her. I added my own name and the date before I passed it on to my grandparents.

Once I figured that out, I felt better about the parties and being squeezed for information. Material things meant little since Grandma and Grandpa bought whatever they needed, but conversation pieces and petty triumphs over their friends? Worth more than gold and gems. Apparently, that counted as currency in their circles.

As I put the finishing touches on brunch, Grandma said, "So tell us about this boyfriend of yours, dear."

Were they genuinely interested, or was this one more piece in what for all I knew was an endless game between them and their friends? That I understood their game didn't necessarily mean I was ready to convert all my life to game chips.

"He's a prince, but his parents are another matter."

"They're not homophobic, are they?" Grandpa glared at me, but I knew it was directed at the Castelreighs.

I thought about that for a moment. The fact that they didn't like a particular gay man didn't necessarily make them homophobic per se. "I'm not sure, to be honest. They used to be much more supportive of our relationship, and I don't know what's changed."

Grandpa frowned. "What about your condition? Are they upset by it? Is he upset by it?"

"I really don't know what to say about Michael's parents." I opened my shirt collar and showed them the leathern collar Michael gave me. "Do you know what this plus sign means?"

"We do, dear. Your mother told us about your... troubles."

That wasn't what I'd expected to hear, and for a bunch of reasons. I'd never had the least idea Mom kept in touch with her parents, for one thing. "Does...does it bother you?"

"It certainly wouldn't have been our first choice for you, *Liebling*." Grandpa sighed. "But listen, we're modern. We get it. It's a condition, not the wrath of God. You look healthy. You'd have to be to do what you do in those boats."

"True fact. I admit, it's a balancing act, and one of the things that worries me about training on the level I'll need to for the national team is whether I can maintain the balance. It's something I'll need to talk to my doctor about before I commit." I thought for a moment. "From what I've read online, there's been at least one Olympic gold medal winner who's been poz, so it should be possible to train at the levels needed without compromising my health, and crew's a noncontact sport, so I don't have to worry about putting my fellow athletes in danger."

I practically saw Grandma relax before my eyes. "That's been our biggest worry, dear. That you'd overexert yourself and get sick again. The fact that you're aware of the possibility is very reassuring."

"I have to be, don't I?"

"Actually, you don't." Grandpa gave me a very direct look. "There seem to be a great many people who move through this world heedless of their own safety and that of others, and I'm not talking about the apparently large numbers of men your age who don't know their own HIV status, or at least not solely."

I thought about that for a while. "The summer before my senior year was a rough one. I grew up very quickly."

"We can tell, dear. More espresso?"

I laughed at that. Espresso appeared to be Grandma's solution to everything, and I had grown addicted in the short time I'd stayed with them. "Yes, but please teach me how to make it. I'll be sunk when I return home if I don't learn. I can already tell I'll need to buy my own machine and grinder."

"Good luck," Grandpa said. "I've been trying for years, but no one makes it like your grandmother."

"I'll settle for even minimal competency," I said as I followed Grandma to the kitchen, our conversation about Michael set aside for the time being. Set aside, but not forgotten.

*

As I checked my e-mail later that evening, the Skype icon started jumping up and down on the dock. I clicked it, and up popped Michael.

"Oh, thank God." I practically sobbed. "You have no idea how glad I am to see you. Where've you been?"

"Where have I—?" Michael all but yelled back.

That wasn't how this was supposed to go. "What? I told you where I was going."

He looked terrible. "I know, but then I didn't hear anything..."

"My phone works, and I've texted you nonstop since I got here. Texted and e-mailed. I've even sent you a postcard." This couldn't be good. I was suddenly terrified because Michael looked scared.

"My parents took my phone away." He chewed on a fingernail.

"What? What's been going on? How are you contacting me now?"

Michael hesitated. "It's been horrible around here. Your parents seem to think I know where you are—"

"You do. If they paid attention to their credit card statements, they would, too, Mom especially. They're her parents, after all." And he hadn't answered my question...

"But, Rem, they blame me for some reason, and Geoff's frantic with worry."

Welcome to the parental blame club. Sucks, doesn't it? Jeez, I couldn't let myself head down that road. "That's crazy, Michael, bone-deep crazy, and why did your parents take your phone away?"

He closed his eyes, sighing. "They found out that we went to the prom together, and since they know you couldn't have bought the tickets, I'm on restriction. So, they took away my phone. My computer too. They'll have to give that back once school starts, but not until then. I'm actually using their computer right now."

I wasn't sure how to respond, in part because I'd thought that crashing the prom was a bad idea, but I couldn't exactly say that. My guy was suffering and crowing "I told you so" wasn't my style.

Okay, it totally was, but not to Michael and not over something this serious. Definitely not when he appeared so beat-up by it.

Michael looked like he wanted to say something else but couldn't. Like he was afraid to tell me. He closed his eyes for a moment. "They found my Truvada."

Oh. Shit.

I hardly knew what to feel. Anger? Defeat? Hopelessness? Extreme hatred?

"Are they trying to break us up?" I'm not sure I wanted the answer, but I had to know.

"The only reason I'm able to contact you now is because there was some kind of accident at one of the dry-cleaning plants. Not one of the stores, but the plants. Is it horrible I'm happy about environmental degradation?" He wiped away a tear, and I'd never felt so helpless.

I touched the screen. What else could I do?

My guy needed ideas right now, so I thought hard and fast. "Okay, so here's what we'll do. First, Truvada works best when you take it every day, but I'm not there, so it's not the end of the world. It's not like we bareback anyway. When we hang up, see if you can find it and then contact Geoff. Explain what's going on and see if he'll hold it for you until I get back. If all else fails, we'll call Dr. Kravitz and get more when I return—"

"Rem! They flushed it."

I swore. "Assholes. As far as Geoff goes, he knows my phone number—"

"Rem, has it never occurred to you that people are afraid of you? That *Geoff's* afraid of you? Afraid of losing you?"

"Then maybe he should've kept his pie hole shut in the first place. He was dead wrong, and until he's man enough to admit it, I have nothing to say to him. I'm not too dependent on you, and that's a fact." Damn. This whole thing pissed me off all over again. "When it comes down to it, everyone knows how to reach me, be it on the phone or via e-mail."

"Even me?" he said in a small, quiet voice.

Was he crying? Fucking hell, he was. I promised to feed the rest of the Babcocks to the bottom-feeders at the port for this.

"Michael, I'm so sorry your parents are insane. I can't believe they were in denial about us having an adult relationship and taking all appropriate steps to protect your health. Regardless of what lies they may have told you, that's a sign of maturity on both our parts. Obviously, I had no idea they'd taken your phone and your computer." I hated to see him cry. Had I ever seen him cry? Damn. I was two thousand miles away, and there was nothing I could do about it but shake in impotent fury. "I'll be home soon. Can you hang on? Will I even be allowed to see you when I get home?"

"I can always sneak out my bedroom window. They still haven't figured that out." He gave me a watery smile.

I thought for a moment. "If you can get out, I want you to go to the library and set up a free e-mail account. Then e-mail me the mailing address of a friend who can receive mail for you. Another thought, Casey and James both owe us big time. I'll send you a burner phone."

"Won't that cost a lot?" Michael frowned. "I mean, I appreciate it and all—"

I cut him off. "Money's not an issue, not with my grandparents, trust me. Besides, I didn't say I was sending you a new iPhone, although I bet they'd pay for it."

Michael stared at me. "You're kidding."

"You have no idea. None. It's insane. I'll tell you—and show you—when I get home." I shook my head. "But that's not the hot issue right now. I don't know how long your parents will be gone, and I want you to meet my grandparents. Can you hang on a sec?"

Michael nodded, drying his eyes.

"Grandma! Grandpa!" I called, carrying my laptop out to the living room. "I made contact with Michael."

After several minutes of squinting, Grandpa said, "I'm sorry, Michael, I simply can't see on Jeremy's laptop screen. It's too small. I presume he has your contact information?"

"Yes, sir." That was my boy, always polite.

"Then he'll call you right back, dear," my grandmother said. "Hang tight."

Grandpa led us into his office, where not one but three studio displays waited. "I have no idea how to use that many screens," I said. "What do you do with them?"

Grandma laughed. "Your grandfather never retired, dear. He's up dark and early monitoring the markets and running circles around men not much older than you. He loves it." She smiled fondly at her husband. "So...three screens, three huge screens."

"They have to be that big at my age," Grandpa said. "Your eyes are worthless after sixty, even with laser surgery."

I still couldn't believe my parents had deprived me of these warm, caring, and hilarious people for all these years. Then it hit me. Mom had done exactly what I was doing—cleaving to her man. I needed to talk to her without anyone else around. Was there some rule that the older you got, the more complicated everything grew?

So, I called Michael back on Skype and made introductions.

"You don't look any different," Michael said.

I snorted. "You do. You're about two feet tall. Grandpa's got these enormous displays to keep track of I don't know how many different markets."

"Money can hold time at bay, but it will win in the end, boys. Always remember that," Grandpa said. "Yes, money makes life very comfortable, but all it really is, is a convenient way to keep score. The only thing that matters is your family, your loved ones."

I noticed a certain pain behind those words, and it made me wonder what it cost my grandparents to be semi-estranged from my mother, their only child. I guess I could vow to reunite them, but from what Grandma said about knowing my serostatus, they maintained some sort of contact. Besides, my plate was full enough, and I couldn't fix the world. Hell, I could barely keep myself out of trouble. Some things were above my pay grade, and one day I knew I'd have to accept that.

After Grandma and Grandpa visited with Michael for a few minutes, they left the two of us alone, but as Michael grew increasingly edgy about getting caught, I knew it was time to go.

"Remember: e-mail, address, and a burner phone." I felt horrible, and I had to wonder, which had been worse—no contact or this?

Michael nodded. "I'll start tomorrow."

"And I'll see what I can do about returning as soon as possible after New Year's Eve."

"You'll deal with your parents?"

"For you, Michael? Anything." I meant it too.

He looked so forlorn. "I'll see you soon."

"Yeah. Soon."

The screen went dark. "Goodbye," I whispered. "I love you."

I pulled myself together. And went to face my grandparents. To thank them, really. I appreciated that they took the time to meet my boyfriend and that Grandpa allowed us to use the screens in his office. I had no idea how to turn them off.

"What's wrong, Jeremy?" Grandpa said when I entered the living room. Guess I hadn't pulled myself together as well as I'd thought.

I fought back more tears. "Michael's very upset. He hasn't replied to any of my attempts to contact him since I left, and now I know why. His parents took away his phone and impounded his computer. I'm actually kind of afraid for him." I promised myself I wouldn't break down, but right then I thought I might break that promise. Michael was the kindest, sweetest person I knew, and for his parents to treat him like this... They were supposed to love him more than anyone else in the world, and that they'd treat him like a felon because of me made me feel lower than something I'd scrape off my shoe. "They've disapproved of our relationship, of me, since I started college, but this level of crazy is new. I don't understand why they're doing this to him now, of all times. It's hard not to think this is aimed at me."

Grandma patted the sofa next to me, and once I'd seated myself, pulled me into a hug. "That sounds very rough, dear."

"I feel so powerless." I sniffled. "I wonder what happened to the Michael who stood up for me, the Michael who protected me when I got so sick?"

I sounded like Geoff did when he grilled me after the Head of the Charles. I wanted to kick myself. Or choke on the irony. "I used to be so fierce too."

Grandpa gave me a look of purest sympathy. "Jeremy, you're young. I know you've seen and done a lot, but you're not even nineteen yet. You don't have to answer every question. Sometimes observing a pattern is enough. Maybe the two of you aren't fierce right now because you don't have to be. I've seen a lot of anger in you, but unless you control it, direct it to a productive end, you're nothing but a pissed-off teenager."

Not even nineteen, yet. I could hear Paul Hardcastle's "19" in my head. Mad and bewildered, yes, but at least I wasn't lost in the jungles of Vietnam, just lost in the thickets of relationships—parents, Michael, friends, crew.

"Your grandfather's right, dear. No one in the history of the world has ever taken an angry teenager seriously, but a young man with righteous arguments and a goal is something to be reckoned with. Maybe it's time to start being fierce again, dear. For Michael, if not for yourself."

"Let me put it to you this way, Jeremy, and this is something I've learned the hard way over decades. Success, however you define it, is a fairly simple thing. Figure out what you want. Determine what it'll cost you." Grandpa smiled at me. "*Then pay the price.*"

I jumped when Grandpa pronounced his steps to success so emphatically, but I found myself nodding. They were right. I'd already spent too much time allowing my parents to call the tune and picking the dance for me. Hell, my presence at CalPac was Exhibit A. Maybe that wasn't the best example, after all. I liked CalPac and no longer wanted to transfer, opening an entirely new can of worms. But my grandparents were right. People took one look at angry teens and wrote them off as pouting hormone cases. As it was, even young adults with well-reasoned arguments stood decent chances of dismissal due to age alone. And I was angry. I could stay angry—at my parents, at my brother, at Michael's parents—or I could grow up and use that anger, that passion, to fuel my plans forward. I could also use that anger to benefit Michael and myself. As Grandpa said, the steps to success weren't all that profound. That didn't mean they were easy, but that they weren't a secret.

"I'm going to have to think about how best to help Michael, because righteous arguments or not, I'm eighteen, and he's still a minor. But your steps to success?" I nodded my understanding. "I think I've been using them in crew without even knowing it."

Grandpa smiled. "It wouldn't surprise me. It's pretty simple. Never easy, but simple."

"I've willingly paid the price for years, but the next step? That's a whole new price altogether, and I admit it scares me. What if I fail?" It was the first time I had ever contemplated failing in crew, but it was bound to happen sooner or later.

"But my dear, what if you fly?" Grandma said.

I couldn't answer that one. I would only fly by dint of excruciatingly hard work, harder than any I'd known before. But then, couldn't I say that about every goal in crew up to this point? I'd spent the summer before my first trip to the Youth Nationals sculling many hours per day, sculling until my hands looked like hamburger from gripping the oar handles tighter than I should've and by putting in more time on the ergs than was perhaps healthy. My caloric intake had skyrocketed, and if I hadn't gotten so sick with what turned out to be HIV that following fall, I would've been in danger of gaining a ton of weight.

I nodded to acknowledge her point. "I also have to talk my parents into paying for it, and right now I'm not speaking to them," I said without considering the implications or the audience. My mind and attention were two thousand miles away in Davis.

Grandpa waved a dismissive hand, but that was easy for him to do. He was richer than God. "Stuff and nonsense. You let us worry about that. We're your grandparents. Spoiling you is what we live for, and we haven't been allowed to do it for far too long. We've got years of pent-up spoiling to do."

That brought my attention back to the here and now. I wanted to smack a hand across my mouth, but barn door? Horses? "More bragging rights?"

"Well, there is that, too, dear." Grandma smiled.

My jaw hung open. "You can't be serious. It's...it's too much."

I couldn't understand how they kept score. Right when I thought I had it figured out, they introduced some new wrinkle to throw me for a loop.

"Why don't you let us worry about that, dear? How much will you need?"

I felt kind of stupid. "I don't actually know."

Grandpa patted my hand. "Why don't I talk to your coach? That'll make things easier. You can name your boat after us or something."

"This is a joke. You're kidding, right?"

Grandpa's eyes held a twinkle. "Am I?"

He laughed, and I laughed, too, but what if he wasn't kidding?

Chapter Eighteen

I called the airline and set my ticket to fly back to Sacramento and Michael on January 2. Grandma and Grandpa had been so kind and generous to me that I could hardly deny them the opportunity to use me in their games with their friends on New Year's Eve. Now that I knew there was a game afoot, I played along a little better. Sure, earlier it bugged me, but I understood it more, now. It made me uncomfortable, but it was something I could do in return for all they had done and would do for me. Besides, it gave me a chance to hang out with Lance and Caden one last time.

"So d'you ever find out what was up with your guy?" Caden said, sucking up a tropical drink through a straw.

"Yeah. His parents put him on some kind of lockdown." I glared out at the party.

Lance made a face. "Shit. What're you going to do?"

"Fly home the day after tomorrow and see what I can do to help him. He's been strong for me in the past. It's my turn." It was true. I needed to deal with the situation at my parents' house first, but then I planned to challenge the Castelreighs.

"Awww, you'll ride to his rescue." Caden punched my arm in what I assumed was intended to be some sort of bluff camaraderie but in fact almost knocked me off my feet.

"How many of those have you had?" I rubbed my arm.

"Six. Why?"

"Next time, use a pile driver. They're gentler."

Lance looked seriously put out. "You're leaving already? That sucks."

"I left a real mess behind with my family, and as Caden so colorfully put it, or would've had he retained his higher brain functions, I need to ride to Michael's rescue, his knight in shining armor on a white steed." I thought about it. "Or in this case, me in a white Civic, but whatever."

"We were just getting to know you," Lance said.

Caden nodded. "I'm sure I could've talked your pants off if you'd been here another week or so."

"Bored them off, more likely." Lance made a face.

I shook my head. They had no idea how deep my devotion to Michael ran. "No offense to either of you, but if you two and Michael and I were the last four gay men on earth, you two would bang each other or die due to terminal semen poisoning."

Lance and Caden looked at each other in horror that was only partially faked, then looked at me and gasped.

"You..."

"...bitch."

Yep, they'd marry one day, I was sure of it. "Be sure to invite me to your wedding, boys."

They gaped, their mouths moving like koi. Lord love a duck, this was better than television. Of course, that was a low bar to reach.

I winked at them and went in search of something to eat. Glancing over my shoulder, I noticed that they trailed along behind me. I guess the last few minutes never happened.

"Seriously, we're going to miss you," Lance said.

I looked around. "You, who? All my fans and admirers? You guys have been great. These parties would've been deadly dull without you, and I'm very grateful you came up and pulled me out of my shell."

Caden giggled. "Remy on the half-shell. Remy the cracked crab. Remy the—"

"We get it." I put my hand over his mouth.

Caden licked it.

"You're kind of disgusting." I wiped my hand on his lapels. "Strangely lovable but disgusting."

"You think I'm lovable?" Caden grinned.

Lance nodded. "But disgusting. Don't forget that."

I made an effort to drag the conversation off such serious topics after that, and Caden gleefully helped. But as the clock struck midnight and the traditional "Auld Lang Syne" nonsense rolled around, I couldn't help but think that new acquaintances were something special too.

I spent New Year's Day packing and visiting with my grandparents. Apparently, they customarily passed the day calling on friends, but I had to wonder. If they called on friends, and if their friends similarly called on each other, how did they find anyone at home to receive visitors? I didn't bring this up. Some things were best left to puzzle out alone.

Before I left, my grandparents sat me down to talk. "We need to discuss money, dear."

Grandpa nodded. "It's a subject that makes a lot of people uncomfortable, I've noticed, but that doesn't make it any less important. Your grandmother and I established trust funds for you and your brother when you were born, and there'll be more for you when we're gone."

I made a noise. Suddenly I couldn't think about that.

Grandma patted my hand. "I know, dear. It's not my favorite subject, either, but if you think about it, it's been there since the beginning. We've had a good run, your grandfather and I, and with a little luck and proper healthcare, we'll have a number of good years ahead of us before we start drooling into our oatmeal."

"We wanted you to know about this, not to depress you." Grandpa chuckled. "The point is, we don't want you and Geoff to worry about money later in life. Our lawyer will know how to reach you, even if it's at your parents' house."

"I...thank you. I hardly know what to say." I didn't think Hallmark made a card for your loaded grandparents promising to set you up for life with their deaths. Awkward.

"Now, how are you set for school?" Grandma said.

This I could handle. "I'm doing very well as far as that goes. I'm on a full-ride scholarship, so it's basically living expenses and spending money. Did I mention the scholarship? I think I mentioned the scholarship. I've been in a constant state of overwhelm this entire trip, so I can't remember who I told what to."

"What about your car? Is it reliable?" Grandpa said.

I laughed. "It's a Civic. So long as I maintain it, it will never die. Geoff got the new-to-him used car when he graduated."

"Well, just in case, here's a credit card for emergencies, dear." I looked at the card Grandma handed me. It was a copy of their Amex Black, the Centurion Card. Amex, the one card no merchant took. Bad, Remy, bad. Don't be ungrateful. "We know Steven's your father, but we also know he can be difficult. If he cuts you off because of this feud you've had since October, use it and call us. We're not going to let you leave the school that's made you so happy. Of course, if it comes to it, you can always transfer to the University of Chicago or anyplace else you need to. Education's too important to let your father's temper get in the way of it."

"Wow. This is all so much. I hardly know what to say. But thank you." They overwhelmed me with their generosity, but they also knew the score. It wasn't my fault I'd been a stranger. "Tomorrow will be...interesting. I'm so glad I had this time with you to buffer the ulcer I'm sure to develop."

"You let us deal with our daughter and her husband. I'll call her to let her know you've been with us this whole time and that you'll be home tomorrow afternoon. By the time I'm done, she won't know what hit her. They don't call it Jewish guilt for nothing, dear. I can play her like a violin."

I'm pretty sure Grandpa's eyes were glistening. "You must come back."

"Every time I can, Grandpa." And now I knew where I'd spend every break in school I had.

*

Penguins and polar bears would've found the atmosphere at my parents' house congenial when I returned, but that was okay. I was the Ice Princess, right? I found it all too easy to slide back into my previous role of sullen teen, despite my talk with my grandparents. I admitted, at least to myself, that my parents and brother—him most of all—had wounded me terribly that fall, and I froze them out in response. I was surprised I didn't see frost on the walls. I spent the first week home sculling at Cap City, alone or in a double with Lodestone, or pointedly ignoring my family. Earbuds were truly a miracle of modern design.

Dad brought it all to a head after I'd been home for almost a week.

"I'm amazed at how long you can hold a grudge, Jeremy."

I felt Geoff watching from the door out of the kitchen. Mom lurked somewhere on the margins. Grandma must've done a number on her because she lived on eggshells where I was concerned.

I threw the stack of plates in my hands on the floor. Hard. It was on. "And I'm amazed at how badly you can misjudge a relationship, most of which is conducted far away from your gaze. Tell me, where and when did you get your data about Michael and me? The summer before school started? Michael and I spent it rowing. I didn't see you at the boathouse.

"Or Geoff? That's rich. His girlfriend keeps his balls in a jar on her dresser, to say nothing of the fact that he left for school a month after I did. He knows nothing about how my boyfriend and I interact. If you're going to bitch me out, you'd better include his codependency issues or face the fact that you're nothing but homophobes despite your protestations to the contrary."

Dead silence.

Oh my God. They *were* homophobes despite their liberal protestations to the contrary and couldn't cop to it.

"That's it, isn't it? You're treating me differently because my relationship's with another man." Suspecting it was one thing, knowing the truth of it was something else, and I'd had no idea.

Dad gritted his teeth in a way I found wholly irritating. "That's the problem, Jeremy. He's not a man. He's legally a minor."

"Are you fucking kidding me? Nothing about our relationship changed the day I turned eighteen."

"Yes, your relationship to Michael did change. I wish it hadn't, but the Brennan trial taught us that." Mom looked worried.

I wanted to throw up. "Did either of you bother talking to Detective Nakimoto? To the lawyers?"

"No, just to the Castelreighs." My dad looked like a thunderstorm.

"I will ruin them."

The silence crashed around us.

Mom looked like she needed a Xanax. "What exactly do you mean?"

"Beware the vengeance of a patient man, Mom." I glared at her like a basilisk. "That's all I'm saying."

Dad pinched the bridge of his nose. "Jeremy..."

"No, Dad. I've had it with every goddamn one of you. Everything was fine before I turned eighteen. Then suddenly I'm a threat to Michael's tender years. Have they actually met their son? Have you? This is un-fucking-believable. How much of this is a smokescreen for fears about HIV, do you think?"

Dad didn't answer right away. "I'm not sure I can answer that, and before you explode—again—I'm not bullshitting you. I truly hadn't considered that."

"It wouldn't surprise me in the least, Jeremy." Mom shook her head slowly. "The Castelreighs, especially Michael's mother, can be...different...where health issues are concerned. She knows I'm a drug rep, so you can imagine what she thinks I do for a living. She and I got into it one day about vaccinations, of all things. It's a thoroughly academic topic, since Michael's far beyond needing childhood immunizations, but if she's not an anti-vaxxer, she's the next best thing. AIDS-phobic? I'm not a gambling woman, but I don't think I'd lose money on this one."

That was just ducky. And Michael hadn't said a thing. I wondered if he even knew. How could he not know his parents were barking mad? But that certainly explained why they turned crazypants on finding his Truvada. Crazypantser?

It was January, it was cold as fuck outside, and dark on top of it. "I'm out of here. I'll be back later."

"Where are you going? You can't run off like this." Dad looked outraged. Welcome to the club, old man.

"Sure, I can."

I took the stairs up to my room three at a time. I had so much old rowing kit here, there had to be something I could wear, and I wouldn't be cold very long once I started sculling.

After I'd escaped, I pulled over and texted Lodestone.

ME: *Sculling. It's that or kill the fam. Just FYI.*

He replied a few minutes later, so I pulled over again.

LODESTONE: *Want company?*

ME: *Sure. No therapy tho. See U at Cap City.*

As I drove on, I thought about my grandparents' advice about angry teenagers. I needed to calm down and approach all of this rationally, if only for Michael's sake. When I returned to my parents' house, I resolved to stop stomping around and start being the passionate young man with righteous arguments that my grandmother told me to be.

*

I had just finished dressing in a pair of comfy sweats and a new Head of the Charles T-shirt when Geoff—I didn't intend to call him Goff, not for a long time, maybe not ever again—knocked on my bedroom door.

"So, I thought about what you said."

"Which time?" I sat on my bed and rolled sweat socks up my feet.

"Boston." He pulled out my desk chair and sat down. Sure, Geoff. Have a seat.

"You thought about it? Or did Laurel make you?" I knew the difference by now.

Geoff glared at me. I saw venom in his eyes, something I'd never seen before. "Sometimes I really hate you."

"I can live with that. Can you?" I used a calm, flat tone I knew he hated. "And you didn't answer my question."

"Laurel."

I didn't smirk at him. I didn't have to. "And?"

"She sat me down and reminded me how it went back in July when we visited campus. You were right. We matched our schedules as closely as possible."

I stared at him. I felt the steel crawling up my spine. I had a boyfriend whom I loved to protect. Magnanimous in victory? Not hardly, not when the damage had been done to Michael, to me.

"And?"

"God damn you! What more do you want?"

Geoff stood up abruptly, stomping off to his bedroom, stopping at the bathroom door.

"I want what you're not telling me." I stood up too.

My brother stared at me, chest heaving. He was livid. "Laurel's furious. She's barely spoken to me since then. Since the middle of October, Remy! We haven't seen each other at all since we've been home. This is your fault, and you'd better fix it."

"My fault? I think not." I was up and in his face in a second, my teeth bared. "You can't pin this on me, and you know it. Don't you dare project your own guilt onto me. If your girlfriend's pissed at you, you'd better be prepared to grovel. You backed our parents against me, you hypocrite, and you have to live with that."

Geoff looked like he was about to hit me.

"Go for it. Gimme your best shot."

Then he swung.

I danced sideways, grabbed his fist, and spun him around. I pulled his arm up behind him and then shoved him into the wall.

"You've been out of football for a year, and you're soft. Meanwhile, I'm still training. Actually, I'm being eyed by USRowing for the national team, so chew on that for a while," I hissed in his ear. "You and the people who spawned us? Y'all made my boyfriend cry. That's not suave."

Then I pulled his arm higher up his back.

"Dammit, that hurts! Let me go."

"If I pull your arm high enough, something will break. Or you'll dislocate your shoulder. I can't remember which."

Then my bedroom door flew open. "Jeremy? Geoffrey! What's the meaning of this?" Dad demanded. Mom was close behind him, her mouth an O of horror.

I turned Geoff around and shoved him at Dad. "The next time your oldest son decides to take a swing at me, make sure he's physically up to the challenge. If this happens again, I'll damage more than his pride."

"Geoffrey?" Mom said.

Geoff sighed, glaring at me again. "Yeah, I tried to hit him. I don't feel like going into it right now."

"Fighting in our home is unacceptable, and I don't care who started it." Dad looked furious, and I couldn't blame him.

"I'm sorry, Dad. Mom, I apologize for getting into a fight with my brother under your roof. This is obviously much more serious than our childhood squabbles, if only because we have men's bodies and strength now," I said as sincerely as I could. "Geoff and I were rehashing something that happened between us right after the Head of the Charles, something we let fester longer than we should've. Geoff, I'm still very hurt and angry about what you said, both then and tonight, but we need to settle this like adults, not street brawlers. Right now, I think you need to call Laurel. Your apologies should start there, but that's only my opinion." I swept them all with a hard look. "That the three of you have upset Michael as much as you have will take me a long time to move past, but I'm a lot angrier about that than I realized, and that's something I need to work on before revisiting the subject."

The three of them stared at me until it unsettled me. "What?"

"Thank you, Jeremy. I appreciate what you said. That showed a lot of insight and maturity. Yes, we're going to have to discuss this, but I think you're right—not right now." Dad exchanged a look with Mom, but hell if I knew what it meant.

Mom looked at Geoff and at me. "Are you boys all right? Really?"

"No, but we will be." Geoff sighed. "I think you're wrong, Remy. Right now, my priority is to apologize to you. Will you excuse us?" he said to our parents.

Mom and Dad looked at us one more time and then left my room, albeit reluctantly, as if they thought fisticuffs would break out again the moment they left us alone.

"We'll be okay." I glanced at Geoff.

He sighed again. "I promise, no more beatings. My ego can't take it."

Once the door shut behind our parents, Geoff turned and looked at me. "You're not going to make this easy on me, are you?"

"Geoff, I spent this fall bereft. My own twin turned on me. It was a terrible time. Mom and Dad I can take or leave, you know that. But you? That hurt." I put all my cards on the table. "I need to know that you're on my side, that you have my back. I don't know what happened, and maybe it didn't matter, but never let it happen again."

As I spoke, Geoff hung his head. "I'm sorry," he said softly. "I...I worry about you. Between the HIV and what felt like a major change in your personality, I got scared. You seemed like you'd junked a major part of who you are to be with Michael, and I didn't recognize you anymore."

"And this fall didn't teach you otherwise?" I said dryly.

He laughed. "That's about what Laurel said. Something along the lines of 'You were worried about him going soft? He cut you off like a gangrenous toe and you're freaking out. Who's soft, now?'"

"Ouch."

"I know, but she didn't stop there. 'You dared to question whether or not his relationship with Michael was healthy and real, and then he kicked you in the teeth before booting you out of his life. What did you think would happen? Michael's not a bad influence. He's the best thing that ever happened to your brother.' It went downhill from there, actually." Geoff looked miserable.

"Downhill? How?" I knew Laurel was the stronger of the two of them, but wow.

"There's no point in repeating it. I was wrong, and she made sure I knew it." He shook his head. "Look, I said some things I shouldn't have, and I was wrong, Remy. I'm sorry."

"Apology conditionally accepted." Geoff met my eyes. He was about to speak, but I shook my head. "For myself, I'll get over it, but Michael's had a shitty fall. The three of you have a lot to do to fix that. You want my forgiveness? Make peace with my boyfriend. He may come across as resilient, but in some ways he's quite fragile, and you in particular dragged him into the middle instead of contacting me directly."

Geoff nodded slowly. "Understood. I'll call him tomorrow."

"I hope his parents let him out of solitary."

"That poor guy." Geoff hesitated. "Will you text Laurel to let her know we've made up? I don't know if she'll believe me."

I frowned. "It's gotten that bad?"

"I'm afraid so."

"Shit. You...you're not going to break up, are you?"

Geoff bit his lip. "I really hope not."

I did the only thing I could. I engulfed him in the biggest hug I had. "That can't happen. You two are supposed to be together for the rest of your lives."

"Thanks, Remy." No, his eyes weren't suspiciously wet or anything. "So...will you text her?"

I whipped out my phone and fired off a text, hoping that Geoff's brother interceding would speak for itself. She called me back within a minute.

"Yes, Laurel. It's really me. We're speaking, we've made up, it's beautiful... No, he still has to grovel to Michael, but give the man a break. It's been a lot for one night... *I'm* worried about you two... Michael may have to wait a few days. His parents are insane, or at least his mom is. They found his Truvada." I actually had to hold the phone away from my ear, she screeched so loudly. "No, my boy's on lockdown. Took all his electronics. I had to send him a burner phone so he wasn't cut off from the world... Right. Geoff'll see you soon."

I ended the call. "Get out of here," I said to Geoff. "I'd apologize to Mom and Dad on the way out. I think we're both in trouble." I thought about it. "Actually, maybe you should ask if you can go see Laurel."

Geoff laughed. "You think we're grounded?"

"You tried to punch me, and they're paying for school. Let's be cautious."

"Just like old times." He grinned at me.

I rolled my eyes. "Don't sneak out the window."

"Can I borrow your car? Mine's in San Diego."

Chapter Nineteen

Geoff left for Laurel's without any hitches, at least not once we assured our parents that we really had made up. Yes, there would be ramifications to fighting under their roof—or for Geoff taking a swing at me, since I'd put a stop to his attempt to start a fight before the fight had started—but I, at least, understood and accepted the consequences. Easy for me; I hadn't thrown the punch.

So, I joined my parents for a quiet evening at home, or what could've been a quiet evening had it been another family. But we were the Babcocks, so you know. Questions, pointed looks, and pregnant pauses.

"Out of curiosity, where did you spend the holidays?" Dad asked once Geoff left.

"Ask Mom. Grandma and Grandpa Fischer. Grandma called her, after all."

Dad turned to look at her. "Oh really, Dina? Did you not see fit to tell me this?"

"You know my relationship with my parents is complicated, and—"

"*Your* relationship with them is complicated? What about mine? I was worried sick about Jeremy, and you knew where he was this whole time?"

Mom held up one hand. "I *suspected*. I didn't *know* until Mom called me the day he came home."

"Sophistry, Dina." Dad shook his head. He was pissed, but for once not at me. "On what did you base your suspicions?"

"The credit card statement. He charged tickets to Chicago. We're going to discuss your penchant for traveling in the first-class cabin one of these days, young man."

Dad sighed. "This family. Dina, you and I will talk later. But meanwhile, tell me, Jeremy. How was it being Fischered?"

I squinted at him. "What's that mean?"

"Bought off, steamrollered into jumping through hoops, forced to be something you're not. Any of that sound familiar?" Dad laughed at me.

I thought about that for a moment. "There was an element of that, for sure, but they also listened to me when I needed to talk and helped me to put a lot of things that'd been bothering me into perspective." I fixed Dad with a beady-eyed stare. "So yeah, they used me in their social-climbing games, and they're footing the bill for my national team training, but they also told me to quit being a whiny brat, grow up, and come home and talk to you about our issues like an adult."

I laughed at Dad's flabbergasted look. Even Mom looked startled, and they were her parents. "I don't actually know what to say to that," Dad finally confessed.

"*You* don't know what to say?" Mom laughed, but it sounded bitter. "Our youngest has apparently gotten out of them the one thing I always wanted. What's your secret, kiddo?"

So, this was uncomfortable, and I avoided the question. "Did you know that the social climbing, the games, all of that is only a way to keep score? They're all rich beyond belief, so merely spending money is irrelevant, and they have to work through proxies. Once I figured that out, them dressing me up like a Ken doll and bragging about my rowing and everything else made a lot more sense, and I came to see the fun in it. I even made some friends I'll keep in touch with at those parties of theirs. If you look at it that way, Grandma and Grandpa are actually proud of our accomplishments."

I looked at them both. "So, the secret? Work with them. Give them what they want to hear, and then the heavens will open up. They're lovely people."

"Wait. Did you say something about national team training?" Dad stared at me intently.

"Did I? Maybe you should call my grandparents. They accepted me and my relationship without any judgment. Something to think about, isn't it?"

With that, I went upstairs. I'd made my point. I was reasonably sure I heard Dad mutter, "I hate it when he's right."

*

The next morning Geoff and I were left to hold down the fort. Surprisingly, we both woke up fairly early. I could've and should've gone sculling but didn't feel like it, and who knew why Geoff was up. He'd crept in fairly late last night, or early this morning, as the case had been. I tried to be quiet and keep the coffee fresh. I'd wasted no time in acquiring an espresso maker on my return, so it wasn't coffee so much as that sticky rocket fuel Grandma had plied me with in Chicago. My skills as a barista only kept growing, but I had room to improve.

"Jeez, Remy, what is this?" Geoff coughed a few times.

I smiled. "Grandma calls it espresso."

"Turpentine's gentler."

"How do you know what turpentine tastes like?"

"Missing the point." Geoff thought for moment. "So, how were they? What was it like?"

"Grandma and Grandpa Fischer? They're delightful. Mom and Dad should be ashamed for letting their issues keep us from our grandparents." I shook my head. "Honestly, it was just the break I needed, even if it sucked being away from Michael while the shit was apparently hitting the fan. That reminds me, I have a box full of Apple products for you to pick through."

"Oh?"

I shrugged. "I guess they thought I needed new computers."

"Plural?"

"I'm afraid so." I smiled. "They haven't seen me—us—for a while and had some indulging to do. There's no way I can use all that. If there's anything left when we're done, I'll see what Michael and Laurel want. Grandma and Grandpa don't appear to know the meaning of restraint."

Geoff shook his head. "Only you can fall from the frying pan into the fire and emerge covered in diamonds."

"I think you're mixing your metaphors there, sport." I hoped he wasn't jealous. I'd ended up in Chicago out of desperation, after all.

"Can you steam milk on that thing? I'd love a latte to buffer that last dose you hit me with. Seriously, are you brewing paint thinner in that?" Geoff gave me an appraising look while holding his little espresso mug out for more. "You've had an interesting fall, haven't you?"

I had some things on my mind and wondered if Geoff had been rehabilitated enough to bounce ideas off or whether he needed to be tormented some more. Then again, maybe being related to me was torment enough. Or perhaps I'd punished him since October, and I needed someone to talk to. Regardless, Geoff provided me with an opening.

"You don't know the half of it. Can I run some things by you?"

Geoff looked surprised and maybe a little pleased, like we were back to being brothers again. "You can't talk to Michael?"

"No, this involves him." I handed Geoff his latte. Who needed Starbucks when you had an espresso machine more complicated than a Kurosawa movie and more expensive than one of those computers my grandparents had given me? I used that contraption to stall by making my own beverage.

"Sooooo?" Like Geoff didn't know what I was up to.

I sighed. "I'm going to rip the bandage right off, then. I don't want to transfer to a New England school when Michael starts college next fall."

I braced myself for the fallout. To his credit, however, Geoff stayed silent, thinking about what I said. "I presume you have your reasons."

"Yes. I hope they don't sound lame when I say them out loud." They probably would. Everything sounded normal inside my head, but I easily became my own echo chamber. At least I was aware of it?

Geoff leaned back in his chair. "Lay 'em on me."

"I guess it's really two issues," I said. "The first is that I've realized over the course of the fall that as much as I love Michael, I can't be involved with someone in high school."

All I had to do was think of that Baby Shark prom and it became so clear.

Geoff looked at me like I was stupid, and maybe I was. "What do you mean? He'll be out in six months, then you'll be a sophomore and he'll be a freshman. Don't tell me you haven't seen those on campus, because they're all over the place."

"It reminds me too much of Josh Brennan—an older man involved with a minor." Jeez, even thinking of that turned my stomach.

Geoff, too, apparently. He reared back like I'd slapped him. "Oh man...that's...that's... You two aren't like that. You two have one of the healthiest relationships I've seen."

"Then how come you—" Damn, this subject was going to make me angry for a long time.

"I was blind, and I was wrong, as Laurel pointed out quite forcefully and at great length."

"I know, but when I first thought of it, it hit me like a tugboat. I ran to the bathroom and puked my guts out." I smiled faintly. "I scared my therapist."

"Yay." Geoff didn't look all that amused. "I'm sure that's one she'll eat out on when she and the other shrinks get together." Then the first and probably most important part of what I said struck him. "Wait—you love him? Remy, that's great. Yet it makes what you told me so sad and horrible. Can't you... I don't know, hang on for six more months?"

I buried my face in my hands. "I know, I know. And he's put up with so much from his parents because of me. I can't turn my back on him right now. Talk about a crappy thing to do to someone, and yes, I really do love him, but..."

I jumped when Geoff put his hand on my shoulder. I hadn't been aware of him getting up. "Nothing's ever simple, Germy, least of all being in love." He pulled out the chair next to me. "What's the other reason you don't want to transfer? What did Mom and Dad promise you? I can't remember."

"In return for being forced to spend my freshman year at CalPac—on a full-ride crew scholarship, by the way—that I could transfer anywhere I could get in for my sophomore year, including Boston University." I looked up. "We didn't really get a chance to discuss it after my races in October, but I toured BU before the regatta. It's a great school, but it's not for me."

Geoff laughed. "You know, there might be other great schools in the Boston area."

"Ass." I rolled my eyes. "That's not actually the issue, though. I like CalPac. A lot. It's a great school. The rowing program is taking me places. I came in with a ton of AP credits, so I'm almost a sophomore without having done much, although I guess that'd be true anywhere. Okay, my roommate's a nightmare, but I've got him under control. I'm building a life here."

"A life without Michael."

I exhaled noisily. "Not necessarily, not if he goes to school on the West Coast, but yes, potentially."

Geoff looked grave. "Have you spoken to him?"

"Jeez, no. I'm terrified. He means the world to me, and this will break both our hearts." Thinking about it made me choke up. "I only recently realized I love him. How can I be thinking about not being with him?"

"I don't know, Remy, but it seems like you are."

"I know." I sighed, thinking. What a terrible thing it was to contemplate your own damnation. Wasn't that what I faced for turning my back on love? What I deserved? All I'd ever wanted was to be somewhere with Michael where we could row and be ourselves. Now it looked as if I had to choose, and when faced with a choice between love and rowing, there wasn't really a choice to make. What did that say about me? Besides the fact that my priorities were seriously deranged.

But Geoff was speaking again. "So, it looks like you won't be coming to San Diego either."

"No, I'm afraid not." Was that not implicit in telling him how much I liked CalPac and how far the crew program could take me?

"We could've had a blast, you know." Geoff shook his head slowly.

I thought about it. Maybe we could've...before October. "Do you think so? Isn't it time to make a break? Get used to not being constantly in each other's lives?"

"You'll always be a part of my life, Jeremy."

"And you'll always be a factor in mine. That's part of being brothers, Geoff, but that's not what this is about." Seriously, why was Geoff making this about him? This had nothing to do with *our* past and everything to do with *my* future.

Geoff looked as confused as I'd ever seen him, and I was right there with him. "Then what's it about?"

"It's about me doing what's best for me educationally. It's about me making it into professional rowing, or as close as my sport comes to the pros." I took a deep breath and pushed through my fears at even articulating it. "It's about facing the fact that as much as I love Michael, I don't think we can be together right now."

Geoff said nothing for the longest time. "Okay, all I can say about the rowing is damn and congratulations. I've known you were a great rower for years, but I'm not sure anyone knew how great you could be—"

"I think Lodestone knows, not that he's talking. Did I tell you I want him to coach me for my push for the national team?"

"That figures." Geoff nodded. "I can't really tell you what school's best for you. I still think UCSD has a lot to offer, but if the CalPac Titans are what you need for rowing, then UCSD's Tritons will just have to cope."

*

Geoff and Laurel left for San Diego and the winter quarter the next day. They took a few Apple products with them, but that still left the bulk of the computer hardware and iPads for me and Michael. I think they struggled with the notion that Apples really did grow on trees, at least where our Fischer grandparents were concerned.

"Doesn't it feel strange to you that grandparents we haven't seen since junior high suddenly shower us with consumer electronics?" Geoff said when I showed him the trove.

I shrugged. "Not really, no. They'd already taken me shopping and treated me like a life-size Ken doll. By the time they convinced themselves I needed a new computer—"

"Or three," Laurel said.

"—or more, I was used to it," I said. "I tried to tell them that I didn't need all of this, but it didn't do much good, as you can see. So, I did the next best thing, and that was bring it all home for us to share."

Geoff frowned at it all. "I'd feel better if I'd been there, I guess."

"Go see them this summer, or even better, spring break." I followed them out to Laurel's car and waited while they strapped in. "Go with, Laurel. Granted, shivering on the shores of Lake Michigan isn't exactly a typical spring break destination, but then, you go to school in San Diego. It'll be refreshing."

"Or bracing." Geoff snorted. "I'll think about it."

Unfortunately, I knew what Geoff's "I'll think about it" meant. It meant it'd probably never happen. "Make sure he does something about it, Laurel, will you? If nothing else, the trust fund they've set up for him might see you two through medical school, so it'd be a nice gesture to feign an interest in them."

Geoff's jaw dropped. "Wait, what? A trust fund? They've set up a trust fund for me?"

"Oh, did that slip out?"

"Remy!" Geoff yelled out of his window.

I grinned and went back to the house. I turned and waved from the front steps. "Don't be a stranger, now."

I wouldn't go so far as to say my brother and I were back to the way things had been before, but at least we'd started.

Chapter Twenty

Life before the spring term at CalPac started had a few bright spots. Michael went back to school about the same time Geoff did, which was about a month before CalPac resumed for the spring semester. As such, he no longer needed to sneak out to see me because he had the perfect excuse to leave the house and it was legally mandated— his last semester of high school. He came to my house whenever he had the chance before, during, or after school. Or I *happened* to encounter him at the Cap City boathouse, where I continued to scull until I was able to get back into the CalPac facilities.

Lodestone thought the entire thing absurd until we explained it to him. Then he knew it was absurd.

"I feel like a pimp," he groused.

I sighed. "I'm not fucking him over a boat, Lodestone."

"He's really not, Coach. Total bottom city," Michael said in a stage whisper.

Lodestone winced. "You two will be the death of me, I swear."

"Then don't lead with sexual innuendo." I examined my fingernails for signs of damage, frowning at my left thumbnail. It actually looked like it was delaminating. I didn't know that was even possible.

"You've only gotten worse with age, Remy. You weren't this dreadful last year, or even at the Head of the Charles. You used to be such a nice boy, and Michael! You've corrupted *him* beyond all hope of redemption." Lodestone shook his head slowly.

I rolled my eyes. The circumstances clearly called for it. "Are you sure?"

"Just look at him," Lodestone said. "I fully expect to see some sort of obscene tattoo the moment he turns eighteen. That, and about five piercings, only two of which will be visible when he's clothed."

"Are you sure I'm the one responsible for the debauching?" I enjoyed this more the longer it went on.

Michael nodded. "He's right, Coach. Quiet waters run deep and all that. Maybe I only *look* innocent, and how do you know I don't already have those piercings?"

"Jacob's ladder piercings and butt sexing give 'Chutes and Ladders' a whole new meaning, Lodestone." I grinned at him.

Lodestone flinched. He actually flinched. "You... you." He shook his head. "I got nothing. Congratulations, Remy. You finally did it. You broke me."

"I had help." I pointed to Michael, who waved.

"One *enfant terrible* was more than enough, but two of you!" Lodestone continued. "Two! How can I be expected to put up with that?"

This was why I liked Lodestone, loved—even revered—him.

Michael slid his arm around my waist. "With your usual grace and dignity, I'd imagine."

"'Usual grace and dignity,'" Lodestone parroted. "Did you have some reason for inflicting yourself on me, Remy, or was this purely a social visit?"

That question made me twitch because did I ever have a reason, even an agenda for being there, and for once it wasn't sculling. Or not sculling alone. "Uh... actually, yes. I need to talk to you about some special coaching."

"Do you, now? This wouldn't have anything to do with an offer dangled in front of you by Pendergast, would it?" Lodestone's brown eyes caught my gray ones and held them. For all my alleged cleverness, Lodestone saw right through me and always had.

"I'll catch you later, Remy." Michael gave me a quick peck on one cheek.

"No, you'd better stay." Lodestone shook his head. "This concerns you too. You need to know what your boy's getting involved with."

Michael and I exchanged looks as we followed Lodestone back to his office. That didn't sound ominous or anything. It made me wonder exactly what the implications of my CalPac coaches' offer were. The chance to compete on a national or even international level had certainly dazzled me, and while I liked to think of myself as a practical soul, I now had the certain sensation that Lodestone was about to pull me rather forcibly back down to earth.

"Have a seat, boys." Lodestone usually pulled a chair around from behind his desk so that the three of us sat facing each other, but not this time. I wondered why he chose to maintain that distance.

"So..." I started, but Lodestone cut me off with a gesture.

"We all know what you're going to ask me, Remy, so let's get to the point. I know what your CalPac coaches have offered you, and I know they've given you permission to approach me about the kind of specialized, intensive coaching you'll need. Frankly, it's amazingly generous of them."

Okay, so much for building up to things, but then, cutting to the chase was more my style. "They get that I respond to you. You took me to the Youth Nationals twice. They think maybe you can take me beyond that too." I looked him in the eyes. "Can you? Will you?"

Then the negotiations commenced. Negotiations? More like my one-time coach and mentor trying to argue me out of pursuing something most people never even dreamed of. Could I honestly say I dreamed of this? I wasn't so sure. It had never occurred to me until Pendergast and Ridgewood had spoken to me about it.

But spoke to me they had. They dangled that brass ring before my eyes, and now I wanted it more than anything. Yet there sat Lodestone, and unless I missed my mark, he appeared to be talking me out of it. What was up with that? Crush *my* dreams, will you? Ha!

"Lookit, Lodestone, will you coach me or not? It's not like you won't be compensated, and you can essentially name your price. So cut the crap, because I know what I'm getting into: I'll have to take a bare minimum course load, my mail will be forwarded to the boathouse, and despite the rats, I might as well sleep out here, because I'll be here more than I'll be at my dorm."

Lodestone gave me a long, serious look, like the one when he'd caught me with Josh Brennan a few years back, but worse because I felt like he was trying to take the measure of me. "Do you, Remy? Do you really know what you're asking of us both? Because I can guarantee you that training on this level is nothing you've ever done before and will require sacrifices not just from the two of us but from our nearest and dearest. I can't say Marissa's thrilled at the thought, but then, she knew she'd be a rowing widow when we first got serious about each other."

I looked at Michael, but before I could open my mouth, he shook his head. "Don't drag me into this. I row, so I have an idea what you'll be facing. And it's not like I can't handle the logistics for our escape to the East Coast."

Oh, bloody fucking hell, that. I didn't know how I kept forgetting it. I didn't want to face telling him about my change of heart, so I let rowing distract me.

Uh...actually, yes, I knew exactly how I kept forgetting. Avoidance.

Lodestone and I kept at each other, but the whole exchange annoyed me. Annoyed? Try pissed me off.

"Seriously, Lodestone, if you don't believe in me and my ability, why're we even here? I'd like to think that after two trips to the Youth Nationals and a handful of gold medals, I'd have proven to you that I've got at least *some* native ability—you've got those on your coaching résumé, right, you hypocrite?—but no, I'm sitting here on the other side of your desk while you play devil's advocate. At least, that better be what you're doing. So cut the bouillabaisse and answer the question—will you coach me or not?" Then I had an idea, a horrible, rotten, evil idea. "Or have we finally found the limit of *your* abilities? If this is more than you can handle, there's no shame in saying so."

For a moment I thought I might have gone too far. Lodestone looked like I'd smacked him upside the head.

"You...little...punk."

Michael watched us both with undisguised amusement...as he had for years.

"What're you laughing at?" I glared at him.

"Two gifted, idiosyncratic men circling around each other. You're going to work with each other, if only because you, Coach, won't stand for someone else monkeying about with your greatest achievement. And you, Remy. You don't actually listen to anyone but Peter Lodestone, at least not for very long, and we all know it."

We both stared at Michael. I mean, he was right, but did he have to say it out loud like that?

I glanced at Lodestone. "Are you going to get this one?"

"Me? He's your boyfriend." I'm sure he tried to hide it, but I knew Lodestone thought it was funny.

"You're delusional if you think I have any control over him." Sure, this whole conversation revolved around training me to work miracles in thirty pounds of carbon fiber, but I was only human.

"Get to the point," Michael said. "I have to be home soon, and this 'Coach kept me after practice' bit only stretches so far before it's too thin to be believable."

Lodestone coughed. "Right. So, here's what we're looking at. I've already mapped out a periodized training and competition strategy that has you peaking at the U23 team selection trials in late June. I've worked backward from that." He shoved a spreadsheet across his desk to me. It bristled with labels, each color-coded, but it gradually resolved into some sense and order the longer I studied it. "You'll notice that if you make the U23 team, there'll be another minicycle to bump you up before the Worlds selection camp."

Lodestone let the reality of the next six months sink in for a few moments before he continued. "You will be lifting, sculling, and erging. A lot. Plan on two practices—two *long* practices—a day that incorporate some combination of those. Plan on regular erg testing. I will assume total control of your diet, and you'll start logging your food intake. If you bite it, you'll write it, whether it's coffee or a steak dinner or cheesecake for dessert."

I looked at Michael, whose eyes held a devilish gleam. "Stop that," I said. Something told me Lodestone didn't really want to know how many calories, carbs, et cetera a load contained.

"What're you two up to, now?" Lodestone said.

"Nothing...yet."

Sure, Michael looked innocent, but no one in the room believed that for a second.

"*Anyway,*" Lodestone said, "before we get any further into this, you're going to have a complete physical and health screening as USRowing defines it. You haven't had one of those yet, which has been an oversight."

I'd expected that, but I had no idea how to go about setting up one that would "count," if that made sense. I mean, sure, I could've gone to see my HIV specialist, but my meds and I got along fine, and we talked about HIV and competition a fair amount. The upshot was that HIV and competition at the highest levels got on well together, and there was at least one gold medal winner who was poz.

"Because of the HIV? I thought I'd told you I'd been cleared—"

"No, because you should've had an ECG long before now. Sudden death is the leading cause of mortality in endurance athletes, and it's usually due to an undiagnosed but preexisting cardiac abnormality."

Lodestone sighed. "This one's pretty much my fault, guys."

My once and future coach paused for a moment, and I could tell he sought for the right words. Experience alone taught him he needed to tell me the truth, but maybe not all of it. "To be honest, I've had to consult with my old coaches at U-Dub. They're the ones who shoved me in the direction of the USRowing health exams. We'll fill out all of these forms, and your doctor here will administer the ECG, but experts in Boston will read and analyze them. USRowing contracts with cardiologists at Mass Gen to read the ECG in particular. They don't want you keeling over on their watch, and neither do I."

"I don't want you dying either." Michael took my hand. "I know how much this means to you, Rem, but nothing's worth that."

"I know, believe me, I know." I'd already faced my mortality once, and I had no intention of going down that road again. Did they not remember? Whatever. I did.

There remained one topic to discuss. I hated talking about money, but it was a reality of adult life. "How much do you need for this? My grandparents will be paying your salary, so don't lowball your needs. Oh, and you may end up talking to them about my equipment needs too."

"Remy? How well off are your grandparents?" Lodestone looked troubled, and I couldn't blame him.

"I have no idea. That they live on the Gold Coast in Chicago is about all I know, and they offered to do this for me." I knew a lot more than that, but really? Talking about money with nonfamily members? Please. I knew I was brash and about as subtle as an uncontrolled chain reaction, but even I had my limits.

"I'll have to give this some thought then. I made some assumptions that may not be true," Lodestone said. "I'll talk to some club members to see if they mind you trying out their boats. I want you to get a feel for what's out there before I—or your grandparents—buy you a single. I may replace those sculls your parents bought you too."

He referred to the pair of oars my parents bought me to entice me back into a boat when I was recovering from the initial infection with HIV. I'd recovered well enough physically, but psychologically? It hadn't helped that a few 'phobes on the Cap City junior crew had made some unhelpful comments either. In one of their rare moments of insight and sensitivity, Mom and Dad had bought me sculling oars.

Replace them? Fine. He knew more than I did, after all.

Then something occurred to me. "How will I get this future boat of mine back east for the trials?"

"You won't." Lodestone made some notes on my training spreadsheet. "You'll rent one, most likely from the manufacturer. Believe me, they've got quite the racket going with this sort of thing. We'd get there early to make the necessary adjustments to the rigging."

I glanced at the time. The sand was almost out in Michael's hourglass. "Anything else? Michael needs to leave soon."

"You two really are joined at the hip, aren't you?" Lodestone smiled.

"Looks like we'd better be now, while we still can." Michael glanced meaningfully at the training spreadsheet.

Lodestone laughed softly. "Don't worry about that. One, I'm not that cruel, and two, it's periodized, remember? That means planned and regular periods of rest. Have you forgotten everything I've taught you about training? We stress the body to provoke deliberate changes, but we have to give the body time to adapt and make those changes. Otherwise I'm just tormenting you. So, get out. I'll see you both tomorrow. Remy, for you that means five a.m."

"We're starting already?"

"Yes."

*

Out in the parking lot, I did my best to get him to take some electronics off my hands, but Michael's reaction to the Apple harvest matched Geoff's.

"I can't take this."

I laughed awkwardly. I felt like I was pedaling things that "fell off the back of a truck" when I showed Michael the bounty of my grandparents' largesse.

"How on earth do you think I can use all of this? You don't think I intend to share it with my parents, do you? I mean, come on."

Michael shook his head. "There's no way I can accept any of this."

"Why not?"

"There's my parents, for one thing." The "duh" went unsaid but hung there in the air like a fart.

Eye roll. "What do they have to do with it? Didn't they impound your computer?"

"Yes…"

He was weakening. I could tell.

"Do you have it back yet?" All I had to do was take baby steps down the primrose path.

"Well…no."

One step after another.

"So, take the computer, and if they bitch about it, tell them you needed one for school and borrowed it from a friend."

Michael nodded. "So, it's a loaner?"

"Don't be ridic, you're telling them that since they've got no connection to reality at this point. Say it's from Laurel. You'll know she'll back you up. Take an iPhone too. They bought me one, but the one I have from my parents is fine. That crappy little burner can't be easy to use." I sighed. "This way, if they try to take this one, you can tell them they're committing theft."

Michael smiled, and I got all tingly. I wondered if he knew how much power over me he really had. "No, it's really not. My thumbs are killing me, and before you ask, no, they haven't given me my real phone back either."

"So, take the iPhone, and get a plan with lots of texting but maybe not so much on the data, because as I recall you don't really download much." It was going to kill me to break his heart about our plan for next year.

"True fact." He looked at his watch. "Okay, I really have to go."

We kissed goodbye for a few minutes, but really, his parents were insane and knew what time his practice ended. The whole situation was insane, really.

Chapter Twenty-One

Looking back, I should've kept Michael in the parking lot longer. I should've boned him in the back of the car. I had never been this tired in my life. Yes, Lodestone had warned me. Sure, I had that colorful spreadsheet. I posted it in multiple places, almost every vertical surface by late February. In fact, a picture of one was the first thing I put in the training log I started keeping for my grandparents for them to show off. Those "off" weeks in Lodestone's periodization? I caught up on sleep, and not even Brady and his petty annoyances could disturb me. Actually, I think he started to feel sorry for me. I wouldn't have thought I'd reached a point in my life in which regular team practices were my easy weeks. It's not like Pendergast went easy on us or anything but given what I was doing on my own time, nothing he threw at me mattered.

Pendergast. It took remarkably little time before it became blindly clear to everyone that I'd outgrown Ridgewood's team. Okay, sure, let's get it out there that I was a rowing prodigy, but anyone who put the butt time in the seat with the kind of attention Lodestone gave me would improve by leaps and bounds. But then, nothing came for free, and as my grandfather had said, I'd determined what I wanted, and I was paying the price. I don't think people understood that.

One morning at practice as I warmed up with the usual JV guys, someone I barely recognized came up. Steven, I think his name was, a senior and a varsity rower. "You're Remy, right?"

I glanced up from my erg. "Yeah."

"Coach says you're with us today."

"Um, okaaay." I glanced at Robbie, the JV team captain, who shrugged, as mystified as I was.

I went back to erging.

"Now, man. We leave earlier than JV."

I climbed off the erg. "Nothing like advanced notice."

"Yeah, whatever. I'm Steven, the team captain. Try not to suck."

Oh, really? Allow me to humiliate you and hand you your ass, bitch. "Try to keep up."

I walked past him to the bay housing the varsity boats. I enjoyed that practice. I wish I could've said I earned his grudging respect, but I think he resented my presence, if not my rise through the ranks. I never did determine if it was because he'd been assigned as my babysitter or if he simply didn't like me. I was told some people didn't. Whatever. I had better things to concentrate on, like rowing. Or seat racing. I wanted his.

Seat racing was both fun and sadistic. It made for faster boats, but it did so by setting members of a squad against each other. Take two fours and fill them with people you wanted to compare. Race them down a set course, usually a kilometer, tracking the times. Then bring the boats into alarmingly close proximity, like the "riggers of one boat touching the hull of the other boat" proximity. Then, through a complicated ballet, switch the people who rowed the same seat in each boat, such as each two seat, for example. Then repeat the process. Sometimes the stronger rower—strength or technique or both—became clear immediately. Otherwise, lather, rinse, repeat. Coaches could tweak lineups this way indefinitely.

I never managed to take Steven's seat, but the fact that I made him sweat for it made his jaw drop. The fact that I did it without appearing to work myself into a lather filled him with disgust. No, I eventually ended up in the engine room in the varsity A boat, and that worked out fine. I pulled hard and rowed my seat without having to think too much. I wondered if that was what Pendergast had in mind.

I might accidentally on purpose have been eavesdropping when Pendergast told Peevie Steevie, "You know he has a decent shot at making the U23 National Team, right? When you bring that to the boat, you can be obnoxious, too, and to be honest? He's not that obnoxious."

I'd have taken the time to savor the moment, but I was ramping up on another of Lodestone's cycles, and what I truly wanted to do was sleep for a week or three. Preferably snuggled up to Michael.

But I swear Pendergast was out to get me one morning. "Remy, do you do any yoga? You've got uncommonly good balance in the boat."

"Yes."

I must've looked a bit hesitant because he laughed. "Relax. I've been trying to get through to these lugs the importance of balance and flexibility. We still have that damn shimmy, and it's costing us time. Maybe if you show them, they'll listen."

"Because I'm not already the odd man out?"

"Did you just whine?"

I nodded. "Probably. I'm exhausted."

"I know, and I know Lodestone's keeping a close eye on you. I am too. Your blood tests and the lactic acid profiles look good, for what that's worth." Pendergast looked so hopeful. I knew how much he and Ridgewood wanted this, and I believed them when they told me—as they did from time to time—they wanted it for me and not for what I could do for the program.

"They'd better?" I tried to laugh, but it only sounded strangled.

Pendergast frowned. "Is this too much?"

I thought about it for a while, or what felt like a while but was only a handful of seconds. "It feels like it if I slow down. If I stop during the day, I fall asleep." I held up a hand to forestall him because he'd opened his mouth. "But I went into this knowing what I was getting into—or knowing as much as I could. In terms of my health, I'm fine. I'm merely tired. A lot. But that's what to expect with periodization and why I'm taking a minimum course load and why Lodestone's in charge of almost everything about my life."

Everything but Michael. The weird thing of it was, now that I was completely absorbed in training, the Castelreighs appeared to be loosening up. Of course, that was easy to do when I was never around... Bastards.

"So," Pendergast said, "the yoga?"

I shrugged. "Sure, why not? I don't have the energy to care whether anyone resents me or not. I mean, anyone else besides Peevie Steevie."

"Peevie Steevie?" Pendergast smirked.

"That's what I call Steve—"

"Oh, I know who you're talking about, and I should pretend I never heard a thing. So how do you want to do this?" my coach—or one of them—said.

I thought about it for a while. "Can you have a single waiting at the dock one day after practice? Oars not extended. I promise I'll make it spectacular."

"You're a natural showman, aren't you?" Pendergast grinned. He did that a lot. It was a good quality to possess.

I shook my head. "No, but if I'm going to make a point, I want it to stick, if not actually hurt."

"Remy, do me a favor. Don't ever go into education." Then Pendergast laughed. The thing was, I wasn't sure he was kidding.

"Don't worry, Coach. I don't plan on it."

I'd forgotten about that part of our conversation when, a few days later, I found a single waiting for me after practice, oars in the riggers but not extended. That made for a very tippy boat. Pendergast met my eye, and I nodded.

"Can you hold the bow for me?" I asked the cox'n as I moved the boat around so that only its bow touched the dock.

"Sure." She gave me a funny look. "What're you up to?"

I gestured toward Pendergast with my chin. "Ask him."

"May I have your attention, gentlemen"— Pendergast nodded to the cox'ns, all women on the varsity squad this year, apparently—"and ladies? I've been harping on balance for some time now, not that anyone takes me seriously. No matter what I say, no matter who I move where, and regardless of what drills I put you through, there continues to be an unacceptable degree of lateral motion in the boat. Some of you have even had the nerve to tell me the kind of balance I'm demanding is impossible. It's not."

While the sun shone bright and clear, someone forgot to tell the weather it was February, usually a time of respite and oddly warm temperatures for all that it was winter. I felt the chill coming off the water, or maybe I was cooling after practice. Either way, taking a bath so Pendergast could prove a point didn't figure into my plans that morning.

Before I overthought it, I scampered down the bow deck, quick and agile as a monkey, to crouch in the seat. Admittedly, Pendergast had been thoughtful enough to provide me with an open-water craft, wider and more stable than a racing single.

I awkwardly turned around to face my assembled teammates on the dock, and being very, very careful, I stood up. I worked consciously to stay relaxed.

In every single of whatever size, there was a reinforced place that was safe to step. I had no intention of going through the hull.

Pendergast grinned at me. "Do you see what he did? No oars, no stability, and he made it down the deck. Okay, so the only reason he didn't go through the decking is that he's fast. But he's centered in the boat, and probably in his mind. So, don't tell me it's impossible to achieve that balance in the boat, because it's clearly not. Go ahead and come back, Remy."

I carefully sat back down and extended the oars. "Wait a minute, Coach."

I stood back up and nudged the seat back. I stepped onto that reinforced place, so thoughtfully roughened by the boatwrights to reduce slippage. Then I carefully assumed vrksasana, the tree pose. Sure, I was showing off and I knew it, but if Pendergast really wanted to ram the point about balance home, I could think of few better ways.

"Find a way to make that happen, guys. Remy, may I see you in my office?"

I nodded as I carefully unfolded myself and sat down. No baths, not in the port and not at that time of year. There was no way to pull myself into the dock. "Can I get an assist?"

Grinning openly, the cox'n holding the bow pulled me in. "Too bad you bat for the other team. You're all kinds of flexible."

"Coach is waiting." I winked as I hoisted the boat to my shoulder and picked up my oars. After putting the equipment away, I knocked on Pendergast's door. "You wanted to see me."

"Shut the door and have a seat."

That didn't sound good, but as soon as the door clicked closed, Pendergast started to laugh. "You should've seen their faces, Remy. I know you were concentrating, but I wished I could've filmed them for you."

I sighed internally—if that was actually a thing. I knew I faced accusations of being the coach's pet, even if my teammates had the wrong coach. Not where I could hear them or anything, but I'm sure they existed. Did that make me paranoid? Of course, just because one was paranoid, didn't mean they weren't out to get you...

I shrugged. "If it works, great. If not, it only gives certain people one more thing to resent." I glanced at my watch. "I need to leave for school."

"Go, go." Pendergast waved me away. "I don't even know if this will work. They're not bad rowers...for a college crew, but they can be better than they are. You're going places, Remy, and if they're paying attention, you'll show them the way."

"Thanks, Coach." I showered and dressed quickly. I'd stopped carpooling in February. My schedule was too finely calibrated to depend on anyone else, so at least I didn't have to worry about missing my ride.

But I thought about team dynamics as I drove back to campus, chugging some bland protein concoction Lodestone demanded I drink after practice. I no longer worried about making friends. Who had the time and energy? But if I'd been concerned about such things, my little display had effectively murdered any chances of that.

Oh well, at least Michael knew me and understood my drives and compulsions.

*

Most people looked forward to spring break. Most people weren't me. The week before? The week before hit one of the rests in Lodestone's periodization, and that made me a happy, happy man. Every day after CalPac practice, I returned to my room and crashed. Lodestone had even arranged with Pendergast so that I could miss some practices. One of those mornings I even bailed on class, I was so tired. Brady, through the benign will of some saint or power or bodhisattva, had chosen to attend to his own education, and I had the room all to myself. I pulled my thick, fluffy duvet up over my head and enjoyed the precious luxury of sleep.

Until someone knocked on my door. I ignored this person for everyone's sake. The people on my floor knew my deal and thought it a cool thing, indeed, so when Remy slept, they let me be. This? This constituted cruelty, and whoever set my phone off? This person needed that phone inserted nasally. Sideways.

Then I checked the damn message. Michael. What the actual fuck?

MICHAEL: *Open the door.*

I loved that boy, truly madly deeply, but at that moment all I could think was that he had better be bleeding profusely, and wasn't that why God made ERs?

Throwing back my duvet, my sweet duvet, and glaring balefully out of the one eye I felt like opening, I staggered to the door and threw it open. "What the ever-loving fuck? Why aren't you in school?"

"Why aren't you?"

Damn, he rocked my world, even when mad. Especially when mad? Weirdly, I thought of the scrawny kid he'd been on that bus to San Diego two years ago. Time had been good to him. I melted.

"I'm sleeping. Or trying." I pulled him inside before I went back to bed. He knew the score. He could join me or find his own seat.

Since Michael followed me so closely, I pulled the covers back. He hesitated for a moment and then climbed in next to me. I squirmed around, positioning him until he was the little spoon. Then I slid one arm under the pillow he'd appropriated and wrapped the other around his waist. With my head against his neck, I was in heaven.

"Are you going to stay awake long enough to talk?" He sounded upset, even a little angry.

"Do you feel lucky today?" I mumbled. I tried to wake up, but when I crashed, I crashed hard.

He sighed. "Not today, Rem."

I struggled to form words. It felt better to rest against him and pretend I was still asleep. With a little more drifting, I would be. "Cut me some slack, Michael. This is the first time I've had a chance to sleep—really sleep—in weeks."

Michael inhaled to reply but then didn't. I lost my battle and fell back to sleep. Michael made it so easy.

When I woke up again, Michael was sitting up. My head was in his lap, and he played with my hair. I looked up at him. "Hi."

He looked down at me, his expression softer than when he'd arrived. "Hi, yourself."

"I'm really sorry." I remembered that he'd come here to talk to me and I'd fallen asleep.

"It's all right." He smiled. "I guess I wasn't lucky."

I looked away. "I'm..." There was no point in finishing the sentence. We both knew.

"I know." Michael was quiet for a moment. "That's what I wanted to talk about."

I felt like I was standing in quicksand, like someone had cut off my air. "What do you want to talk about?"

"I never see you." Michael sounded so anguished.

"That's not true. We see each other at practice." I winced. It sounded stupid as I said it.

"Boats passing on opposite sides of the river doesn't count, and you know it." Michael's voice could've cut metal.

I sighed. What could I say? "Michael, you knew what I was getting into. You were right next to me in Lodestone's office when he laid it all out. Did you ever think there might've been a reason you were included?"

I sat up and pulled at Michael until he let me hold him. My man needed comfort, and I was at least a little more alert.

"Hearing it was one thing but living it has been something else." He sounded so sad, so much younger than he was. I tended to forget that for all his balls of brass, Michael was still seventeen, still so young. We both were.

I held him tighter, thinking hard about what to say. Had I been selfish the last couple of months? I'd been following Lodestone's schedule as written, and I knew Michael had a copy of it somewhere, and not only that, I'd e-mailed him a copy.

Was there some way I could carve more time for Michael? With twice-daily practices, school, and homework, I didn't see how. We engaged in an awful lot of parallel play as it was, doing our homework together or otherwise spending time doing our separate things in close proximity, and when it came down to it, the fact that I now shouldered more commitments was not the only reason we saw less of each other. Yep, his psycho parents could always try lengthening his leash.

I sighed, trying to think of a diplomatic way to bring up all of this. I was the adult, and I knew I needed to be strong for him. Yes, I felt nothing but constant exhaustion, but my guy was hurting. While I kept hearing the echoes of my grandfather's words about paying the price for what you wanted, I hated that Michael, rather Michael and I as a set, had to be a casualty of that.

"Michael, I'm not sure how I can exist on less sleep than I already am, but I'll look at what I'm doing every day to see if I can possibly carve out more time. Maybe we can lift together or something?"

He at least appeared to give it some consideration, which encouraged me.

"But I need you to work on your end too." I still held him, so I twisted around so I could see his face.

Michael didn't look happy, but he was far from a stupid man. "My parents?"

"Your parents. A nine p.m. curfew for a high school senior is idiotic, and while the 'my friends all get to stay up later' argument has never worked in the history of ever, maybe if it starts getting in the way of study groups, it'll get their attention."

"I'll see what I can do. I've applied to enough competitive schools that I can't afford to let my grades slip, even this late into the year." Michael sighed. "It sucks being smart."

I looked at him like he was crazy. "No, it really doesn't."

"Yeah, but if you're stupid, you don't know you're stupid." At least Michael was smiling again. "So, what're you going to do with the rest of your day?"

My first thought was *you.* I reached for him. "The question is, what're *you* going to do?"

The more practical thought was *get you back to school so you don't get in trouble.* Grown-up, remember?

I looked at the clock. I bet I could fit him in and still get him back to school before lunch ended.

Chapter Twenty-Two

I couldn't maintain this pace, but what form the fall would take remained to be seen. When it came, it came ugly, because even I had my limits, and I could only trip out on lactic acid for so long before it all came crashing down on me. Rowing at least once a day, weights and erging, weekly testing on said ergs, it was all bound to take its toll. Lodestone did his weekly lactate tests, but I knew it had built up in my muscles. Figuring that out took no special skill, and I could tell because all my major muscle groups—including ones I'd never use for rowing—were mildly fatigued all the time, even during recovery periods. I went back and forth on including things like this in my training journal—on the one hand, it sounded like whining; on the other, this was what it felt like.

While I personally had a difficult time believing I was supposed to feel like this constantly, I had to trust Lodestone. After all, he was the one with the USR coaching certificates and the info pipeline to the University of Washington, one of the major rowing powerhouses in this country. Without faith in Lodestone, I'd have bailed, pure and simple.

One morning after CalPac practice, I trudged up the dock, my mind anywhere but there. Second declension Latin nouns? The Krebs cycle? Then I fell down and broke my crown, as the rhyme went. If only. Instead, I fell to my knees and split the right one wide open. Blood everywhere.

So not suave.

"Whoa, dude, are you all right?"

I forced myself up. Exposing my teammates to poz blood was not an option. Jeez, that stung.

Even Peevie Stevie seemed sympathetic. "I'll get the first aid kit. Someone help him to the locker room."

"There's a spill kit in Coach's office." I sighed. "I'll need that too."

Laurie, bow seat in the A boat, looked at me funny. "What's a spill kit, and why do you need one?"

"Never mind, Remy said he needed it, so he needs it," Jonah called over his shoulder as he helped me to the locker room. Jonah rowed at six, right in front of me. "Can you do what he said without arguing?"

Jeez, here it came. "There's bleach in there. Wear gloves and douse any place my blood spilled with the bleach."

"Some people simply cannot follow directions," Jonah whispered to me.

I snickered.

Jonah sat me on a bench in the locker room and then ran to get the first aid kit. First thing he did? Snapped on the nitrile gloves. Then he unfolded spill pads under my right leg. They looked like puddle pads left over from when someone trained a puppy, but they'd catch blood too.

"Poz?" Jonah said softly.

"How'd you know?"

Jonah laughed. "You're acting like your blood's radioactive. It doesn't take a Rhodes scholar to figure out. Besides, my aunt's a nurse, and she's poz. Needle stick on a medical mission in Africa. She couldn't get the postexposure drugs in time."

"Doctors Without Borders?"

"Baptist missionary."

When I went still, Jonah put his hand on my leg. Above the cut, but still. "Remy, I'm not judging. I've got my faith, but if God handed out diseases as punishments, we'd all be on Obamacare."

"Thanks."

"Thank my aunt. She's a good, godly woman, and if she caught HIV, it couldn't be divine wrath." Jonah didn't say anything for a moment or two as he carefully cleaned up my knee. "It took me time to reconcile it all, but I got there."

"So now what?" I said. The ball was in his court, I supposed. I wasn't sure how to handle really religious people. Would he freak out about the fact that I was gay? Love the sinner, hate the sin? Because that was bullshit, but I'd take it over open warfare in the boathouse.

"Now you hold the edges of the cut together while I apply the butterfly bandages to it." Jonah frowned at the supplies in the kit. "I'm thinking two."

I laughed. "You're kind of awesome."

"I know, and I know that's not what you meant." He elbowed me. "Look, I know my religion hasn't made itself any friends in the gay community, and personally I don't get why Christians have chosen those verses to freak out about over the ones about disobeying your parents or women being virgins on their wedding nights or any number of other things—"

"Like divorce."

Jonah nodded. "Like divorce, except maybe there are so many divorced people that advocating killing them would be socially unacceptable, and same with the nonvirgins, but gays and lesbians? You're what, ten percent of society?"

"At most. I think it's actually less than that." Why did I feel like I was confessing a secret to an enemy spy? Maybe because with Jonah, I felt like I was hearing the first honest talk about this, and besides, he knew I was poz and didn't care. He'd gloved right up and went to work on my cut without flinching.

"Really? That only proves my point. There aren't enough of you to fight back." Jonah shrugged. "Seems kind of cowardly when I say it out loud."

I thought about what he said. "Do you really think that's it?"

Jonah shrugged. "Unless you want to talk about the ick factor."

"Don't take this the wrong way, but I don't think you want to know what I get up to behind closed doors any more than I want to know what you do." I smiled so he didn't think I was being an asshole.

"As it so happens, I'm saving myself for marriage."

While I'd never heard Jonah engage in any locker room talk, all that really meant was that he was a gentleman. I never kissed and told either. He looked so serious and pious when he said it, I knew he had to be kidding. I stared at him for a while to make him squirm.

"I don't see any purity ring."

Jonah burst out laughing. "Damn you and your observational skills. Why do you think no one gets after the virginity thing?"

I leaned over and rolled everything up in the spill pads before depositing the bundle in one of the red biohazard bags I found in the first aid kit. I held the bag open, and Jonah put his gloves in there.

"What do we do with that?" he said, frowning.

"I'll take it to my doctor's office. He'll dispose of it." I stood up. "I think I'd better get out there and see what's going on with the spill on the dock."

Jonah nodded. "That's not a bad idea. I've never seen anyone so dense. What's so hard about 'Dump bleach on the red spots'?"

"I don't know, but I'm about to find out." I sighed. I did that a lot now along with yawning, but then, sleep was but a dream.

"I want to see this," Jonah said with an easy laugh.

"At least HIV is fragile. Can you imagine if it were something like TB that lingered in the air for hours? I bet I still end up scrubbing at it."

"HIV theater?" Jonah suggested.

"Or maybe virus theater?"

Jonah countered with, "Theater of the absurd?"

"What about Grand Guignol? That was sufficiently gruesome."

"No way, dude, that's only if you start slicing people open and transfusing them on stage."

I looked at Jonah. "What?" he said. "I'm a theater minor."

"Are you sure you're straight?"

"Well, there was that one guy back in high school. He gave righteous head."

I elbowed him. "Stop it."

All too predictably I faced a backlash of both HIV-phobia and homophobia, but as this was California Pacific, no one said anything outright, if only to avoid a fast trip to the student judiciary council. No, whispers and hisses never seemed to see the light of day.

Jonah took the bully by the horns one morning before practice. "Would whoever's been sounding the HIV horn kindly shut up? It's no secret Remy's gay, so unless you want to ride him bareback, you're not going to catch HIV. It's also no secret he's got a boyfriend, so even if you do, you're shit out of luck. He's loyal that way, unlike some of you. I hear what you say in the showers, you know."

I giggle-snorted before I could catch myself.

"Something funny, Remy?" Steven said.

I nodded. "Kind of, yeah. This nonsense is a distraction. My viral load is undetectable. You're not going to catch HIV from me."

"We don't want your disease." I didn't hear who muttered it. Maybe Pendergast had, because he was watching all of us.

Jeez, the stupid was burning hot. "Great, let's not shoot up together, then."

Keith, a rower I almost never spoke to, shook his head. "Do you think it's that easy for us to accept?"

"It should be," Jonah said. "This far into the twenty-first century it should be. He's poz. It's not the cheese touch. If he bleeds, he takes precautions. You all saw that. Some of you had a hard time following directions, but you saw how careful he tried to be."

"Aren't you all religious and shit?" This was from Austin, someone I really never got a reading on. He rowed at three. Three was where coaches buried lousy rowers.

Great, it was already out of hand. "No, he believes in God. A little respect, please. We're a crew—or supposed to be. We all have an HIV status, and mine happens to be positive. You can't catch it from toilet seats, using the same drinking fountain, or being in the same boat with me. The virus doesn't survive long in the open air, so pouring bleach on it was more along the lines of virus theater than a medical necessity. I take my medication as directed and take care of myself, so my viral load is zero. To spell that out for the nonreaders among you, that means I'm functionally uninfected, although there is as of yet no cure."

That whole time, Jonah had been shaking his head, and Pendergast looked like he'd been ready to murder someone. "Wonderful, boys. Five and six seats appear to be adults, but the rest of you? The jury's still out. Do you mind if we row boats today? Be on that water in ten minutes or less."

Pendergast stalked off muttering to himself. Steven looked over at me and crossed his eyes. What the hell did that mean? Did Peevie Stevie have a sense of humor? No way.

*

I stopped measuring time like normal people. I followed only Lodestone's training plan and had gone so far as to map all my school dates and deadlines onto that. It made everything easier to tolerate. I needed any advantage I could leverage.

I had endured one of Lodestone's weekly erg tests when I heard something I was fairly sure I wasn't supposed to. For starters, the way I worked off the horror of a six-thousand-meter test on a rowing machine was by rowing it out, a nice long piece afterward, no pressures, no demands, only me and the ergometer and, usually, my iPod. But since I'd spent that test listening to something moderately appalling to help me test well despite the constant fatigue, I wasn't listening to anything. I used the earbuds to block the sounds of the erg—it was noisy—but otherwise it was me and my thoughts.

And then Lodestone pulled Michael into his office. They left the door open. Why shouldn't they? As far as they knew, I was in my own little iPod-generated world, me and Kill the Wendybird.

"So, talk to me, Michael. What's going on?" Lodestone said.

I heard Michael sigh. "It's all so stupid."

"I see. Can you narrow that down?" Lodestone said. "Maybe to Mrs. Zimmer's class?"

"I should've known she'd call you." Michael sounded bitter.

Lodestone sighed. "When you've been five minutes late every day for twenty days in a row on purpose, then yes, she calls me. She knows your parents are...difficult, so she's doing you a favor. Please don't roll your eyes, Michael."

Michael grunted. "Look, I'm already into Brown, so high school is borderline irrelevant at this point. So long as my As don't turn into Fs, I'm golden."

"I don't think it's quite that—" I lost the thread of the conversation at that point, but if I slowed down to hear better, I'd give myself away. Damn.

"—it didn't even make sense. I mean, what, I'm not gay but my fag boyfriend is?" Michael was saying.

"No, I agree, Davis isn't nearly as liberal is it's reputed to be, but I also know Davis High is being very careful about hate speech, particularly in the wake of a certain recent lawsuit. If you report that comment, they'll be all over it."

Michael exhaled noisily. "It's…it's everything, Coach. I'm done with Davis, and we all know it. I'm ready to blow this Popsicle stand and start the next phase of my life, and can I do it already?" His voice had risen steadily until he all but yelled. "I look at each page on the calendar, and it's one goddamn day after another with the same stupid routine that goes nowhere fast, and in the meantime there's Remy, pulling on the erg or rowing in a boat eight hours a day, happier than a pig in shit, and I never ever see him. I can only sit here with a fixed smile on my face and pretend to be the supportive, loving boyfriend for so long, you know."

No one said anything for a while, at least that I could hear. This was a good thing, because my mind spun faster than the flywheel on an erg in a two-thousand-meter test. I knew Michael was restless and yeah, maybe not so happy with my training. I had some idea how unhappy he'd grown, but it sounded like more than that. Of course, Brown was news. Interesting. That wasn't in Boston, the city where we'd planned to go to school, the city where I'd realized I couldn't go and lacked the stones to tell him. Oh what a tangled web and weaving and deception or something. Stupid commonplaces.

Why did my grandparents' words keep coming back to haunt me, over and over and over? Sac up and grow up, Remy. That's not what they'd said, but it's what it had all amounted to. I'd let this go on so long it would blow up in my face when I dealt with it. There would be no other possibility.

"—so no more of this passive-aggressive nonsense, Michael, d'ya hear me? If you have a problem with crew, you talk to me. If you have a problem with Remy and his training, you talk to him, or you ask him to come see me together with you."

"I guess. It's... I know how much he wants this," Michael said.

"Not wants, he needs it."

Michael sighed. "I know he does, which is why I don't want to say anything. Why does everything have to be so difficult?"

"Welcome to the grown-up world you're in such a hurry to join," Lodestone said. I could tell he was trying not to laugh. "You have to consider your partner's needs, maybe even more than your own. But then again, your own needs have to matter too. Short-term sacrifice is one thing—so long as you both know the score—but obliviousness to your own suffering isn't fair either."

"Do I have to grow up?" Crap, Michael was whining. That never boded well for my immediate future.

Lodestone cleared his throat. "There's a lot I could say here, but I'll stick to yes. Now go wait for that boyfriend of yours. He should be done sooner or later."

I pretended to be engrossed in my rowing as Michael emerged from Lodestone's office. When he came over to me, I waited a couple of strokes before I looked up and smiled. "Oh, hey." I stopped and yanked the earbuds out. "What's up?"

I could be an awful little liar.

"Will you be done soon?" Michael seemed so quiet, but duh.

"How about now?"

"You've recovered from whatever it was you were doing?" However resentful he might've felt, Michael at least appeared genuinely concerned that I take care of myself.

I nodded. "I need to stretch, but really, I've had enough of the ergometer for one day. Or a hundred."

As I stretched—more of a short yoga routine—I said, "Let's go back to my parents' place. I'm training like a fiend, but spring break starts Monday, and the dorms are closing."

"Again?" Michael made a face.

I nodded. "Apparently the school saves a ton of money by shutting off the utilities. Since I'm speaking to my parents these days, I'm going home. Besides, Geoff's here, and you haven't seen him and Laurel for a while, have you?"

Michael cocked his head to one side. "Am I allowed over there?"

"Oh yes. I won that round." I grinned viciously. Dumbest thing my parents ever did. Depending how cranky I felt come October, I might even throw a little commemorative fete right before I left for Boston.

"I get the feeling"—a frown marred Michael's handsome face—"you don't lose many."

"It may look that way, but that's because I'm careful with the ones I'm involved in." I stood up and gathered my gear before taking a long, slow drag off my water bottle.

"You didn't used to be. You used to fly off the handle and not back down." Michael smiled faintly, remembering. "Then you'd drop a cluster of R-bombs, and it'd be the zombie apocalypse."

I snorted. "I got lucky, and my opponents were usually lazy or careless. Now? I'm trying to choose more wisely."

"Uh-oh." Michael looked afraid. "Heaven help the rest of us. You being a loose cannon was our only advantage, you know."

I was almost positive he was joking.

Chapter Twenty-Three

Mom and Dad were out doing...I wasn't sure what, but I took the opportunity for what it was and enticed Michael into the shower with me. We both needed to clean up and wash the stink of practice off us, right?

"What are you two doing in there?" Geoff singsonged when he heard us.

"Conserving water!" Michael sang back, since I couldn't. It was rude to speak with your mouth full.

After we dried off and made ourselves comfortable in sweats, I dragged us back up to my bedroom with a tray of food. Geoff and Laurel were in the living room, and this way we stood a chance at privacy—a slim one, but a chance, nonetheless.

"So, what's college like?" Michael said when we were settled on my bed, like old times, almost.

I sighed, for once lately a sigh of relief. "You'll love it."

"I thought so. I've been watching you all year." Michael hooked my foot with his. "I can't wait to get out of here and head east."

And there it was, probably the best opening I'd have. Time to take my lumps.

"I heard your conversation with Lodestone. I've got something I need to say." I closed my eyes to the sadness I felt. When I opened them, I saw Michael staring at me, utterly unsurprised.

"I figured there was something going on."

"What? How?"

Michael caressed my cheek. "Sweetheart, you are one of the most complicated people I know, but in some ways you're also one of the simplest. Things haven't been quite right for a while. Is it you, is it me—"

"Is it history?" we finished together.

"We're both too young for Psychic TV."

Michael tapped me on the nose with his finger. "Remy? You're stalling."

I exhaled noisily. "Give me a moment. This isn't easy." I thought for a bit. "Okay, we've always had the Plan, right? Where we both go to school in Boston?"

"Yes..."

"I can't go to school there, and from the sounds of it, you're not either."

Michael frowned. "No, not exactly, but Brown's not that far away. What do you mean you can't go to school there? Did you not get into Boston University?"

"I didn't apply."

And the silence crashed down around us.

"There's no way I heard you right."

"Apparently you were never going to go to school in Boston either." Why did that feel like a betrayal? I had no right to feel that, but why?

Michael shook his head. "I applied for schools in New England because you were going to go to Boston. I mean, look at a map, Providence isn't that far from Bos—what the hell, Rem? You're not even going to BU. That's a pointless objection. It's nothing but a smoke screen. Your parents even promised you that you could transfer to BU. So, what gives?"

"I toured it before the Head of the Charles last fall. There's no way I can make it work. The crew's top notch, of course, although now I'm training for the U23 team, I don't know about that, but academically I couldn't see myself there. I still can't." I hunched my shoulders, like I could hide in bad posture or something.

"When the hell were you planning on telling me this? When?" Michael looked furious, and I couldn't blame him.

"I don't know. I've been meaning to for a while." I tried not to sound as pathetic and stupid as I felt. "Why can't you go to CalPac?"

"I don't *want* to go to CalPac." Michael looked at me like I was a moron. "I'm sick of this area. You were the one who said he heard everything when Lodestone scragged me for skipping class. You've been so hung up on BU I thought I was safe looking east. Then I was recruited by Yale and Brown, and I'm very attracted by Brown's acceptance and social activism."

I made a face. Great, just what the world needed, another social justice warrior. "What's its crew like?"

Michael groaned. "The men's crew is fine, Rem."

"'Fine'? That's a ringing endorsement." That one slipped out, and as soon as it did, I knew I'd fucked up.

"Not everyone walks around with an oar up his ass, and as I recall, you didn't want to go to CalPac either. Your parents pulled a fast one, and the only reason we all weren't treated to one of your famous hundred-megaton R-bomb clusterfucks is because you were still too sick for an explosion like that. They gave you a contract for BU, but you're the one who's breaking it."

"Sometimes plans change. I didn't expect to like—no, love—California Pacific, and then—"

"That's right, Rem, sometimes plans change. I would like to have been informed when ours did, but apparently I didn't get that courtesy," Michael said, all but spitting in his rage.

Everything Michael said was true. Okay, the R-bomb crack hurt, but Michael had a right to his feelings, and I had no right to blame him for being pissed at me. But when the one thing I thought I could cling to turned and savaged me—with or without justification—I knew why I'd put off telling him. This fucking killed me. He was—had been—my source of support, the one thing in my life I knew I could count on. Yes, I lived for crew. I had to in order to sacrifice everything else for a shot. Without Michael to share it with, it felt hollow.

I wanted to lash out. I wanted to make him feel as bad as I felt right then. Instead...

"Michael, I'm really sorry. All I can do is apologize."

"What if it's not enough? This is my life. Our lives. Don't you think I should've been informed?"

"Yes."

"Would you stop being reasonable about this?" Michael shouted.

Damn, he looked sexy when he was furious. It was totally inappropriate right then, but he really needed to hold me down and punish me.

Reel it in, Remy. I shifted uncomfortably.

Michael glanced down. I pretended not to see it.

"So now what?" Michael pulled his attention back up to my face. At least it was a struggle. Yay for maturity. Damn, it sucked, and not in the fun, tingly way. "Are we still together?"

My eyes pricked, and I shut them against the tears I knew were there. "I want us to be." I opened them and let the tears run down my cheeks. "But I think the ball's in your court."

"So...long distance? How will that work?"

At least he was giving it some thought.

"After this summer, yes. Long distance, I guess." I sniffled. "Lots of phone calls. Visits when we can."

I felt him searching my face. "Is this really what you want, Jeremy?"

"You're what I want, so this?" I took Michael's hand. "This is what it'll take to be with you."

"You've never been an easy person to love, Jeremy, but you've always been worth it." Michael was crying too.

That was it, game over. My own waterworks started in earnest. "You love me?"

"How could you not know this?" Michael glared at me.

"Maybe because you never told me?" Not that I had any kind of ground to stand on. "But I love you too."

"You do?" Michael sounded so small, so lost.

"Oh, Michael." I still held his hand, so I used it to pull him into me. "You have amazed me since the moment we met, but it's taken me until this year to realize how much I love you."

After that, we held each other. I think we'd both said what there was to say, at least for now.

Eventually Michael roused from his near slumber in my arms. "So, this is it."

"Looks like it." I felt incredibly tender toward him.

"Okay, then," he said softly.

I nodded. "Okay."

Michael leaned over and kissed me, but chastely, a quick press of his lips against mine. When he left, he didn't look back.

*

The only time I felt as depressed as I did then was after my HIV diagnosis. Not right after, because my denial knew no bounds, but later, in the hospital after reality and I had gone head-to-head and reality won. But after talking about colleges and plans for the future with Michael... yeah, that. I knew I had to do it, but it had sucked, and far worse than I'd thought it would. What else could I do? Part of me wanted to scream "It's not fair!" but realistically speaking, life wasn't. The fair happened every year at Cal Expo and featured unicorns farting glitter and rainbows. This grown-up stuff I'd discussed with my grandparents operated by different rules: figure out what you want, figure out its price, pay the price. What I'd wanted and needed was to come clean to Michael, and while I'm not sure I could have predicted the exact price, I'd expected him to be angry, and lo and behold...

I knew Geoff and Laurel would see both my side and Michael's. Were I to ask Caden and Lance, both would tell me I was an idiot for bringing it up: Lance, an idiot for waiting this long, and Caden, an idiot for telling Michael in the first place. Caden, at least, had ulterior motives but cheerfully confessed them. I learned early in the academic year never to trust Brady with anything personal. With a start, I realized that other than Lodestone, there was no one else close to me to tell. Had I let no one else get close?

It was a sad panda who climbed into his single the next morning. I rowed my pieces with Lodestone dogging me the entire way, and while I gave it my all, Lodestone didn't look too impressed.

"Way 'nuff." His barely amplified call through the megaphone sounded more like a grunt. He zoomed up close to me, turning his launch perpendicular to my shell and drifting in like dandelion fluff at the last moment so I could catch him. He reached out and grabbed the earlobe nearest to him and then stuck it. Acting quickly, he captured the welling blood. He had to in order for the lactate tests to mean anything. Highly trained fools like me processed lactic acid so fast that if he waited until we finished everything and put the equipment away, I'd have worked it all out.

"What's with you? You were anywhere but in the boat."

I put my head on my knees. "I don't know how much longer I can keep this up."

"Take it in, Remy. Put everything away, and I'll see you in my office."

I all but fell into one of the chairs in front of Lodestone's desk maybe twenty minutes later. Wordlessly, Lodestone handed me a mug of coffee and gave me a few minutes to drink it.

"Okay, Remy, talk to me. What's going on?"

I snorted. "Well, other than literally falling to my knees with exhaustion after a CalPac practice and splitting one of them open—single-handedly setting off rounds of gay and HIV panic in the process, I might add—I think Michael and I broke up."

"Okay, you need to back that up and go into a lot more detail on both, because that made no sense at all."

I'll give Lodestone this much credit... He looked horrified, and as I spoke, he shook his head.

"Remy, you lovable idiot! That training plan was always provisional. You were supposed to check in with me after every cycle to let me know how you were feeling physically and emotionally."

I looked at him dully. "You never told me that."

"I expected you to read the information I gave you. There was a lot more on that training plan than brightly colored boxes." He looked at me, his jaw hanging open. "You haven't read that training plan. It's March, and you haven't read the training plan. Jesus fuckcakes, Remy. You're not eating enough, you're still working out like you were in January, you're not even resting at the right times."

Lodestone looked stunned, and if I weren't a shuffling zombie whose grades had dropped an entire letter or in some cases two, I'd marvel that I'd finally done it to him. "I can't believe this. You didn't read the training plan. I've gotta call Pendergast and Ridgewood. Go home, Remy. I don't want to see you for a few days. I'll call you. Expect e-mails with a revised training plan. Do nothing but scull lightly and never for longer than forty-five minutes. No weights and no ergs."

I stood up as I made ready to go.

"Lodestone...I'm sorry."

He looked stricken. "Oh, Remy." He stood up and engulfed me in a hug. "Remy, kiddo. No. *I'm* sorry. You...you're just oblivious. Like always."

I rested my head on his shoulder. I noted absently that my head reached farther up his kind-of-massive chest than the last time we had to do this, after Lodestone had to hit my reset button the last time, when Cisco died during my first trip to the Youth Nationals. Lodestone was the only coach I'd walk through fire for, and we both knew it. Apparently, I already had. Huh. I felt safe there in his arms, like he'd protect me. It was absolutely nonsexual even though he was so hot he needed Nomex underwear. No, it was more paternal, because we were closer in many ways than I'd ever be with my own father. Somehow, he knew, and he rocked me for a moment. Or maybe he'd always known, which was why we'd always been close.

"Go get some sleep," he said softly. "And call Dr. Kravitz. I want to make sure this hasn't done anything to your health. It was never supposed to be like this, and a blood test will put my mind at ease on that score, at least."

*

The new training plan arrived within a day, and with it a much-improved outlook on almost everything. Everything, that was, but my relationship with Michael. I put a great deal into my training log, but I left the relationship issues out. Grandma and Grandpa paid for a lot, but that didn't include a total lack of privacy.

So, for all our pretty talk, as March turned into April, Michael and I barely spoke. I escaped into my usual limbo of compartmentalization, only not quite. Memories of Michael pierced that featureless gray and prevented me from truly tuning out and focusing on nothing but training and school, and this made me epically cranky. Nothing worked right, not in the boats, not in the lab, and not in the classroom. Brady resumed his goading, even bringing his football buddies in on it, or trying.

Hard luck for my roommate, the first time some of Brady's friends from the football team—he'd actually succeeded in making good on that threat—tried to hassle me was also the last time. Why he and they'd waited until the middle of the most challenging training of my life was anyone's guess, or maybe that's why Brady had held off until then. Most crimes are crimes of opportunity, after all, so why not wait to strike until I appeared defenseless? Brady knew the toll the stress had exacted, and since my darling roommate hadn't seen Michael around, I can only assume he figured the worst had happened and made a lucky guess.

I suppose I was relatively slender for my size. It's not that Lodestone's training plan made me bulk up: quite the opposite, in fact. I'd actually lost body fat, and extra muscle was nothing but more weight to haul down a race-course. Actually, given my screw-up with the training plan, I'd probably lost muscle mass, too, and with my luck, the lean muscle I needed for crew. So, Brady's football jocks? I must've looked like easy pickings. Oh well, I'd held them off in high school; I knew I could deal with them in college.

"Look into these cold, dead eyes. Do I look like I care?" I stared until one or two started squirming. "I'm overtrained, my grades are dropping like a rock, and my boyfriend's not speaking to me. What do you think you can possibly say or do that will bother me? And before any of you says 'fag,' remember that this is CalPac, and I'll have your asses in front of student judicial before the *g* comes out."

"Whoa, dude. No need to get personal," one of them said.

"Then think before you decide to be Brady's bully boy. Ooh, it's alliterative. Can you spell 'alliterative'?" Jeez, I was being a dick, but with the bit between my teeth, there was no help for it. Rather, I didn't feel like stopping.

"Probably not. We're here to play football, and it's a safe school."

I frowned. "Way to take the wind out of my sails."

"I know." Grinning, the player who spoke up said, "Right bastard, aren't I?"

"Now you sound like a rugby player." Seriously, what was going on here?

He shrugged. "It's something to do in the off-season."

"Don't make friends with him, Scott," Brady said from where he sat on his bed, "he bites."

Scott looked me up and down. "Maybe I like that. So, if this boyfriend of yours makes the radio silence permanent, look me up."

"Dude! What did I just say?" Brady threw down the book he'd been pretending to read.

Scott started pushing his fellow players out of the room. "Like you ever had a chance, Brady."

I frowned. This wasn't suave. I didn't want this Scott person. I wanted Michael. "You'll have to get in line. There seems to be a rower at UC Davis who's interested, but I won't give him the time of day either."

"Wait, what?" Scott demanded, but it was too late. I shut the door after them all.

I closed my eyes and shook my head to clear the hooey, but it didn't seem to work. When I opened my eyes, Brady still sat on his bed, glaring at me as fiercely as ever, and Michael still refused to return my calls.

Chapter Twenty-Four

It all came tumbling out in San Diego at the Crew Classic. The big spring regatta put me and Michael in close quarters, like rats in a coffee can, and the fact that we shared a coach certainly didn't help matters. No, this wouldn't be at all awkward, particularly since I refused to leave San Diego without resolving this. The thing that only Lodestone understood about me and the Crew Classic was that it didn't matter. Sure, CalPac thought it was a huge deal, and yes, I'd pull on that oar for them, but for my training goals? We were two-thirds of the way through Lodestone's training plan, two-thirds of the way to the U23 selection camp. This? This was a rest week in one of the periodization cycles. Lodestone planned it that way so he could devote his energy to Cap City's junior crew and its gentlemen's crew, as the varsity boys called themselves.

Me, I had plenty of time and energy to devote to righting things with Michael. I'd flown down on Wednesday evening, two days before the regatta, for no reason other than to distract Geoff and maybe to bust his roommate's chops. I mean, if the shy and skittish little forest creature wasn't going to come out, I might as well be über-gay in front of him. That I wore that beat-up "I'm Not Gay But $20 is $20" T-shirt when I met him on Thursday was entirely coincidental. I'd once used it to irritate Michael, so it should work on Geoff's roommate, Craig, every bit as well.

"You're terrible." Laurel struggled not to burst out laughing when she met me, Geoff, and Craig after whatever lecture she had. We picked up her roommate, Olive, and took off for a campus restaurant they swore campus food services hadn't gotten its hooks into.

Craig and his poor wounded sentiments had taken one look at me and lost the power of speech. He turned bright red and stayed that way for the rest of lunch my first day in La Jolla. He eventually responded to my attempts to draw him out, but usually in short sentences. I could only blame myself.

Olive nodded slowly. "So, you're Remy. I've heard about you."

"And you're Olive. I love that you both have botanical names. Someone in the housing office has a sense of humor."

"Thank you, Captain Obvious."

"You're welcome, Blunder Woman."

I liked her instantly. I could tell she'd give as good as she got and wouldn't put up with my crap, which in all honesty constituted nothing more than boundary pushing.

Olive reached out, and I bent my arm so she could take it. "I'm keeping him."

"Okay, am I the only one who's suddenly nervous?" Geoff said.

"No," Laurel and Craig said together.

Olive and I grinned like we'd known each other for years. Oh, we would have so much fun together, I could already tell, and based on her maniacal grin, she thought so too.

"Let's get them fed," Geoff said. "Maybe if they're in a food coma, the rest of us will stand a fighting chance."

After we'd eaten, Craig excused himself to use the bathroom, and I followed him. Yes, that's the sort of thing that gives a boy a bad reputation, but since mine seemed to be rock bottom these days, what did it matter?

"Wait...what're you doing here?" Craig asked when he noticed me at the urinal next to him.

"It's a bathroom, doll face. I should hope I don't need to explain its function to you, a college student."

Someone in one of the stalls snickered. Maybe I should've been quieter.

"Asshole!" Craig hissed.

Okay, so this was turning out not to be one of my better ideas. "If you wanted to tap it, all you had to do was ask. I shaved and everything."

More laughter.

I was done, but I guess I was making Craig pee shy or something. He looked tormented.

"Why're you doing this to me?" He looked so sad. I felt terrible, but how much worse was it to live in a prison of your own devising? I still remembered.

I leaned over and whispered in his car, "Because it's okay, it really is. No one will judge you, least of all anyone sitting at that table out there. Least of all me. Talk to Geoff, okay? Talk to someone."

Then I gently wiped a tear away with my thumb because Craig started to cry.

I got out of there as quickly as I could. Craig took a few minutes to rejoin us, and I covered for him. It was the least I could do. I'd originally planned to bunk with Geoff, but after that I figured a hotel would be a better bet. I'd made a grown man cry—not one of my prouder moments—and I owed him some space.

The five of us spent another hour or so together, but the four of them had classes at various points throughout the afternoon, and I didn't need them to entertain me. We made plans to meet for dinner later, and then I shifted for myself. I knew my way around the city and I'd rented a car, and if nothing else, the UCSD campus was easily one of the most beautiful in the ten-campus system. The Geisel Library—as in, Dr. Seuss—appeared to defy gravity, and I could've looked at it for hours. I eventually ended up at the Fashion Valley Mall, because why not? San Diego's climate was warmer than Sacramento's, and I'd once scored a stadium-length wool coat in charcoal gray for a song, because who needed that in San Diego? This time I found a pair of leather pants at the Nordstrom Rack. They fitted my ass like a glove too.

Friday morning was mine. I studied and read, since I couldn't afford to let my grades slide any more. Sure, crew was the reason, but I was still on a scholarship, and keeping my grades up was imperative. Besides, the Geisel Library was every bit as fun inside as outside. Geoff, Laurel, and Olive knew I'd be busy starting in the afternoon but also knew I'd welcome them with open—if perhaps sweaty—arms all weekend. I'd told Craig he could come by any time he wanted, but I knew the score. I'd likely never see him again and had only myself to blame. Still, I hoped he would at least consider my words. He'd ultimately be happier if he did.

After lunch it was regatta ritual time. It was also time to hunt my alleged boyfriend down. I'd allowed this foolishness to go on long enough. I wanted to rant and scream and call him names, maybe kick a little dust in his face. After all, wasn't that what he'd been doing to me? It certainly appeared one of us was going to have to be the bigger man, however.

I'd already checked out of my hotel—Geoff had been disappointed I hadn't stayed with him, but once I'd explained it, he'd understood—so I took my team duffel bag and changed at the race venue. CalPac unisuit under baggy shorts and one of my inevitably tight T-shirts, and off I went. I had a race-course to walk.

But first...

I stopped by the Cap City encampment. It wouldn't hurt them to make the walk. "Any of you guys want to walk the course with me?"

Instead of the nods of recognition that usually greeted me—even the ones I'd never rowed with had gotten to know me while I'd trained with Lodestone—dead silence greeted me. They looked at me like I was some kind of alien invader or enemy to be killed, like an escapee from the latest first-person-shooter game.

Lodestone looked up from the boat he'd been tinkering with. He met my eye and frowned. I shrugged imperceptibly.

"We'll do it later," someone—I didn't see who—said.

So that's how it would be. "Michael, a word, please?"

"Can't it wait?"

Whoa. Petulance and hostility. My favorite flavors.

"No." Glaciers were warmer than my tone, and the temperatures on Mission Bay dropped a good thirty degrees. If he wanted to treat me like that, he could, but he would reap what he sowed.

Michael rolled his eyes. Huh. I wonder where he learned that...

He stomped up to me as I walked a little way away. "What?"

"Can we please not do this this weekend? You haven't responded to anything I've done to try to contact you, and—"

"Figure it out, Jeremy."

That hurt. "The last time we spoke, we were still boyfriends, and nothing you've *said* has changed that." Of course, he apparently wasn't speaking to me... "We're leading parallel lives. We do the same sport at the same boathouse with the same coach, we're at the same race, but we're ignoring each other, and it's stupid. Everyone knows what's going on, so how about you cut the crap, act like a grown-up, and treat me with the respect you'd treat a total stranger, m'kay?"

I admit I might've spoken a little louder than conversational volume, but maybe other people needed to hear that.

Without waiting for his answer, I walked off. I pretended not to hear the "Whoa! A little aloe for that burn?"

I cranked *Parallel Lines*, and off I went for my walk of the venue. The cover art for *Parallel Lines* was piano keys, but puh-leez. I'd bet money I'd once seen a cover featuring two lines of coke on a mirror. Given what went down during the 1970s, that was probably more appropriate. But... Debbie Harry. All gay men have their divas. Blondie's mine. Cher? Meh. Madonna? Whatevs. Give me Blondie or give me death. I don't care if she's old enough to be my grandmother. We don't go there.

The Crew Classic was rowed down two thousand of the finest meters the back end of Mission Bay offered. The back end provided the most sheltered waters, although some years *sheltered* was a relative term. I'd seen rainy and windy and sunny and hot, with everything in between. Spectators watched along Crown Point Shores, and if they were loaded, they did so from the tents, otherwise they sat on the grass with binoculars or squinted at the jumbotrons. That's where I found the vendors, and as per Remy Babcock tradition, I bought T-shirts for everyone who mattered. This year I bought one for Craig as an apology, and for my grandparents, since they footed all kinds of bills.

Let the children stare. We were at a regatta, and they'd all seen me row my single. They could all kiss my fine uni-clad ass as I walked the racecourse. When I reached the end of the sidewalk, I stopped. Quite a bit of the race-course remained, but I had no way to walk to it, so I made do with looking at it and remembering the conditions all the different times I'd rowed on Mission Bay. I spotted SeaWorld off in the distance. Funny. When my boat sat at the starting line, SeaWorld would be *right there*. I'd probably always have a soft spot for the park for that reason alone. I found an out-of-the-way spot to sit down and composed an admittedly lengthy text to Geoff and Laurel to warn them about what just transpired with Michael. Sure, they knew what had happened between the two of us, and more important, what hadn't happened since, but there was no point in letting them stumble into this weekend blind, not when they were expecting to host both of us.

> ME: *Sorry, lovelies. It's already shaping up 2B a nightmare, and I've done my best.*

> LAUREL: *Thanks for the heads-up. We'll handle it as it comes. Maybe if we give U each someone 2 vent 2, you'll move past this.*

I didn't feel that optimistic.

ME: *Maybe. Let me know when U can make it down from La Jolla and rescue me from team dinners.*

LAUREL: *We're bringing Olive.*

ME: *You'd better ;-) Craig 2 if he's not afraid of me after lunch.*

LAUREL: *Didn't G tell U? Craig came out yesterday. So B nice.*

My dear brother had clocked his roommate within five minutes of meeting him last fall. Then he'd spent most of the school year trying to coax the shy and timid Craig out of the closet. I was sure the aggressively heterosexual Geoff singing the virtues of out, loud, and proud confused Craig no end. But apparently perseverance paid off. Or me being a jerk in the bathroom had.

ME: *I'm always nice.*

LAUREL: *Nice looking, maybe.*

ME: *I'll text U as soon as I have more info about the team circle jerk.*

Then I reported to the CalPac base of operations. I had a long afternoon of practice rows.

*

I hated team dinners. Always had. The fact that I now rowed for a collegiate crew changed nothing. Colossal wastes of time, team dinners. Every special snowflake wanted to be heard, yet somehow, we always ended up eating spaghetti or pizza, two of my least favorite foods. All carbs did for me was make me hungry again in two hours. Can we say "insulin spike"?

By this time, the CalPac teams had moved into the cluster of rented houses spread out along Grand Ave near Mission Beach. Awesome sauce.

As I made ready to leave, Pendergast scragged me. "Wait, Remy, where're you going? You'll miss the team dinner."

"My twin brother goes to UCSD, Coach. That's why I flew down early. We hardly ever see each other anymore."

"Hold on, there's more than one of you? Why didn't you warn us?" Steve crossed his eyes and stuck out his tongue. Was that his signature move? Now that he'd removed the board from his ass, he was turning out to be an okay guy.

"Introduce me tomorrow then." Pendergast sighed and waved me away.

"I will, I promise. You'll like him. We're nothing alike," I said as much to Steve as my second coach.

Pendergast laughed before he could stop himself. "You're terrible."

"Geoff's not, and his girlfriend is the nicest, kindest, sweetest person you'll ever meet...as long as you're not competing for a space in med school with her." I liked Laurel. I knew her, but I liked her.

"Tomorrow at the venue, and even if you eat better than we do, you still owe me a double run."

I smiled. "Does Lodestone know?"

Pendergast nodded. "I cleared it with your daddy."

I couldn't get out of there fast enough. Too bad the neighborhood was so dodgy, so different from where I'd stayed in high school with the Cap City junior crew. In high school, the crew stayed in some of the nicer areas around Mission Bay—mansions, once even in Crown Point Shores above the race venue. Literally million-dollar views. In college? Mission Beach. Not too terribly far from the bay, but jeez, an entirely different world. Bar fights at 3:00 a.m. and tattoo parlors as far as the eye could see.

Next year? I was so staying up in La Jolla with my brother, whether I'd terrified his roommate or not. Maybe he and Laurel would shack up by then. That was something to look forward to, I supposed.

The CalPac team was still up when I got back.

Jonah looked up from his book. "How was dinner?"

"Do you mean how was the restaurant, or how're my brother, his girlfriend, and their roommates?"

"The latter," Jonah said.

I flopped down next to him on a ratty-looking sofa. "I apparently committed the grave sin of being overwhelmingly attractive in front of my brother's babygay roommate."

"What," Steve said, "is a babygay?"

"My brother finally talked him out of the closet, so...babygay. Geoff's been trying all year, then apparently, I show up and swamp this Craig creature with my studliness or tight clothing. Or something. I stopped paying attention to complaints about my wardrobe years ago. You know how it is."

Pendergast looked up from the papers he'd been focusing on. "Jeans that're too tight through the quads? Regatta T-shirts that don't go down far because you're too tall and don't fit because your shoulders are too broad? We've all been there. You could always try buying clothes that fit. That's what my wife tells me, at any rate."

"Why? I'm eighteen and have no idea what I want to do or be when I grow up." Seriously, where'd he get this stuff? "Okay, maybe I'll go into nursing, so...scrubs. Problem solved."

Jonah shook his head. "He's got you, Coach. Admit it."

"What if you want an office job?" Pendergast wasn't giving up. I could see that.

My phone buzzed, and I pulled it out. Geoff. "Trust fund."

I swore I heard Steve mutter "Let it go" as I typed out a message. I started humming the song from *Frozen*.

GEOFF: *Did you have 2 dress like a go-go boy?*

ME: *What're U vaporing on about now?*

GEOFF: *How U dressed. How U always dress.*

ME: *At least I didn't wear the leather pants.*

...

ME: *That's what I always wear, U know that. My clothes have always fitted like that :-(Michael liked them.*

GEOFF: **snort* Craig did 2. I thought he was going 2 cream his jeans right there at the table.*

Looked like Geoff added someone new to our group texts.

ME: *My entire team backs me re clothes btw.*

GEOFF: *Biased sample.*

ME: *Tell Craig not 2 touch himself when he thinks about me.*

GEOFF: *Don't be gross.*

ME: *But you know he's going 2.*

GEOFF: *I *know* damn U. Now I have 2 bleach my brain. I hate U.*

Then Jonah grabbed my phone.

"Hey! I was using that."

"Hay is for horses. What do you eat?" he said.

I blinked, nonplussed. "That is possibly the dumbest thing I've ever heard."

"Geoff's your brother?" Jonah ignored my verbal jab as he scrolled through the conversation.

"Oh jeez, now I have to bleach my brain too." Jonah handed my phone back.

I shook my head at his foolishness. "No one made you read my messages. Now that I think about it, for someone who's a devout Christian, you probably shouldn't be swearing 'Jeez.'"

"Now what're you going on about?" Jonah said.

"Don't you imagine it's a shortening of Jesus?" I shot him a bland look. "I mean, I haven't checked the OED or one of those *Why Do We Say It?* books, but it only stands to reason."

"Wow, look at the time." Pendergast checked a watch that wasn't there. He clapped his hands. "Off to bed, everyone! We start early."

Steve chuckled. "Coward."

Chapter Twenty-Five

Saturday morning dawned cool and still. A marine layer wrapped the sky and the city in a thin fog, but most of us racing knew it would burn off by midmorning, and we'd have a glorious day of rowing. The weather app on my phone held potentially dire things for later, however, and I tried not to take it as a portent. Relationship troubles, newly out gay man, who I hoped was more careful than I was—what else could go wrong?

I tried to put it out of my mind. I knew Geoff and my San Diego friends were somewhere around the venue before they'd texted me. I'd already told them not to buy T-shirts or anything because reasons. Geoff knew what that meant.

The regatta organizers liked to group schools and clubs geographically, so CalPac's boats were close to UC Davis's and Cap City's. Because we didn't see enough of each other on the water and in the parking lot? Oh well. The thing I hated about this was that I was preternaturally aware of two men I needed not to be aware of, Michael and that Randy dude. Michael had well and truly etched himself into my mind, and even if we were over, it would take a while to root him out, but Randy? He baffled me. I made jokes about people being into me because I otherwise had no idea how to deal with it. I was just Remy Babcock, rower and misanthrope, and not all that lovable when it came down to it. These people... *They* needed to have their heads examined. *I* needed to start carrying my therapist's cards to hand out.

I'd recently come back from my first run of the morning and sat on the ground to stretch. Pendergast wanted two runs, but he never specified when he wanted them. One run to cool down after the first heat for one of the invitational cups, plus fours races, with stretches after. I'd missed many of the CalPac women's heats by virtue of being on the water myself, and vice versa. We all knew the deal. At least we could see the novices row. The finals for the invitational cups would be held tomorrow afternoon, probably in time for the predicted rain. Yay.

Another run later in the day would satisfy Pendergast. Actually, I think he only wanted to know I took him and CalPac as seriously as I took Lodestone's training. Speaking of Lodestone, ordinarily I'd have spent the afternoon cheering on a certain high school crew, but under the circumstances, I'd spend it with the coach, instead.

So, there I sat underneath CalPac boats to stay out of the sun, and whose voice should I hear but my brother's. And Michael's.

"Hi, Geoff." Michael sounded wary.

"I'm still your friend, too, Michael, or I'd like to be." Geoff sounded sad.

"I...I wasn't sure whose side you were on."

Geoff sighed. "Is it already down to sides?"

"I don't know," Michael said. "I didn't think so, but then Remy called me out in front of my team."

"Did he? Or did Remy ask to talk to you?" I loved my brother, oh yes, I did.

"He told you."

"Yeah, he did. He's not a bad guy, Michael, and I don't think he'd try to humiliate you on purpose." Geoff paused. "Do you want to talk to me? Because I'm not on one side or the other. It makes me sad that you see sides. I don't think he does."

"Are you going to run right to him?" Michael sounded bitter.

"Believe it or not, Michael, as much as I love my brother and hate seeing him hurt, I've been your friend as long as he has."

Michael didn't say anything for a few ticks, and then laughed. "You know, I'd almost forgotten that I'd met you both at the same time."

"It's still true though."

"I guess it is," Michael said.

"So, talk to me. What's going on? When you left our house, you left as Rem's friend and boyfriend. You don't seem like you can stand the sight of him right now."

Michael's turn to sigh. "I...I feel smothered by my relationship with Rem all of a sudden. I'm, like, graduating from high school in two months, and I'm tied to someone I never see."

"His training?"

"His training," Michael all but growled.

"Wait, Rem said you were there when Coach Lodestone explained it all." Geoff sounded puzzled. "It's not like you could say you were surprised."

"There's knowing and there's living, I guess. I want a boyfriend who's committed to me, not a sport." Michael didn't sound as angry anymore, but damn. He knew all of this when we started dating. Hell, we started dating because of rowing. What did he expect?

"When it comes down to it, he and I want different things. He's a rowing phenomenon, and that's amazing and wonderful and he should go for it, but I'm just an ordinary mortal," Michael continued. "I row well...for a high school and eventually collegiate rower. I know the meaning of balance. Your brother doesn't."

Geoff snorted. "You've got that right."

"You don't know the half of it, Geoff, you really don't. He's incredibly dependent on me, and he's like an addict where rowing's concerned. Seriously, keep an eye on him. He should never drink, and if he *ever* starts using drugs, book the room in rehab, because he'll crash if he doesn't kill himself."

"That's kind of harsh, don't you think? What you see as the possibility for addiction, his coaches see as dedication and determination."

You tell him, Geoff.

"The line is very, very thin," Michael said. "He seriously scares me sometimes. You don't get to be as good at something as he is without being touched by the gods, Geoff. Or crazy."

"He lives life pared down to his essence. I wonder if that means the rest of us have to pick up the slack for certain things." Geoff paused. "I've had some time to think about this. I wonder if what my parents saw as dependence on you was more like you taking over for him, like maybe he depended on you for certain things so he could reach that much further in rowing."

"Okay, maybe. Don't get me wrong, I dug that dependence at first. Rem's an amazing guy, and if he was that into me, maybe I was too. Reflected glory, you know? In some ways, Rem's a titanic figure, but in a lot of ways, he's really not. That I could be strong for him meant a lot to me." Then Michael broke off. He sounded like he was choking up a little. Ouch. "But you don't know what it's like having the responsibility for someone's happiness, shit, for his life, heaped on your shoulders when you were as young as I was. You don't.

"My parents are psycho, Geoff, but that doesn't mean they're always wrong. In some ways, being with Rem—as awesome as he is—robbed me of experiences this last year or so. Robbed me of being a kid."

Geoff didn't say anything right away. Then, "I think you're being overly dramatic. You were in high school, not elementary school. Yes, him being poz certainly taught you and me things we never wanted to know, but robbed you of being a kid? Come off it."

"Remy taught me things about myself. He taught me to be strong. He taught me to be toppy and dominant—"

"Overshare!"

"Like you didn't know that about him."

"Yeah, okay, I have to give you that one," Geoff said.

Michael coughed. "I love your brother, and I think I always will, but I'm not even eighteen. It's ironic, but because of our experiences, there are more out guys at Davis High. I'm young. I'd be lying if I said I didn't want to play with some of them. They've made it known they want to play with me."

"Michael, you haven't—" Geoff sounded pissed.

"Of course not. But I don't see me and Rem together through the summer either." Michael paused. "Geoff, I'm seriously conflicted, and that makes me scared and angry, and—"

"Taking it out on your boyfriend?"

I'd heard enough. Whatever else Michael might've had to say to Geoff, I couldn't listen anymore. I fell backward, away from the Cap City boats, closing my eyes and wishing the world away. My heart shattered in my chest, and with every breath, the shards cut me more.

I grabbed my duffel bag and executed an awkward half roll, half tumble underneath the boat that had sheltered me and then skulked between boats. I hadn't gone very far before I ran into someone. Literally.

I looked up into the palest blue eyes I'd ever seen. I knew the owner of those eyes. Whatshisname. Randy. The Davis rower.

He grinned down at me. "So, you're a subby bottom?"

I groaned. "Lord, is there any way this whole race didn't hear that?"

"That was your boyfriend, wasn't it?" he said softly.

I nodded. I didn't trust myself to speak right then. This whole scene was the opposite of suave.

"Who was the other guy?"

"My brother."

"Oh shit."

"Yeah, kind of."

"You think he was hitting on your brother?"

"No. I'm sure of that much. My brother's straight as an arrow, and Michael knows it."

"Next on *The Jerry Springer Show*." Randy extended a hand and pulled me up. "I'm getting you out of here, and before you can say anything, we have the same race schedule. I checked."

"You're thorough." I thought about it. "Or creepy."

Randy flashed a big surfer's grin. "Why not both?"

"You said something about getting me out of here?" Because that sounded better by the second. While I'd exaggerated when I'd said the regatta had heard my humiliation, in a way it felt like it. If nothing else, the venue itself had. I needed to be anywhere but there.

"Yeah. Anyone you should tell?"

"Both coaches, I guess. If I make them look for me, either could make me regret it." I fired off a couple of vague texts. As an afterthought, one to Steve, as well, since he was team captain.

"Where are we going?" I said, sighing.

"Wherever's in walking distance. I think there's a nice café about six blocks up that way." He pointed away from the race venue.

Funny thing about rich neighborhoods. They don't like businesses bringing down the tone of the place, so for all the million-dollar mansions in Crown Point Shores? There's nowhere to eat.

Now I felt stupid. "I...um. I thought you had a car or something."

The big guy—not as bulky as Michael and nowhere near as big as Lodestone, but more massive than me—started laughing. I mean, really laughing. Like, holding his sides laughing.

"Oh, Remy. You're the best. Let me explain one of the differences between UCD and CalPac, okay? We're a state school. Most of us aren't nearly as rich as you guys. I'm dirt poor. Go easy on me."

Okay, I'd only thought I'd wanted to die and crawl under the ground. Now I truly had to. "Could you shoot me? This whole day needs to go away."

Randy hadn't earned the full story, and if I kept making these assumptions, he never would, apparently, because how can you be friends with someone when he acts like a rich idiot? I'm not a rich idiot, or at least not rich, even if I have loaded relatives who'll set me up when they die.

"I'm really sorry, but for starters? I'm at CalPac on a full scholarship, so be sure to throw that into your calculations, okay?" I didn't plan to tell him my parents probably could've swung it even if I'd only earned a partial scholarship. "How else do you think they could pay for two kids in college at the same time?"

Randy winced. "Ouch, a direct hit. But damn, a rowing scholarship to CalPac? How good are you?"

"Can we not talk about that right now, since that appears to be one of Michael's many grievances? Maybe later." I sighed. "And I do have a rental car. Let's go."

"Wasn't I supposed to rescue you?" Randy bumped my shoulder. Last fall at the Charles that would've scared me, but now it didn't.

"Let's not quibble. You're successfully distracting me, and right now that means a lot."

It occurred to me that I could've called or texted or whatever Laurel—this seemed a bit much to dump on Olive or Craig—but Randy was right here, and he'd offered. Besides, he'd heard it all. No further explanations needed.

When Randy saw the rental, he fake coughed into his hand. It might've sounded like "private school rich kid," but then again, maybe he only had a racking cough like a barking seal. Just in case, I pounded on his back. No one was going to choke on my watch.

When he glared at me, I looked back in wide-eyed innocence. "Easy there, big guy. I was afraid you were choking on phlegm or something. Are you okay?"

"Well played, sir. Well played." Randy winked at me.

"I'm going to violate my training diet. Wanna help?" I had a thing for Starbucks, and a Frappuccino wouldn't kill me.

Randy looked at me askance. How quickly they learned. "What would this entail, exactly?"

"A chemical shitstorm in a twenty-ounce cup." That was what Brad St. Charles called them, and after I'd looked up the ingredients online, I knew how right he was.

"I bet you think that counts as actual trouble, don't you?" Randy shook his head slowly. "So sad."

After that I certainly wasn't going to tell him my phone had an app on it that located any Starbucks within a ten-mile radius. Let him marvel at my amazing homing skills.

"Do you trust me?" I asked when we arrived at a Starbucks nowhere near the race venue. Fortunately, San Diego was a compact city, so driving us north a few minutes to the gayborhood in Hillcrest was an easy thing.

"Do I have a choice?" Randy smiled when he said it.

I sent him to find a table while I ordered us two of the biggest, stickiest drinks they made.

"Thanks for rescuing me." I set down two large doses of sugar, dairy fat, and caffeine.

Randy glanced up at me, one of the gentlest looks I'd seen in a long time. "You clearly needed it."

He extended his hand. "Allow me to formally introduce myself, since that time in Boston barely counted. Josef Randolf Deburgh, at your service. Everyone calls me Randy."

"Jeremy Babcock, but everyone calls me Remy." I shook Randy's hand. Given the vibes coming off him, I was definitely not at his service.

Randy stared at my throat. "So, tell me about that collar and cross."

"This? Michael gave me the collar, and given what you overheard earlier, it means about what you'd think. But the cross? It's not a cross, it's a poz sign." At Randy's blank look, I said, "I'm HIV-positive."

"Oh. How'd that happen? You're so young."

I cocked one eyebrow. "How'd it happen? The usual way. Shall I draw you pictures? Maybe interpretive dance? Or a puppet show?"

Randy blushed very prettily. "I...um. There's no saving this, is there?"

"It's not like this is a date, so no hard feelings." Did he look disappointed? Too bad. He heard it all, and at no point did Michael—or I—say anything about a breakup. Life support, maybe, but we weren't dead yet.

"You know," Randy said, "you're one of the least approachable people I've met."

I laughed. "Me? I'm harmless."

"Dude, for a moment there, I thought you said you were harmless."

"Treat me as you would any highly venomous creature." Then I had an idea. "Do you mind if I bury my face in electronics? I'll only be a moment."

"Be my guest."

I felt Randy watching me as I pulled a MacBook Air out of my team duffel. I waited for it to boot, and then waited for the Wi-Fi to realize that Starbucks was trying to tell it something. "Cancel that," I muttered, clicking the "go away" button.

I fooled with my phone, setting it up as a hot spot. So much faster. "You can talk to me while I'm doing this. I thought of something to do to send an unmistakable message."

"Do I want to know, or do I need to be able to tell the police I had no idea what you were doing?" Randy sounded amused. I think he thought I was funny.

I looked up. When he smiled, dimples appeared. "You're hilarious. It's pretty simple. I told Michael we were leading parallel lives, so it was stupid for him to pretend I didn't exist, especially given the way we left it. So, I'm sending him Blondie's *Parallel Lines* through iTunes."

"Lives, lines. Parallel lines never intersect. I like it. Do you think he'll get it?"

"If he doesn't, we have no business being together. Here, check out the track list. Some of the cuts are perfectly titled too." I turned the computer around.

Randy perused them while I finished setting up the hot spot. "'Hanging on the Telephone'? 'One Way or Another'? 'Heart of Glass'? Going for subtle, I see."

"I know, right?" I took the laptop back and sent the "gift" off to Michael through iTunes.

"How do you know he's got an iPhone?"

"I gave it to him," I said with a shrug. At Randy's look of disbelief, I said, "It's a long story, trust me. Anyway, the next time he opens iTunes—sometime in the next fifteen minutes, knowing him—it'll download, assuming he can get a Wi-Fi signal."

"Right, you're perfectly harmless. Too bad you didn't include 'Call Me.'" He held up his blended coffee drink. "To gifts with messages."

"And lives without complications."

He gave me a funny look. "Are you actually from this planet?"

"Probably not. My dad thinks I'm a changeling."

When our legs tangled under the table, I didn't move mine. Was I playing with fire?

"Right, a changeling."

We chatted for a while, about nothing and everything. It all took my mind off my present circumstances.

When Laurel texted to find out where I was, I replied, *Ask G.*

"My future sister-in-law," I told Randy. "My brother will propose to her as soon as she feels it's time."

He laughed. "Really?"

"Really. Geoff's always been a beta male, and this way they'll both know who's in charge. Laurel's good for him, because without her he'd only wander aimlessly." I knew they'd do so well together. They actually gave me hope for the institution of marriage.

"Yeah, but what does she get out of it?" Randy said.

"She's ambitious and intends to go far, and with Geoff behind her to keep the lights on and dinner warm, she'll always know where home is."

Randy nodded. "But what about you?"

"I told you. I'm the changeling."

That only appeared to frustrate Randy, but it was the truth.

My phone pinged again. I read it and smiled, then slid it across the table. "It's from my coach, or one of them. He's Michael's too."

> LODESTONE: *Remy, U magnificent bastard, that was perfect. He's not foaming @ the mouth, but U can fix that. Full Frontal's "You Think You're A Man."*

"How does your coach know about *Queer as Folk*?" Randy said.

"Dude, I'm pretty sure they let straight people watch it too. Besides, Divine sang it first."

> LODESTONE: *Now get your ass back here. You and your new playmate have responsibilities this afternoon.*

Chapter Twenty-Six

Randy and I were back at the races in the morning. Men's and women's varsity rowed their grand finals for the invitational cups, and later, the petite finals, a polite term for the best of the losers. Okay, that was me being horrible. One of the things I'd always appreciated about crew was the repechage, a chance for those eliminated in the heats to compete against each other for a lesser first place, the petite finals. Weather conditions—and in San Diego, the tides on the bay—as well as personal physical conditions contributed to the quality of the race, so it was only fair to take that into account. JV also raced on Sunday, and I liked to cheer them on. That Cap City's ladies' and gentlemen's crews raced later in the day no longer meant jack to me. I planned to be busy—very, very busy—de-rigging CalPac boats.

"How long are you going to let this go on, Remy?" Lodestone said softly from where we watched the national team's coxed fours row a shortened exhibition race. In other words, we watched my competition show off. Laurel, Geoff, Olive, and even Craig joined us that morning too.

I sighed. "I've done everything I can. I can't make Michael stay in a relationship that he doesn't want to be in. I also can't make him end it like an adult either."

Lodestone nodded. "I know, but I hate to see it end this way. You two really do care for each other."

"I still love him," I said softly. "That's what makes this all so difficult."

Geoff bumped my shoulder with his. He still looked a little shell-shocked. The revelation that I'd heard everything Michael had revealed to him yesterday shook him. Welcome to rowing, Geoff. You never know what's lurking behind or under every boat. "I'm sorry. I think Michael feels trapped," he whispered.

"Maybe he should try talking to me. I'm not the one trapping him."

"You kind of are."

"We'd part friends if he said even half of what he told you to me. We could've parted friends when we spoke weeks ago." I shook my head. "What happened yesterday? That was childish crap that I don't have time for."

"As opposed to your iTunes message?"

"He earned it."

"You two." Geoff shook his head slowly. "You really pissed him off with that."

"Good. Maybe he'll think twice about trying to bullshit me in front of his team or anywhere else." Suddenly I couldn't even pretend to be in a good mood anymore.

Geoff sighed. "Could you please not do this to him?"

"Him?" I stared at my brother. Really?

"Yes, him. He's going through a lot right now."

"And I'm not? Goodbye, Geoff. We're not doing this again. Call me when you regain your sanity." I paused. "And remember who you shared a room with for the first nine months of prelife."

The exhibition row ended, and I caught myself looking around for Randy, but I suspected my posse had frightened him off. It was just as well. There was too much unfinished business between me and Michael for me to play any more footsy underneath the table.

Boats waited for me to de-rig them, and I realized that the R-bombs were loaded and ready. With an Irish goodbye, I headed for CalPac's boats.

"Remy, wait!"

I stopped, and Craig of all people caught up to me.

"Yeah?" I tried to soften my demeanor, I really did. He flinched anyway. "I'm sorry, it's been..."

Craig shook his head. "No, I get it. I...uh, wanted to say thank you."

"For terrorizing you in the bathroom?" I cracked a smile.

He smiled back. "No, for the T-shirt."

I laughed. "You're welcome. Maybe it'll remind you of the weekend you came out and that there'll always be people who'll support you. Like me."

"And you didn't terrorize me—"

"Yes, I did. That wasn't cool."

"Okay, you did, but when I stopped shaking and I thought about what you said, I realized you were right." Craig looked very serious. "Thank you for the push. I'm still scared, but... I think it'll be okay."

I hugged him. "Sorry for the sweaty rower hug, but it's all I've got. Make your roommate give you my e-mail and cell phone number. You can always reach me if you want to talk."

"Thanks."

I turned to go.

"Remy..." Craig looked seriously tongue-tied. That poor guy, it was no way to go through life. Maybe coming out would help him fit into his own skin better.

"Yeah?"

"I...I hope my first boyfriend's as cool, as kind, as you are." Craig blurted it all out at once like he was afraid I'd run off.

"Make sure he is." Yep, right on time, the ol' Remy blush, from my forehead down well below what was covered by my unisuit. "And Craig? I expect to find a text from you by tomorrow evening at the latest so I know you have my contact info, okay?"

"Okay." And then Craig blushed. He struck me as a good guy. We were both college freshman, so why did I think of him as a kid?

Oh well. Boats, and with them my fragile mood.

"So, there he is." Jonah greeted me as I walked up. "You look like someone stomped your kitten. What's up?"

I made a face. "How much detail do you want?"

"Not much," Steve said. That actually made me happy.

"Thank you. I'm sick of thinking about it." Seriously, such a burden to let go of for now.

"Oh wait, there was a Davis rower looking for you. You could tell us about him," Steve said.

"Or maybe not," I said.

Jonah grinned. "You have such an interesting life."

"Wanna trade?"

Steve handed me the nearly universal 7/16" wrench. "Not right now. Get busy. Nice collar, by the way."

"Gladly." I ignored the rest.

I buried myself in the familiar work of preparing boats for transit. One of the things I liked about CalPac's rowing program was that although we had the money for a rigger to do all of this, the coaches required that we handle it ourselves. So, there's that for your "spoiled rich kids' school" comment, Randy. Except to tell him I'd have to find him, and that'd be dangerous. Oy, so many puzzles. Being an adult sucked. I couldn't wait to tell my grandparents that.

So, when Lodestone walked up with a certain devastatingly handsome and incredibly aggravating Cap City rower in tow, I was already wary, with a glare capable of pulverizing granite at the ready.

"A word with you, Mr. Babcock, if you please?"

Steve waved me away. "You might as well, Remy. You've had the most fascinating weekend of any of us. I think I speak for everyone in our boat, however, when I say that we all want the details."

"I'm almost positive I can make you regret those words," I muttered.

While Michael looked positively mutinous, Lodestone only said, "Thanks, Remy. Hopefully, this won't take long." He led us over to a set of picnic tables far enough away from any rowers to avoid fueling the inevitable networks of gossip. Seriously, rowers gossiped worse than any demographic I knew of. Social media meant it would spread to the entire regatta within twenty minutes tops.

"Look, the two of you need to work this out or set it aside. I refuse to let this travel back to Sacramento." Lodestone more or less forced us to sit by pushing down on our shoulders. "Remy, I know you'd sworn you'd deal with this, but your efforts didn't look all that successful from what I saw and heard. Michael, you're a senior in high school and about to leave the gentlemen's crew, and frankly, I expect better of you—"

"You can't talk to us—"

I smiled slowly, maybe a little ruefully. I put my hand on his arm. "Michael, he can, and he's right."

I wondered if Michael was aware he'd said "us"? It gave me hope he still thought there was an "us." I wanted there to be an "us." Based on the glint in Lodestone's eye, visible to me despite his sunglasses, so did he. My respect for that man knew no bounds, and things like this were one of the reasons why.

Michael might not have realized how expertly Lodestone manipulated us, but I did. Had I been manipulated if I saw it happening? Whatevs. Lodestone had played Michael like a virtuoso, and I couldn't even applaud. I'd text Lodestone later.

I felt Michael settle under my hand. Interesting.

Michael looked at his phone. "We don't really have the time to talk now, you know."

"I know. Can we get together back home? That's where the hard work will have to happen anyway." Lodestone appeared disinterested, but I knew him very well. He all but vibrated in place.

Michael nodded. "Yes, but maybe wait until after AP tests?"

"Fair enough. I won't ask for things to go back to the way they were, but Michael? I insist on civility."

Michael's shoulders slumped. "I'm sorry. This has been a rough time for me, Rem... Can I still call you that? That was always our special nickname, and I haven't exactly been a good boyfriend, or even much of a friend."

Michael sounded so lost, even a little confused. But he was right. He hadn't even been much of a friend. I found that the sound of "Rem" on his lips didn't sit well. For what it was worth, I still refused to call Geoff "Goff," and he'd been my twin my entire life.

"If you want to, you can." I didn't really want him to.

"I understand," Michael said sadly. "Some things have to be earned."

Then Michael looked like he remembered something. "Remy? I know how rude I was to you, but please don't send any more musical messages. That hurt, especially in public."

Lodestone started coughing and had to excuse himself.

"I see your point, but then again, that was part of *my* point, Michael. I'd asked to speak to you alone, and you tried to humiliate me in front of your entire team. I know a bunch of those guys, and that wasn't suave. I'm willing to bet you won't do that again."

"I won't do it again because I'm graduating, but damn, Rem. Remy. Is this how far we've sunk? I never thought you'd do that shit to me." Michael sounded more sad than anything.

"This is the most you've said to me since we talked about our futures. Hell, this is *all* you've said to me, and let us not forget that conversation I overheard between you and my brother, so yes, this is how far we've sunk," I said. "Maybe I ought to load up Scruff and have some fun myself, you know, so long as you're cruising Davis High."

Michael gasped. "Damn your brother—"

"*Overheard*, I said. You really need to check the area around you before you spill your guts. I was under a boat, stretching." I stood up. "I think we've about exhausted the possibilities of this conversation. Michael, we'll talk in Sacramento. Lodestone, I'll look for the latest training plan in my inbox."

I texted Lodestone a thank-you as I walked back to CalPac's boats.

*

I hit the water as soon as I returned home. In the meantime, boats had been re-rigged and stored, and both CalPac and Cap City essentially wound down for the summer. Lodestone's efforts to whip me into shape for the U23 trials, however, kicked into an even higher gear, but that's as it should've been. Unbeknownst to me and Michael, however, Lodestone was far more of a meddler than any curtain-twitching neighborhood busybody. He had contacted our parents.

"We're adults. How long do you think we're going to have to put up with Lodestone busting our chops?" Michael said as we left Sacramento behind.

I shrugged. "He was your varsity coach and is still my coach. Probably forever."

I never found out what made the difference with the Castelreighs. Maybe Lodestone impressed on them how upstanding a person I was, or perhaps Michael himself had it out with them. In the end, I think what tipped the balance was that Michael himself lost patience, because long before AP tests, Michael and I headed up to a timeshare that the Castelreighs owned at Lake Tahoe for a long weekend. I hid my shock well. The Castelreighs?

Letting "us" use it? To work on our relationship? That they hated? And skipping two days of school? Michael must've kept a set of dolls with pins in it. What could I say, voodoo got shit done.

In its way, the weekend was like old times. Eventually. The drive was actually fun. Mountain roads in an Audi? Oh yeah. Teenage males in an Audi? Stupid. Fun, but stupid. German engineering totally mastered Echo Summit and semis ate our dirt. But other than that, the tension between us could've killed a small dog. Maybe playing *Parallel Lines* was a bad idea.

The timeshare—the whole lodge, actually—occupied prime real estate a block from the Nevada border along South Lake Tahoe Boulevard and a block from the lake itself. Given the weather at that time of year, Michael and I planned to take advantage of the lodge's offerings during the day—I couldn't wait to try windsurfing. Kayaking? Meh. Why bother? It was half of what the two of us were used to doing. Maybe trail riding? We'd still have plenty of time to drag ourselves down with dreary conversations.

When we checked in, we found that someone reserved us a one-bedroom unit. Alrighty then. Subtle hint, anyone?

The first night, Michael and I got right down to it.

"What happened to us?" I said.

Michael sat next to me, radiating more anger than I'd ever felt from him. "Don't tell me you don't know."

"I really don't know, Michael." I sighed. "It's been commented on many times by many people that I don't 'get' anything that isn't made of carbon fiber. Can we proceed from that? Please? I'm not a mind reader."

"Obviously not."

The next several days would fly right by, oh yes, they would.

"Uh...for starters, we're not going to school in the same place. I mean, Boston? What the hell? Were you ever going to tell me?" Michael's tone answered many questions I had no intention of asking. "Yes, obviously I wasn't going to go to school in Boston, but Providence is roughly fifty miles from Boston. Fifty. That's sixty to ninety minutes, depending on traffic. It's even shorter via train, and we could study."

"How many times do you want me to apologize? Because if you're never going to forgive me for that, there's no point in me even trying," I said.

Michael stared at me, I guess dumbfounded that I dared to speak. He'd met me before, so I could only assume in his anger he'd forgotten certain essential parts of my personality. This would only get more "interesting" from there.

"I deserved to know, dammit."

Oh lordy, he crossed his arms over his chest. "You're right, you did. I should've told you as soon as I returned from Boston."

"Can you be quiet and let me speak?" Michael snapped.

"Would you have applied to any West Coast schools if you'd known? Stanford? The Claremont McKenna colleges? Given the costs of the University of California, those're supposed to be viable options these days. Maybe Willamette University? I've heard amazing things about it. University of Washington? Go Huskies!" My question cut right through the baloney, because if he had no intention of going to any West Coast school, then he was full of shit and merely wanted to fight.

"That's not the point, Remy!"

And we had a winner.

I looked to the heavens and prayed for patience. "Then what is the point, Michael?"

"I gave up the best part of high school to be with you, Remy. Don't you get that?"

At least he'd stopped yelling at me. I'm sure the neighbors appreciated that. "Can you explain how exactly that worked? Sure, there were all those cute party boys you wanted to screw, which apparently you held off doing since we were together—and thank you for that. But maybe high school just *was*, did you ever think of that? Would your high school experience have been any better without me, or simply different? I thought we'd had some good times, but maybe not."

Michael stared at me, I guessed in disbelief since I hadn't shut up.

"Stop being logical!" he bellowed.

Oh, that was just too *too*. "I'm sorry, what?"

"You heard me, and stop that. It's a delaying tactic, and I'm not stupid."

I—somehow—kept my temper leashed. Had Michael forgotten what I could be like? Or maybe he wanted me to fight back? Sure, hatefucking was hot, or so I was told, but I hoped that's not what he was shooting for. "Of course, I heard you. You're screaming in my face. I'm also trying here. Would you please start acting like the grown-up the law thinks you're going to be in a few months?"

He gave me a look of purest hatred. "It's all so easy for you, isn't it? Wall off your emotions and keep pulling on the sculls."

"No, it's really not, but my sculls don't scream at me, and they don't tell me we're still together one minute and then refuse to talk to me the next, cutting me off for over a month." There was a very good reason I kept a lid on my temper, because if I took the lid off, bad things happened. Michael might be bigger than me, but I was innately more vicious. I felt the R-bombs trundling toward the bomb bay doors... "Do you realize how much shit I've put up with to be with you? How much guff my family's given me because of you? How much garbage I've put up with from your family? I've got the transcript from that chat we had at Christmas. Want a copy? That'll be exhibit A at your mother's competency hearing, by the way, and yes, I know all about her anti-vax, anti-science bullshit."

I got all up in his grille, my face nothing but a mask of contempt, and I bared my fangs. I tried to take the beatings I was owed without complaint, but this? Oh hell, no.

"Listen to me, little boy. The summer you couldn't decide whether you liked me or not is the summer I cared so little about my life without you in it that I fucked anything that moved and got HIV. Because without you, it didn't matter. Without you, nothing mattered. And you think I don't care about you? That I don't love you? That somehow our relationship has been one-sided and you're some kind of martyr to my rowing? I hate to burst your bubble of whining self-pity, but I am not the author of your present misery. You've done that all by yourself. I took the best part of high school? Which part would that be? The part where your friends dry humped me on the dance floor at a prom neither of us had any business attending? Or the part where we were almost busted for drugs because they took molly? Or the part where you turned coward because you thought Gutslinger was going to run right to your nutso parents? Or maybe the part where I showed you what it meant to be a man? That part of high school? At no point do I recall you putting up much of a fight, *Michael Castelreigh*, and at times you even begged.

"So, if you can't come up with better reasons than 'You beast, you horrid beast,' then shut up or I will shut you down, because I've been nothing but loving and loyal to you, and the best boyfriend—the best partner—I've known how to be. Like that jerk of a character said in *Angels in America*, failing in love is not the same as failing to love, so don't you fucking dare make them out to be the same."

I swore I heard clapping through the walls. Michael sat there, his mouth hanging open.

I glared at him. "Don't sit there like statuary. Say something before I kick a response out of you. Because right now? I hate the sight of you."

"I don't even know where I'd start." He laughed, but it wasn't a humorous laugh. "Wow. Have you been saving that up?"

"No, Michael." I calmly gathered the spare set of bedding to make up the sofa bed in the sitting room. I had no plans to share a bed with him. "I've reached my limit. I've put on a cheerful face, and made allowances because I assumed you're as afraid of your future as I am of mine. I've done everything I could to be understanding, but that's over. Now? It's on. Now you'll see why my family and everyone else is terrified of me. You let me know tomorrow whether or not you want to do what we came up here to do."

I left Michael sitting by himself in the bedroom, adrift in a king-size bed as I ostentatiously prepared not to sleep with him. I closed the bedroom door because at long last, I had had enough. I heard nothing from the bedroom. Good. Maybe I'd shocked him into maturation. Lord knows after my diatribe I'd be lucky if he still breathed. Sorry, Mr. and Mrs. Castelreigh, your son was being a butthead, so I cut him down to size. I'm sure he'll grow back.

I bedded down for the night, lying there in the dark and wondering where I'd gone so wrong and what I'd done to make Michael hate me so much. Neither of us deserved this.

"Remy... Jeremy? I..." Michael whispered from the bedroom doorway. "Can we talk? I don't know what happened to us. I really don't, but I'm scared. I thought we'd be together forever and now? We're not."

And whose fault is that? I didn't stop talking to me, now did I, sugar?

He stood in the shadows, arms wrapped around himself, like he was holding him because I wouldn't. I closed my eyes. I didn't want to cry. "Michael, I am so sorry," I said, my voice thick. "I never meant to hurt you."

"Awww, jeez, Rem, don't cry. You...you're my everything."

He had once been mine.

Now he was crying too.

I held the covers open, and Michael all but dove into bed with me. We held each other through the storm, shaking like leaves in the wind.

Chapter Twenty-Seven

We woke up tangled together, more like a puppy pile than anything erotic. Morning breath never had excited me. I watched Michael sleep for a timeless now. Even in repose he looked bothered. "Tormented" sounded so gothic, but I could tell he hadn't had a restful night, but then, neither had I.

Michael opened his eyes, sleeping to awake all at once, and he smiled. "Hi."

Then realization dawned. I felt him tense up.

"Still happy to see me?"

"Oh, Remy. I'm happy we're talking, but I'm sad at the circumstances."

He pulled me to him, and I went willingly, resting my head on his chest. "I know what you mean."

"Promise me something." Michael kissed the top of my head. "Promise me we can talk this out and that we'll stay friends."

Given that I'd thought we were still together up until the Crew Classic, that was an easy promise for me to make. "That's all I've ever wanted, Michael. Maybe sometime, when you're ready, you'll be able to tell me what happened."

"Maybe." He sighed. "I have to figure it out myself first."

Frustrating, but since Michael had been honest enough to say it, the least I could do was accept it. This was progress. "Fair enough."

"Thanks, Rem," he said softly. He knew full well I could go all grand inquisitor without notice. He ran his hands up and down my back in a way that made me yawn and stretch like a cat.

Then he stopped. "You're still wearing my collar."

"Yes."

Michael didn't say anything for the longest time.

"Thanks." He was trying not to cry, which set me off. Then he lost his battle. We were such a mess.

After we recovered, we started talking about inconsequential things, and then things that made us laugh.

"Okay, I have to say one thing."

I craned my neck to look up at him. "What's that?"

"Don't send me another album to make your point. Jeez Louise, *Parallel Lines*? And those track names? Thanks for not sending me 'Call Me.'" Michael shook his head, but I saw the smile playing about his lips.

I sat up and glared at him. "Why am I the only one who didn't think of that?"

"What're you talking about?"

"After I heard you rip my heart out with Geoff, a friend from the UCD men's crew got me out of there and was sitting with me when I sent my little hint from Blondie. He told me I should've sent you 'Call Me' too."

Michael grinned. "Face it, Rem. While you are an amazing and talented man, you can't think of everything."

"We'll see about that."

"You scare me, Rem." He pulled me back down to his chest.

I sighed in contentment, even if it was a shallow thing. I knew how fragile it was. "What do you want to do today?"

"Laze around in bed?" He sounded so hopeful.

"Windsurfing? Hiking?"

Michael groaned. "Dude, seriously?"

"Whaaat? I'm the one training for national competition. You, you're just lazy. C'mon, we're up here in paradise, let's not waste it." I started tugging on his arm. "Up, up!"

Michael sat up. "Do I get to shower first?"

"What's the point? I promise to soap you down when we're done."

"Really?" Suddenly he sounded interested.

I got out of bed and stretched in the most provocative way I could. That I happened to have slept last night in a pair of assless Andrew Christians and one of my perpetually short T-shirts convinced Michael to climb the rest of the way out of bed. "We could stay in today. I'm almost positive I can give you a workout right here."

"You want it, you earn it." I bent over my suitcase and started pulling out clothes appropriate for active recreation.

Michael was still fussing and grumbling while I called the concierge. "Yes, that's right... I'm fine, thanks. How're you...? Good. Do you have information on windsurfing...? You do? There're places affiliated with the resort? That's suave, very suave. We'll be down in fifteen minutes." I looked at Michael, hopping around with one leg in his shorts, trying to get the second leg in. "Make that twenty."

*

Windsurfing rocked, and despite the fact Michael all but batter-dipped me in an SPF so high it had an exponent, I still looked a little red. The lake acted like a giant mirror for the sunlight...just like the river we both rowed on. Shocking, that. Even if we couldn't get close enough to each other to talk while on the water, Michael and I heard each other laugh all afternoon, and we both felt the lighter for it.

We were tired by midafternoon, and the winds had died anyway, so we opted for a late lunch on the beach along with an equally late donning of UPF-50 shirts. I eyed Michael's burrito jealously.

He laughed. "Sorry, no Mexican food for bottoms."

"I'll have you know that power bottoms are the backbone of our society."

"That you may be." Michael leaned over to kiss my nose. "But you still don't get to eat anything that could race right through you."

I glared at him and vengefully ate my chicken sandwich. A few minutes later, I looked up to find Michael smiling at me.

"We have to stay friends, Rem. *We have to*. We're all strained and trying not to say things we don't really mean and shit like that, but I cannot imagine my life without you in it. I can't."

I swallowed the lump in my throat. "I have to have you in my life too. I've known you since I was in the third grade."

Michael frowned. "I thought we met when *I* was in the third grade."

"At this point, does it really matter?" I shrugged. "I can text my brother if you want. He probably remembers."

"Don't worry about it. We've known each other forever. That's what counts." He sighed, and I leaned into him. Michael put his arm around me, and we watched the shadows crawl across the mountains as the afternoon passed.

The weird thing about the conversation Michael and I had about our future was its episodic nature. Throughout the weekend, one or the other of us spouted off with some thought or other about it, like our future was too precious and painful to confront head-on, so we sidled up to it or looked at it only out of the corners of our eyes, lest it blind us.

So, the next night, as we soaked away the aches that came of horseback riding—seriously, neither of us would be able to walk right for a while—we hashed out the bare bones of our split. Even thinking those words to myself made it real in a way I didn't want to face, but I knew I had to.

We promised to stay together through the end of summer, and we promised to be friends, no matter what. That included talking out any weirdness that cropped up.

"You realize this will include seeing other people, right?" Michael pointed out.

Well, that certainly didn't take long, did it? "Yes, but is it okay if I can't talk about that right now?"

"Only if you promise we discuss it before I head east for school. I think I'm heading out midsummer, but I'll keep you posted."

"That's fair. It's... I don't share well, and it's going to take me a bit of time to get used to the idea that you're not mine anymore." Ugh, so not a thought I wanted to have.

Michael stared at me until I squirmed. So that's what it felt like. I'd done it to other people often enough. "You realize that works both ways, right? And that however much we're together this summer, I have to reconcile myself to sharing you. That fine ass of yours is no longer mine alone to tap."

My mind went immediately to Randy. Somehow, I knew that when I was ready, he'd be first in line. Unless I was in Chicago, in which case I'd have to pepper spray Caden. If he were there. Then there was that Johnny-come-lately, Scott.

"Right then, you thought of someone, didn't you?" Michael said sadly.

I sighed. "Three, actually."

"I always knew if we ever split, you'd only be single if you wanted to." Michael looked miserable.

"I didn't want to be single."

"I know."

Neither of us said much after that. We settled back and looked at the Milky Way. That much, at least, seemed permanent, even if it really wasn't. It was nothing but dead light, light that took so long to reach Earth that the stars that produced it could've exploded into nothingness and we wouldn't know it for millennia.

Yeah, good times.

Michael knew I was down that night and to his credit didn't try to cheer me up. He only held me until we both fell asleep.

The next morning, we were both still subdued.

"Do you want to hang out here for the day? You don't seem up for anything too active," Michael said.

"I thought about trying to go for a run once it warms up. I figured the altitude would be character-building." I handed Michael my phone that showed him how cold it was outside.

He pulled me back down under the covers. "Character-building. Right."

It turned into a lazy day, which I needed, and that run took place much later in the afternoon.

Michael looked up from his e-reader when I staggered in and snickered. "Your character looks much improved."

I flipped him off. Cussing him out required more air than I could've spared. I grabbed two bottles of water from the fridge and then flopped gracelessly to the floor.

"You'll douse yourself if you drink those lying down."

I glared up at him and did it anyway. As cooling as the water was, Michael was basically correct, so I flipped him off again.

Michael laughed. "Nice, Rem. Real nice."

I closed my eyes to hyperventilate in peace, but when I opened them, there was Michael, grinning at me.

"You stay there, I'll cook dinner."

I ended up showering to get the stink off me, but I appreciated the thought.

We ate on the patio. Sure, it only overlooked the pool, but it could've been worse. It could've overlooked the motor court.

"So, how're you doing?"

I sighed. "I'm kind of angry about things right now, but I love you. I may not be in love with you anymore, but I love you."

Michael brought his chair around by mine and rested his head on my shoulder as we watched the sun set. Of course, given Lake Tahoe's position in a bowl in the mountains, the sun went down early, and we had plenty of time left for our evening.

"I worry that your future boyfriends won't understand your need to dominate. And that you won't be able to speak up for yourself. Isn't that weird? A toppy guy with a need to be in control who has a hard time asking for that?" I'd never worried about it, because that was Michael and I understood him, but what about other men?

Michael shrugged uncomfortably. "I was lucky you perceived that. You saw things in me no one else did."

"We were each other's first in so many things. I worry that you'll end up compromising on things that might be more important than you realize." I took a deep breath. "But I guess there are rights boyfriends have that even superclose friends don't. I can say that I worry about things like that now, but I have to trust you to find your own way later. Fuck."

I turned away. This would kill me, kill us both, and possibly end our friendship.

"I'm amazed that even after I destroyed our relationship, you can still care about things like that for me, but I shouldn't be." Michael touched my cheek, like he still found wonder in me.

I gasped. "Michael, you didn't destroy—"

Michael put his hand over my mouth. "I did, Rem. Jeremy. I did. I can see that now. I don't know why, but I did. You were only ever honest. Maybe not timely, but honest. You may turn out to be the best thing that ever happened to me. I'll always wonder about that."

That was it, that was fucking it, and I collapsed into his arms, sobbing for us both.

Michael kissed my forehead. "I will destroy anyone who doesn't treat you like the prince that you are. And if he has a problem dating someone who's poz? They will never find his body."

Then he snorted out a laugh. "Hell, if you're worried about me not getting what I need, you could always approve my first couple of college boyfriends. Let's be honest, it's not like you won't be in Boston every year."

"You're terrible." I wiped my eyes. "What if I hold you to that?"

*

I finished my freshman year at CalPac. While my grades never returned to what they'd been before I started training for the U23 team, without the distraction of a dying relationship, I pulled them up. That is, I pulled my grades right back up, but the damage had been done. At least training was my sole stressor once school got out in May. The intensity of my training sucked, however.

"This is it, Remy. This is the final push," Lodestone said.

I raised one eyebrow. "Unless I make the U23, in which case I compete for a spot for the Worlds."

"There's that. Now, you've got an erg test, and unless you like erging when it's hot, let's get going."

I sighed and loaded up obnoxious music. It took something vile and loud to keep me pulling as fast as I needed to in order to rock a 2k erg test.

On the whole, I preferred the distraction Michael had brought to my life, if only because he had brought a certain amount of happiness with him. I was more or less settling in to being friends with him, rather than boyfriends. I hadn't told my family, yet. I knew I could avoid the issue until Michael graduated. No one accomplished anything the last month or so of his senior year, but given the Castelreighs' objection to our relationship, his absence around Chez Babcock would not be commented on, not for a while at any rate.

Had Geoff planned to come home for very long this summer, the story might've been a different one. Geoff listened to our parents, however, and planned to work on unpaid internships—were there any other kind anymore?—before returning home to visit for a week or two. Then he'd head back to San Diego in time to pick up a job and some summer school credits. Without him around the house, however, I delayed fessing up as long as possible.

Given what my dad termed "our new, more mature relationship," Mom and Dad were happy to let me row, rest, and row some more so long as I contributed around the house. I couldn't have explained to anyone how this differed from the cooking and cleaning I'd always done, but whatevs. If it made them happy and that led them to leave me alone, it was a win for all of us.

But May turned into June all too quickly, and with June came Davis High's graduation. Naturally, I wasn't invited, not that I'd expected to be.

"So, what're you doing to celebrate graduation?" I asked Michael over lunch, now that I'd become a man of leisure. Heh.

Michael sucked on his soda in a way that made me sigh nostalgically. "Grad Night, I guess."

Grad Night was an all-night all-inclusive party sponsored by parents and subsidized by local businesses, and its intention was to keep new graduates from wrapping their cars around utility poles in a drunken stupor.

"Don't sound so excited. People'll get the wrong idea." I thought about it for a moment. "I went to Grad Night. It wasn't terrible."

Michael frowned. "Davis isn't where I'm supposed to be, and I don't intend to stay in contact with too many people from my class, so why should I spend one last night with them?"

I didn't have a good answer for that. "Not even some of those out guys you want to play with?"

"Remy..."

"I'm trying to signal my maturity and acceptance through humor."

I said this while totally deadpan.

"I don't know whether to punch you out or laugh."

I snorted. "As if you could. Knock me out, I mean."

"No, I couldn't hit you."

Michael pulled out his phone and fiddled around with it for a while. Then he looked back up at me. "Do you want to go out that night?"

I blinked. "What night?"

"The night I graduate, Remy," Michael said patiently.

Holy mixed signals, Batman. "Won't you have family or whatever underfoot?"

"I'll be at Grad Night, remember?" I could've sworn his eyes twinkled. "Besides, your plan Bs are always way better than everyone else's main events."

"I see. Will it be you, or will I be entertaining others?" And everyone thought I was the sneaky one. No, I was the noisy one. Michael was far more devious when he wanted to be.

"Like I'd share you, and Remy?"

"Yeah?"

"I'm over eighteen, you know."

"I haven't forgotten."

"Really?" Michael looked so skeptical.

I blushed, stop-sign red and everything. "Okay, I totally forgot, but I promise it wasn't anything passive-aggressive."

"You can make it up to me the night I graduate then."

We'd broken up?

Chapter Twenty-Eight

I spent the evening of Michael's high school graduation with my parents, or at least the early part of the evening. Despite my plans for later, I wasn't particularly nervous, and not even waiting for Michael's text changed that. Part of that came down to good planning, but I also knew nothing I did could change the fact that Michael had made his decision. Tonight was a gift for a good friend, not an attempt to win him back, even if I stood a reasonable chance of getting dicked.

Mom looked around in satisfaction at the three of us ensconced before the television. "This is nice. We never did this when you were younger, did we, Remy?"

"You and your brother were always rushing off somewhere." Dad shook his head at the memory.

ME: *watching TV with the olds. Help meee.*

I laughed. "I'm too tired to dash off somewhere. I'll get back to you later this summer, okay?"

"I'd say you were too young for this, but I've seen those training plans Coach Lodestone sends you," Dad said. "I'm pretty amazed you don't fall asleep driving back and forth from the port. Who are you texting? Could you not pay attention to us, the people who're physically present?"

"I was texting Geoff about this. It feels like he should be here." I put the phone down. "Is this where I admit I nap in my car after practice sometimes?"

"No." Mom sounded very emphatic about that.

Dad rolled his eyes. I came by it honestly, at least. "Which would you prefer, Dina? That he nap, or that he drive tired?"

"Why do I have to choose, Steven?"

"Did you just whine, Mom?"

"You have to choose because our son is an adult who's maturing very nicely and who's training for something most people never get a shot at." Dad looked at me. "And yes, Remy, she whined."

"On that note, I'm going to bed. As we've established, I get up early." Actually, tonight I needed a disco nap because their almost nineteen-year-old son planned to sneak out after his ex-boyfriend texted him to make that ex's graduation from high school memorable. No, there wasn't anything weird about that, nothing at all.

I had everything ready to go in my car, even the food. I'd asked Lodestone for permission to use the boathouse, which he granted. That permission allowed me to set up a fair amount ahead of time. I think he hoped Michael and I would patch things up, and I didn't burst his bubble. He was too involved as it was. Lodestone meant well, but I needed to set limits.

When Michael's text set my phone off—I hadn't bothered to change his custom tone—I felt like I'd barely drifted off. It was almost midnight.

> MICHAEL: *Leaving Grad Night. Ready 2 make the magic happen?*
>
> ME: *See U @ the port.*
>
> MICHAEL: *The port?!*
>
> ME: *Plan B, baby.*
>
> MICHAEL: *UR 2 much.*
>
> ME: *U told me 2 do something. U didn't set any parameters :-p*
>
> MICHAEL: *OMG*
>
> ME: **grin**

*

By the time Michael arrived, I had the table ready, right down to the plates and candles. I reheated the food in a portable microwave, kept warm in insulated bags on the drive in. Beverages cooled in a small ice chest. Nothing alcoholic. I'm sure I could've lifted wine or something from my parents' collection, but neither of us was legal, and I was a rules follower. That said, I'd placed candles everywhere, and they were all lit, bathing the boathouse in a soft golden glow. The old rattrap had never looked better.

I also had boats ready in slings on the dock. The full moon kissed the flat water with a wide path of silver. It was a glorious night to row, and fortunately for him I had workout gear for us both. The river looked amazing lit up like that, and none of us at Cap City or CalPac ever saw it.

Despite the fact we both rowed, we had rarely sculled together. In some ways this night was as much a goodbye, a farewell kiss, as it was anything else. We'd both grown up at the Cap City boathouse, and while I suspected I'd always be kicking around here in one form or another, I already knew that Michael would never be back, just as I thought "we" would never be together again. While melancholy, I could bear it. Because something was sad was no reason to avoid it. Besides which, I had other, more pleasurable things planned too.

I stared out at the river while I waited for Michael to walk in the door.

"What the... Remy?" Michael whispered.

"Hello, Michael." I turned around to greet him. Michael's jaw dropped when he saw me. I wore the suit my grandparents had purchased for me at Christmas, and I knew it looked like it had been shrink-wrapped to my frame. I wanted the night to be special for him.

While more casually dressed, Michael looked good. But then, he always did. Biased much, Remy?

"Wow, Rem. This is...this looks amazing."

"I wanted to make it perfect for you."

Michael took me in his arms. "It looks like you succeeded. What is this?"

"A late dinner, then a midnight row under the full moon, followed by...?"

Michael spun me around. Like a record, baby. I really needed to let the '80s music go. "A row? I didn't bring—"

"Oh, Michael. Give me some credit."

He laughed. "You brought something for me?"

"What do you think?" I gestured to the candlelit extravagance around us. "If I can manage this much, I think I can be trusted to handle workout clothes."

"Of course, you can." Michael kissed my forehead. "I shouldn't have doubted you. Care to tell me what we're eating?"

"Nothing too fancy," I said, my eyes twinkling in the candlelight. "Your favorite dinner, maybe."

"How on earth did you make fettuccine carbonara at the boathouse?"

"Not just fettuccine carbonara," I said smugly. "Fettuccine carbonara with peas, and I didn't make it here. I made most of it at home. I only finished it here."

I shepherded Michael to the table. "Ordinarily a crisp white would be the perfect thing to serve as a counterpoint to the heaviness of the cream in the fettuccine, but we're minors, so we have lemon- or lime-flavored fizzy water."

"How do you know that much about wine, Rem?"

"I'm a closet lush, Michael."

"I'm serious."

"My mom's a budding wine snob, and I made my parents the same thing for dinner." I smiled. "They were the test market for a new recipe."

"Of course."

"Do you doubt my sincerity, Michael?"

"I believe that you can be sincerely full of crap."

I raised my glass. "Eat up, Michael. Your pasta's getting cold. And congratulations, by the way. This is only the beginning, you know."

"What is?"

"Your life. High school is largely irrelevant."

He laughed. "You've learned that in the year since you graduated?"

"No, I suspected it for years before I graduated. It's been confirmed in the last year. I..." I stopped to choose my words carefully. "I know that next year will see us in places we hadn't anticipated, but I hope you know that I want only good things for you. The best things."

"I know. I wish things had been different, but they're not." Michael looked at me over the table, the candles making his eyes appear dark brown, almost black. "I do know that you'll be impossible to forget."

"That's all anyone can hope for." I sounded much lighter than I felt. This long goodbye to my happily ever after? It sucked.

After that, we both consciously pulled back from the serious talk, or at least exchanged it for something less emotionally charged. Michael told me about preparations to start at Brown in the fall, at least what prep he could do this early. I updated him on how training was going. I was in the midst of my last push, so Michael was surprised that Lodestone had allowed me to eat what I'd made for dinner.

"He doesn't know." I whispered like the boats themselves might give it away.

Michael pretended to be shocked. "You mean the ultradiligent Jeremy Babcock lied to his coach?"

"No, I simply didn't tell him." That comment deserved an eye roll, and an eye roll I gave it.

"A lie of omission is still a lie, Rem."

Give me strength... "Does this mean you'll be foregoing that trifle I made for dessert out of solidarity with my much-violated training diet?"

"Don't be absurd. I'm not the one who'll be rowing his ass off in mere weeks." Michael leaned over and thumped my forehead.

I rubbed the spot. "Then don't say such stupid things. Honestly."

"Why don't I serve dessert?"

I glared at Michael. "Don't trust me not to dump it on you?"

"Actually, that hadn't occurred to me, but now that you mention it..." Then Michael looked at me. "A plastic bowl? Really?"

"We're in a boathouse, Michael. I certainly wasn't going to risk Mom's crystal trifle bowl."

Michael shook his head slowly. "Now I know how much you really care."

That hurt. All I could do was stare. I'm sure I wore a wounded expression.

"Too soon?" he said quietly.

"Soon?" I closed my eyes, waiting for the sting to pass. "Try never."

"I'm sorry, Rem."

For what, I wondered. There were so many things. I'd always been a bolter. Given a choice, flight usually struck me as the best bet. If I escaped into my single, I'd ruin my suit. If I literally ran... Well, who could run in a suit? "I didn't deserve that."

"I know you didn't."

"Any of it, Michael," I snapped.

He sighed. "No."

When I didn't say anything for a while, he sighed again. "I'll clean up."

What I longed to say was "You sure can fuck up, so why not?" What I said was, "You don't have to. I'll do it. Tonight's my gift to you."

"Why're you so forgiving, Remy?"

I stopped and looked at Michael. "I'm not, really. But I'm trying not to invest further emotional resources into what's essentially a dead relationship."

"Now that hurts."

"I didn't say it to hurt you, Michael, but what do you want from me? We're no longer romantically involved, and that was not my idea. I'm doing the best I can to work on my feelings in a healthy manner, but it's too soon to say things like that. Maybe you'll never be able to say things like that to me. Forgive me for not finding the humor in that yet."

"You've always been so damn pragmatic," Michael muttered as he put food in the containers I'd brought it in.

Yes, and that was the eighth cardinal sin. Besides, he'd known that since before we started dating. Did he think I'd changed? People usually become more themselves, not less.

After we'd finished cleaning, Michael approached me like he feared an explosion of R-bombs. "Rem, I'm sorry. I didn't mean to kill the evening."

"I know you didn't." But you did, Blanche! You did. Sometimes I wished I'd never seen *Whatever Happened to Baby Jane?* But you did, Remy, you did!

Michael put his hand on my arm. "Let's go sculling. That always makes you feel better. I hope you know I didn't mean to derail the evening you were awesome enough to plan for me."

"I know you didn't." He was trying, and that was sweet. And he was right. For me, at least, sculling cured a multitude of ills.

"I don't know what you plan to do with that suit, which looks fantastic on you, by the way."

I smiled. "I brought hangers. It cost more than my car. There's no way this deserves to be wadded up in a bag."

We dressed for sculling by candlelight, Michael and I, and something about that made it erotic. Stripping, sure, but putting on stretchy technical fiber clothes? That was a new one.

After we snuffed the candles, we launched. The moon rode high in the sky, and we managed to scull in the middle of its path. In the ordinary course of things, all the rowing clubs observed a right-hand traffic pattern to avoid collisions, but it was well after midnight, and no one else was on the river.

Michael had been right. I felt much better for being on the water, but then, I almost always did, especially when there was no tyrant in a motorboat running drills. While Michael knew how to scull, he was nowhere near my equal in skill, and awareness of that prevented me from turning this into another practice. It was good for me.

But all good things, as the saying went, and we returned to the boathouse. I made sure the boats were properly wiped down and put away, not only because I knew Lodestone would check, but because I owned one of them. Enlightened self-interest for the win.

Michael and I stood on the dock, watching the moon on the water. It would never not be magical. Michael had his arm around me to keep me warm.

"Remy?" he whispered.

"Yeah?"

"Make love to me?" The way Michael said it made me think he knew the memory would have to last him the rest of his life.

I tipped his chin up and kissed him softly. "Sure, Michael."

"Can I confess something?"

I'd have thought the time for confessions had long since passed us by. "Um...okay."

"I've kind of always wanted to do it in the boathouse." Michael buried his face in my neck. He only did things like that when he thought his requests were somehow sketchy. Given what I liked people—him—to do to me, I'd have hoped he knew he could ask me for anything.

"Me, too, actually." I was the one with all the experience getting sexed up in public, after all.

Michael looked at me, no longer looking quite so vulnerable.

"I don't think it's really going to be making love, is it?" I said.

"Maybe not so much." Michael reached for me.

I nibbled on the shell of one ear. "Does fucking like dogs work for you?"

Michael groaned as I palmed the bulge growing beneath his shorts. "You have no idea."

Rowing kit turned my crank. One of the fun things about it was its variety. That night Michael wore an old pair of rowing trou, a pair of shorts that covered the same territory as a square-cut Speedo. So that bulge of his? It was in very real danger of exceeding the limits of the trou's ability to contain it. A trashy hookup in the boathouse sounded really hot right then.

Michael grabbed my hand and pulled me up to the boathouse. "Now."

As soon as we were inside, I grabbed Michael. He wanted to be mauled, and I wanted to make the night memorable. One of the coaches had left a boat guts-down in slings, so I shoved him back against it and kissed him hard as my hands began their relentless assault on all parts of his body.

I bit my way down Michael's neck, pinching and tweaking his nips. I refused to be gentle, but rough appeared to work for him, based on his groans and little gasps. I felt him grab at me, but I had him so worked up he couldn't concentrate long enough to reciprocate. Not that I minded. I'd planned tonight for him.

I never drew blood for obvious reasons, but I knew Michael would feel this for a few days. Happy graduation, Michael. Good luck finding someone to do *this* to you. Yeah, hatefucking rocked, all right.

The poor, overburdened trou lost the fight to keep Michael's junk contained. So, I made it official and pulled the short shorts down far enough to reach things. Then I spun Michael around. "Bend over, hands on the boat. Don't move unless you're told to."

I fell to my knees. Damn, he had a fine ass, and I intended to mark it up. I reached through his legs, and the moment I wrapped one hand around his cock—loosely, so loosely he'd barely feel it—I bit down on one cheek of that lovely ass, and bit down hard.

Michael screamed wordlessly.

Before he felt too much pain, I tightened my grip on his cock and ran my tongue across his pucker, barely a flicker.

"Ohhh..."

I laved the bite while stroking him, kissing it to make it better before I returned my attention where it belonged, to the world of possibilities in between the firm muscles of his glutes.

With no particular pattern, I licked, I nibbled, I bit, nothing Michael could predict, and as he started pushing back onto my tongue, I bit the other cheek, loosening my grip on his cock. I wanted him off-balance and sobbing with need.

"Rem. Killing me."

I reached forward to catch the precum flowing from his cock in a steady stream. It made such a pretty puddle on the floor of the boathouse. I used it to slick up his hole before I used my stubble to make him beautifully insane again.

"Isn't that the idea?"

Damn, I loved the smell of sweaty jock. It dove straight to my own dick, stoking my need.

"Take me bare?" Michael begged.

I ran my stubble around his most sensitive area a while longer. "Are you still taking Truvada?"

"Nooo." He panted, trying to get his breath.

I loved rimming him.

"My viral load's undetectable, but don't be a fucking moron." I slapped his ass. "I'll be right back."

I ran to my bag and grabbed my supplies and then dashed right back. Then I caught more of his precum and fucked him with my fingers. Hard.

"Remmm!" He stood on his toes to get away from me, but his cock never stopped leaking.

I put some lube in the tip of the condom and rolled it on. Then I slicked Michael up. I planned to fuck him hard and fast, but not dry.

I lined myself up at his entrance. "You ready?"

"Uh huh. Get in—"

I didn't wait.

"Meee!"

Then Michael didn't have room to think. If I'd known that boats in slings gave us the perfect angle for me to hit his sweet spot, we'd have done this sooner. I grabbed his hips and hammered that spot instead, over and over and over.

I felt the heat of my climax growing down in my guts and then rising like a phoenix from its flames as the burn coiled up and around my spine.

"Almost, Rem."

I nailed him harder. "Can you cum without touching yourself?"

"Shit...yes! Damn! Remmmm!"

I felt Michael clench around me, and fucknation if he wasn't shooting onto the boathouse floor.

My rhythm faltered, and I followed right behind him as the burn exploded across my brain. The force of my orgasm seared my cock as I filled the condom with shot after shot, pain as much as pleasure.

I shook as I collapsed against Michael's back, boneless and nerveless and trying to catch my breath.

"Damn, Rem. That was..."

"Oh yeah."

I forced myself to stand, holding on to the condom as I pulled out. My legs felt wobbly as I stepped back, but postcoital cuddles were for lovers. I hated that this was what Michael and I had come to. But here we were.

Still, I pulled him up and kissed his cheek. "You okay?"

"More than." Michael sighed, half closing his eyes. "Too bad I have to move."

I smiled. I knew what he meant. "We could make you a nest on the safety bags that go in the launches."

"Can't you see Lodestone looking from me to the stain on the floor when he shows up in a few hours for your practice?" Michael shook his head. "Awkward."

I held up a bag with all-purpose cleaner and paper towels. "That's what this is for."

"Damn, you're intense."

"So I've been told."

Michael pulled his trou up. "I won't be able to sit for a week."

I handed him the cleaner and towels. "Go for it."

"Me? You made the mess."

"No, I caused you to make the mess." I winked at him. "There's a difference."

"A rather fine one."

"That's not my DNA on the floor."

Michael smiled at me and went to work. After that he helped me load everything into my car, and I locked up behind us. No one would ever know we'd been there.

"Well..." I felt incredibly awkward. "Congratulations again."

Michael pulled me to him, putting his hands on my shoulders. "Thank you. I had an incredible night. When I asked you to do something fun for me, I had no idea you'd go all out. This was...magnificent, Rem. Truly astounding. Just like you."

I wanted to scream. If I were so damn magnificent and astounding, why was I single?

"Thanks, Michael. I...uh, I need to go. I have to get up in a few hours for more torture."

"Oh, Rem. Why didn't you say anything sooner? Somehow, I thought tomorrow...this morning, I guess, was a day off." Michael looked upset, I'll give him that much.

"Michael, the U23 selection camp is in roughly two weeks. There's no off until afterward." I hugged him. "I have to go."

I got into my car and drove off. I saw him in the rearview mirror, watching me. I felt like I'd turned tail and run, but I hadn't been lying. I had to be back at the boathouse in four hours. It was a toss-up whether I should've slept in my car or not. But I needed distance right then.

I swore one thing as I drove home. Despite our pledge to each other to stay friends and stay in each other's lives, I had to step back. Friends was one thing, but that kind of friend? No, not ever again.

I thought about e-mailing Randy to see if he wanted to get some coffee or something, because I needed to talk, but then I realized I wasn't in the right frame of mind. He was a great guy who struck me as wanting more than coffee. I also realized that sometime I might be up for more than coffee with him. I didn't want to poison that stream with venting about the ex. I hated thinking about Michael that way, but he seemed intent on forcing my hand.

I decided I'd e-mail Lance and Caden, instead. Caden would never happen, no matter how hard he tried, and a description of Michael's grad night would surely torture him beyond all reason.

Chapter Twenty-Nine

"You're under a lot of pressure these days, Remy. How're you doing?"

I sat in the chair in Alicia's office. I spaced my therapy appointments at wider intervals when I started my training for the attempt at the U23 team, because there came a time when trying to squeeze even therapy into a tightly packed schedule itself provoked · anxieties.

"No towers with high-powered rifles!" I snorted. "Seriously, I'm meeting my obligations and keeping my sense of humor. More or less. So, I think I'm ahead of the game."

"Careful there. If I thought you were in any way serious, there are a whole bunch of annoying and intrusive questions I'd be asking you right now."

I rolled my eyes. So much for cutting back on contemptuous gestures. "'A danger to himself or others'? My questionable sense of humor is a coping mechanism, and you know it."

"I do know it, which is why I'm not interrogating you." Alicia flipped through her notes. "How're you doing post-Michael?"

"He dumped me, but he's quickly becoming the Ex Who Won't Go Away. Please note the caps." I growled. "He's trying to have it both ways. He wants to be friends and joke about the breakup, but it almost seems like he expects me to still be the boyfriend too."

"Can you tell me about that?"

I tried to get a read on Alicia, but damn, I'd hate to play poker against her.

"Well, take his grad night. He wanted—basically told me—to come up with a surprise for him."

"So, did you?" She scribbled notes so fast her hand was a blur.

"Yes, and I hate myself for it now too."

"But you did it?" Alicia phrased it as a question, but it wasn't, not really.

"I did. I planned the perfect romantic evening, and when he made a stupid joke about me not caring, I unloaded on him."

Alicia stopped writing and looked up at me. "Why do you think that was?"

I hated therapist doublespeak. "Because I'm finally accepting the fact that we're done, and I don't like it. I'm allowed my feelings too. If he wants to stick around and make jokes about dumping me, then he gets to hear about it."

"That's a healthy attitude, you know."

Oddly enough, for all her fevered note taking, Alicia hadn't resumed writing.

"I guess. He felt bad for saying anything. Then I felt bad for ripping into him."

"Who's responsible for Michael's feelings?"

"Um...not me?"

"Is that a question or a statement, Remy?"

Gag, therapists. "It's a statement. I'm not responsible for Michael's feelings."

"And if you don't think it's healthy to be around Michael anymore, then I recommend you don't be around Michael anymore." Alicia resumed writing.

"It's not that easy." That sounded pitiful even to me.

"Actually, it is that easy. Say no when Michael asks. If you feel compelled to say yes, you need to ask yourself, what are you getting out of it? The reality is, if you find yourself in a pattern you don't want to break, on some level you're getting something from it." Alicia pierced me with one of those looks of hers. "It may not be healthy—in fact, I'd bet on that—but you'll be getting something out of it. You need to ask yourself what that is. Once you figure that out, at least you can make an informed decision."

"Even if it's only that I'm really not ready to be cut loose?"

Alicia nodded. "Even if it's only that. There's nothing wrong with that, by the way. He broke up with you, not the other way around. You're going to be looking for closure for a while, but don't mistake closure for something it's not, or with jumping when he whistles for a real relationship. It's not—it's being used."

*

"We're going to starve to death when you make that selection camp," my dad said after his second helping of the vegetable casserole I made for dinner.

I handled a fair amount of the cooking, since they worked and I was generally ravenous after my second daily practice. My training diet was protein heavy and, while not vegetarian, derived a fair amount of that protein from nonmeat sources. My parents adapted.

Mom made a face. "I don't relish going back to takeout."

"Don't worry, I'll leave you with plenty of frozen leftovers, all in individual portions and clearly labeled." I smiled. I enjoyed being needed.

"Have you given any thought to what happens if you don't make the camp?" Mom said.

"Honestly? Not even a little bit. Between practicing and finishing school for the semester, I've barely kept my nose at the waterline. Anything more and I think I'd have gone under." I hadn't told them this next bit. "I almost did as it was, until I fell apart at Lodestone, and it turned out I hadn't been reading my training plan right. I'd been overtraining—working way too hard—until Lodestone caught my mistake. As it was, my grades slipped."

"Be careful, Rem." Dad frowned. "You need that scholarship."

"I know, Dad. I brought my grades back up, and I met with my coaches about it. They told me not to worry. I think it helped that I went in knowing there was a problem and having a solution in hand."

Mom beamed at me. "I love how much you've grown up this year."

I squirmed. Not the most comfortable subject for me.

"It's true, Jeremy. Don't be afraid of the compliment. Your brother's always gone with the flow, but you? You've always been a fighter, and that's both good and bad."

"What does that mean?"

"Only that not everything is a battle, but you see it that way," Dad said. "When something is a battle, however, you'll conquer it. When someone crosses you? You'll render him down to stew meat, probably before he knows what's coming. See the difference? It can be a tremendous waste of resources, but in troubled times, chances are you'll come out on top. As for your brother, it can take a fair amount of effort to get his attention, and it may be too late by the time something rouses him. That's why Laurel is so good for him."

I nodded. "That makes sense. So, what I'll need in a husband is someone to balance out my appetite for destruction."

"I'm not sure I'd put it that way, but yes." Dad laughed. "You have a lot of drive, and you'll go where you want to go in life. You're highly intelligent, and you're not patient with people you perceive as less intelligent. So yes, you'll need someone who can handle your rough edges and interpret the rest of the world for you. If nothing else, someone who'll take you everywhere twice—the second time to apologize."

"Someone like Michael. Where's he been, by the way?" Mom said.

I flinched. "Yeah, about him…"

"Yes?" Mom said.

"Okay, this won't be easy, and it brings up a bunch of subjects I've needed to discuss with you anyway." I took a deep breath. "We broke up. Actually, he dumped me."

Mom and Dad exchanged one of those "parental looks."

"I'm sure I speak for your mother, too, but I'm very sorry to hear that, Jeremy. I know how much he meant to you." Dad looked like he meant it too.

"We'd had a plan whereby I'd transfer to BU and he'd go to a school in Boston as well, but then I toured BU before the Head of the Charles and learned it wasn't the school for me. Then I spent the time between then and earlier this spring chewing out my entrails trying to screw up my courage to tell Michael." I sighed. "That wasn't all I screwed up, I guess. The excrement hit the fan a few weeks before the Crew Classic. He still can't tell me exactly why it was a deal breaker, particularly since he won't be going to school in Boston himself, but there it is. Anyway, that's a long way of saying I'm not transferring."

My parents looked shocked, I'll give them that.

"That's actually a fairly brief way of delivering a lot of news at once," Dad said. "So. Michael. How do you feel about this?"

"Obviously, I wasn't too happy, but you can't make people stay in a relationship. I'm talking it over in therapy, and we're trying to stay friends, Michael and I." I stopped pretending to eat, not even bothering to push food around on my plate for all that I'd cooked it.

Mom raised one eyebrow. I've heard it's a heritable trait, so maybe I got it from her. "Interesting choice of words—trying to stay friends."

"I know, right?" I laughed, even though it wasn't funny. "I'm trying not to find the way he handled it offensive—not talking to me for weeks, then being an asshole before getting over himself and expecting us to be almost like we were before, only not boyfriends—while he's trying not to get angry at me for being angry."

"Jeremy Babcock—life in hard mode" was all Dad said.

"I don't go out of my way to make things hard, honest."

Dad laughed. "No, I don't suppose you do. It seems to happen nonetheless."

"Tell me about it," I said ruefully. For years I'd tended to do my thing without bothering my parents about it. Partly that was a twin thing. Geoff and I had kept in nearly constant contact with each other as we'd grown older and grown into our high-school activities, because it felt more natural to us than letting our parents know. Eventually they'd stopped fighting it and started asking us. But now Geoff and I lived on opposite ends of the state, and I lived very close to our parents. Maybe I needed to mend some fences. "I don't suppose…"

"What, Jeremy?" Mom said.

"That is, I know it's not much notice and all that, less than two weeks, but is there any way you might come out to see me race at the selection camp?" Why did this matter to me? I didn't know, but somehow it did suddenly.

I held my breath while my parents looked at each other.

"Awww jeez, never mind. It was a stupid question. Forget I asked." I couldn't get away from the table fast enough.

"Remy!" Mom called after me. "Come back."

"Coach Lodestone already gave us the dates," Dad said. "We've been waiting for you to ask."

That stopped me in my tracks. "Oh."

"Actually, speaking of asking, that's what we did. We wanted to be there to support you, but you know what it's like for me to move patients. It's just easier not to book them during a certain window of time." At my obvious relief, Dad continued, "We'll get this family stuff down, you'll see."

I laughed. Whether it was from nerves and anxiety or Dad's joke, I couldn't tell, and maybe it didn't matter.

Mom nodded. "We're trying, and that's what matters, right?"

"Right. I'm going to assume that if Lodestone gave you the dates, he's also given you information about where to stay and things like that?"

"Correct." Mom nodded. "I'm so glad you want us there."

"I'm starting to find I need my family, after all."

"I'm assuming you don't mean just for money? And speaking of, what do you want to do about that contract since you're not going to BU?" Mom said.

"I've kind of got a plan for that, if you're willing to at least consider the notion."

"For someone who's barely kept his nose at the waterline, you've given a surprising amount of thought to your future." Dad was always a shrewd one. He might not always have paid attention to what his family did, but he wasn't stupid. "We're certainly willing to listen, aren't we, Dina?"

"We'll always listen, yes," Mom said.

"It's occurred to me that barring anything unforeseen, my undergrad education's essentially being paid for by CalPac, right?"

"Assuming you keep your crew scholarship, yes, and by all reports that's not going to be an issue." Dad made "keep going" gestures.

"So, I wondered if maybe you'd be willing to at least help pay for a graduate program, instead." Then I held my breath.

My parents looked at each other and basically shrugged. Huh.

"We'd have to see what it'd cost, of course. What kind of program are you thinking, or is it too soon yet?" Dad said.

I knew my parents. They'd always preferred the concrete to the airy-fairy, especially Dad. "I've been looking at nursing, as a matter of fact. It would make use of my biology major, and it's attracted me since I contracted HIV."

"I can think of worse reasons to go into a field, Steven," Mom said.

Dad nodded. "So can I. Registered nurse? Nurse practitioner?"

"Probably an RN at first, but yes, eventually I'd like to be a nurse practitioner. The people who've helped me the most have been NPs."

"Oh, yes, Heath and Jerry," Mom said. "What do you call them, your HIV godfathers?"

I smiled. "Something like that. They've been inspirational, but the fact that UC Davis now has a school of nursing as part of its medical school has also been a factor in my calculations. Despite my best efforts, this area has gotten under my skin. I'd be able to stay in the Sacramento area and still pursue my education. Between City College, Sac State, and now the nursing school for the nurse practitioner education, it's all covered. If CalPac weren't paying for my education, it'd make sense to transfer somewhere that offered a bachelor's degree in nursing. Since CalPac doesn't, that's not an option. I still think we'll come out financially ahead this way."

"You really have been thinking about this," Mom said. I could tell she was impressed.

"Yep. While I may be clueless about what to do for the rest of my summer, I more or less have my future mapped out."

"I can see that. I have to tell you, I'm as impressed by that as the fact that you don't seem to want to be a rowing bum." Dad started stacking dirty plates.

"Okay, so here's the deal with rowing, and it's a secret to no one in this family. I'm good, possibly with the potential to be great. I want to see how far it'll take me." I leaned back in my chair. "But even if it takes me to the Olympics a couple of times, crew isn't one of the sports that lands endorsements, and even endorsements aren't enough to set people up for life. At most, I might be able to sell myself as a motivational speaker, and that's not what I want to do. Can you even see that? Remy Babcock, demotivational speaker. I won't tell you how to do something, but I'll tell you you're an idiot for ten grand. So, I'll ride the carbon fiber for a while and when it's time to get off, I will. I'll always be involved in the sport in some manner, but do I want to be a collegiate coach? I'm not even sure I can say that. So...nursing."

"Interesting" was all Dad said.

"Seriously, Dad. That's what a lot of people who compete on the levels I'm heading for do when they reach the end of it. But I can't honestly say I want to line up for Pendergast's or Ridgewood's jobs. Perhaps you're thinking 'bullshit,' or I'm burned out by training, and maybe you're right." I shrugged. "I'd still rather plan on nursing and kicking around Cap City and rowing for fun. Doesn't that sound like a better way to live? It does to me."

Mom laughed at that. "I think Geoff once said you've never been young. That proves it."

"I don't know if I'd go that far, Dina, but I'll say this. Remy, I don't think your mother or I can argue with anything you've said, nor is there a reason to. Speaking as your father and as a therapist, I think you've got a healthy attitude toward crew and your future possibilities." Mom nodded as Dad kept speaking. "While we'd have to see what Geoff has planned before we can commit to paying for all of nursing school, don't think we're not aware that your undergrad education—all of it—is costing us less than we'd pay for a year or two at BU."

"Your father's right. I know that CalPac wasn't your first choice, and that you in fact attended it under duress, but not only are you thriving there, you're happy. That should free up money for education beyond your bachelor's."

"All right, then. All I can do is thank you for listening. I know you don't owe me anything, so...thanks for being willing to consider it." I hoped they'd see their way to at least help to defray the costs. I was reasonably certain they would, as I knew they'd been saving for my education—Geoff's too—and that they weren't touching that money, or at least not much of it.

Dad slowly shook his head. "When'd you turn into the reasonable one?"

"This year. I've grown up a lot."

Then Dad shocked the hell out of me. He hugged me. "You certainly have, and I'm proud of you."

"Stop it, Steven. You'll scare him."

Ladies and gentlemen, my parents.

Chapter Thirty

Lodestone and I flew out to West Windsor, New Jersey, a few days before the selection camp started. I wanted to get the lay of the land, as it were, to say nothing of rigging my boat to my satisfaction. Lodestone had spoken to my grandparents and explained the cost-benefit analysis of renting another boat versus paying to ship the boat I'd trained in across the country. They had clearly found that analysis compelling because I would be rowing my own single at the camp.

I felt some serious guilt where my grandparents and the cost of this were concerned and said as much to Lodestone. "I wish I'd kept receipts or something, maybe set myself up as a nonprofit."

"Oh, Remy." Lodestone patted my cheek in the most patronizing way possible. "For starters, nonprofits don't actually work that way. Then there's the fact that Cap City actually is a 501(c)(3) organization."

I connected the whole thing in a flash. "So that's why my grandparents have funneled everything through you. It's actually being funneled through Cap City's treasury so they can deduct all of this."

"That and so my payroll deductions are on the up-and-up, but essentially, yes."

"So, who owns my boat?" I wasn't entirely sure I wanted to hear the answer, but I knew I needed to.

"That's the thing. Cap City's board started to balk at that point, and your grandfather stepped in to deal with them personally. I don't think they knew what hit them. I still want to know how rich they are." Lodestone made an adjustment to the pitch of the oarlocks, squinting at them like that would make a difference. "Apparently the glory of having an athlete and coach training at the highest levels wasn't enough. Whatever. I don't know the details, only that one of the board members who's a lawyer—family law, I think—went toe-to-toe with your grandfather's business attorney. I'm told the results weren't pretty, but oops. Sucks to be them. So, the boat's yours, I don't know what your grandfather worked out, and the board got spanked."

"Heh."

"Try not to gloat. It's unbecoming."

I laughed. "Says the man who just gloated."

"Hush, you."

The fun and games weren't only on the water, and they started before the trials did. Both my parents and my grandparents arrived a day or two ahead of time, and for whatever deranged reason, both couples assumed that

Marissa Lodestone would play hostess. Peter Lodestone and I both rolled our eyes at the notion, since Marissa was there for one reason, and that was to see if Peter's coaching had paid off. I'd known Marissa since I was a high school freshman and she was Lodestone's girlfriend. Really? Play hostess? "Play" was right, because she didn't have a domestic bone in her body. Anything domestic occurring in the Lodestone household happened because my coach was a rowing bum. For her part, Marissa simply turned her cochlear implants off by removing their processors—I'd seen her do it before—and pretended she couldn't read lips.

Me? The work of six months was focused on the next few days, and I had no intention of running interference between my parents and grandparents. Grow up, already. Or maybe I imagined everything, since I could've made a diamond by clenching coal between my teeth. Also, I've been accused a time or two of being completely self-absorbed. I preferred to think of it as being of singular focus. Everything unrelated to rowing I ignored more than ever. After, I'd play host, maybe even interpret for Marissa if she were still playing that game. My sign language might've been rusty, but I still remembered it.

The selection methods themselves were quite simple and yet incredibly nerve-racking. Over the course of the selection event, we were run through trials boats and selection camp boats. Trials boats consisted of coxed fours, quads, and everything smaller, right down to my beloved single. The smallest selection camp boats, on the other hand, were the coxless fours, but mostly? The mighty eights. Sure, they weren't the men's and women's eights from the Olympic teams—seriously, watching the Olympic men's eight always sent shivers down my spine—but many of the people who made the U23 eights would end up in serious contention for Olympic boats. Actually, there was no distinction between athletes rowing eights and scullers. All athletes at the selection camp tested for all boats, and anyone making the cut? His or her shit didn't stink, and that was the end of it.

No pressure.

Imagine my surprise when the morning of the first day of the tests dawned pleasant and free of humidity. Wasn't the East Coast supposed to be hot and humid in the summer? California bias, much, Remy? Maybe—just maybe—USRowing had selected the site in New Jersey for a reason, and that reason was highs in the 70s and 80s with low humidity and no bugs. Regardless, it was a beautiful day to be handed my ass, and that started a trend that didn't let up the entire time. At least, that's how it felt to me. Nothing clicked, and I felt like a novice on the first day of learn-to-row camp.

My family made soothing noises for the entire camp, but Lodestone understood that platitudes and I mixed as well as gasoline and phosphorous-bearing laundry detergent. That is, a sticky, flammable combination that was a close approximation to napalm. Then again, Lodestone knew me better than my family too.

Someone must've tipped off Geoff because he texted me. Actually, the entire San Diego contingent texted me, including Craig. Michael even called. As much as I loved them all for encouraging me, I couldn't wrench my attention away from the Hindenburg-like flaming wreck of all my work. I had to keep my head in the boats.

Finally it was over. I felt... I wasn't sure, actually. My feelings were too complicated to sort out, at least at first. I knew I'd eventually debrief with Lodestone, and in the meantime, I only prayed I'd escape without too many "Awww, poor baby" comments from my family.

Not long after the apocalypse, three of the national team coaches approached me. For some reason all I could think of was *Macbeth*. The fact that all three wore black technical fiber shirts or warm-up pants hardly helped to rein my imagination in.

"Hi, Jeremy," the first Weird Sister said. "We wanted to congratulate you for your strong performance."

"It wasn't strong enough." So yeah, that was graceless.

The second Weird Sister sighed. "I was afraid you'd see it that way."

I cocked my head. "I didn't make the cut. Is there some other way to see it?"

"Actually, yes, and that's why we're here. We've been watching you, Remy. I think you knew that. You're still growing and maturing, and we expect to see you back here next year," the first Weird Sister said. "Your erg tests are great. Fantastic, even. But like the stupid saying goes, ergs don't float. There's something missing with your performance on the water. We think you can get this, and that's why we want to see you next year. In fact, we expect to see you at the identification camps and national team testing."

"That's something, I guess." I tried to rally. I was tired—no, not tired, exhausted, like the fatigue of the last six months came crashing down now that I could let go.

The third Weird Sister nodded. "The one thing we want you to work on is your ability to blend with other rowers. You're a demon in that single, but you don't mesh well with others yet. We want to see more of that. One of the criteria is the athlete's ability to match the style and technique of the rest of the crew, and that's just not there. You may want to cry shenanigans, but we're as disappointed as you are."

I thought for a moment. I really hated it when Pendergast was right. I sighed. "It's not the first time I've heard that. I trained so hard in my single..."

"I don't doubt it," the third Weird Sister said. "I'm going to guess, based on what I've seen and what Lodestone's told me, you're enough better than the other guys at CalPac that the single's the only way to challenge you. That's another reason we want to see you again."

"It's not an automatic invite like the Head of the Charles, but if it were, you'd have one. Speaking of, you did a great job in that quad, but...what happened?" the first Weird Sister said, curiosity overcoming manners. "It's like you've lost ground or something."

I snorted. "I've known some of those guys for a long time, and two of them are like older brothers to me. It took almost nothing for me to synch up with them."

"Your coach has film of all of this, some of it he took, some of it's ours. But here's the deal," the second Weird Sister said. "We don't want you to watch it for a while, okay? Take a break, and don't look at it until you can think about crew without bitterness."

"What?" The first Weird Sister smiled ruefully. "You think we don't understand the thought process? Trust me, every single one of us understands what you'll feel soon, because we've been there. Go home, do something else for a while, and try to remember that you didn't get here by being a crappy rower."

I nodded. Sure, I didn't get here by being a crappy rower, but I was leaving here without being on the U23 team. I needed some time. I wasn't ready to shrug off six months of the hardest physical and mental work I'd ever done, six months to which I'd sacrificed everything, possibly including the most meaningful relationship of my life.

And it'd all been flushed down the shitter. When I thought about it, and it was impossible not to, it hardly seemed real. I knew one thing at that moment. I needed not to be where I was.

Mom and Dad approached. "I need to cool down. I'm going to go for a quick run, okay?"

Dad wasn't stupid. "Sure, Remy. We'll meet you back at the hotel."

I took off before anyone else could catch me. Anyone except Lodestone. Sometimes I hated him.

He caught up to me easily. Of course. He hadn't rowed his guts out for four solid days. "Don't shut them out, Remy. They're concerned."

"Doesn't a boy at least get to be mad about this in private without people getting their emotions all over me? I've got enough of my own to deal with." That sounded so bitchy.

"Someone else, maybe. Not you. You get broody and keep things inside."

Could Lodestone not have the decency to sound winded when he was hectoring me?

"Well, fuck you very much for that. I've just been humiliated in front of the elite of our sport, an elite I'm not a part of. Maybe I'd like not to deal with them right now."

I picked up my pace. So much for a cooldown. Of course, that bastard had to match me.

"You get to feel your feelings—"

"Well, thank you so much, Dr. Phil!"

"Did you ever think I might be upset too?"

"Bully for you! Did I ask you to come for a run with me? I'm angry and pissed, and I'm running to get away from people. Six goddam months, Lodestone! I should've worked harder. Could I have worked harder?"

Lodestone yanked on my collar so I had stop.

"Bastard. That hurt."

"Brat."

"Whatever." Actually, I signed *W-E-M-L*, and if he hadn't figured out that meant Whatever, Major Loser yet, there was no hope for him. How long had he coached teens for Cap City?

Lodestone rolled his eyes. "Just tell me to fuck off, because that's what that means."

He asked for it... "Fuck off."

Lodestone stared at me. "You can be such a shit."

Did he seriously not know not to yank my chain when I was in one of these moods?

"You told me to tell you to fuck off. You must feel very satisfied right now."

"I should beat you for that."

I grinned, showing lots of teeth. "You know I like that. So, don't tease if you're not going to follow through."

Then he laughed and stuck out his tongue.

"Real mature there, Lodestone."

"I coach teens. What do you expect?"

I sighed. "I don't know. Not to be handed my ass?"

"Rem, I know it doesn't seem that way now, but you weren't handed your ass, I promise." Lodestone put his arm across my shoulder and tried to turn me around.

I resisted. "Seriously, could I have worked harder? Or smarter or something? I don't play well with others?"

"No shit. Like that's news?" Lodestone snorted. "But this isn't a question we can answer now."

"I know. I need a break. I feel like... I feel old. Why do I feel old?" I wanted more than anything to collapse against my coach and let him take care of me.

"Rem, look at me. Jeez, you're stubborn." Lodestone forced me to turn and look at him. "You feel old for a bunch of reasons, not the least of which is because you've been focused on this for half a year and it's over. No, not like we wanted it to be, but it's over."

When he was sure he had my attention, he continued. "Take a break. I mean it. Do nothing physical for a week, maybe two. Three if that feels right. You've hovered on the edge of being overtrained for months, now. That's why I've watched you so carefully."

I nodded. "Yeah. I'm...done."

"You are, Rem. That's part of why you're so upset right now. Yes, dreams crushed, but also? You're on the brink of collapse. I can almost guarantee you that with a week's rest, you'll feel a lot different about this. That said, I was serious about not working out for a while, and when you do, I don't want it to have anything to do with rowing."

I looked at him like he was crazy.

"I'm not kidding. Sure, you need to stay in shape, but give those muscles a rest. Give your mind a rest." Lodestone looked like he was thinking for a moment. "Cross-train, like running or biking. Swim. You don't even have to be very good at it to keep your cardiovascular conditioning up."

I tried to imagine my life without the constant training. I failed. How pathetic.

"Yeah, okay. Do I want to do this again? Do you?"

Lodestone made a face. "Do not make this decision now. Promise me. I don't want you thinking about it for at least a month. People will ask you what you're going to do. Lie to them."

I smiled. "What're you going to do? Don't say go to Disneyland."

"Screw you. Disney *World*. I'm taking my wife to Disney World. It's closer to where we are right now, and I want to be reacquainted with her."

When we returned to the rowing course, I did what I needed to do. I marched right up to Marissa. "Thank you," I signed.

"What're you thanking me for?" she signed back.

"For letting me monopolize your husband, to say nothing of your family time, for the last six months."

She smiled at me. "We knew what we were getting into."

"I'm glad. I had no clue."

"LOL," Marissa said with her fingers. "Thanks for being aware of it. That means a lot."

I had no idea Internet slang worked so well with signing, or maybe that was all Marissa. I guess it was like any foreign language. What I learned in school was the formal version. Marissa once told me I sounded "Victorian."

What people actually spoke was the fast, shorthand version, the casual form of the language that evolved rapidly. I only signed with Marissa, which meant my signing was perpetually rusty.

Marissa gave me a hug. "I know you worked hard, Remy. I'm sorry it didn't go the way you and Peter planned."

"Me, too. Have fun at Disney World. I'm going to sleep for a month and eat like a hog."

With her laughter echoing in my wake, I went in search of my relatives.

Chapter Thirty-One

"So, how'd it go?"

Randy and I met up for coffee during a break in between work and classes. Everyone had found a way to keep busy this summer, everyone but me. Or at least that's how it felt.

Okay, maybe "coffee" was an exaggeration. More like iced tea or blended coffee drinks, because July in the Sacramento Valley? Almost hot enough to make blacktop bubble.

Randy sounded so eager, so excited for me. I felt like an asshole for bursting his bubble. I groaned and buried my face in my hands. "I was slaughtered. I had no business being there."

He listened to my tale of woe and misery and then did something completely unexpected. He leaned over the table and slapped me. Lightly, because he was a friend.

"Shut it." His pale-blue eyes looked so cold. I'd never seen him like this.

"That hurt!" I rubbed my cheek. I'd thought he seemed like such a shy, even diffident, guy, and now this?

"Self-pitying spew makes me sick to my stomach."

I stared at him, openmouthed. "Dude, I—"

"Had a chance to do something that the vast majority of rowers will never do because they're not that good, which you are through some combination of genetics, drive, and skill. You? From what you told me, you missed the cut by a hair, and the coaches told you that you'd damn well better keep trying. Wasn't that about the extent of it?" Randy cut his eyes to the side, like he couldn't stand the sight of me a second longer.

"When you put it that way..."

"Not me, Remy, the USRowing coaches."

I sighed. Then I smiled sheepishly. "I guess I sound pretty bratty."

"You sounded spoiled and petulant, and that's a terrible look for anyone." Then Randy looked me with his amazing blue eyes. They sparkled. "Especially you."

Oh crap. I knew right then that Randy was going to be trouble.

Like I couldn't have figured it out before.

Randy glanced down at his watch. He wore one of those huge diving watches. "Damn, is it that late?"

"How would I know? You're the one with the watch."

"I have class in ten minutes. Catch you later," Randy said. He took off, ruffling my hair on the way by.

I almost missed that, Randy. Could you flirt a little harder?

Because life couldn't ever settle down, right? On my way home, I stopped by the supermarket. As I'd told Mom and Dad, I could at least leave their freezer filled since I wouldn't be working that summer. I didn't count reading in the shade by the pool as working.

Later, over dinner, Mom asked me, "How are you, Rem? Really?"

"I'm upset. Who wouldn't be? But—" Dad inhaled to say something, but I got there first. "—I'm getting over it. There's not much point to stewing over the past."

"You took the words out of my mouth, Rem." Dad smiled.

I shook my head. "A friend helped me get some perspective earlier today, I'll admit that. Why he brought home what everyone else who's said the same couldn't get through, I can't tell you."

"Critical mass? Whatever the reason, I'm glad you're feeling better," Mom said. "Now tell me, where are you finding these recipes?"

They were going to hate me for this... "Your kitchen. You have three shelves of cookbooks. Most of them? Their spines have never been cracked."

The two weeks before I left for Chicago passed at a stately pace, and that suited me fine. I finished my training journal and sent it all off to iPartwithmymoney to be bound into a book suitable for display on coffee tables everywhere. Grandma and Grandpa not only deserved a copy, I planned to deliver it personally. That meant paying for a rush job, but by that time, what was a few more dollars compared to how much the entire enterprise had cost already?

I saw Randy a few more times, but the man truly was busy. I never asked, but I suspected he was working to pay for as much of school as possible. As much as I wanted to play at obliviousness, I knew perfectly well what his intentions were. But me and Michael? I couldn't shake the idea that we had unfinished business. I don't know why I thought that. It wasn't as if I expected us to get back together, but until I felt like a free man, I knew I wouldn't pursue anything with anyone else. I couldn't. That was how I operated. Or didn't. Whatever.

So, when Michael texted me to tell me he planned to drive himself across the country before school started, I felt obligated to say goodbye. Just for old times' sake, I brought him a going-away present, a picture of our Cap City gentlemen's eight at the Crew Classic from my senior year.

MICHAEL: *So do U want to come over?*

ME: *A neutral location seems the better part of valor.*

Which is how we ended up meeting for Chinese food, our default lunch.

"So," I said, obviously trying to make conversation after the silence had dragged on too long, "driving yourself across the country?"

"It's going to be great! I've mapped out every cheesy roadside distraction I can find." Michael grinned. I hadn't seen him this happy in a while, not since grad night. Actually, I hadn't seen him since grad night, period.

Apparently, Michael and his parents had already flown out to Providence to make sure all was in readiness, so all Michael needed to do was get himself to Brown before school started. How his overprotective and frankly insane parents could let him drive across the country solo escaped me, but nope, not my place to speak up.

"I'm almost afraid to ask, but how're you doing after the selection camp?" Michael looked like he was braced for an explosion.

"Obviously, I'm disappointed, but I'm following Lodestone's advice and not thinking about it or making any decisions about going through the training process again for a while." I shrugged. "Until I can think of sculling without screaming, I'm cross-training, and not even that very intensely." I thought about it some more. "I'll drop Lodestone an e-mail and see how he's doing, maybe see if he's ready to go out for a strictly recreational row. So anyway, to answer your question, I really am fine."

Michael smiled. "That's great, Rem."

We made chitchat through the rest of lunch, but that's all it felt like, small talk. Is this what we'd come to? As we said our goodbyes in the parking lot, Michael stopped. "Wait, I've got something for you."

He took off for his car before I could say, "Me too."

Michael handed me a box when he returned. "What's this?"

"Just stuff."

I opened it up. It was the Apple harvest. "What? Why?"

"I don't feel right keeping them."

"Really." I smelled a rat, or rather, two of them.

Michael squirmed. "Okay, my parents figured out where they came from and weren't comfortable with me accepting that kind of gift from you, especially after we broke up."

"Way to cut the cord, *Mikey*. You're sure to do well in college." Then I realized I wasn't done, not nearly. "I notice you're only returning all these fine electronics after they've gotten you through the end of high school. That's convenient."

"The fuck?" Michael looked wounded, but c'mon. What did he expect me to think? His parents could've replaced—or returned—his computer at any time.

"What're you going to use in college?" Seemed like a logical question to me.

Michael crossed his arms. "I don't have to answer that."

"You're right, you don't. It pretty much answers itself." I started to walk away, but then turned around. "I cannot believe I went to bat against my family for you, for this. You didn't even have the balls to end this like a man. You just did the fadeaway."

"You did not say that." Michael reached out and grabbed my arm to stop me from leaving. "You wanna know what I can't believe? I can't believe I put up with your temper. I can't believe I put up with your cluelessness and arrogance, with your complete obliviousness to anything but crew, but most of all I can't believe I spent two fucking years with someone who went and got himself goddam AIDS because he fucked everything that moved one summer but was too stupid to use condoms. Good luck, Jeremy, you're going to need it."

Michael turned on his heel and stormed off, leaving me too stunned to say anything. Maybe there was nothing for me to say. I sat in my car for a long time after that, despite the heat. I had enough sense to put the windows down, and thank goodness I'd parked in the shade.

I could've lived with us no longer being romantically involved. In fact, I'd been living with that since April. But this...this hatred. How long had he—had we—been saving it up? I likewise could've lived with the death of the relationship if only we had stayed friends, but that line about us always remaining friends had so obviously become a lie, and it made me sick. The tempest that had spun up in the place of friendship had sown only devastation, and I knew I'd only reap self-recrimination and sorrow for...I had no idea how long.

*

Grandma and Grandpa Fisher soothed me considerably when I visited them only a few days after the blowup with Michael.

Just like last time, Grandpa met me outside baggage claim. "Lord, it's every bit as bad as last time, only in the other direction," I bitched.

"Hello to you, too, Jeremy." Grandpa looked amused.

"Yeah, hi, Grandpa. Seriously, what's with the weather around here? Does it always suck?" I flapped my polo shirt.

"It's always worse near the airport. It's a bit cooler by the lake."

I raised one eyebrow. "Enough to make a difference?"

When Grandpa stalled, I knew I had my answer.

"The rain helps cool it off."

"Doesn't that make it muggier?"

Grandpa nodded. "No climate's perfect, Jeremy."

"I suppose not." I thought of Lake Tahoe in the spring and summer and kept my mouth shut, if only because the lake during winter could get brutal, or would, if it ever snowed again. "Besides," I said with a grin, "I could've checked an atlas, right?"

"Right."

We laughed and headed for the parking garage.

I knew more or less what to expect this time and couldn't wait for more of that jet fuel Grandma tried to pass off as coffee. It might help me weather the rest of the day. I didn't want to crash after lunch, but early morning flights from Sacramento somehow seemed worse than red-eyes.

I spent the rest of the day visiting with my grandparents, which, after all, was the reason for my visit.

"You were so right about the steps to success, Grandpa, but I also learned that sometimes, paying the price isn't enough, is it?"

Grandpa shook his head. "No, it's not. I'm sorry you learned that lesson so young, but in a way, I'm also not. When it happens to you later, you won't be shocked, and it won't set you back, will it?"

"I can only hope not, right?" What else could I say?

"Now tell us about that young man of yours," Grandma said. "I was surprised we didn't see him at the selection camp."

I made a face. "We broke up in April, allegedly staying friends, but it's been downhill ever since until right before I left. We're not friends anymore, and we're not even civil these days."

"Oh, that's too bad." Grandma looked concerned, and I could tell she wanted more information. Grandpa shot her a warning look, however.

I took pity on her and gave them the edited version. "So, it's not like I have to worry about Michael running around poisoning the social well."

"At least he's that mature." Grandma shook her head.

"I'm not sure I'd say that; it's simply that we no longer have any friends in common." I thought about it for a moment. "I don't actually have that wide a social circle anymore. I'm going to have to work on that when school starts. It narrowed down during training an awful lot."

I got up. "Speaking of which, I have a gift for you. I'll be right back."

When I returned from my room, I presented them with the bound training journal. It had turned out very well, I thought. "Whether I succeeded or not, I count this as a success. I did something most people will never get the chance to do," I said, thinking of Randy.

Grandma clapped her hands. "Look at this, Howard. He brought visuals. No one—not one single person—has *ever* gotten visuals like this from their children or grandchildren."

I had to smile. They both looked so smug. "So...any parties we should attend?"

"Oh, we'll find a way to make sure this is seen, never fear. In the meantime, can we have copies of these pictures?" Grandpa said.

"Of course. I have most of them saved to online accounts. Ten minutes with your computer—and only one of those giant screens, please—and you can have as many of those pictures as you want."

"There's no time like the present." Grandpa hauled me to my feet. Jeez, he was strong. "I think we'll take the lot of them, and then I'll transfer the best to our phones."

As it turned out, there were a number of parties—cocktail, garden, and other sorts. I almost felt sorry for their friends. Almost.

A few days later, I met Lance and Caden for lunch. I was so glad my visit with my grandparents coincided with their visits to the Windy City.

We updated each other on our lives, and I'd been naïve in the extreme to think I'd escape without updating them about my relationship or lack thereof.

"Score! My turn!" Caden yelled in the middle of the restaurant.

I touched his cheek. "Oh, Caden. You'll be the first person I call if I ever want to have another sleazy bathroom hookup."

"Awww, thanks. That's the nicest thing anyone's ever said to me." Caden's eyes popped. "Wait, you said 'another'?"

"I don't know, did he?" Lance sipped his tea and smiled enigmatically. He turned to me. "You need to deal with this in person. Don't let it die like this."

I shook my head. "Lance, it's already over. It has ended, past tense."

"Yeah, you guys are over all right, but you meant too much to each other for this kind of hate." Caden sighed. "What you two had was what I was looking for, and if you guys couldn't make it work..."

Who are you, and what've you done with the real Caden? I almost said that aloud. "You surprise me, Caden."

Caden grinned. "I know, right?"

"Just when you think you can write him off as a complete himbo, he says something like that." Lance sighed and shook his head.

"You know I'm right," Caden said around a mouthful of bread.

"That's the aggravating part. You really are." I thought for a moment. "I don't know how to make this work, or even if I want to do the heavy lifting, not after what he said. This breakup has been the gift that keeps on giving, and I'm tired of it."

"So much for being the adult." Caden toasted me with his beer.

"Sometimes," I said, "being an adult is knowing when to walk away."

Chapter Thirty-Two

I thought about their words as I stood in O'Hare, looking for my gate. I had almost run out of summer. In fact, I needed to report to CalPac and Coach Pendergast for preseason training. I'd had my fun with my post selection-camp summer, but the real world beckoned.

When my phone rang, I pulled it out. I recognized the number all too well. "Hello, Michael."

"Hi," Michael said softly. "I... Thanks for answering. Under the circumstances, I thought you might've deleted me and sent all my calls to voice mail."

"You probably shouldn't give me notions. Why'd you call?" Damn, I sounded cold, but then again, given our last conversation...

Michael sighed. "Can't I call my ex-boyfriend?"

"Under the circumstances, no." There it was. I'd found my gate.

"I guess... Where are you? It's awfully noisy."

"O'Hare."

"Visiting your grandparents?"

I rolled my eyes. "No, I visited my grandparents. Now I'm on my way home."

Michael started crying. "I'm so s-s-sorry I said those things to you. I'm the worst human being ever."

I held the phone away from my ear and squinted at it. "Have you been drinking?"

Maybe I was being drunk dialed for the first time in my life. Awesome.

"N-n-no. I feel so horrible. How can you stand me?"

News flash, Michael...

I probably shouldn't say that to him.

"Oh, Rem, what've we become?"

Pretty much what you wanted us to become in April with your juvenile and immature handling of our breakup. Instead, I said, "Where are you?"

"Ohio. Some place called Austintown."

That sounded improbable. "On purpose?"

"It's right outside of Youngstown, but I was too tired to keep driving."

I cared in spite of myself. "How far are you from Rhode Island? I don't actually know the geography." Or care. "Are you in any condition to make this drive?"

Michael was well and truly crying by this point in time. I knew then I wouldn't be making that plane to Sacramento, so I got up and started looking for someplace quieter. I thought he'd be closer to Providence than that.

When he'd wound down a bit, I tried again. "When did you leave?"

"A couple of days after we fought, maybe a week." Michael sniffled. "I couldn't exactly get my act together right away."

I pulled my laptop out, and using his home address as the starting point, I mapped out Davis to Providence. I remembered that Michael had planned a route that included every horrible roadside attraction, but I figured the direct route would give me a rough idea how long the drive would take. Hmmm, forty-four hours. How did mapping programs come up with something that exact? How did they take local traffic into account? Or people's driving speeds? Or weather? Good lord, Michael was driving across the Midwest during the summer. Didn't they have tornadoes and killer hail?

"And you're outside of Youngstown, you said?"

"Right. Why?"

"I'm looking online to see how long a drive you have left... Okay, you're right outside Pennsylvania, so you've got all of that state, plus New Jersey, to go before you leave the 80 and drive around New York City—please, Michael, drive around New York—and then head up into New England on the 95. In other words, according to the maps, about three hundred and seventy miles."

Michael groaned.

"It could be worse. In our terms, that's only from home to LA." Listen to me being all Pollyanna for my ex.

"Yeah, with LA traffic in the form of New York."

This whole conversation made me uncomfortable. I felt like I should apologize, but at the same time I didn't want to. I hadn't been dishonest, just unforgivably blunt. In other words, me but more so.

Okay, so Dad's words about needing a partner to buffer me or take me everywhere twice made a lot more sense. I realized something. It wasn't so much that I was an emotionless bastard. I had simply compartmentalized again, sealing all of this off. I disliked messes, and was this ever a messy sitch. Suddenly I knew if I didn't handle this right, it really would be the end, and I didn't think I wanted that, not really. I only wanted the slop to stop. So untidy.

"All right, Michael, here's what we're going to do. You're going to take a long, hot bath to relax. Eat something, even if you don't feel like it, and then go to bed. If you can face the road when you wake up, great. Get going. Otherwise, take a slow day tomorrow."

"Yes, all right. I can do that. What're you going to do?"

I'd hate myself later for this, I was sure. "I'm going to get on an airplane. You're going to call me the minute you reach Providence. Got that?"

"Yeah, I... I can do that. And, Remy?"

"Yes, Michael?"

"Thanks, Rem."

"Get some rest, Michael. You'll feel better tomorrow."

I really needed to do something about him calling me Rem. He'd forfeited the privilege.

I could say what I wanted to about being an adult and forgiveness, but I realized right there in the middle of O'Hare that I needed to be there for Michael. So, I found the United service desk.

"I need to be in Providence, RI, and reasonably soon. How possible is that, and what's it going to cost?"

*

In the end, it turned out not to be all that expensive and relatively quick. I caught a flight into Boston that left only a couple of hours later and then drove down to Providence. Thanks to traffic, I could've walked faster, but oh well. I was there long before Michael would arrive, so I looked around. Thanks to the magic of the Internetz and the wait for my flight to Boston, I booked a hotel room close to Brown. Then I called Mom and Dad and explained it all. They thought I was doing the right thing, and that made me feel better about it.

After breakfast, I packed some workout gear in my messenger bag and hit Brown's campus. I'd looked up the men's crew, too, and dropped an e-mail to the men's varsity coach. Practice wasn't until later this afternoon, so I had a day to kill with exploring and reading. Brown looked like a great school from what I saw in one day's visit. You know, for a nest of social justice warriors.

Later in the day, I made my way to the Marston Boathouse, an old fish-processing plant that had been renovated extensively. I loved it the second I walked in the door. Introductions were made, and the men's varsity coach found a place for me in one of his boats, doing exactly what I should've been doing at CalPac. Maybe that would make Pendergast feel better about my absence. The row was fantastic for all that I'd stayed away from crew since late June. When I'd explained that particular fact to the coach, his response was, "Great, none of these guys have rowed all summer, either. Hop in and have some fun."

I hung out at the boathouse after practice to shoot the breeze, since clearly, I wasn't the only guy batting for my team on the Brown crew. Truly, a fine end to a good day. Or maybe not, since some of the guys planned to show the guy from CalPac a good time.

My phone rang. "Hey, Michael."

"Hi, Rem." Michael sniffled.

"Are you okay? Have you been crying?"

"Only a little," Michael mumbled.

That made my soul hurt for him. I could stomp and pretend to be an asshole, but the reality was I wanted us to be friends. That's how I'd tried to leave it when Michael had gotten so justifiably angry with me for not telling him about nixing BU, and it was how I'd tried to leave it after Lake Tahoe. Even if we couldn't make it work as boyfriends, we were supposed to be friends. I held up my index finger to indicate "one minute" to the guys from Brown's crew and then walked a little ways away.

"Where are you?" Michael's voice burned with curiosity, livelier than I'd heard it in recent days.

"The Marston Boathouse." Why did I blush? He couldn't see me.

"You're in Providence." It sounded like an accusation.

I laughed. "Kind of, yeah. Where're you?"

"New Jersey." Michael sighed.

"I'm glad you didn't tackle New York City."

"What?" Michael yelped. "I thought you wanted me to do it in a day. I felt horrible for letting you down."

"I was trying to be encouraging. But Michael? We're not boyfriends anymore, and you didn't let me down. If you were too tired, you totally made the right call. The thought of driving in New York terrifies me, so there's that."

"Something terrifies Jeremy Babcock? I thought you were fearless." A bit of the humor had returned to Michael's voice.

"Michael…"

"I'm sorry. It's been a rough day." He sounded defeated, and that was so not suave.

"Don't worry about it."

Michael giggled. "I should've known you'd find the boathouse."

"That was kind of a given, wasn't it?" I had to smile.

Then Michael actually laughed. "More like a natural law."

It was almost like old times, except it wasn't. "Go to sleep, Michael. You'll feel better in the morning."

"You always know exactly what to say to make me feel better," Michael said softly. As fond of me as he sounded right then, he had let that genie out of the bottle, and he could never put it back.

I needed to smother this in the cradle *now*. "That's because I'm going to be a nurse when I grow up. I'm practicing for that."

"Of course, you are." Michael yawned. "I'll see you tomorrow, I guess. And, Rem?"

"Yes?"

"Thank you."

"Good night, Michael."

*

I'd stayed out later than I'd planned to last night, but even though I used my fake ID and appearance to get into the good bars that catered to the over twenty-one crowd, I played the "I don't drink because they clash with all the drugs I take" card. Let them think I had a more interesting social life than I did.

I went to the boathouse planning to erg, but a twink with dirty-blond hair accosted me. "Are you Jeremy Babcock?"

"Uh...yes."

He was kind of cute. Okay, scratch that, he was hot in a twinky way that I hadn't known until that moment I liked, but daaaamn.

He stuck his hand out. "I'm Zach Jackson. Mike asked me to come find you and show you around."

All bemused, I shook Zach's hand. "Oh, he did, did he? He hasn't even gotten here yet."

"He'll get in sometime tonight. He didn't want you wandering around for another day." Zach smiled like he was super confident, but I bet if I pushed, I could scrape through it easily. That seemed pointless, however.

"Well, I'd planned to erg..."

Zach held up a Kindle. "Allowances have been made. Knock yourself out."

"You don't mind? I won't be more than about forty minutes, plus stretching and showering after." This would give me time to figure out what was going on too.

"I can see the look on your face. Mike texted me a couple of pictures of you last night. That's how I knew how to find you." Zach smiled. "You're kind of an open book."

"Or you can read minds." And Mike? That was interesting. "Okay, I'll go change and get busy."

"I'll be waiting."

And sure enough, a bit less than an hour later, after I'd worked out, stretched, and cleaned up, there was Zach.

Zach and I chatted over breakfast. Zach hailed from Providence, and he'd met "Mike" that summer. I'd had no idea Michael had been out here that long, or had even had the time to find someone, because by the time we were through with breakfast, I'd figured out that if Zach and Michael weren't already in a relationship, they soon would be. But certain other things weren't adding up.

"Uh-oh, I can see that look in your eyes," Zach said as we found a place in a coffee shop.

"I have a look in my eyes?" Of course, I had a look in my eyes, but the hell if I'd admit that to some prefreshman I'd only met that morning.

Zach nodded. "Mike warned me about it. It means you're getting all broody overthinking things."

"Exactly what did 'Mike' tell you, anyway?" I almost felt bad about pumping this kid for information, but if Michael wanted to send this Zach off to the Big Bad Wolf—apparently that was me—he had to assume the lamb would be gnawed on, if not slaughtered outright.

Zach's eyes grew round. "You're mad, aren't you?"

I stared at him. Then it clicked. This was all an act, and Zach was playing me. "And you are so full of shit."

Zach pouted.

I rolled my eyes. So much for cutting back on gestures of contempt. "Stop it. Your cover's blown."

"What gave it away?" Zach's voice dropped half an octave.

I shook my head. Were the games starting already? "Any number of little clues, but mostly the fact that Michael can't stand vapid innocents any more than I can."

"Damn. I'll have to work on that."

"Save it for dumber people too."

Zach shook his head. "He warned me you're spooky smart, but he also said you were oblivious to everything but crew."

"It cuts in and out. So, what's with the games?" I hated games.

Zach squirmed. "Do I have to answer that?"

"No, but I'm assuming Michael had a reason for introducing us. Maybe we should try to get along?"

"I know, but can we ease our way into this? You have to admit, this is pretty weird." Zach picked up his coffee and started drinking.

I knew I faced a choice. I could keep picking, or I could acknowledge that yes, whatever Michael was playing at, this was truly bizarrissimo, and Zach and I needed to make it work.

"It really is." I let out a jittery breath. "I'm a little nervous, to be perfectly honest, and I can be a little overbearing when I get that way."

"No, really?"

Smell that, kids? That's sarcasm.

"It's true!" I squealed.

"You're kind of intimidating, you know that?"

"Me? I'm harmless." I wanted to see if he'd fall for it any more than Randy had.

The fact that he snorted coffee out of his nose put paid to that. I handed him some napkins. "Seriously?"

Once I stopped being deliberately difficult and Zach stopped playing games, we actually got along pretty well. I saw why Michael liked him.

So, I spent the day getting to know the guy who was probably my replacement. Not that I had any grounds for complaint. After all, I knew Randy waited for me back in Davis, ready for whatever I was ready for.

It was still odd.

"Can I tell you something?" Zach fidgeted with a napkin, ripping it into smaller and smaller pieces. I had to wonder if he was always this nervous, or if this was something I brought out.

"Sure, go for it."

"I see why Michael still talks about you." Zach looked everywhere but at me.

That...no. "Oh, I *am* sorry. That's so wrong."

Zach looked puzzled.

"We're over, and he's with you, or so I'm assuming. I'm old news. Hell, he dumped me."

"Does he know that?" Zach sounded dejected, and I was surprised how that cut me.

This? This was crap. "We're putting a stop to this, you and I."

"What?"

"You heard me. You like him, and I'm presuming you're looking for more than sex because there're apps for that."

"Kind of, yeah." Zach looked so shy. I felt like such a perv, but all I could think was there was a certain something there that would pull Michael in. Jeez, it pulled at me, and I could tell for a fact Zach was a catcher too. What would we do together, play pat-a-cake?

The entire idea that Michael appeared hung up on me pissed me off, especially when he had this toothsome morsel in front of him. "When he gets here, the three of us will go out, and if he appears to be paying too much attention to me, I'll redirect him in a way that makes it all too clear what we both think of it."

"I'm not sure I can do that."

I grunted irritably. "Start being sure, because I'm more than capable." I leaned over and looked Zach dead in the eyes. "He broke my heart. It sounds like a cliché, but there it is. I've repaired it and moved on, trust me, but he doesn't get a do-over, and he doesn't get to carry on like there's the slightest chance in hell we'll get back together."

"Then why're you here?" Zach looked so confused.

"To salvage our friendship." Maybe it was only my febrile imagination, but Zach seemed relieved. "You thought I came here to get him back, didn't you?"

"You flew out here for that? Must be nice." Zach ignored me, instead rubbing his fingers together like he was separating Benjamins.

I shrugged. Talking to a near-stranger about money? As if. "I was already in Chicago, so continuing on to Providence wasn't that big a deal."

And that's all you're getting, Zach. You want the rest? Buy the rights. Besides, he was at *Brown*, which wasn't exactly on the list of budget schools.

"Why are you being so helpful?" Zach said.

I ignored that. "Do you like him?"

"Oh yeah." Zach looked at me like I was crazy. "I mean, have you met him? Have you seen him?"

I snorted. "Dude. I watched him go through puberty. I don't know how long he was out here this summer, or if he managed to escape from his parents, but have you gotten him naked yet?"

"I'm working on it." Zach's eyes flashed with hunger.

I nodded my approval. "I'm biting my tongue here, and not to tell you how to conduct your relationship, but ohmuhgaaaw. Get on that. As it were."

"I'm starting to see why he was anxious about leaving us alone."

"Was he? That's funny." I pulled a piece of paper out of my messenger bag and scribbled down every possible way to contact me. "Use 'em if you want to."

Then I had an idea. I pulled out my phone and sat next to him. "Selfie!"

"Are you going to send it to him?" Zach giggled.

"Of course."

*

As it turned out, the men's head coach had made some calls, so when I showed up at the boathouse the following morning, I was greeted with open arms. A single? Sure! I realized overnight that I needed to scull, if only to escape my emotions. Michael and I were kaput but spending the previous day with Zach had made my head spin. No one had come right out and said it, but I knew what was going on. I was being asked to give my blessing to Michael's next relationship. Maybe Michael and Zach weren't even sure of it themselves, but like I'd told Zach, my obliviousness cut in and out.

Just like old times, really. Remy can't handle an emotion? Wind him up, watch him go! But it felt so good to scull again, and I felt restored as I glided back to the dock two hours later. The cast around the boathouse had changed while I'd sculled, so I had to introduce myself to everyone all over again, mostly to answer the question, "Who are you and why do *you* get to row that single when almost no one else even gets to look at it?"

Since I'd already learned "Because I really am that much better than you" didn't actually go over that well, I came up with something better, something that brought up the fact that I was good enough to compete for a spot on the U23 team, but not good enough to win one. Self-deprecation always worked like a charm. I stood around chatting with people. I liked crew and I liked rowers, so why not? I'd probably see these people in a few months in Boston and maybe next spring at the Crew Classic, if not other West Coast races. Rowing was a small world and being polite cost nothing.

When I emerged from the Marston Boathouse calm and clean, I found Zach and Michael waiting for me.

"Took you long enough." Zach tapped his watch.

"I'm sorry, if I'd known you were waiting, I wouldn't have spent that much time shooting the breeze." Then I thought for a moment. "You could've come in, you know. In fact...the men's novice coach is inside. He also works with walk-ons and new recruits. Let's go."

Over their protestations, I dragged them both behind me. No time like the present, after all. When we emerged from the boathouse twenty minutes later, they could only shake their heads.

"What just happened?" Zach looked baffled.

Michael laughed. "Jeremy Babcock, that's what."

"I have no idea what you're talking about." I hid my smile.

"Only you, Remy, could walk into any boathouse in the country, introduce us, and walk out with me having a spot on the novice team and a promise for Zach to try out coxing." Michael grabbed me in a one-armed hug and kissed the side of my head.

I met Zach's eyes. No, that wasn't awkward at all.

"He's over there." I shoved Michael away from me and pointed him toward Zach.

Michael blushed like I usually did. "Subtle, Rem."

I stopped walking. "No, it wasn't, and it wasn't meant to be. You wanted me to get to know Zach? Fine, he and I have struck up the beginnings of a friendship. This is a good thing. I'm here to make sure you and I stay friends, but this? This stops here and now."

"Okay, I get it." Michael glared at me.

"Do you?" Set eyebrow on stun. "You've got Zach ready to give you everything, but you need to put down that torch because, Michael? It's never going to burn again."

No one said anything for a moment, and then Zach looked up at me. "Thank you, Remy."

"You're welcome. I've got your back, at least until Michael here wakes up to what's staring him right in the face." I smiled at him and then looked at Michael and shook my head. "You fool. He's crazy about you."

Michael looked like he wanted to rip into me. "You... I know, Remy. This isn't how I thought things would go, you know?"

"Believe me, I know." I took a deep breath. "Why don't you guys go talk about things? I'd like to meet for lunch. Maybe you could text me, Zach?"

"Okay, now *that* was subtle, Rem," Michael said.

I snorted. "No. You seem to miss subtle. I'm going to keep smacking you upside the head until it sinks in."

"I'll text you, Rem," Zach said, apparently picking up on the familiar nickname. Gag. That was supposed to be for my intimates only. Oh well, I'd clearly lost that battle.

I knew a dismissal when I heard one, and since I'd gone to a certain amount of trouble to engineer this one, I took it, tipping a wink to Zach. I spent the rest of the morning exploring and playing unabashed tourist in colonial Providence. Eventually the three of us ate a late lunch. I didn't ask and they didn't tell, and that, after all, had been the point of my efforts.

The other thing I did that afternoon was change my flight. Again. The only people I told were my parents. All Zach and Michael knew was that I planned to return to

Boston the next day. I'd never told them when I'd planned to leave.

"I'm glad we didn't leave it strained, but I have to get ready for school to start, and I've missed too many practices as it is."

Never mind the fact that I'd been rowing and erging at Brown. It was a plausible excuse, and I needed one right then. Zach and Michael needed me not to be underfoot, and a gentleman always knows when to leave a party. After all, the message I'd been trying to get Michael to understand was that I wasn't supposed to be a part of that relationship. The best way I could think of to ensure that was to be three thousand miles away. But mostly, I had myself to think of. Michael and I were past tense. He would always be special to me, but we were moving on, and I didn't need a ringside seat to his new main event. Why subject myself to that kind of pain? We'd all done our best, after all. Maybe it was time to trust that.

*

A few weeks into the semester and I'd settled in nicely. I'd scored a single dorm room, which suited me well. Randy and I took things slowly. We were busy, both of us with crew, he with work, and me with the possibility of extra training on top of regular practices.

Lodestone, my grandparents, and I debated whether I should train for the U23 trials again or not. Grandma and Grandpa were all for it, as was Marissa Lodestone. Peter Lodestone and I, along with Coach Pendergast, were still analyzing the previous training program and the video of my performance at the selection camp to see how they could be improved upon before we made any decisions. Of course, the fact that we were analyzing everything spoke volumes about making said decisions, but it provided a fig leaf I needed.

One evening when I should've been asleep but was instead reading on my iPad, the Skype icon started dancing frantically.

"Lovely." I tapped it and up popped Zach.

"Can we talk?" Zach looked miserable.

I kissed sleep goodbye. "Sure. What's up?"

Zach explained the situation. Basically, he and Michael—or Mike, as he preferred to be called now—had been going at it hot and heavy, and then Mike had brought out the rope.

"Rope, Remy!"

Hmmm, rope. "Then what?"

"I started giggling. Good grief. What was next, a flogger?"

Damn, I missed that. "So, Mike froze you out after you cut him down during sex. You don't see a connection?"

"Didn't you hear what he did?" Zach looked at me like I was crazy. I tried not to look horny.

"Oh, Zach. Where do you think he learned all of that?"

Then Zach turned bright red. "You're kidding."

"Nope."

He sighed. "Why am I talking to his ex-boyfriend about this?"

"Because this is what you signed up for when you met Mike, I guess. You can roll with it or you can let him go, because I'll always be involved in his life. Apparently." No matter how hard I try not to be. "I'm not going to be your go-to guy whenever you have a problem, and you'll come to know him better than I do, but right now? I'm your map."

I felt bad for Zach, I truly did. This aspect of his boyfriend must've come as a complete shock to him.

"It's..."

"He's really toppy and very, very dominant. He also likes to tie people up, among other things. Do a little reading, maybe see if that's something you can't learn to enjoy. I'm not saying you have to like it as rough as I do, but it's something he realized he needed when we were together. Give him a chance, and he'll fuck you like a raging god."

Zach's eyes had grown progressively wider as I'd spoken. "I have to go."

And this, I thought, was why the aliens won't visit us.

Epilogue

I loved fall in Boston. I loved the Head of the Charles.

I loved the fact that this year, it was free of last year's drama. This year, the most vexing problem I faced was that I could only row in two races and there were three I wanted to participate in. I wanted to reprise last year's quad in the Directors' Cup Challenge. I'd had way too much fun last year to take a pass this year. Besides, I loved those guys, even if I owed Brad St. Charles an oar handle in the kidneys. But I could only race in a single—provided it was an open event—or race in the eights with CalPac's varsity crew.

"I vote for the eights," Lodestone said. "The biggest objection at the selection camp was your ability to blend in with crews. Take every chance you can to work on that. We both know what you can do in the single."

Pendergast nodded. "It only makes sense, Remy. You've got plenty of time to rock the single, but only three years to row in a varsity eight. Besides, you know I'll enter you in what sculling events I can. The rule about one event only here at the Charles is pretty rare."

They were right, and I opted for the eight. For that matter, once I graduated from CalPac, I could enter as a sculler for as long as the Charles would have me. As a collegiate rower? Pendergast had a point. Three years including this one, assuming I graduated on time.

I also loved the chance to socialize at the Charles, at least now that I'd been here before and knew more people beyond my own teammates. Thanks to the Crew Classic, to my time at the selection camp, and to my visit to Brown, I knew people from all over the country, and we all converged on Boston during that one weekend in late October. Between these people, plus friends from the Cap City masters and my CalPac teammates, I had a great time.

The best part of the regatta? When Randy shyly took my hand and I just as shyly let him. Michael saw it and gave me a thumbs-up where Randy couldn't see it. I was glad for Michael's approval, but I'd already realized that I would continue to see Randy with or without it, as I suspected Michael would date—and nail—Zach whether I liked Zach or not. As it happened, I thought Zach was perfect for my ex. Assuming he stopped snickering when Michael tried to tie him up.

We'd all figure it out, I knew that much.

Acknowledgements

Trish Barnaby and Alma Pagan helped me with details and information about Chicago. Online research never compares to eyewitness information, and I haven't been to Chicago in forever. Likewise, Lisa Schwidock answered questions about New Jersey in the summertime. Little details make for a richer story.

Josh Robbins, owner of Imstilljosh.com, provided help and information about life with HIV, and I'm grateful. He's also a really nice guy, and his blog is worth checking out for that reason alone. If you're newly diagnosed with HIV, Imstilljosh.com is a great place to start.

Tricia Blocher. As always, I'm grateful to her. Any errors about rowing and training at the highest levels that exist in this book belong to me alone.

About C. Koehler

Christopher Koehler always wanted to write, but it wasn't until his grad school years that he realized writing was how he wanted to spend his life. Long something of a hothouse flower, he's been lucky to be surrounded by people who encouraged that, especially his long-suffering husband of twenty-nine years and counting.

He loves many genres of fiction and nonfiction, but he's especially fond of romances, because it's in them that human emotions and relations, at least most of the ones fit to be discussed publicly, are laid bare.

While writing is his passion and his life, when he's not doing that, he's a househusband, at-home dad, and oarsman with a slightly disturbing interest in manners and the other ways people behave badly.

Christopher is approaching the tenth anniversary of publication and has been fortunate to be recognized for his writing, including by the American Library Association, which named *Poz* a 2016 Recommended Title.

E-mail
christoarpher@gmail.com

Facebook
www.fb.me/Christopher.tells.stories

Twitter
@christopherink

Website
www.christopherkoehler.net/blog

Other NineStar books by this author

The CalPac Crew Series
Rocking the Boat
Tipping the Balance
Burning It Down
Settling the Score

The Lives of Remy and Michael Series
Poz

Coming Soon from C. Koehler

First Impressions

Henry Hughes nudged his Tesla Roadster into the second of his assigned parking spots beneath the Capitol Towers, the one in which he'd had a charger installed, praying he didn't dent or scratch the pricey plaything.

He struggled to leverage his muscular frame out of the door, and finally just climbed out the top. There was no way this would work long-term. He was way over six feet tall and built like a linebacker. Maybe the other space was larger? He'd already noticed his assistant's more serviceable SUV parked there. He made a note to talk to her about it, but then he realized if he did, she'd relinquish the larger space without a peep, or worse, buy a smaller car. Then he thought about the hassle of moving the charger. It'd be easier to keep climbing out of the top of the car.

The parking was a pain in the ass—and not the good kind—but to keep a place in Sacramento. Since it wasn't his primary residence, a house with a yard simply wasn't practical, not even one of the adorable bungalows in the neighborhoods east of downtown. So, there he was with a condo and the adventures in parking.

Even with the occasional headache, Sacramento still beat San Francisco, and it was the only city of any size close to Alpenglow, his spread near Lake Tahoe. What was his alternative, some village of less than fifty people on US-50? Now entering, now leaving!

The door opened at his touch, and he sighed. There could be only one explanation.

Lillian.

She had arrived early to freshen the place up for him.

It was thoughtful and so like her, and so unnecessary. He wasn't helpless, just an emotional wreck. He lied to himself and pretended the joke was funny.

"Hello?" he called, shutting the door behind him. He walked into the foyer and through the French doors that led to the formal living space beyond. "Lillian?"

"In here, Henry."

Lillian Desmond rose to shake his hand when Henry entered the room because she was respectful like that. She was tall, a bit shorter than him, at least, and while her face was lined by sun and a storied career in law enforcement and paramilitary groups—the details of which he still found improbable despite vetting them thoroughly—she wore her fifty-odd years lightly. He suspected she could put him on the ground in seconds if she wanted to but was nice enough not to demonstrate it. She kept her graying-blonde hair out of the way in a no-nonsense bun, and that plus the reading glasses perched on her nose made her look like a schoolmarm.

"Welcome home." Her reading glasses slid down her nose as she looked him in the eye. It made him wonder what he'd done and what the consequences would be.

Henry looked around. "It doesn't really feel like home. It's more like a hotel suite I own, which is weird, because Alpenglow doesn't look this impersonal and it's actually a hotel. Sort of."

"And whose fault is that? Maybe you should spend more time down here this fall. You work awfully hard." Lillian gave him a hard look. "Take some time off."

"I don't work any harder than you, and you'll take time off when you die." He hated talking about his work habits because they inevitably led to discussions about his personal life. Or the lack thereof. "Who knows. A bit of a break might be nice."

Also from NineStar Press

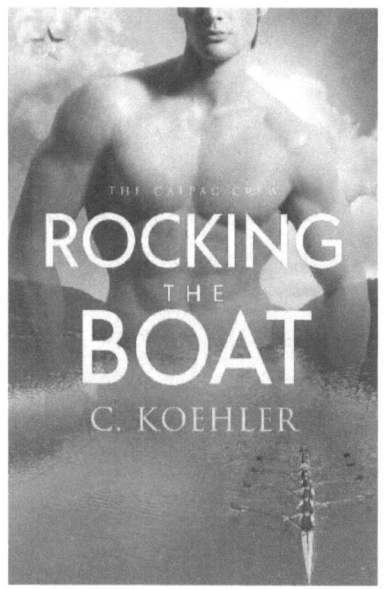

Rocking the Boat by C. Koehler

Nick Bedford coaches the men's rowing team at California Pacific College, a small liberal arts school in Sacramento. He's quiet, dedicated—and closeted. He struggles with professional ethics and NCAA rules as he denies his attraction for Morgan Estrada, one of his rowers. While they may not be far apart in age, the difference between coach and athlete leads Nick to worry about exploitation.

But Morgan has desires and a mind of his own, and what he wants is his coach. As the spring racing season advances, Morgan feels his coach's eyes on him. Morgan may be gay, and while he's not out to team, he hasn't hidden it, either. It may be a coach's job to check out an athlete's form, but Morgan hopes Nick's interested in more than his technique.

Morgan corners Nick in the boathouse, and Nick admits that while he wants Morgan he can't have him. Morgan laughingly points out that he's not bound by any of those rules and he wants Nick. Nick and Morgan start a relationship, but Nick worries whenever they're in public: what if someone sees? An anonymous complaint from a rower to the athletics director sends Nick's worries into overdrive just as the crew prepares for the make-or-break race of the year.

Stranded with Desire by Rick R. Reed and Vivien Dean

CEO Maine Braxton and his invaluable assistant, Colby, don't realize they share a deep secret: they're in love—with each other. That secret may have never come to light but for a terrifying plane crash in the Cascade Mountains that changes everything.

In a struggle for survival, they brave bears, storms, and a life-threatening flood to make it out of the wilderness alive. The proximity to death makes them realize the importance of love over propriety. Confessions emerge. Passions ignite. They escape the wilds renewed and openly in love.

When they return to civilization, though, forces are already plotting to snuff out their short-lived romance and ruin everything both have worked so hard to achieve.

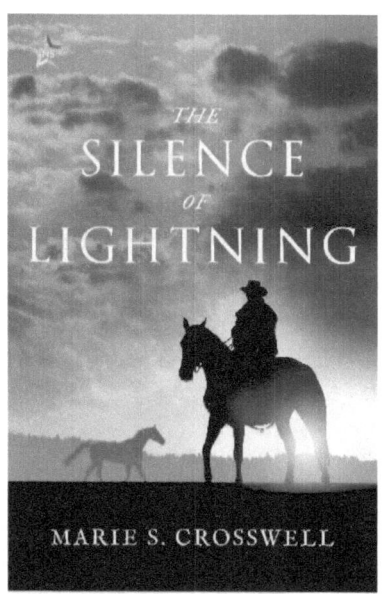

The Silence of Lightning by Marie S. Crosswell

Former pro-rodeo champion Smith Rose and his cousins Cooper and Christa Boone live a quiet life together in the town of Cody, Wyoming—until the summer of 2015 shakes them to their foundations.

Stuck in an unhappy rut since his retirement from the rodeo five years prior, Smith is forced to reckon with his past, present, and future when his former friend and lover John Henry Walker shows up at Smith's bar. Meanwhile, the Boone sisters face a threat they never would've predicted when an out-of-town stranger begins to stalk

Christa after meeting her at a party. While trying to support her sister and their cousin, Cooper secretly agonizes over her fears of their little family splitting apart and where that would leave her.

When Smith, Cooper, and Christa's problems converge in a dangerous confrontation, will the three of them survive?

Connect with NineStar Press

www.ninestarpress.com

www.facebook.com/ninestarpress

www.facebook.com/groups/NineStarNiche

www.twitter.com/ninestarpress

www.instagram.com/ninestarpress